TO CATCH A KILLER

Nele Neuhaus is one of the most widely read German mystery writers and the author of *Snow White Must Die*, *Big Bad Wolf* and *Ice Queen*. More than four million copies of her books are currently in print. She lives near Frankfurt, Germany.

Also by Nele Neuhaus

Snow White Must Die
Big Bad Wolf
Ice Queen

TO CATCH A KILLER

NELE NEUHAUS

Translated by Steven T. Murray

PAN BOOKS

First published 2016 as *I Am Your Judge* by Minotaur Books,
an imprint of St Martin's Press, New York

First published in the UK 2016 by Macmillan

This paperback edition published 2016 by Pan Books
an imprint of Pan Macmillan
20 New Wharf Road, London N1 9RR
Associated companies throughout the world
www.panmacmillan.com

ISBN 978-1-5098-2132-7

Originally published in 2014 as *Die Lebenden und die Toten* by
Ullstein Buchverlage GmbH, Berlin.

1 3 5 7 9 8 6 4 2

A CIP catalogue record for this book is available from the British Library.

Typeset by Ellipsis Digital Limited, Glasgow
Printed and bound by CPI Group (UK) Ltd, Croydon, CR0 4YY

Visit www.panmacmillan.com to read more about all our books
and to buy them. You will also find features, author interviews and
news of any author events, and you can sign up for e-newsletters
so that you're always first to hear about our new releases.

For Matthias,
forever and for always

TO
CATCH A
KILLER

WEDNESDAY, DECEMBER 19, 2012

Outside temperature, 3°C. No wind. No rain in the forecast. Perfect conditions. A.m.

8:21 a.m.

He saw her coming. Her pink cap shone like a beacon in the early slate-grey light of the winter day. She was alone, as she was every morning. Only the dog trotting next to her, a dark, lithe shadow among the leafless bushes. Her route was always the same. She walked down Lahnstrasse, past the playground, then crossed the wooden footbridge over the Westerbach, turned right, and followed the paved path along the stream until it branched off to the left towards the school, which was the furthest point on her morning walk. From there she headed back via Dörnweg, which cut straight through the fields, then turned left after about a kilometre and crossed the wooden bridge to her house.

The dog did his business on the grass in the playground near the swings, and she conscientiously scooped up the poo and tossed the bag into the rubbish bin on the corner.

She walked past him not twenty metres away but didn't notice him. From his hiding place, he watched her cross the bridge, its wood glistening with dew, and vanish beyond the trees. He had prepared himself to wait about half an hour, and was lying comfortably on his stomach under the dark-green rain poncho. If necessary, he could lie there for hours. Patience was one of his strong points. The stream, only a thin rivulet in the summer, rushed and gurgled past his feet. Two crows hopped round him curiously, stared at him, and then lost interest. The cold was seeping through his thermal trousers. A dove cooed in the bare branches of the oak tree above him. A young woman jogged past on the other side of the stream, light on her feet, perhaps exhilarated by the music she was listening to in her earphones. In the distance, he heard the rattle of a local train and the melodious triad of a school bell.

Among the sombre grey, brown and black colours of winter, he discerned a flash of pink. She was coming. His heart rate quickened as he looked through the telescopic sight. He calmed his breathing and slowly moved the fingers of his right hand. She turned onto the path that curved towards the bridge. Her dog was trotting about a metre behind her.

His finger was on the trigger. He scanned the area to his left and right, but there was no one in sight. Except her. She followed the bend in the path and presented the left side of her face to him, exactly as he had planned.

He would lose a bit of the rifle's precision by using a silencer, but at a distance of less than eighty metres, that was no problem. The sound of the gunshot would have attracted too much unwanted attention. He breathed in and out, totally relaxed and focused. His field of vision contracted, settling on the target. He smoothly squeezed the trigger. The recoil that he'd anticipated jolted his collarbone. Only a fraction of a second later, the Remington Core-Lokt .30-06 round burst her skull. She sank silently to the ground. Bull's-eye.

The ejected cartridge lay steaming on the damp ground. He picked it up and stuck it into his jacket pocket. His knees were a little stiff after the time he'd spent lying on the ground in the cold. With a few movements, he stripped down the rifle and stowed it in his sports bag. He folded up the poncho and stuffed it in the bag as well. After he had checked that no one was round, he left the bushes, walked across the playground, and headed off towards the Wiesenbad pool, where he had parked his car. It was 9:13 a.m. when he drove out of the car park and turned left onto the motorway.

AT THE SAME TIME . . .

Chief Detective Inspector Pia Kirchhoff was on leave. As of Thursday of the previous week, until 15 January 2013. Four whole weeks! Her last really long holiday was almost four years ago. In 2009, she and Christoph had gone to South Africa, and since then, they'd only had time for brief trips, but now they were flying almost to the other side of the globe, to Ecuador, and from there by ship to the Galápagos Islands. Christoph had often been hired as a guide by the organizer of the exclusive cruises, and Pia would be going along for the first time – as his wife.

She sat down on the edge of the bed and dreamily looked at the narrow gold ring on her finger. The official at the register office was a bit miffed when Christoph put the ring on her left hand, but she had explained that the left side was closest to the heart, after all, so they had decided to wear their wedding rings on their left hands. That was only half the truth, because there were also other quite pragmatic reasons for this decision. For one thing, in her first marriage to Henning, she had worn her wedding ring on her right hand, as is customary in Germany. She wasn't excessively superstitious, but she didn't want to be reminded of her divorce or tempt fate unnecessarily. And second – and this was the main reason for her decision – it was extremely painful if someone gave her a firm handshake and almost crushed her finger with the ring.

She and Christoph had secretly and quietly been married on Friday at the register office in Höchst, which was located in the garden pavilion of the Bolongaro Palace. Without inviting friends, family or witnesses and without telling a soul. They weren't going to announce their marriage until after they returned from South America, and then they'd throw a big party next summer at Birkenhof.

Pia tore herself away from gazing at the ring and went back to trying to stuff the piles of clothes on the bed into two suitcases as efficiently as possible. They wouldn't need thick jumpers and jackets. Instead, they were taking summer clothes. T-shirts, shorts, swimsuits. She was also delighted to be escaping winter and all the Christmas festivities, which had never much appealed to her. Instead, she would lie in the sun on the deck of a cruise ship, reading a book or simply loafing for once. Of course, Christoph would have a lot to do, but he'd have free time, too, and the nights would be their own. Maybe they'd send postcards to their parents and her sister and brother – yes, especially to him and his arrogant wife – and tell them that they'd got married. Pia could still hear the disapproving comment of her sister-in-law, Sylvia, when she learned of her divorce from Henning. *A woman over thirty has a better chance of being struck by lightning than of finding another man,* Sylvia had pessimistically prophesied. Pia had in fact been struck by lightning one sunny morning in June six years before, in the elephant paddock of Opel Zoo. And that was when she and Dr Christoph Sander, the director of the zoo, had met for the first time and instantly fallen in love. For the past four years, they'd been living together at Birkenhof in Unterliederbach, and quite soon had concluded that they wanted to do so until they died.

The mobile phone on the kitchen table rang. Pia ran downstairs to the kitchen and looked at the display before she took the call. 'I'm on holiday,' she said. 'Actually, I'm about to head out the door.'

'"Actually" is an extraordinarily vague word,' replied Oliver von Bodenstein, her boss, who occasionally had the nerve-racking habit of being too literal and nitpicky. 'I'm very sorry to bother you, but I have a problem.'

'Uh-oh.'

'We have a body, and it's close to your neighbourhood,' Bodenstein went on. 'I'm in the middle of an urgent matter. Cem is out of town, and Kathrin is off sick. Could you possibly run over there and take care of the formalities for me? Kröger and his people are already on the way. I'll be there to take over as soon as I'm done here.'

Pia quickly went over her to-do list in her mind. She was on schedule and had made all the arrangements necessary for a three-week absence. She could finish packing in half an hour. She knew Bodenstein wouldn't ask her unless he really needed her help. She could put in a couple of hours without going into panic mode.

'Okay,' she said. 'Where do I have to go?'

'Thank you, Pia, I really appreciate it.' She could hear the relief in his voice. 'It's in Niederhöchstadt. The best way is to turn off the dual carriageway towards Steinbach. After about eight hundred metres, there's a road across the field on your right. Turn there. Our colleagues are already on the scene.'

'Got it. See you later.' Pia ended the call, pulled off her wedding ring, and put it in a kitchen drawer.

As usual, Pia had no idea what to expect at the site where the body was found. When she called to say that she was on her way, the detective on watch had simply told her that a female body had been discovered in Niederhöchstadt. Near the exit to the town, she turned right onto a paved road through the fields; from far off, she could see several patrol cars and an ambulance. As she came closer, she recognized the blue VW van of the evidence team and other, unmarked vehicles. She parked on a small patch of grass in front of a thicket, grabbed her beige down jacket from the back seat, and got out.

'Hello, Ms Kirchhoff,' a young uniformed colleague standing at the cordon greeted her. 'You'll have to go round behind the bushes to your right.'

'Good morning and thank you,' she replied, and followed the path he'd indicated. The bushes created a little grove in the midst of the open field. As Pia went round the corner, the first person she encountered was Chief Detective Inspector Christian Kröger, head of the evidence team of Hofheim Kommissariat-11.

'Pia!' Kröger shouted in amazement. 'What the hell are you doing here? You're on—'

'Holiday,' she said with a smile. 'Oliver asked me to get started out here for him. As soon as he arrives, I'm gone. What have we got?'

'Nasty business,' said Kröger. 'A woman was shot in the head. In broad daylight and less than a kilometre from Eschborn police station.'

'When did it happen?' Pia asked.

'Shortly before nine, apparently,' said Kröger. 'A cyclist saw her collapse. Bam, just like that. He didn't hear a gunshot. But the ME thinks she was shot with a rifle, fired from some distance away.'

'Shit. Is Henning here yet? I didn't see his car.'

'No, fortunately we've got a new guy. Ever since your ex clawed his way to the top medical job, he hasn't had time for any outside jobs.' Kröger grinned. 'Which is fine with me.'

He harboured a deep dislike for Henning Kirchhoff, and the feeling was mutual. The two often were as touchy as vying prima donnas, though it never affected the thoroughness of their work. That was the only reason everyone else put up with their childish wrangling as they questioned each other's competence. Their verbal battles at various crime scenes had long been legendary.

After Professor Thomas Kronlage retired the previous summer, Henning became director of the Institute of Forensic Medicine. The university had wanted to consider outside applicants, but Henning's qualifications in the field of forensic anthropology were so valuable that it had given him the director's post so it wouldn't lose him.

'What's the new guy's name?' Pia asked.

'I forget,' muttered Kröger. 'Sorry.'

The man in the white overalls who was squatting next to the body slipped back his hood and stood up. Not that young, Pia saw, but his shaved head and thick moustache made

7

it difficult to guess his age. A bald head did make a man look older than he really was.

'Dr Frederick Lemmer.' The medical examiner took off his right glove and held out his hand. 'Pleased to meet you.'

'Same here,' Pia replied, shaking his hand. 'I'm Pia Kirch-hoff from K-Eleven in Hofheim.'

The site where a dead body has been discovered was no place for polite conversation, so Pia let the brief introduction suffice. She prepared herself for the sight that awaited her and stepped closer to the body. The knitted pink cap and the white hair of the victim formed surreal splotches of colour against the grey asphalt, brown mud and a blackish pool of blood.

'*Schindler's List*,' Pia muttered.

'Pardon me?' Dr Lemmer enquired somewhat testily.

'The movie with Liam Neeson and Ben Kingsley,' Pia said.

The ME grasped at once what she was referring to and smiled. 'You're right. It does look a bit like that. The film was in black-and-white, and only the girl's coat was red.'

'I'm a visual person. For me, the first impression of a crime scene is always important,' Pia explained. She put on latex gloves and squatted down. Lemmer did the same. In her many years at K-11, Pia had learned to preserve an internal distance. That was the only way to bear looking at gruesomely muti-lated and disfigured corpses.

'The bullet penetrated the left temple.' Dr Lemmer pointed to the clean entry wound on the victim's head. 'When it exited, it blew off almost the whole right side of the skull. Typical of a large-calibre semi-jacketed round. In my opinion, the murder weapon was a rifle, and the shot was fired from a long dis-tance.'

'And since in this area, it could hardly be a hunting accident, I would assume it was a well-aimed shot,' said Kröger, who was standing behind them.

Pia nodded and studied what was left of the victim's face. Why would a woman between sixty and seventy years old be shot on a public thoroughfare? Was she a victim of opportunity, simply in the wrong place at the wrong time?

Some of Kröger's people, in their white overalls, were using metal detectors to comb through the thicket and adjoining fields, searching for the projectile. Others were taking photographs or recording measurements with an electronic device in order to track the direction from which the shot had been fired.

'Do we know who she is?' Pia got up and looked at Kröger.

'No, she had nothing with her but a house key. No wallet, no mobile phone,' he said. 'Do you want to talk to the witness? He's sitting in the ambulance.'

'Yes, in a minute.' Pia looked round and frowned. Empty fields and pastures. In the distance, the TV tower and the skyline of Frankfurt glittered in the pale winter sunshine that had fought its way through the thick cloud cover. About forty metres away, tall trees lined a stream. Through the bare branches, she saw a playground and beyond it the first houses of the Niederhöchstadt district of Eschborn. Paved roads with streetlights ran through the fields. A park-like recreational area, ideal for riding bikes, jogging, speed-walking and—

'Where's the dog?' Pia asked suddenly.

'What dog?' Kröger and Dr Lemmer asked in surprise.

'This is a dog lead.' Pia bent down and pointed to a worn, dark-brown leather lead, which was wrapped round the woman's shoulders and torso. 'She was out here walking her dog. And since we found no car key on her, she must live nearby.'

*

'I'm so glad that I've got three weeks' holiday.' Karoline Albrecht gave a contented sigh and stretched out her legs. She was sitting at the dining room table in her parents' house with a cup of her favourite tea in front of her – rooibos vanilla – and she could feel the stress of the past weeks and months gradually sloughing off her and making way for a much-needed rest. 'Greta and I will get cosy at home, or else we'll just sit round here with you and eat cookies.'

'You're most welcome.' Her mother smiled at her over the rims of her reading glasses. 'But didn't you two want to fly off to somewhere in the sun?'

'Oh, Mama, I think I've flown more than Carsten this year – and he's a pilot!' Karoline grinned and sipped her tea. But her cheerfulness was all an act.

For eight years, she'd been an executive partner at an international management consulting firm, responsible for the restructuring and internationalization of companies; and two years ago, she'd been promoted to head of management consulting. Ever since then, she had spent most of her time in hotels, aeroplanes, and the VIP lounges at airports. She was one of the very few women to hold such a high position, and the obscene amount of money that she earned seemed almost immoral. Her daughter, Greta, was at boarding school, her marriage had ended long ago, and all her friendships had fizzled out over time for lack of attention. Her job had always been her highest priority; even when she passed her university entrance exam with a grade-point average of 4.0, she had wanted to be the best. She had completed her degrees in business administration at elite universities in both Germany and the USA, graduating with honours. And afterwards, her career had proceeded at a meteoric pace.

But for the past couple of months, she had felt empty and exhausted, and with the fatigue came doubts about the meaning of her work. Was what she did really so important? More important than spending time with her daughter and occasionally enjoying life a little? She was forty-three and had never really lived. For twenty years, she had rushed from one deadline to the next, living out of suitcases and surrounded by people who meant nothing to her and vice versa. Greta felt comfortable with Carsten's new family; she enjoyed having siblings, a dog, and a stepmother who was actually closer to her than her own birth mother. Karoline was on the verge of losing her daughter, and it was her own fault, because she had made herself dispensable in her daughter's life.

'But you do enjoy your job, don't you?'

Her mother's voice tore Karoline Albrecht out of her reverie.

'I'm no longer so sure about that,' she replied, setting her cup on the table. 'That's why I'm taking a leave of absence next year. I'd like to spend more time with Greta. And I'm thinking about selling the house.'

'Really?' Margarethe Rudolf raised her eyebrows but didn't seem particularly surprised. 'Why is that?'

'It's much too big,' said Karoline. 'I'm looking for something a bit smaller and cosier for Greta and me. Something like this.'

She had chosen to leave the house as it was when she bought it: stylish, luxurious and energy-efficient, 4,300 square feet of living space with exposed concrete floors and every conceivable comfort. But it had never felt really homey, and she secretly yearned for her parents' comfortable old house where she grew up – with its creaky wooden stairs, high ceilings, battered checkered floor tiles in the kitchen, bay windows and the outmoded bathrooms.

'We should drink a toast to your new life,' her mother suggested. 'What do you think?'

'Sure, I'm on holiday, after all.' Karoline smiled. 'Have you got a bottle in the fridge?'

'Of course. Champagne,' her mother said with a wink.

A little later, they were sitting across from each other, clinking their glasses in a toast to Christmas and to Karoline's decision to make some fundamental changes in her life.

'You know, Mama,' she said, 'I've been so driven, wanting desperately to live up to the perfect image that everyone had of me: disciplined, reasonable, organized down to the last detail. But it was stressing me out because I wasn't doing all that out of genuine interest, but only because everyone expected it of me.'

'You've set yourself free now,' her mother concluded.

'Yes. Yes, I have.' Karoline took both her mother's hands. 'At last I can breathe again and sleep soundly. I feel like I've been living underwater for years but suddenly surfaced and realized how beautiful the world is. Work and money aren't everything in life.'

'No, sweetheart, you're right about that.' Margarethe Rudolf smiled, but her expression was sad. 'Unfortunately, your father has never come to that realization. Maybe someday he will, after he retires.'

Karoline doubted it.

'You know what, Mama? We're going shopping,' she said firmly. 'And we're going to cook together on Christmas Eve, the way we used to.'

Touched, her mother smiled and nodded.

'Yes, let's do that. And why don't you bring Greta over tomorrow evening, and we'll bake cookies. Then you two will have something to munch on when you're here for Christmas.'

Half an hour later, Oliver von Bodenstein showed up at the scene where the body had been discovered.

'Thanks for covering for me,' he said to Pia. 'I can take over now.'

'Oh, I don't have anything to do today,' she said. 'If you want, I can stay a while.'

'I won't turn down an offer like that.'

He grinned, and it occurred to Pia how much her boss had changed in the past two years. After the break-up of his marriage, he had often been distracted and unable to concentrate, but now he had regained his former sense of authority and his keen perception; he had also begun to treat himself with greater forbearance. In the past, Pia had been the one who liked to follow her hunches and energetically push things forward, while he did things correctly and by the book, putting the brakes on her. Now it sometimes seemed that they had switched roles.

Only someone who has suffered an existential loss and survived is capable of maturing and making fundamental changes. Pia had read this sentence somewhere, and it certainly seemed valid – not only for her boss, but for herself as well. In a relationship, you could fool yourself for a long time, close your eyes to reality, and act as though everything was fine. But inevitably, the day would come when the illusion would burst like a soap bubble and you would be faced with a choice: to go or to stay, to merely *survive* or to truly live again.

'Have you already talked to the witness?' Bodenstein asked.

'Yes,' said Pia, pulling on her hood. The wind was icy. 'He was riding his bike along Dörnweg. That's the name of the road that connects the sections of the town. He came from Eschborn and was heading in the direction of Niederhöchstadt. He was about the same distance away as the electrical tower over there when he saw the woman collapse. He thought she'd had a heart attack or something, so he rode over to her. He did not hear a gunshot.'

'Do we know anything about the victim's identity yet?'

'No. But I think she must live in the area, because she had a dog with her and had no car keys.'

They stepped aside to make room for the hearse.

'We also found the bullet,' Pia went on. 'It was fairly deformed, but it's definitely from a rifle. Dr Lemmer says it's a semi-jacketed round. Hunters as well as the police use this type of ammunition because of its superior stopping power. In the army, they're banned in accordance with the Hague Convention on Land Warfare.'

'Dr Lemmer told you all this?' Bodenstein asked with a slightly mocking undertone. 'Who is he, anyway?'

'No. Believe it or not, I happen to know something about this type of gun,' Pia replied sharply. 'Dr Frederick Lemmer is the new medical examiner.'

They heard a whistle. Pia and Bodenstein turned round and saw Kröger down by the stream, waving both hands in the air.

'Christian has found something,' Pia said. 'Let's not keep him waiting.'

A moment later, they crossed a wooden bridge and stepped onto the lower part of a playground. Swings, seesaws, multicoloured climbing frames, a zipline, sandpits and a pond to play in were scattered over the spacious area higher up the Westerbach stream.

'Over here!' Kröger shouted, excited as always whenever he made a discovery. 'He must have been lying in these bushes. The grass is still flattened, and there . . . over there . . . do you see it? The impression left from a bipod. Fading a bit, but still recognizable.'

Pia had to admit that she didn't see anything but wet clumps of grass, old leaves and damp soil.

'You mean the perp lay here in wait for her?' Bodenstein asked.

'Yes. Precisely,' said Kröger with a vigorous nod. 'Whether he had this particular woman in his sights or just wanted to shoot somebody at random, I can't tell you, of course. But I do know one thing: the guy is not some amateur, firing blindly out here. He deliberately set out to ambush his victim, using a silencer and a nasty type of ammunition—'

'Semi-jacketed round,' Bodenstein muttered, and winked at Pia.

'Right. So you already know,' said Kröger, annoyed at being interrupted. 'Anyway, I think this is where he waited, probably wearing some sort of ghillie suit.'

'A gilly – what?' Bodenstein asked.

'Jeez, Oliver, you're acting a bit slow on the uptake,' Kröger said impatiently. 'A ghillie suit is a camouflage outfit that hunters or snipers use to conceal the shape of the human body. It allows the shooter to blend in with his surroundings. Never mind. What's important is that somebody lay here with a rifle that he rested on a two-legged stand to steady his aim. The rest is up to you to figure out. Anyway, try your best not to bother my team. Just let us work in peace.'

He turned on his heel and left them standing there.

'He thinks you were trying to make fun of him,' Pia told her boss.

'I had no idea what he meant by a ghillie suit,' Bodenstein defended himself. 'I mean, it was only after he explained that I realized I've heard the term before.'

'In other words: you forgot,' Pia said, helping him out.

'No need to rub it in.'

Bodenstein's mobile rang.

'I'm worried about all the spectators.' Pia nodded towards the group of onlookers that had already begun to form and was growing by the minute. Some people were even holding their mobiles high and taking pictures, although there was nothing to see besides the red-and-white crime-scene tape and the officers from the evidence team. Other people just watched, discussing the scene with each other, exhibiting the age-old fascination with horror that seemed to be an innate human trait. Pia was always surprised to see how a violent death drew crowds.

She went over to a colleague who was restraining two women with a couple of small children from entering the playground.

'But we come here every Wednesday morning,' one of the mothers complained. 'The children look forward to it all week.'

The uniformed officer frowned in irritation.

'In a couple of hours, they can use the playground again,' he said. 'Right now, it's closed.'

'Why? And what's going on with the bridge? Why is it

closed, too?' the other woman wanted to know. 'How are we supposed to get back across the stream?'

'Just take the road over to the swimming pool. There's another bridge down there,' the officer advised her.

'This is outrageous!' mother number one exclaimed, incensed. The second woman also turned aggressive and started talking about a police state and their right to freedom of movement.

'Officer,' said Pia, 'please extend the cordon over to the intersection and from there to the dual carriageway. If there are any problems, call for back-up.'

The pugnacious mother took advantage of the policeman's momentary lapse of attention and pushed her buggy under the crime-scene tape.

'Stop!' said Pia, blocking her way. 'Please leave the restricted area.'

'Why?' The woman's eyes were flashing, and she jutted out her chin, looking for a fight. 'What harm will it do if our kids play in the sand for a while?'

'It will disturb official police work,' Pia said coolly. 'I'm asking you politely to leave.'

'In Germany, we are entitled to freedom of movement!' the mother insisted. 'Now look what you've done. The children are upset because *the police* won't let them use the playground. You just don't understand!'

Pia was tempted to tell the woman that she was the one who was acting unreasonably and escalating the situation so that the children were upset. Not the red-and-white police tape. But she didn't have time, and it wouldn't do any good anyway.

'For the last time,' she said firmly, 'please leave the restricted area. If you do not, you will be impeding a police investigation. We will then have to take your name and personal information and institute legal proceedings. I'm sure you don't want to set a bad example for your children, or do you?'

'We come here every Wednesday all the way from Kronberg, and now this happens!' The mother glared at Pia, snorting with rage when she got no further reaction, and then retreated, cursing all the while. 'We're going to file a complaint! My husband knows important people in the Ministry of the Interior!'

A woman who obviously had to have the last word. Pia let her have it and secretly felt sorry for her husband.

'Incredible,' said the officer standing next to her, shaking his head. 'It just keeps getting worse. People think they can do whatever they want. Courtesy has become an alien concept.'

Bodenstein was waiting a short distance away. Pia left her colleagues to deal with the curious onlookers and went over to her boss. She crossed the playground, the wet grass squishing under her shoes.

'We're going to ring all the doorbells and find out whether anyone knows a white-haired lady with a dog,' Bodenstein said. 'Just in case someone is at home and not standing round down there, gawking.'

They started at the first place on a street lined with terraced houses. Before Bodenstein had a chance to ring the bell, Pia noticed a dark brown Labrador that was cowering in fear between two parked cars across the street.

'I bet that's the dead woman's dog,' she said. 'Maybe I can catch him.'

She walked slowly towards the dog, squatted down, and

reached out her hand. The dog was no longer young, judging by his greying muzzle. And he didn't care much for strangers. He jumped up, squeezed through the bushes behind the cars, and took off down the road. Bodenstein and Pia followed him, but when they turned the corner, the dog was gone.

'I think I'll just ring a few doorbells,' he said, opening the gate of the first house. No one home. There was no response at the second one either. He finally had success at the third house.

The front door opened a crack, and an elderly woman peered at them suspiciously over the safety chain.

'Can I help you?'

'We're from the criminal police.' Pia had her police ID ready. She and Bodenstein had often been mistaken for Jehovah's Witnesses or unwanted sales reps. In the background, they heard a man's voice. The woman turned round.

'It's the police!' she yelled, then shut the door, removed the chain, and opened the door all the way.

'Do you happen to know whether anyone on the street owns an old dark brown Labrador?' Pia asked.

Behind the woman, a white-haired man appeared wearing a knitted cardigan and slippers.

'That might be Topsi, Renate's dog,' said the woman. 'Why do you want to know? Did something happen?'

'Do you also know Renate's last name and where she lives?' Bodenstein ignored her questions.

'Oh, sure. Her last name is Rohleder,' the woman replied eagerly. 'I hope Topsi hasn't been in an accident. That would break Renate's heart.'

'She lives at number 44,' the man put in. 'Up the street. The yellow house with the white bench in the front garden.'

'Actually, it was her husband's house.' The woman lowered her voice to a confidential whisper, and her eyes were flashing. 'But when he left her, back then, seven years ago, and only three days before Christmas, Renate's mother, Ingeborg, moved in with her.'

'The police don't want to know all that,' her husband rebuked his gossipy wife. 'The Rohleders own the flower shop on Unterortstrasse, in the town. But Ingeborg is certainly at home. She usually takes the dog for a walk round this time.'

'Thank you for the information,' Bodenstein said politely. 'You've been a big help. I'd appreciate it if you didn't phone the flower shop quite yet.'

'Oh, of course not,' the woman hastened to assure him. 'We're not that close to Renate anyway.'

Bodenstein and Pia took their leave and walked up the street. Number 44 was the last house in the row, and it stood out from the rest with its cheerful facade painted a sunny yellow. Under a carport of light-coloured wood stood an old but well-kept Opel. The small front garden had been carefully prepared for the winter. A few plants were wrapped in canvas sacks to protect them from the snow and cold; Christmas ornaments decorated one bush, and a string of lights had been draped round a boxwood. A Christmas wreath hung on the front door, and there they saw Topsi shivering as he waited in vain for someone to open the door.

The bell over the door rang, and warm, humid air and the over-powering scent of flowers and fir boughs met them as they entered the flower shop. Outside above the display windows was an old-fashioned sign: ROHLEDER FLOWERS – ESTABLISHED 1962.

The shop behind the steamed-up windowpanes was

crowded with customers. There were flowers and all sorts of ornaments in open display cases, on wooden shelves and in baskets. Behind a long counter, three women were busy putting together bouquets.

Bodenstein invariably associated the smell in flower shops with mausoleums at cemeteries, so it took a lot of willpower not to turn on his heel and leave. Flowers growing in gardens and meadows were beautiful to behold, but he couldn't stand the sight of cut flowers in vases. They made him feel sick.

He walked past the customers, despite the protests of an elderly matron who was next in line to pay for the tiny Christmas star she was holding in her hand.

'Uh-uh, young man, that's not polite,' she complained in a quavery voice, giving him a good bump with her walking frame.

'Thanks for calling me a *young* man,' Bodenstein countered dryly. On days like this, he felt especially old. Having to give someone the news that a loved one had died violently was as difficult after twenty-five years with the criminal police as it had been the very first time he did it.

'I'm ninety-six years old,' said the old woman with a hint of pride. 'Compared to me, you're all a bunch of young whippersnappers.'

'Then by all means, do go first.' Bodenstein stepped aside and waited patiently until the Christmas star was packed up and paid for. Pia, who'd been looking round the shop, stepped up beside him.

'Can I help you?' The ample blonde with a little too much eye make-up, and hands that were cracked from working with flowers and water, gave him a cheerful smile.

'Yes. Hello. My name is Bodenstein, and I'm from the

criminal police in Hofheim. This is my colleague Pia Kirchhoff. We'd like to speak to Renate Rohleder.'

'That's me. What can I do for you?' The smile vanished, and the thought involuntarily shot through Bodenstein's mind that she wouldn't be smiling again for a long time.

The bell on the shop door announced new customers, but Ms Rohleder offered no greeting. Her eyes were fixed on Bodenstein's face, and she seemed to guess that some disaster was about to change her life.

'Has . . . has something happened?' she whispered.

'Perhaps we could speak somewhere else?' Bodenstein asked.

'Of course. Follow me.' She raised one end of the narrow wooden counter, and Bodenstein and Pia slipped through, entering a small, hopelessly cluttered office at the end of the hall.

'I'm afraid we come with bad news,' Bodenstein began. 'This morning round nine o'clock, the body of a woman was discovered in the field between Eschborn and Niederhöchstadt. She had white hair and was wearing an olive-green jacket and a pink cap . . .'

Renate Rohleder turned pale as chalk, an expression of incredulity spread over her features. Not a sound crossed her lips; she simply stood there with her arms hanging limp at her sides. Her hands closed into fists and then opened again.

'The woman had a dog lead with her,' Bodenstein went on.

Renate Rohleder took a step back and sank onto a chair. Stunned disbelief followed on the heels of silent denial – *this can't be, there must be some kind of mistake!*

'She was going to come to the shop to help out after she took Topsi for a walk. There's always so much to do before Christmas. I meant to call her, but I didn't get round to it,' she murmured tonelessly. 'My mother has a pink woollen cap. I gave it to her for Christmas three years ago, along with a pink scarf. And when she walked the dog, she always wore her old Barbour jacket, that ugly, stinking thing . . .'

Her eyes filled with tears.

Now the shock was setting in as she realized the finality of what had happened.

Bodenstein and Pia exchanged a brief glance. The pink cap, the Labrador, the olive-coloured jacket. There was no longer any doubt that Ingeborg Rohleder was the victim.

'What happened? Did she . . . Did she have a heart attack?' whispered Renate Rohleder, looking at Bodenstein. Tears were running down her cheeks, which were streaked with mascara. 'I have to go to her! I have to see her!'

She jumped up, grabbed her phone and car keys from the desk, and snatched a jacket from the coat rack by the door.

'Ms Rohleder, wait!' Bodenstein seized the trembling woman by her shoulders and held her steady. 'We'll take you home. You can't go see your mother.'

'Why not? Maybe she's not even dead, but only . . . unconscious or . . . in a coma!'

'I'm very sorry, Ms Rohleder. Your mother was shot.'

'*Shot?* My mother was *shot?*' she whispered, stunned. 'That can't be possible. Who would do something like that? My mother was the kindest, friendliest person in the world.'

Renate Rohleder staggered and her legs gave way. Bodenstein just managed to grab a chair for her before she collapsed. She stared at him, and then her mouth flew open in a terrible, shrill cry of despair that would echo in Bodenstein's ears for hours afterwards.

*

It was a manageable group that had gathered in the conference room of K-11. Bodenstein and Pia sat on one side of the oval table, Dr Nicola Engel at the head, and Kai Ostermann took a seat on the other side so as not to infect anyone with his germs. He was sniffling and coughing non-stop and in a truly pitiful state. Outside the windows, it was already dark by the time Bodenstein finished his report.

'We should consider taking this public,' Engel said. 'Maybe someone saw the gunman leaving the playground. Thanks to the eyewitness, we at least have a firm time frame.'

'I think that's a good idea, but at the moment, we're completely understaffed,' Bodenstein countered. 'Pia is on holiday and only jumped in today to help out. If we set up a telephone hotline without more manpower, I'll be the only one free to work the field.'

'What do you suggest we do instead?' Engel raised her slender plucked eyebrows.

'So far, we still don't know whether Ingeborg Rohleder was shot because she was the intended target, or whether she was merely a target of opportunity,' Bodenstein replied. 'We have to find out more about her circle of friends before we take this public. We spoke with her daughter, the staff of the flower shop and a few neighbours. The deceased woman seems to have been popular with everyone, and apparently had no enemies. As things stand, we can see no personal motive for the murder.'

'Think back to the case of Vera Kaltensee. That started the same way,' Pia put in. 'In the beginning, we thought she was popular, respected and above reproach.'

'You can't compare the two,' Bodenstein argued.

'Why not?' Pia said with a shrug. 'Anyone who is seventy years old has a long past in which all sorts of things could have happened.'

'I could do some research on the victim,' Ostermann croaked.

'Definitely do that,' Bodenstein said, nodding. 'Maybe the ballistics report on the bullet will tell us something about the murder weapon.'

'Good.' Nicola Engel stood up. 'Please keep me in the loop, Oliver.'

'I will.'

'So, good luck.' She went to the door but then turned. 'Thanks for jumping in today, Ms Kirchhoff. I wish you a lovely holiday and a Merry Christmas.'

'I hope you have a nice Christmas, too,' said Pia. 'Thanks.'

Ostermann pushed back his chair and walked shakily to his office, coughing all the way. Pia followed. There was a whole row of medications on his desk, with a thermos of tea and a box of tissues.

'I haven't had a cold this bad in a long time,' Ostermann moaned. 'If we didn't have a murder case right now, I'd just stay home tomorrow. You'd better leave, Pia, before you catch what I've got and sit round on the cruise ship coughing and sniffling.'

'Jeez, Kai, it makes me feel terrible to leave you alone with this,' she said.

'Ah, bullshit.' Ostermann sneezed and blew his nose. 'I wouldn't feel guilty in the slightest if I'd booked a holiday, and *you* had to sit round here, half dead.'

'Thank you. You say the sweetest things.' Pia flung her

little leather rucksack over her shoulder and gave him a grin. 'So I'll just wish you a speedy recovery and Merry Christmas. Ciao, pal!'

'Say hi to the sun at the equator for me.' Kai Ostermann waved and sneezed again. 'Now, get the hell out of here!'

THURSDAY, DECEMBER 20, 2012

Bodenstein had not slept well. After tossing and turning for half an hour, he was wide awake and decided to get up before he woke Inka, who was sound asleep next to him, snoring quietly. He left the bedroom without turning on the light, pulled on a fleece jacket over his pyjamas, and went downstairs. In the kitchen, he turned on the brand-new coffeemaker that he'd given himself as his favourite Christmas present and set a cup under the nozzle.

Two people out sick in K-11, Cem Altunay and Pia on holiday and a murder case that didn't seem like it would be cleared up anytime soon. The flu season had run riot among his colleagues, so there weren't even any reinforcements to fall back on from other investigative units.

The grinder in the coffeemaker rattled, and a few minutes later, the coffee ran into the cup and a marvellous aroma filled the kitchen. Bodenstein slipped his bare feet into his short lambskin-lined boots and stepped out onto the balcony. He took a sip of coffee – he had never had better – and sat down on the synthetic cotton sofa under the protruding eaves. He wrapped himself in one of the woollen blankets that he took from the neatly folded pile on one of the easy chairs. The air was frosty cold, but so clear that Bodenstein could see the running lights of an aeroplane landing at Frankfurt Airport. The view over the Rhein-Main plain, from the city past the industrial park in Höchst to Frankfurt Airport, was always spectacular – day or night, in summer and winter. He loved sitting outside like this, losing himself in his thoughts and letting his gaze roam free. He had never regretted for a single second buying this semi-detached in the Ruppertshain district of Kelkheim. For him, it meant a return to normal life, which had been abruptly shattered after his divorce from Cosima four years ago. The only constant during that chaotic time had been his job, and he still had that only because Pia had saved his arse several times. His inability to concentrate had led to some serious mistakes, which he was ashamed to acknowledge, but she had never wasted one word on castigating him or attempted to expose his errors in order to nab his job as the head of K-11. Undoubtedly, she was the best colleague he'd ever had, and the thought that he would have to solve the murder of the old lady from Eschborn without her made him more uneasy than he wanted to admit. The sliding door opened. He turned his head and was astonished to see his eldest daughter, Rosalie.

'Hey, sweetheart, why are you up so early?'

'I couldn't sleep anymore,' she said. 'Too many things running through my head.'

'Come here.' Bodenstein scooted over a bit. She sat down next to him. For a while, father and daughter enjoyed the view and the quiet of this early winter morning. He could sense that something was bothering her, but he wanted to wait for her to bring it up herself. Her decision to take a position as sous-chef in one of the best hotels in New York at the age of twenty-four was courageous, especially for Rosalie. Since childhood, even the tiniest change had brought on abdominal pain. She had finished her training as a chef the previous year by winning best in her class, and her mentor, the star chef Jean-Yves St Clair, had advised her to spend some time abroad to gain experience.

'I've never been away from here for longer than a week or two,' she began quietly. 'And I've never lived alone before. Only with Mama or with you. And now America, all of a sudden, New York!'

'Some birds leave the nest earlier, some later,' Bodenstein replied, putting his arm round her shoulders. She tucked her legs up and snuggled against him under the warm blanket. 'Plenty of young people move out to pursue their studies but still cling to their parents' lifeline for years. You've been making your own money for a long time and you're very independent. Besides, you've pretty much managed the whole household. Do you know how much I'm going to miss that?'

'I'm going to miss you, too, Papa. I'll miss everything here. I'm not much of a city person.' Rosalie leaned her head on his shoulder. 'What am I going to do if I get homesick?'

'First of all, I don't think you're going to have much time for feeling homesick,' Oliver said. 'But if it does happen, you can Skype with the people you're missing, or even call them on the phone. At weekends or whenever you have a couple of days free, you can go out to Long Island or up to the Berkshires. They're only a few hours away from New York. And if I know your mother, she's bound to go and visit you.'

'I suppose so,' said Rosalie with a sigh. 'I'm looking forward to New York, and to the job and the new people. And yet I still feel queasy about the whole thing.'

'If you felt any other way, it wouldn't be normal,' he

replied. 'In any case, I'm incredibly proud of you. Back when you first started studying to be a chef, I was convinced that it was only an act of defiance on your part and that you'd soon throw in the towel. But you not only toughed it out, you turned into an excellent chef.'

'There were times when I felt like giving up,' Rosalie admitted. 'I never had time to go out with my girlfriends to parties, concerts or clubs. But somehow they were all so . . . aimless. And I was the only one who found her dream job.'

Oliver smiled in the dark. Rosalie was truly a lot like him, and not only when it came to her attachment to her hometown and her sense of family. Like him, she was also prepared to take responsibility and to make sacrifices to achieve something that was meaningful for her. From her mother, on the other hand, she'd inherited a great deal of ambition, which he somewhat lacked. It put her in a position to overcome all obstacles.

'And that's a valuable thing. Only if you really love doing something do you have a chance of being successful and finding fulfilment in your work,' Oliver said. 'I'm convinced that you've made the perfect decision regarding your future. The year in America will present you with all sorts of opportunities.'

He turned his head and rested his cheek on top of Rosalie's head.

'Whenever things get stormy in your life and you need a calm harbour, there will always be a place for you here,' he said softly.

'Thank you, Papa,' Rosalie murmured, and then yawned. 'I'm feeling better already. I think I'll go back to bed for a while.'

She sat up, gave him a kiss on the cheek, and went back inside.

Children turn into grown-ups, Bodenstein thought with a hint of wistfulness. Time went by so fast! Lorenz and Rosalie had long ago left their childhood behind, and Sophia had already turned six a couple of weeks back. In eighteen years, when she would be as old as Rosalie was today, he would be almost seventy. Would he be able to look back on his life with satisfaction? He was offered Nicola Engel's job a year and a half ago, after he'd taken over temporarily during her suspension, but he had declined. Too much administrative paperwork, too much politics. He wanted to work as an investigator, not a pen-pusher. Only later did he realize that with this decision he had taken from Pia any chance of climbing the professional ladder of the Regional Criminal Unit. Having been Chief Detective Inspector for two years, she had all the necessary qualifications to be an excellent leader of K-11. But as long as he held the post, she would have to be satisfied with being merely part of his team. In the long run, he didn't know whether that would be enough for her. What if one day she decided to transfer somewhere else so she could take a step up the career ladder? Bodenstein downed the last of his coffee, which had by now turned cold. His thoughts returned to the murder case that he had to solve. He would find out in the next few days what it would be like to work without Pia.

Like her boss, Pia Kirchhoff got almost no sleep that night, and for similar reasons. She just couldn't get yesterday's murder out of her head. Some of her colleagues claimed that they could dismiss all thought of work from their minds as soon as they drove home, but she seldom succeeded in doing so. At some point, she got up, got dressed, and tiptoed downstairs. The two dogs yawned and crept out of their baskets, which were in the living room, and followed her outside in the cold, more out of duty than with any real enthusiasm. Pia checked on the two horses standing sleeping in their stalls and sat down on the bench in front of the stable.

According to the initial reports, Ingeborg Rohleder was a nice elderly lady who had worked her whole life in the family-owned flower shop and had been generally well liked in her hometown. Neither the neighbours who had been questioned nor the shocked employees at the flower shop could imagine why anyone would want to put a bullet into Ingeborg Rohleder's head. Was it a case of mistaken identity, or had the woman been a random victim of the shooter? This idea was far more alarming than any other. In about 70 per cent of all murder cases in Germany, there was some connection between the perpetrator and the victim, and often the perp was from the victim's close circle of acquaintances. Usually it was a strong emotion such as jealousy or rage that played a part, or the fear of being caught for committing another crime. A pure, unspecified desire to kill that resulted in the murder of a random victim was very rare. And such cases were extremely difficult to solve. If there was no connection between perp and victim, the police had to rely on happenstance in the form of an eyewitness, a genetic fingerprint or some other detail. Recently, Pia had attended a seminar in which one topic had been the development of violent criminality involving firearms. Even she had been astounded by how few killings in Germany – only 14 per cent – were actually committed with a firearm.

Pia shivered. There wasn't much traffic on the nearby motorway on the other side of the small riding stables at this hour, only occasional headlights flashing by. In less than two hours, that would change tremendously. Pia glanced at the two dogs, who sat in front of her, shivering pitifully, obviously regretting having left their comfortable baskets.

'All right, come on, let's go back inside,' she said as she stood up. The dogs dashed off ahead of her and slipped into the house as soon as she opened the door. Pia took off her jacket and boots, went back upstairs, and snuggled back under the covers.

'Ooh, what's this block of ice?' Christoph murmured when she nestled next to his body, warm with sleep.

'I was just outside for a few minutes,' Pia whispered.

'What time is it?'

'Twenty past five.'

'What's wrong?' He turned over to face her and took her in his arms.

'I can't get the dead woman from yesterday out of my head,' said Pia.

Late last night, she told Christoph why she'd gone to work even though her holiday had already started. No one could appreciate that sort of dedication better than Christoph, who also performed his job as director of Opel Zoo with passion and commitment. When they were shorthanded, he often gave up his weekends and days off.

'The woman was a nice old lady, popular with everyone,' Pia went on. 'The perp used a rifle with a silencer.'

'And what does that mean?' Christoph stifled a yawn.

'We've just begun our investigation, but I have a feeling the woman wasn't specifically targeted,' Pia explained. 'And that could mean that we're dealing with a sniper who just shoots at people at random.'

'And now you're worried because so many of your colleagues are off sick or on holiday.'

'Yeah, that's right. I'd feel a lot better about going away if Cem and Kathrin were there.'

'Listen, sweetie.' Christoph wrapped his arms more tightly round her and kissed her cheek. 'I understand if you'd rather stay here in a situation like this. For me, the trip is more work than holiday—'

'But I can't let you go off on our honeymoon alone!' Pia protested.

'We can always go on a honeymoon later,' Christoph countered. 'It wouldn't be very relaxing for you if your conscience was bothering you the whole time.'

'I'm sure they can handle things without me,' Pia said without much conviction. 'Maybe the whole case will be solved by today.'

'Why don't you sleep on it.' Christoph pulled her even closer. The warmth of his body had a relaxing effect, and Pia could feel sleep overwhelming her.

'Sure,' she murmured. 'I could do that.'

And then she dozed off.

He leafed through the newspaper, reading each page carefully. Nothing. Not a word about the murder in Eschborn. He didn't find anything on the Internet either – neither in the news nor on the police blotter. Obviously, the police thought it better to keep the case out of the media for the time being, which was just fine with him. In a few days, that would change. But until then, the public's ignorance would protect him from accidental witnesses, and he could move about freely.

He was content with his strategy. Everything had gone

exactly as planned. In the car park at Wiesenbad in Eschborn, a few mothers had been there with their kids, but nobody had paid any attention to him when he put the sports bag with the rifle into the boot of his car and drove off.

He pulled up the German Weather Service site on his iPad. He'd been doing that several times a day for weeks and months now, because the weather was an extremely important factor.

'Shit,' he muttered.

The weather forecast for the next three days had changed since yesterday. He frowned as he read about heavy snowfall extending down into the valleys starting on Friday evening.

Snow was bad. He might leave tracks in the snow. What was he going to do now? A precisely worked-out plan in which all the risks had been considered and reduced to a minimum was essential for his success. Nothing was more dangerous than improvisation. But the damned snow threatened to ruin his calculations. For a while, he sat at his desk, summoning in his mind all the details of his plan. It didn't help. The snow was a serious threat, so he would have to change his timetable. Immediately.

'Jeez, Kai, you belong in bed,' said Bodenstein as he entered the K-11 conference room and looked at his only remaining colleague.

'In bed is where people die,' Criminal Detective Superintendent Kai Ostermann said with a wink. 'I feel better than I look.'

He grinned and coughed, and Bodenstein gazed at him sceptically.

'Well, at any rate, I'm grateful that you haven't left me in the lurch,' he said, sitting down at the big table.

'The ballistics report came in a few minutes ago,' Ostermann croaked, shoving a few stapled pages over to him. 'The bullet was a Winchester .308 calibre. Unfortunately, it's a rather common calibre that's used by the army, by hunters and target shooters, and also by us. Every ammo maker has this calibre in its catalogue, and most also produce variants.'

The heating was turned up full blast, and Bodenstein was already breaking out in a sweat, but Ostermann, who had wrapped a scarf round his neck and wore a down gilet over his jumper, didn't seem to notice the heat at all.

'This cartridge is a Remington Core-Lokt, 11.7 grams, which is the bestselling centrefire cartridge in the world for hunting. The weapon from which the bullet was fired has not yet turned up.'

'So no real clue, then.' Bodenstein removed his jacket and hung it over the back of the chair. 'Any news from the evidence team?'

'No. The shot was made from a distance of about eighty metres.' Ostermann coughed, popped a sage cough drop into his mouth, and continued in a whisper. 'No problem for a trained marksman. No traces were found at the crime scene or the spot from which the shooter fired, other than the blurred outline of indentations left by the bipod. He must have picked up the cartridge casing and taken it with him. After evaluating the statements taken from neighbours and employees at the flower shop, we have to conclude that nothing of note happened during the past few weeks. Ingeborg Rohleder seemed the same as always and gave no sign of feeling threatened.'

Bodenstein was coming to the depressing realization that

so far, they knew nothing at all except for the calibre of the murder weapon and the type of cartridge used. He didn't like resorting to such a measure, but because so many of his colleagues were off sick, he had no choice but to ask Commissioner Engel for reinforcements from other investigative units.

'I'm asking myself seriously, how we—' he began when the door behind him opened. Ostermann's eyes widened.

'Hello,' said Pia behind Bodenstein, and he turned round.

'What are you doing here?' he asked in surprise.

'Am I interrupting?' Pia looked from him to Ostermann.

'Oh no, no, not in the least,' Bodenstein hurried to assure her. 'Come and have a seat.'

'Don't you have anything better to do on the day before you leave on holiday?' Ostermann whispered hoarsely.

'No.' Pia took off her jacket and sat down with a big grin. 'I've taken care of everything. And then I thought I'd just help you solve this case quickly before I take off for three weeks in the sun.'

Kai Ostermann grimaced, and Bodenstein took off his jumper before rapidly summing up the facts that he and Kai had been discussing.

'That's not much,' said Pia. 'Is there any chance of finding out where and when the ammo was purchased?'

'No,' said Ostermann, shaking his head. 'It's found in every gun shop and hunting catalogue in the world.'

'And so far, we have no clue as to the motive,' said Bodenstein. 'It could be a sniper who shoots people out of a pure love of killing.'

'Or maybe Ingeborg Rohleder had some dark secrets that nobody knows about,' replied Pia. 'We should do a complete rundown on the victim's circle of acquaintances and past history.'

'Agreed,' Bodenstein said with a nod, and stood up. 'Let's drive over and see Renate Rohleder. Then we'll stop by forensics. The post-mortem is scheduled for eleven fifteen.'

Renate Rohleder seemed almost as distraught as she'd been yesterday. She sat red-eyed at her kitchen table, kneading a handkerchief in her left hand and with the other mechanically petting her Labrador, who was nestled at her feet. Her blonde hair, which yesterday had been artfully pinned up, now hung limp over her shoulders. Her face was puffy and bare of make-up, as if she'd been crying the whole night.

'Why isn't there anything in the paper?' Renate asked with a reproachful undertone instead of responding to Bodenstein's polite greeting. She tapped her finger on an open newspaper. 'Nothing on the radio either. Why not? What are you doing to find the person who murdered my mother?'

Visits to the loved ones of a murder victim were always difficult, and Bodenstein had experienced every kind of reaction in his twenty-five years at K-11. When a murder happened in a family, most people eventually managed to regain some semblance of a normal life, but the early days were always marked by shock, chaos and breakdowns. He and his colleagues often served as lightning rods in this emotional state of emergency, and Bodenstein had long since acquired a thick skin.

'It's still too early to involve the media,' he replied calmly. 'We don't have enough facts to ask the public for help. News reports filled with pure speculation would not be in your best interest.'

Renate Rohleder shrugged and looked at her smartphone, which was beeping melodiously every few seconds.

'I suppose so,' she whispered. 'I can't even go to the shop. People mean well, but I . . . I simply can't stand hearing all these expressions of sympathy.'

In a glance, Bodenstein took in the state of the kitchen and assumed that Ingeborg Rohleder had kept the house in order while her daughter ran the flower shop. After twenty-four hours, her absence was already noticeable. Still on the table were the remains of a breakfast: a plate full of crumbs, an open jar of marmalade with a spoon stuck in it, and soggy tea bags lying on a saucer. Dirty dishes were stacked in the sink along with a saucepan with burnt food stuck to the bottom.

'We're very sorry that we have to disturb you in your grief,' Pia said. 'But we need to know more about your mother and her circle of friends. Where was she from originally? How long did she live here in Eschborn—?'

'Niederhöchstadt,' Renate Rohleder corrected her, blowing her nose again and glancing at the display on her phone.

'In Niederhöchstadt. Did she have any enemies, or were there any difficulties in the family? Had she changed recently, was she nervous or feeling threatened?'

'You don't seriously mean that someone shot my mother on purpose!' She sounded almost hostile. 'I already told you: she didn't have any enemies. Everyone liked her. She came here in the early sixties from Sossenheim, opened the flower shop and nursery with my father, and she has lived here ever since. Happily and peacefully, for more than fifty years.'

She picked up her mobile phone, which kept on chirping and lighting up, and held it out to Pia.

'See? Everybody, absolutely everyone is offering their condolences, even the mayor.' Her eyes swam with tears. 'Do you think that would be happening if my mother wasn't well liked?'

'It's possible that your mother had some kind of secret in her life, something that happened a long time ago,' Pia persisted. Bodenstein knew that she was thinking of the Kaltensee case. The idea wasn't that far-fetched. At the very start of an investigation, when they were still fumbling about in the dark, it was important to explore all avenues. That's why he hadn't contradicted Pia when she'd mentioned earlier in the car that, unlike him, she didn't believe in random killings. The crime statistics were on her side. Murders committed simply from a desire to kill without any real motive were extremely rare.

'Ms Rohleder, our questions are in no way intended to disparage your mother's memory,' Bodenstein now intervened to reassure her. 'Our sole purpose is to find the person who killed her. In our search for a motive, it's common practice to begin by carefully examining the victim's circle of friends and relatives.'

'But there can't be any conceivable reason for killing her,' Renate Rohleder insisted. 'You're wasting your time if you're trying to find the motive in my mother's life.'

Pia wanted to ask something else, but Bodenstein signalled with a quick shake of his head that he found further questioning to be pointless.

'Thank you, Ms Rohleder,' he said. 'Should you think of something that might help us, please don't hesitate to call.'

'Of course.' Renate Rohleder blew her nose again, using the already soaking-wet handkerchief. Bodenstein stuck his hands in his jacket pockets for safety's sake, in case the woman offered to shake hands with him when they left. But she was completely focused on the sympathy messages coming into her phone almost every second.

They left the kitchen and walked down the hall to the front door. Bodenstein turned up the collar of his coat. They had left the car in the car park back at Eschborn police station on the main street.

'*Niederhöchstadt*, not Eschborn!' Pia snorted. 'Good God, when was the local government reform? Fifty years ago?'

'Nineteen seventy-one,' Bodenstein said with a smile. 'People are just proud of their old villages and want to hold on to their own identity.'

'What crap.' Pia shook her head. 'All these hick towns would have gone broke long ago if they'd remained autonomous.'

At the street corner, a few elderly people had paused to stare at them with undisguised curiosity. Bodenstein greeted them with a nod.

'At least now they have new fodder for the village gossip mill,' Pia said caustically. 'Maybe Ingeborg Rohleder was shot because she told someone she was going to live in Eschborn.'

'Why are you so sensitive about that?' Bodenstein cast a sidelong glance at his colleague. 'Or were you hoping that Renate Rohleder would mention a name and we could immediately arrest somebody?'

They reached the police car park, and he beeped to unlock the doors of their unmarked car.

'Of course not.' Pia stopped. Then she smiled wryly, shrugged, and opened the passenger door. 'Well, maybe. I'd feel better about going on holiday if the case were solved.'

*

At precisely 11:30, they entered Dissection Room II in the basement of the Institute of Forensic Medicine on Kennedyallee. The body of Ingeborg Rohleder lay washed and naked on the metal table. Professor Henning Kirchhoff and Dr Frederick Lemmer had already begun with the external postmortem examination.

'Pia?' Henning cried in astonishment. 'What are you doing here? I thought you were on holiday.'

'I am,' she said. 'But almost everyone is off sick at K-11, so I jumped in just for today.'

'I see.' Henning pulled down his mask, raised his eyebrows, and grinned. A bit mockingly, Pia thought.

'We're on a flight tomorrow evening at seven forty-five,' she reassured him. 'The bags are already packed.'

'That doesn't mean a thing,' said Henning. 'I bet you a hundred euros that you don't go.'

'You've already lost that bet,' Pia retorted. 'And while all of you will be freezing your butts off here, I'll be relaxing in the sun and thinking of you.'

'Not going to happen. Remember, I know you,' Henning teased her. 'So, just in case you let Christoph go alone, you're cordially invited to come have Christmas dinner with us. We even put up a tree.'

'I'll be on that plane tomorrow!' Pia snapped in annoyance. She hated that Henning knew her so well and always had such an easy time seeing through her. She'd actually prefer to call off this holiday that she'd been looking forward to for so long, but she refused to admit it to herself. And she certainly didn't want to hear it from her ex-husband.

Bodenstein smiled and held out his hand to Henning's new colleague, who had been following the exchange with some amazement.

'Don't mind these two. They were married once,' he explained. 'Oliver von Bodenstein, K-11 Hofheim.'

'Frederick Lemmer,' the other man answered. 'Pleased to meet you.'

'Can we begin?' Pia asked indignantly. 'We don't have all day.'

'Why not? Your plane doesn't leave till tomorrow,' Henning needled her, grinning at the dirty look she gave him. Then he turned to the body.

The post-mortem uncovered no decisive new facts. Ingeborg Rohleder had been as healthy as could be, and if she hadn't been shot, she would have lived many more years. The projectile had entered her temple above her left ear and exited a few centimetres higher through her right vertex, which confirmed Kröger's theory about the path of the bullet. The gunman had been positioned down by the stream. He came out of nowhere and then disappeared into thin air.

'How do you like this one, Mama?' Greta had slipped into a short jacket edged with fake fur. She twisted and turned, casting a critical eye at herself in the mirror. The jacket suited her. She was slim, with seemingly endless legs, which meant she looked fabulous in that sort of jacket, unlike many women of Karoline's generation, who had already been getting pudgy even at Greta's age.

'It looks great on you,' Karoline said.

Greta smiled radiantly as she looked for the price tag, which was hanging out of one sleeve.

'Oh no!' Her eyes widened in consternation. 'I can't buy this.'

42

'Why not?'

'It costs a hundred and eighty euros!'

'I'll get you the jacket for Christmas if you like it.'

The girl looked dubious but then turned back to glance in the mirror, torn between reason and desire. Finally the jacket ended up in the shopping bag with three pairs of jeans, a jumper, and a hoodie. Greta was overjoyed, and Karoline was pleased.

When was the last time she'd been shopping in the city five days before Christmas? It must have been twenty years ago, if not longer. Karoline used to love pushing her way through the crowds with her best friend. She loved the kitschy Christmas decorations, the rousing Christmas carols, the vendors' booths that stood on every corner and the aroma of roasted candied almonds in the cold December air. When she picked up Greta from boarding school early in the afternoon to take a walk into town, she'd been thinking of Goethestrasse, but Greta insisted on going to the shopping centres on the Zeil. For three hours, they had ploughed their way through overheated and overcrowded department stores. She felt happy watching her daughter prowl the aisles with shining eyes, looking for Christmas presents for her girlfriends, for Nicki, Papa and her half sister. Greta also enthusiastically tried on clothes that her mother secretly found largely impossible. To Karoline's surprise, even the crowded stores were fun, calling up long-forgotten memories from her youth.

Back then, she'd had so much time. Her mother had always been generous and never chided her if she sometimes came home late. How amazing it felt not be under pressure from any sort of deadline. Her smartphone was back in the glove box of the car, and she didn't even miss it.

43

At five o'clock, they lugged their loot in a zillion bags to the car, which was parked in an underground garage, to drive back to Oberursel. Baking cookies with Grandma – that was something Greta still loved doing at thirteen.

'Do you really want to stop working?' she asked her mother as Karoline manoeuvered the black Porsche out of the parking spot.

'You don't believe me, do you?' Karoline gave her daughter a sidelong glance and saw the doubt in her eyes.

The girl sighed.

'I like it at boarding school, but it would be much nicer if I could live with you and Papa – during the week, too. But . . .'

'But what?' Karoline stuck the ticket in the reader, and the barrier rose up.

'Papa said that the world would have to end before you would ever stop working,' replied Greta.

Bodenstein and Pia were feeling rather frustrated when they arrived back at the station in Hofheim. A photo of Ingeborg Rohleder hung on the bulletin board in the conference room, and next to it, Ostermann had written her name and the time of the murder. That was all they had. The canvassing of the neighbourhood, which some of their colleagues had done, had turned up nothing. The statements of witnesses had been helpful only in pinning down the exact time of the fatal gunshot. No one had seen the shooter. Evidence techs had searched the crime scene meticulously within a radius of 250 metres, but except for the faint impression of the bipod, they had found nothing: no fibres, no shoeprints on the frozen ground, no cartridge casing, no skin scrapings and no hair. The perp remained a phantom, and his motive a riddle.

'How should we proceed now?' asked Ostermann with a rasping cough.

'Hmm.' Bodenstein studied the map on the wall and rubbed the back of his neck in thought. Where did the perp escape to? Was he audacious enough to get away by crossing the playground and the Rhine highway and walking right past Eschborn police station? Or did he take the Lahnstrasse, then the footpath to the viewpoint and get into a car there? Those were undoubtedly the two fastest escape routes, but there were other options as well. Walking to the car park near the swimming pool, for instance, or going further, past the tennis courts to the fairground, which was used for parking by the employees of many of the surrounding businesses. In any of these places, he could have unobtrusively got into a car and disappeared down the road.

'We should inform the public and ask for help,' Pia said, and Ostermann nodded in agreement. 'We're probably not going to find any more facts relevant to the crime than the ones we already have.'

Inwardly, Bodenstein argued against it, because he was afraid of the immense amount of time it would take to handle the usual phone calls from idiots and all the spurious leads that would have to be checked out. He really couldn't afford wasting any time, given the extreme shortage of investigators at his disposal, but there seemed to be no alternative. Pia was right – at the moment, they weren't expecting to turn up any more facts. Still, there was a slim chance that someone may have seen something that had seemed unimportant at first.

'Okay,' Bodenstein said at last. 'We'll go to the press. And hope for the best.'

The spot was ideal. The fir branches hung low over the flat roof covered with moss, and the road was a dead end. By six in the evening, it was pitch dark. On the right side of the road were only meadows, and her house was the last one, right at the edge of the little wood located between the outskirts of the village and the old state road to Königstein. She had turned on the light in the kitchen ten minutes before and then gone upstairs. The old house had huge, old-fashioned lattice windows and no roll-down shutters, only wooden folding shutters, which seemed to be only for decoration; they probably hadn't been closed in years. From his perspective, the house looked a lot like a doll's house. He could see into every window and follow exactly what she was doing. He knew her daily routine, which hardly ever changed except in the most minor ways. In no more than ten minutes, she would go back to the kitchen and start preparing dinner for herself and her husband.

The temperature had dropped by a few degrees since yesterday. The snowstorm predicted for late evening would be a long time coming. The cold didn't bother him. He was dressed for it. He glanced at his watch. The digital display jumped to 18:22. At that moment, she entered the kitchen. Through his Kahles ZF69 rifle scope, he could see her as if she were standing right in front of him. She bent down, then turned round and took something out of a cupboard. Her lips moved. Maybe she was listening to music and singing along, as many people do when they're alone. His index finger was on the trigger. He was breathing deeply in and out, concentrating intently on his target. Then, as she turned in his direction, he squeezed the trigger. In the same second that the bullet crashed through the windowpane and burst her head wide open, he flicked his eyes reflexively to the right and saw a

*second person in the kitchen. Good God – she wasn't alone!
A shrill scream pierced the air.*

*'Shit!' he muttered. Adrenalin was pumping through his
body, his heart hammering. He hadn't counted on anyone else
being in the house. The woman hadn't been singing, she was
talking to someone! Swiftly, he disassembled the rifle and
stowed it in the bag. Then he put the used casing that had
been ejected in his jacket pocket and crawled to the edge of the
roof. Under cover of the tree branches, he slipped down from
the roof of the transformer substation and vanished sound-
lessly in the dark.*

The whole project in the kitchen turned into a gigantic mess.
Like a spurting fountain, the hot liquid sprayed her face, hands
and arms.

'Damn!'

She looked down at herself and saw that she was covered
with orange spots. The pumpkin and carrot juice would be
almost impossible to get out of the light-grey cashmere of her
favourite jumper. Pia swore a blue streak because she'd forgotten to put on an apron before she stuck the hand blender in
the saucepan and turned it on. The juice had also spattered
the Ceran cooking surface on her convection stove top, the
floor and half the kitchen. Normally she wasn't so clumsy
in the kitchen, but she was feeling out of it, and this was the
first time she was making pumpkin soup with ginger and
coconut milk. The recipe had sounded good and promised to
be child's play, but the pumpkin had almost done her in when
she was unable to cut it up as easily as described in the recipe.
After she had sawed on the gourd in vain with a meat knife
and almost sliced her finger, she marched outside with the

obstreperous sphere and without further ado set it on the chopping block next to the shed and quickly split it apart with an axe. She finished dicing up the pumpkin in the kitchen.

'I'll be a laughing stock if I can't even make a simple pumpkin soup,' Pia muttered, turning off the blender. Stupidly enough, the recipe page was so covered with orange liquid that she could no longer decipher how much coconut milk to put in the soup.

Outside, a car drove up, and a minute later the front door opened. The dogs greeted Christoph with happy barks.

'Wife at the stove,' he called cheerfully as he came into the kitchen. 'That's the way to start a holiday!'

Pia turned round and smiled. After more than four years, her heart still skipped a beat whenever she saw Christoph.

'I planned to have dinner ready long ago, and surprise you with a delicious soup. The recipe said it was easy and would take only twenty minutes. But it all started going wrong when I had to use brute force to break up the pumpkin into small bits.'

Christoph's eyes surveyed the kitchen, which Pia had transformed into a battlefield. He tried not to grin, but then he couldn't help laughing. Ignoring the pumpkin-carrot splatters, he took her in his arms and kissed her.

'Yum,' he said, licking his lips. 'Tastes good!'

'It's only missing the coconut milk. And the coriander.'

'You know what?' Christoph took the blender from her hand. 'Let me finish this while you clean up and set the table.'

'I was hoping you'd say that, beloved husband.' Pia smiled, gave him a kiss, and got ready to clear away the chaos she'd created with her cooking experiment.

Fifteen minutes later, they were sitting at the table, and the soup actually did taste fantastic. Pia talked non-stop about all sorts of trivia, which was out of character for her, but she was trying to avoid having Christoph ask whether she'd been at work today. She was torn between her desire to spend three weeks with her husband and the awful feeling that she was letting down her boss and colleagues. The dilemma was tormenting her, because normally she was not a person who put off making unpleasant decisions. At first, Christoph went along with her evasive manoeuver, but finally he brought up the awkward subject.

'Have you decided yet whether you're flying with me or staying here?' he asked casually as they were clearing the table.

'Of course I'm going with you,' she replied. 'My bags are all packed.'

'Did you and your colleagues catch the murderer?'

'Unfortunately, no.' Pia shook her head. 'There are no clues, no witnesses, no obvious motive. Maybe the woman was just in the wrong place at the wrong time, and there's no connection between the victim and the perp.'

'You mean, she was shot at random?'

'It's possible. That sort of thing is rare, but it does happen.'

'So now what?'

Pia began to fill the dishwasher.

'The boss wants to take the case public in the hope that somebody somewhere might have seen something. So there's absolutely no reason for me to stay here,' she said, keeping her voice cheerful, though she felt the exact opposite. 'It won't really matter whether I'm here to help them or not.'

*

'I just came from Wiesbaden,' Dr Nicola Engel announced as she sat down on one of the visitors' chairs in front of Bodenstein's desk. 'At the office of the State Criminal Police, I happened to run into the head of Operational Case Analysis. He said it might be possible to send over one of his people, as reinforcement and to lend us another perspective.'

'I see.' Bodenstein took off his reading glasses and looked at his boss expectantly. Nicola never 'happened' to run into anyone, and her use of the phrase 'might be possible' was only a rhetorical trick to make him feel that she had asked his opinion. In reality, she had undoubtedly already arranged everything without consulting him.

'Andreas Neff is an experienced case analyst,' she went on. 'He was in the States for a while and learned the latest profiling methods.'

'I see,' Bodenstein said again. The idea of working with a stranger on this case didn't exactly please him, but since Pia was leaving on holiday tomorrow and Fachinger was still off sick, he desperately needed some back-up.

'What do you mean by "I see"?' Nicola Engel asked. 'I thought you'd be happy to have some help.'

Bodenstein gazed pensively at his boss, who years earlier had once been his fiancée. A lot had happened since the incidents in the summer two years ago, which had resulted in her arrest and suspension from the force because of serious accusations made by their longtime colleague Frank Behnke. Behnke claimed that Dr Engel had ordered him to liquidate an undercover investigator during a raid fifteen years earlier, to stop him from spilling the beans about the connections between some high-ranking personalities and a paedophile ring. The arrest of the leader of the criminal police had created quite a stir, and naturally, the press had jumped all over it.

But Dr Nicola Engel had not allowed these accusations to stick. She finally revealed to Bodenstein what she until then had resolutely kept secret. In 1997, he was also working in Frankfurt K-11, but he had only peripheral knowledge of the events. Nicola now told him that in reality it wasn't Frank Behnke, but she herself who had been the victim of a plot that extended into the highest political levels. When she became a danger to the people pulling the strings, they had threatened her and then had her transferred to Würzburg in Bavaria. Knowing that the statute of limitations never expired for murder, Nicola Engel had decided to put the case on the back burner until some later time when she would be able to expose what really happened.

Her testimony before an investigative commission had provoked dramatic results. The former acting chief of police and a retired judge from the Federal Constitutional Court both committed suicide. Other individuals involved had been arrested and had confessed, so that after fourteen years, the murders of Erik Lessing and two members of the Frankfurt Road Kings were finally resolved. After this, Engel had been reinstated and returned to her position, while Frank Behnke was sentenced to life in prison for the triple murder.

After Engel returned to the Regional Criminal Unit in Hofheim, which Bodenstein had headed temporarily during her absence, she had a long conversation with Pia and Bodenstein to thank them specifically for their actions. With this burden finally lifted from her soul after fifteen long years, a great change was apparent in Engel. Working with her was entirely different, more collegial and, at times, even convivial.

'I'd be happier if I had my whole team working on this,' Bodenstein now replied, shutting down his computer. 'But perhaps a case analyst would be a good idea. We're fishing in murky waters, and we're no further along than we were yesterday.'

Engel stood up, and Bodenstein followed suit.

'I'm giving you carte blanche,' she assured him. 'If you need more people, just tell me, and I'll take care of it.'

His mobile rang.

'All right.' He nodded to his boss. She left the office and he took the call.

'Papa!' Rosalie shouted in his ear. 'Mama just dumped the dwarf on me, and she wasn't supposed to do that till tomorrow!'

'I'm not a dwarf,' Sophia protested in the background, and Bodenstein had to smile.

'Calm down,' Rosalie said to her little sister; then she turned back to her father. 'Mama has to leave today for Berlin, because her schedule got changed somehow. But what am I supposed to do now? I have so many things to get done, and I can't leave Sophia alone. What am I going to—?'

'I'll be home in half an hour,' Bodenstein interrupted his elder daughter. 'Then you can take off.'

He took his coat from the closet, grabbed his briefcase and turned off the light in his office. As he walked, he punched up his contact list on his mobile and tapped in the number of his ex-wife. Once again, this was so typical of Cosima. She was always so wrapped up in her own plans and impulsive ideas, so she had never paid much attention to what anyone else needed to do – her husband and her children came second.

*

Pia put away her buzzing mobile when she saw that the caller had blocked the number. At seven thirty in the evening, it could only be somebody she didn't know, or the police dispatcher. In twenty-four hours, she would be sitting on the plane to Ecuador, and she didn't want the decision that she had finally made to be jeopardized by anything.

'Don't you want to take that call?' Christoph asked.

'No.'

She had already given the horses their evening hay, and now she wanted to curl up on the comfortable sofa and watch a DVD with Christoph while they finished off at least one bottle of wine. 'Did you choose a movie?'

'How about *In Bruges*?' Christoph suggested. 'We haven't watched that in a long time.'

'Please, nothing with guns and dead bodies,' said Pia.

'Well, that eliminates almost everything we have in our video collection,' he said with a grin. He was dead set against letting Pia talk him into watching *Steel Magnolias* or *The Devil Wears Prada*. Before he found some football match on the Sky Channel or a deadly boring documentary on Arte, Pia agreed to watch a James Bond movie. They were always entertaining, and it would take her mind off other things.

Her mobile buzzed again.

'Go ahead and take it,' Christoph said. 'It seems to be important.'

Pia sighed, grabbed the phone, and said hello.

'Ms Kirchhoff, please forgive me for bothering you,' said the officer on duty. 'I know you're on holiday, but I can't reach anyone else from K-11. We have another body. In Oberursel this time.'

'Shit,' Pia muttered. 'What about Bodenstein?'

'He's not answering his phone. But I'll try him again.'

'Where do I have to go?' She met Christoph's gaze and shrugged to signal her regret.

'The address is An der Heide 12 in Oberursel,' said the officer. 'I've already notified the evidence team.'

'Got it. Thanks.'

'And thank you.' He had the decency not to wish her a good evening, because obviously she wasn't going to have one.

'What's up?' Christoph asked.

'If only I hadn't taken that call.' Pia got up. 'There's another body, in Oberursel. I'm really sorry. I hope the boss shows up soon so I can make a quick exit.'

Bodenstein was ecstatic that he had to play only a minor role in his ex-wife's chaotic life. It had taken him years to admit that he didn't find it 'exciting' but rather terribly exhausting to adapt to her constantly changing plans. Cosima had no qualms about rescheduling appointments that had been made weeks before, if something more interesting suddenly popped into her head. And she expected her family and friends simply to accept the way she impulsively changed her mind. 'Flexibility' and 'spontaneity', two words that she promoted as positive traits, were in Bodenstein's eyes nothing more than proof of her inability to organize her life.

'I wanted to take a taxi, but they couldn't send one for an hour!' Cosima said as Bodenstein loaded her luggage into the boot of her SUV in the car park of the Zauberberg building in Ruppertshain. 'It's totally outrageous.'

'If you'd ordered the taxi yesterday, I'm sure it wouldn't have been a problem,' was all he said as he closed the boot. 'Have you got everything?'

'Oh dear, where's my handbag? Did I have it with me or not?' She opened the boot again. Bodenstein got in behind the wheel and turned to Sophia, who was in her car seat.

'Are you all strapped in?' he asked.

'Sure. Even a baby could do it,' replied his younger daughter.

'Ah, here it is!' Cosima shouted, slamming the boot closed, then jumping into the passenger seat. 'God, I'm frazzled.'

Bodenstein refrained from commenting. He started the engine and drove off. Some things would never change.

Cosima babbled on during the whole trip, through Fischbach and Kelkheim, down the B8, and didn't shut up until they turned at the Main-Taunus Centre and got on the A66 to Wiesbaden. Bodenstein glanced to the right and saw in the dark the lights of Birkenhof, where Pia lived with her partner. Maybe the profiler that Nicola had forced on him would really help solve the case quickly. But he felt rather lost without Pia, Cem and Kathrin. During his career with the criminal police, there had been very few cases that went unsolved. He had the unpleasant feeling that the murder of Ingeborg Rohleder might one day end up as a cold case in a box in the archives. Seldom had the evidence been so scanty as it was in this investigation.

'Are we there yet, Papa?' Sophia asked from the back seat.

'Almost,' he said, signalling to turn right. A few minutes later, they could see the lights of Frankfurt Airport. He had driven Cosima out here countless times when she was going off on a trip. He could find the way in his sleep. As usual at this time of the evening, all hell had broken loose at the airport, but Bodenstein got lucky and nabbed a ten-minute spot in front of the departures hall. He got out, found a baggage trolley, and loaded suitcases and bags on it while Cosima said goodbye to Sophia.

Then they were standing face-to-face.

'Kind of like the old days, don't you think?' Cosima smiled, a little embarrassed. 'Merry Christmas, Oliver. And thanks for everything.'

'Don't mention it,' said Bodenstein. 'And Merry Christmas to you, too. Give us a call on Christmas Eve, everybody's coming over to my house.'

'Ah, I wish I could be there,' Cosima said with a sigh, surprising him. She didn't seem very happy. The feverish euphoria that had always gripped her when taking off on a trip to work on a long-planned film project was missing.

Suddenly she took a step towards Bodenstein and hugged him. It was the first time in years that she'd touched him, but it felt strangely familiar. She still wore the same perfume.

'I miss you,' she whispered, giving him a kiss on the cheek. The next instant, she grabbed the handle of the baggage trolley, blew Sophia a kiss, and took off. Amazed, Bodenstein watched her go until the glass doors of the departures hall closed behind her and she disappeared in the crowd.

When Pia arrived at the designated address with the help of the satnav, she had a feeling that it was going to be a long evening, because the whole cavalry had turned out in the quiet cul-de-sac at the edge of the fields: several patrol cars, the medical examiner, ambulances, the forensic team and a crisis intervention team. Blue lights flashed mutely in the night. Pia left her car behind a dark-coloured Porsche with Frankfurt plates and walked through the light snowfall to the blue VW van with the side door open.

'Hello,' she greeted her colleagues, who were already pulling on overalls and unloading the equipment they needed for their crime-scene work.

'Hi, Pia.' Christian Kröger jumped out of the van.

'So what do we have?' she asked.

'A woman was shot,' said Kröger. 'Her granddaughter was standing right next to her. Her daughter is also in the house. They're both being treated for shock and emotional trauma.'

That didn't sound good. Not good at all.

'Who is the dead woman?'

'Margarethe Rudolf, sixty-four. I think her husband is a doctor.' Kröger pulled up his hood. 'The ME just got here. Two of my team are still inside, but I need to examine the outside before the snow or any curious neighbours mess up the place.'

He grabbed two metal cases.

'Why outside?' Pia asked. 'I thought it happened indoors.'

'The woman was standing in the kitchen,' Kröger said. 'But the gunman shot through the window from outside. Head shot with a large calibre. If you ask me, it looks a lot like our killer has struck a second time. Sorry, but I've got to hurry.'

Pia nodded and took a deep breath. So it wasn't a domestic dispute after all. Although that would have been bad enough, the alternative might be even worse. She gazed through the whirling snowflakes at the old house. What could be waiting for her inside? Why the hell had she answered her mobile? Right now she could have been lying comfortably on her sofa and watching a movie, but instead, her damned sense of duty had brought her here. At last, she gave herself a kick in the butt, crossed the street, and followed the paved path to the front door, which was ajar.

'Where do I go?' she asked one of the uniforms who was standing in the foyer.

'Straight ahead and then take a right. In the kitchen,' he replied. 'The victim's daughter and granddaughter are in the house. The deceased's husband, Professor Dieter Rudolf, isn't here yet, and as far as I know, he hasn't been informed. I say this only so that you'll be prepared.'

'Thank you,' Pia said. This was completely different from doing crime-scene work at some anonymous place. Here, they were in the presence of family members who were in shock. She was glad that a crisis intervention team had arrived, along with a psychologist and a priest.

'Hello,' she said as she entered the kitchen.

'Hello, Ms Kirchhoff,' Frederick Lemmer said, looking up and nodding to her. 'She's been dead for about an hour,' said the ME. 'A single shot that struck the right side of her head. She must have been turning her head left at that instant. The bullet exited at about the same height and went through a cupboard door. In my opinion, the same calibre as the one yesterday.'

The woman lay on her back. She was wearing a blue-and-white striped apron over a brown top and a thin knitted cardigan. Her facial features were almost beyond recognition, so destructive had been the effect of the bullet. There was blood and brain matter all over the cupboards and all the way up to the ceiling. Pia had learned in her day-to-day experience as a murder investigator, as well as in numerous police courses and seminars, to keep her head functioning in situations like this and to close her heart, but the sight of the bag of flour in the victim's left hand made her swallow hard. Her eyes took in the rest of the room. On the counter below the window stood sugar and butter, eggs, crumbled chocolate and shredded coconut, along with a bowl, a mixer and metal cookie cutters – Christmas trees, animals, stars.

'She was just getting ready to bake Christmas cookies,' Pia said in a hoarse voice. Rage flared up inside her. How ice-cold would a person have to be to do something like this so close to Christmas and in the presence of a child?

Somewhere in the house, a phone rang, but no one picked it up.

'Are you guys finished?' Pia asked her colleagues from the evidence team.

'We're done with the body,' said one of the officers.

'You, too, Dr Lemmer?'

'Yes.' The ME closed his bag and stood up.

'Then I'd like the body to be transported immediately,' Pia ordered. 'And get a crime-scene cleaner in here straight away. Things are already bad enough for the family.'

'Will do,' one of the officers said with a nod. 'I'll tell the morgue guy outside.'

Pia stayed behind in the kitchen alone. She examined the shattered pane in one of the rectangular wooden lattices of the window, through which the cold wind was blowing. Death had occurred in a fraction of a second, and Margarethe Rudolf had felt nothing – no fear of death, no pain. From one moment to the next, her life was over. But her granddaughter had witnessed the whole thing.

Pia glanced at the clock. Eight thirty. Where was Bodenstein?

She had to talk to the girl and her mother, although she would have preferred to be spared the task. But there was no sense in putting it off any longer.

Pia heard loud voices outside. She went into the hall and saw a slim, white-haired man in a dark coat who was trying in vain to get past two officers. 'Let me through at once! This is my house!' the man cried in outrage. 'What's going on here?'

Pia went over to him, and the two officers stepped aside.

'Dr Rudolf?'

'Yes. And who are you? What happened? Where's my wife?'

The men from the morgue carried in the zinc coffin to remove the body and then paused respectfully.

'I'm Chief Detective Inspector Pia Kirchhoff,' Pia said. 'Could we please speak privately—?'

'First I want to know what's going on here,' the professor interrupted her. Fear flickered in his eyes behind the lenses of his gold-rimmed glasses. 'My daughter's car is outside. Where is she?'.

In the doorway of the living room, a woman with blonde hair appeared. Pia judged her to be in her early to mid-forties. Her face was rigid, her eyes glassy and her expression vacant, either from a sedative or the effects of the shock she had suffered.

'Karoline!' Professor Rudolf squeezed past Pia. 'Why won't anyone answer the phone?'

'Mama is dead,' the woman said tonelessly. 'Someone shot her . . . through the kitchen window.'

'How did he react?' Bodenstein wanted to know twenty minutes later. He apologized for the delay by explaining that he'd first had to drop off his little daughter at home.

'He totally collapsed.' Pia was still shaken by the intensity with which the professor had reacted to the horrible news.

'Did he see his wife's body?'

'We couldn't prevent it.' Pia shivered in the cold. 'He shoved right past us and went in the kitchen. It took four men to tear him away from her body. At least his daughter was able to stop him from locking himself in his office and doing harm to himself out of sheer despair.'

They were standing in the street by the evidence team's VW van as the snow began to come down even harder. The corpse had been taken away, and the crime-scene cleaners had shown up and were working in the kitchen. The ambulances and the medical examiner drove off. A few curious neighbours had gathered on the pavement underneath a streetlamp, watching as the daughter left the house and got in the Porsche with the Frankfurt plates. On the advice of the psychologist, she had not permitted Pia to speak with thirteen-year-old Greta, who had witnessed her grandmother's murder. Pia had accepted that. It seemed unlikely the girl could have seen much, or at least nothing that would be helpful.

'She's leaving her father here alone,' Pia remarked. 'That's odd.'

'Maybe he wants to be alone,' Bodenstein said. 'Every individual reacts differently to a catastrophe like this. Besides, isn't it better for the girl not to stay in that house any longer? By the way, where is she?'

'Her father picked her up earlier. The parents are separated, and he lives in Bad Soden,' Pia told him. 'I've sent some colleagues out to talk with all the neighbours; maybe somebody saw something.'

'Very good.' Bodenstein rubbed his hands and stuck them in his coat pockets.

Kröger came over to them.

'We found the spot where the shooter fired from,' he said. 'Do you want to have a look?'

'Of course.' Bodenstein and Pia followed him round to the back of the house. The woods began just beyond the property. In one corner stood a shed, and on top was a tent illuminated by floodlights.

'He was up there,' Kröger explained. 'Fortunately, we were able to put up the tent before the snow started, in case there was any evidence to secure. And as a matter of fact, we found impressions of a reclining body in the moss growing on the roof. He used a bipod this time as well.'

'Can we get up there and look?' Bodenstein asked.

'Yeah, sure. We've already finished with it.' Kröger nodded and pointed to the ladder that was leaning against the wall of the shed. Pia climbed up after her boss. They squatted next to each other and looked over at the house. In the summer, the hornbeam hedge would block the view, but now they could see through it into the big window of the house.

'Without a doubt, it's an ideal spot, but not easy to find,' Bodenstein commented. 'He must have cased the whole area very carefully.'

'The line of sight was about sixty metres,' Kröger said to the two detectives standing next to him. 'Afterwards, he could have escaped in two ways: either taking the path between the back gardens and along the edge of the woods to the car park for the training centre of the Federal Institute of Labour; or he could have gone down here past the barrier to the Hotel Heidekrug. The hotel closed last Sunday and won't open again until the end of January, so no one would have noticed his car. And from there, it's only a few seconds' drive to the road to

Königstein, which leads up the hill to Highway B455. An absolutely perfect escape route. Only someone out for a walk could possibly have seen him.'

'How sure are you that it's the same guy as yesterday?' Bodenstein asked.

'Pretty sure. The bullet that we pulled out of the kitchen cupboard was the same calibre, at any rate. And we couldn't find a spent cartridge here either, just like yesterday. He must have taken it with him so he wouldn't leave any evidence behind.'

They walked slowly back to the cars.

'It sounds like the murder was carefully planned,' Pia said.

'You're right,' Bodenstein agreed, deep in thought. 'The woman was definitely not shot at random. Let's go back inside and try to talk to the professor. We can interview the granddaughter tomorrow.'

FRIDAY, DECEMBER 21, 2012

Not much was going on in the car park of the Seerose Industrial Park. Except for the supermarket, the discount warehouse and the bakery, the businesses wouldn't open for another hour, and the office workers from the nearby office complexes mainly came over during their lunch hour and after work. This early in the morning, the customers were mostly pensioners or people on their way to work in Frankfurt, stopping to pick up breakfast or a cup of coffee. He waited patiently in the queue at the counter of the bakery, and even let someone go first because he wanted to be waited on by the nice young Turkish woman who worked the early shift every morning. Unlike her surly colleagues, she always seemed in a good mood. Right now, she was bantering with the two men in orange jackets who had left their refuse truck parked across several parking spaces. Who knew why they had done that?

'Good morning!' She gave him a smile that was as charming as it was insincere. 'One loaf of the usual? Farmer's bread, sliced?'

As a good saleswoman, she knew the preferences of her steady customers.

'Good morning,' he replied. 'Yes, that's it. And also a pretzel stick with plenty of salt, please.'

The loaf of bread would turn old and hard, like all the bread he'd bought from her in the past few weeks. He didn't come here for the bread, but she couldn't know that.

'Certainly,' she said. A lock of dark hair had come loose from her tight ponytail to curl over her forehead. Her face was attractive, with full lips and very white teeth. A lovely young woman. A bit too much make-up for his taste, and she didn't really need it. But above all, she was a woman with regular habits and an extremely regular routine, which made things easy for him.

'Do you have time off after Christmas?' he asked casually as she slid the pretzel stick into a paper bag.

'Unfortunately, no.' A woebegone look flitted across her face, but then her usual smile returned. 'But in the new year, we'll be going on holiday. Then you'll have to get along without me for three weeks.'

In two sentences, she had shortened her life by at least three days. Originally, he had intended to let her have Christmas and New Year's Eve, but her holiday plans now forced him to revise his timetable. But he still had some leeway in the schedule.

'That'll certainly be a big challenge for me.' He put a ten-euro note on the counter and smiled, well aware that she wouldn't pick up on the ambiguity of his words.

'Well, until then, you'll be seeing me a few more times.' With a coquettish giggle, she handed him the paper bag with the bread and the pretzel, still warm, and gave him his change.

'See you tomorrow!' She gave him a flirtatious wink as he left, before turning to beguile the next customer with her laugh. Her friendliness was not directed at him personally. But even if it had been, it wouldn't have done any good.

Pia Kirchhoff stepped out of the shower and reached for her towel. Christoph had left the house a quarter of an hour before. He had taken his suitcase and assured her that she didn't have to worry about him. Antonia and her friend Lukas would drive him to the airport in the late afternoon and bring his car back to Birkenhof sometime later.

'Of course, I understand about work,' he'd told her the night before. 'In your place, I would have made the same decision.'

He had long since realized that he'd be flying to Ecuador alone. Just as Henning had said. In principle, and Pia had to admit this, all three of them thought the same way. They were all 100 per cent committed to their jobs.

Back when she was still married to Henning, Pia had often felt annoyed that his work was more important to him than his private life. Henning hadn't wanted her to get a job, but she'd spent weeks, alone and bored, in their apartment in Sachsenhausen. In the evenings and at weekends, she'd gone to one of the dissection rooms at the Institute of Forensic Medicine just so she could see her husband. The last straw that had prompted their separation, in March now eight years ago, had been a cable tramway accident in Austria; specifically the fact that Henning had neglected to say goodbye to her when he left. She had moved out of the apartment – and he hadn't even noticed until two weeks later. Subsequently, she had made the two best decisions in her life: to buy Birkenhof and to return to her old job with the criminal police. She wanted to be free, and she had promised herself never to put her own desires in second place again.

Then she'd met Christoph and fallen head over heels in love, first with his chocolate-brown eyes and then with his incredible personality, although in his own way, he was just as crazy as Henning. But the biggest difference was that now she, too, had a profession that she felt passionate about. She seldom saw her job as a constraint, and often enough, there were periods when she left work precisely on time and could devote herself to her animals and the farm. Yet occasionally situations like this would come up, of course, and Christoph never complained when she had to work almost round the clock. Nor would it ever occur to Pia to grumble when the zoo needed him on-site, as had often been the case in recent months while the new elephant house was being built.

Pia stared at her face in the mirror and let out a big sigh.

She had known that Christoph would understand and not be disappointed or angry, and although she was relieved, she was sad about his reaction. For the first time, they were supposed to celebrate Christmas and New Year's Eve as a married couple – but now she would sit round at Birkenhof while

Christoph spent the holidays with strangers thousands of kilometres away.

Just a little while ago, as he gave her one last hug before
leaving to finish up some work at the zoo, she'd felt as if her
heart were about to be ripped out of her chest. At that
moment, she had doubted her decision. Could two dead people
whom she didn't even know be more important to her than the
man she loved above all else? What if something happened to
Christoph on the trip? What if the plane crashed or the ship
sank and she would never see him again? How would she be
able to stand that? She already missed him so much that the
pain was physical. Ever since they met, they had never once
been apart longer than a day.

Pia got dressed and drew her hair into a knot at the nape
of her neck. So far, Bodenstein knew nothing of her decision to
cancel her holiday. None of her colleagues expected that she
would sacrifice her time off to assist in a murder investigation,
and apart from her boss, none of them would ever consider
doing the same. She could still phone Christoph and tell him
that she would fly with him after all. She turned off the bathroom light and went downstairs. Her mobile was on the
kitchen table. All she had to do was pick it up and press the
speed dial to reach Christoph.

But then she thought about the husband and daughter of
the woman who was killed yesterday. And Renate Rohleder.
Their bewilderment and horror. Pia also thought about the
young girl who had seen her grandmother's head blown off.
Damn.

All the seats were taken in the waiting room behind the
guardhouse on the ground floor of the Regional Criminal Unit.

Previously, Chief Commissioner Nierhoff, Nicola Engel's prede-
cessor in the post, had preferred to use this space for his numerous
press conferences because it was the biggest room in the building.
This morning, the 'Sniper' Special Commission was convening
for the first time, and the room was already fully equipped with
tables, a telephone, the inevitable whiteboard, PCs, printers and
a fax machine. Twenty-five officers were jammed into the space,
sitting and standing. They'd been brought in from various investigative units to join the special commission, which also included
Dr Nicola Engel, the head of the regular police in the building;
case analyst Andreas Neff from the State Criminal Division; and
Bodenstein and Ostermann as the last contingent from K-11.

After a very brief statement to the press was issued, which
Bodenstein had done last night, the newspapers and online
news services were already writing sensationalist headlines
such as: SECOND SNIPER MURDER! IS AN INSANE KILLER ON
THE LOOSE? And the public was understandably nervous. To
the annoyance of police colleagues manning the switchboard,
people were already calling the general emergency number
for information, so the first order of business was to set up
an emergency phone number especially for this case. Since
Ostermann was hardly saying a word, Bodenstein took over
describing the situation to his assembled colleagues.

'On Wednesday morning at round eight forty-five in the Niederhöchstadt district, seventy-four-year-old Ingeborg Rohleder
was shot dead,' he began. 'So far, we have no indications of a
motive for the crime. The gunman used a rifle and Winchester
.308 ammunition. That's a very common calibre, so it's impossible to ascertain where, when and from whom this ammunition
was purchased. At first, we assumed that Mrs Rohleder was
merely a target of opportunity, but last night at round six thirty,

a second muder was committed in Oberursel in a very similar way—'

There was a knock on the door, and someone came in. The others began whispering to one another.

'Hey, Pia,' Matuschek from Fraud called out. 'What are you doing here?'

'Couldn't get along without us, eh?' another said.

There was loud laughter.

'I thought you're supposed to be on holiday,' said a third.

Pia set her rucksack on the table.

'How about if we all agree,' she said frostily, looking round the room, 'that for the time being, a certain word beginning with the letter *H* will not be part of our vocabulary.'

Everyone nodded. Bodenstein, who once again had hardly slept a wink all night, felt a deep sense of relief when he realized that Pia had decided not to go on her trip.

'Seems pretty stupid to me,' someone muttered. 'Coming to work instead of flying off on holiday? It would never occur to me to do that.'

'That's precisely why you have the job you do, Officer Probst,' Pia retorted. 'And you'll keep the same rank until you retire.'

Bodenstein's gaze met Nicola Engel's, and he noticed a brief smile flit across her face.

'Sorry for interrupting, boss, please continue.' Pia nodded to Bodenstein and took a seat on the chair that Ostermann had requisitioned with a snap of his fingers from another colleague.

'Thank you,' he said, and turned back to the group. He gave a brief rundown of events surrounding the two murders and summed up the facts they knew so far.

'Both victims were women of retirement age. As far as the family backgrounds of the victims go, so far, there do not seem to be any parallels or points of contact,' he concluded. 'The husband of victim number two is a general practitioner; the daughter of victim number one is a florist. That's all we really have at the moment.'

'Thank you very much,' Chief Inspector Neff said, and then took the floor. 'It's not much to go on, but we have to assume that there is little information to be found. To me, both situations seem to demonstrate the random behaviour of the killer. I see some parallels to the case I was on when I was in the United States. In October of 2002, over a period of three weeks, two men shot people at random, killing ten of them, in the Washington, DC, area. The targets were seemingly chosen totally at random. They killed for the sheer joy of killing.'

'Who is this guy?' Pia whispered as Neff recounted the story of John Allen Muhammad and Lee Boyd Malvo.

'The secret weapon from Wiesbaden,' said Ostermann, rolling his eyes. 'Offering assistance to the hick cops.'

'That's Andreas Neff, case analyst from the State Criminal Police,' Bodenstein added in a low voice.

'A *profiler*?' Pia frowned. 'What's he doing here?'

Ostermann shrugged mutely.

'Dr Engel made the decision,' said Bodenstein. 'And I'll take all the help I can get.'

Pia waited until Neff had finished his lecture.

'After what happened yesterday, there's no way I'd believe that our perpetrator is shooting victims at random,' she objected. 'The very location of the crime scene last night tells me it wasn't a crime of opportunity. The victim's house is located behind a tall hedge at the end of a cul-de-sac. The killer not only had to find a suitable spot from which to fire, but he also had to scout out his exact escape route. There must be some connection between the two victims, even though we're not yet able to see it. That's why we should examine closely the background and social circles of both victims.'

Neff had listened politely to her and now nodded, giving her a smile.

'Naturally you should do that,' he said. 'I have merely presented my assessment of the situation. It's possible that I'm wrong, but—'

'Thank you very much for your preliminary evaluation, Chief Inspector,' Bodenstein interrupted him, and stood up. 'Ms Kirchhoff and I will be interviewing Ms Rudolf's relatives today. You're welcome to go with us if you like.'

Then he assigned various tasks to other colleagues and ended the discussion. Kai Ostermann made no secret of what he thought of Neff.

'Have fun with the smart-arse,' he croaked. Bodenstein gave him a dirty look.

Pia had nothing against taking Neff along with them. She had never worked with a case analyst before, but she'd heard that profilers often noticed details that could contribute decisively to solving a case. One thing was clear: time was tight. The perp could strike again at any moment.

'In order to carry out an analytical reconstruction of the crime, what investigators most lack is time. I'm sure you know that. So it was a wise decision to include me in the investigation at this early stage.' Chief Inspector Andreas Neff walked round the unmarked car, opened the passenger-side front door, and was about to get in.

'You sit in the back,' said Pia, stepping in front of him.

Neff looked at her, then shrugged and smiled. He was a slight man, about an inch shorter than Pia, with an ordinary-looking face, the kind that was easily forgotten. But his small stature seemed to have had no effect on his high opinion of himself.

'You know, this is something that I often encounter.' He sat down in the back seat. 'As a case analyst with the State Criminal Police, I don't belong to any specific team. We are deployed only where our colleagues have no idea how to proceed. And that means we're not particularly popular at first, because who wants to admit to failure.'

Pia didn't know what he was getting at.

'What is it you often encounter?' she asked.

'People send me signals, sometimes not very subtly, that I am basically unwanted,' he replied. 'I've studied human behaviour for years. The act of human communication consists of only eight per cent speech, and ninety-two per cent body language. From your body language, I deduce a sense of uncertainty towards me. You cover up this uncertainty, of which you are probably unaware, with an aggressive attitude. Many female colleagues do the same. They already feel isolated because of their gender, and this is compounded by a feeling of physical inferiority. The fact that I'm relegated to the back seat while you sit in the front is a display of dominance on your part, intended to put me in my place and clearly indicate my subordinate rank on the team.'

'Is that right?' Pia was stunned. 'I do not feel physically inferior to you. Nor am I uncertain.'

'Yes, you are,' Neff insisted. 'But I'm familiar with this reaction, and I understand your behaviour. You see, when a person such as myself is constantly examining and analysing even the smallest detail, over time, that person develops an acute sensitivity for the power structures of a team. In the United States, they're far ahead of us with regard to equal rights in the workplace and the acceptance of women on the police force. Here in Germany, we are limping along, decades behind.'

Pia saw that Bodenstein was having a hard time keeping a straight face.

'And is it your expert opinion that I'm uncertain only because I'm sitting in the front seat of the car?' she interrupted Neff's screed. 'Or am I, per se, uncertain because I'm a woman?'

'Both.'

At first Pia thought Neff meant this to be a joke, but he was nodding his head in earnest.

'It's also a matter of *how* you demonstrated your position of power with regard to me. By saying "You sit in the back", you meant it to be a command, not a polite request. In addition, you stepped in front of me, which means you were giving your command physical emphasis as well.'

'Ha!' Pia said, shaking her head. 'Now, just a minute. I sit in the front because there's no satnav in this car and I know the way to the crime scene. You don't. Besides, I always sit in the front.'

'Ah yes,' said Neff. ' "I *always* sit in the front." What does this seemingly benign sentence actually tell us about you and your attitude? You are inflexible. You insist on routines because they suggest security. Furthermore, it signifies that you're afraid of change and innovation. I could go much deeper with this analysis, but let's leave it at that.'

Pia said nothing, although she had a caustic retort on the tip of her tongue. She did feel unexpectedly uncertain, and that made her angry. Neff seemed to take her silence as affirmation of his theories. He began talking about the profiling methods that he had learned during his time with the FBI.

'With serial killers, in particular, there are certain patterns that, statistically speaking, can and must be linked to specific socioeconomic classes,' he pontificated from the back seat. 'As profilers, we draw our conclusions based on criminological expertise, with the help of clues, crime-scene information and circumstantial evidence. In this respect, it is unfortunate that I've seen only photos from the crime scenes. Normally, I prefer to be able to get a feel for the crime scene in person.'

Bodenstein signalled and turned off at the Königstein roundabout in the direction of Kronberg. They drove past Opel Zoo, and for a few seconds, Pia considered asking her boss to let her out. She could still take the plane to Ecuador and the Galápagos Islands instead of being insulted by this know-it-all shithead.

'Excuse me for interrupting your lecture,' she then said to Neff. 'But do you happen to have any questions? Yesterday I was at the crime scene only an hour after the woman was killed.'

'I'm well aware of that. I did read the case file, after all,' Neff replied, sounding peeved. 'Of course I have questions that I will ask. I *am* part of the team.'

On paper, maybe, Pia thought to herself, doubting that Andreas Neff was at all capable of participating in a team effort.

'Please allow us to handle the interview with the victim's

relatives.' Bodenstein finally intervened after not uttering a peep for the past fifteen minutes.

'Why is that?' Neff protested. 'I must—'

'We are the investigating officers, you are the external case analyst. That means your role is to observe and analyse what you observe,' Bodenstein explained in a calm voice. Pia could have kissed him for making Neff finally shut his trap.

Margarethe Rudolf was from Oberursel, which was where she had lived her whole life. The lovely old villa had belonged to her parents, but when they passed away early on, she and her husband had moved in. Like Ingeborg Rohleder, Margarethe Rudolf was a woman who had been both well liked and respected. She was involved with the church congregation, the sports club and the cultural circle; she had played bridge, led a literary group and was active in the Lions Ladies Club. Among her extended circle of acquaintances, there was absolutely no one who could have wanted her dead – this was something that her husband and daughter stressed again and again. Both were in utter shock, and no one could blame them.

'I'd gladly offer you a cup of coffee, but . . . but my daughter and I . . . we simply can't manage to do . . .' Dr Dieter Rudolf, a slim man in his early sixties with snow-white hair, didn't finish the sentence, but Bodenstein and Pia understood what he meant. The crime-scene cleaners had done their work well, and not the tiniest fleck of blood could be seen in the kitchen, yet it had to be terrible for them to even go into that room.

The professor answered all their questions with composure and made a great effort to preserve the outward appearance of normality, just as his daughter did. Two people who were used to having their personal and professional lives in perfect order. Karoline Albrecht was wearing the same outfit as the night before, a sure sign that she hadn't had any sleep.

The house was already lovingly decorated for Christmas. On a sideboard stood a whole orchestra of hand-carved little angels next to a 'smoking man' incense burner with a yellowish beard. Pine boughs in a tall glass floor vase were decorated with Christmas ornaments. The heavy dining room table was dominated by a tasteful Advent wreath, with the last candles still unlit. In front of the tall mullioned windows that faced the snow-covered garden hung large and small Christmas stars in red and white.

An imposing Nordmann fir outside on the covered terrace waited, probably in vain now, to be decorated. Nothing in this house would ever be the same. It was bad enough to lose a loved one because of a heart attack or a serious illness, but a murder was beyond comprehension.

'Ms Albrecht,' said Pia gently, 'we would like to speak with your daughter, Greta.'

'What's the point of that?' Karoline Albrecht retorted. 'It was dark outside, and the light was on in the kitchen. She didn't see anyone.'

'Where is your daughter now?'

'With her father and his family in Bad Soden. A familiar place and a little normality are very important for her right now.'

She stopped talking and pressed her lips together. Her father touched her arm, and Karoline Albrecht placed her hand briefly on his. Although they were sitting right next to one another, they seemed oddly lost and not like people who were especially close to each other. An unexpected death in the family, especially a murder, often made relatives forget their animosities and come together in order to lend each other solace and support. But such an event could also bring long-smouldering conflicts to light and totally shatter families. Pia decided not to insist on talking with Greta at this time. With a brief nod of her head, she signalled to her boss that he should take over.

'Had you noticed any change in your wife in recent weeks?' Bodenstein asked. 'Was there anything she might have observed? Or did she feel threatened in some way?'

'No.' The professor shook his head absent-mindedly. He sat there rigidly, his strikingly slender hands clasped as if in prayer. A light shadow was on his cheeks, and the look in his dark eyes was veiled, his expression impenetrable.

'Was there a workman in the house that your wife didn't know, or someone who wanted to read the electric or water metres?' asked Bodenstein gently. 'Was anything out of the ordinary, or had anything unusual happened?'

The professor thought about this briefly. 'Not that I know of.'

'Does the name Ingeborg Rohleder mean anything to you?' Pia now asked. 'From Niederhöchstadt?'

The professor frowned in thought. 'No, I'm sorry. I've never heard that name.'

'Ms Albrecht, would your mother have told you if anything strange was going on?' said Bodenstein, turning to the daughter. 'How was your relationship with your mother?'

'Good. And very warm,' Karoline Albrecht replied. 'I've always worked a lot, but I phoned Mama every day. Sometimes only briefly, but occasionally we would talk for an hour or more. She is . . . She *was* always the steady rock in my life.'

Her voice quavered, but she had her emotions fiercely under control. 'I . . . I'm quite sure she would have told me if there were anything on her mind or worrying her.'

Pia sensed what it must be costing this woman to keep her composure. In addition to her grief over her mother, she was clearly concerned about the emotional welfare of her daughter. At some point, her strength would inevitably run out, and the floodgates of despair would open. Pia hoped for the sake of both Ms Albrecht and herself that this would not happen right now. That sort of emotional meltdown could seriously hinder future contact with the woman. She would be ashamed of her behaviour, and that would not make another conversation any easier.

Bodenstein, Pia and Andreas Neff, who had actually kept his mouth shut, got up. Karoline Albrecht also stood up.

'My mother was a dear person who never hurt anyone. Nobody would have any reason to kill her.' She uttered an inarticulate sound, half laugh, half sob, and then her father, too, lost his iron self-control and began to weep. 'There are thousands of people who deserved to be shot instead of my mother!'

On the drive back, Pia took the wheel. She didn't want to go past the zoo again, so she turned off towards Bommersheim. From there, the L3004 led directly to the junction with the A66 at the end of Miquelallee, and she avoided driving through town with all the traffic lights and drivers creeping along at less than thirty kilometres an hour because they didn't have snow tyres on.

Usually, she and Bodenstein shared impressions after an interview, discussing the answers, reactions and behaviour of the people they had questioned. But this time, Andreas Neff prevented any such exchange of ideas. He started talking as soon as he hit the back seat, dissecting every sentence spoken into its smallest components. He didn't seem to take even a single breath.

'Good Lord, I can't form one clear thought with all your babbling!' Pia finally yelled at him. 'Are you a psychologist, too?'

'Never in my life has anyone called my observations and analyses "babbling",' Neff replied, offended. 'I have learned that things can best be brought into a cognitive perspective by exchanging opinions with one's colleagues immediately following an interview.'

'Just imagine, we came to that realization years ago,' Pia snapped. 'I would appreciate it if you kept your mouth shut for the next ten kilometres.'

Before Neff could say a word, the phone rang and Bodenstein pressed the speaker button, but when he saw the caller's name on the display he took the call on his mobile. He listened, grumbled agreement a couple of times, and ended the conversation without saying goodbye.

'Engel?' Pia asked.

'Mm-hmm.'

'Bad?'

'You could say that.'

'Because?'

'Pressure from IM.'

'The media, huh?'

'Yep.'

After working together for seven years, Pia and Bodenstein

were like an old married couple, and they sometimes communicated in telegraphic style.

'I take it this rudimentary type of communication is
intended to exclude me,' Neff grumbled in the back seat.

'Not in the least,' said Bodenstein, astonished at his in-
sinuation. 'Dr Engel called to tell us that after all the media
reports, the public is starting to panic, and the Ministry of the
Interior is concerned. In plain speak, that means we're getting
pressure from above. Satisfied?'

'Hmm,' Neff grumbled.

Pia glanced at the clock on the dashboard. Four forty-three
p.m. By now, Christoph must have left for the airport, and she
wouldn't see him again for three endless weeks.

'There's certainly not much happening on the road today,'
Bodenstein said. 'Normally at this time on Fridays, we'd be sitting in a traffic jam forever.'

'You're right,' said Pia. 'You think it's because of . . . ?'

'Afraid so,' Bodenstein said with a nod.

'It's terrible the way the two of you massacre the syntax of
our beautiful language,' Neff carped.

'For real?' Pia sounded surprised.

'Totally,' Bodenstein said with a grin.

And then they both laughed, although there was nothing
really to laugh about.

The police had tried in vain to find witnesses in Oberursel
and Niederhöchstadt, and to coax any information out of the
victims' acquaintances. They were feeling frustrated. All day
long, they had gone from one house to another, knocking on
doors, gleaning nothing but regretful denials and shrugs. Even
on the hotline, not a single sensible tip had come in.

Professor Rudolf had never heard the name Ingeborg Rohleder, and likewise Renate Rohleder had no idea who Margarethe Rudolf was. The only similarities that seemed to exist between the two victims were that they were both women and each had a daughter.

The crime scene investigation in Oberursel had produced no leads, just like the one in Niederhöchstadt the day before.

'No traces of the projectiles, no cartridge casings, no footprints and no clues about the killer, who remains a phantom,' Christian Kröger concluded his disappointingly brief report.

'Unfortunately, I have nothing more to add,' Bodenstein said. 'Apparently, there were no striking warning signs such as threats, anonymous phone calls or the like for either victim. It seems that we're dealing with two rather hopeless cases, and we'll have to wait for "Inspector Coincidence" to check in. Or for the perp's killing instinct to expose him.'

Silence descended on everyone seated at the table in the conference room.

'I don't regard these cases as hopeless as the rest of you seem to do,' Andreas Neff piped up.

'Well, great,' Pia muttered, rolling her eyes when he stood up, straightened his tie and buttoned his jacket.

'For me,' Neff began, 'a clear pattern is already emerging. The perpetrator is proceeding arbitrarily, true, but having made thorough plans. We must also assume that he is a very intelligent person who, although impulsive, has his impulsiveness well under control. He is no longer young, but no more than about thirty, because he must be able to run and climb well. The type of victim is also beginning to crystallize – women between sixty and seventy-five. And although a case analysis has little to do with psychology, but is based on criminology, I will venture the prognosis that the perpetrator is a man with a pronounced mother complex.'

He gave a self-satisfied smile and looked round the table expectantly.

'What are we supposed to do with that?' Ostermann whispered to Pia. 'Maybe issue a bulletin: "Warning, all women over sixty! Don't go outdoors and keep your blinds shut when you're at home."'

Pia just shook her head and made a face. She hoped that Dr Engel, who was on the phone out in the hall, would soon notice what a pompous arse this guy was. Pia was listening with only half an ear, because she was eagerly awaiting a call from Christoph.

'Pardon me saying so,' Kröger replied, 'but that's utter nonsense. With the few clues we have, you can't possibly work up a profile of the perp.'

'Maybe *you* can't,' Neff snapped, still smiling. 'But I can. From the FBI, I learned—'

'I was in the States for two years, and I learned a lot over there, too,' Kröger cut him off. 'Above all, that you don't rush to make prognoses before all the facts are on the table. You can only evaluate the whole picture once every single detail is considered.'

'And that's exactly why I've been called in,' said Neff genially. 'To keep the big picture in mind, because people like you often get rashly tied up in details.'

Kröger's face turned red. Surly muttering was heard from the other officers. Even though Kröger sometimes acted like a prima donna, his skills were indisputable. His meticulous work methods and his keen perceptions had often contributed to solving a case.

'So, that's enough of that,' Bodenstein intervened when he felt that Neff had gone too far. 'Inspector Neff, I'd like to have a word with you in my office. The rest of you can go. Have a pleasant evening. But please remain available. Tomorrow morning at ten, we'll meet for our next discussion.'

'Oowee-oowee,' Kai Ostermann whispered. 'Engel's secret weapon is going to be on Christian's shit list.'

'Mine, too,' said Pia. 'A shame he has to put on that macho act. I really think that a profiler could help us a lot.'

SATURDAY, DECEMBER 22, 2012

Kathrin Fachinger looked as though she'd just been snatched from the jaws of death. Her thin face was pale and she had dark circles under her eyes. She dragged herself into the conference room and dropped into a chair.

'Watch out that the sniper doesn't shoot you down,' Kröger said cynically. 'You look like your own grandmother.'

'Why don't you take a look in the mirror. You're not as fresh as the morning dew either,' Kathrin countered, sounding annoyed. 'I put in extra hours to help you out, and the first thing you do is insult me.'

'Christian didn't mean it personally.' Ostermann grinned. 'But Engel's secret weapon posed a theory yesterday.'

'Who?' Kathrin asked, and sneezed.

'The FBI genius from Wiesbaden,' Kröger said in a disparaging tone. 'He knows everything, does everything better, and he claims that he pretty much solved the DC sniper case all by himself.'

'Andreas Neff, a case analyst from state police headquarters. He's supposed to support our investigation,' Pia explained. 'He analysed both cases and is firmly convinced that the perp is targeting elderly women.'

'Great. Thanks a lot!' said Kathrin, her eyes shooting daggers at Kröger.

She was the youngest team member in K-11. With her smooth, girlish face, angular glasses and petite figure, at first glance, she looked much younger than twenty-six. But her non-threatening appearance was misleading. Kathrin was self-possessed and fearless. A few years back, she'd been the one who resolutely read Frank Behnke the riot act and finally made sure that he was suspended from the force.

'What kind of cop is that?' she asked.

'You'll meet him in a minute,' replied Kai, who was leaning on the windowsill and looking down at the car park. 'The poor man's Dale Cooper is heading this way.'

'Let me give you a quick rundown of the meagre results from the ballistics tests,' said Kröger, flicking through the reports he'd brought with him. 'After examining the two bullets, it's clear that they were fired from the same weapon. Unfortunately, the weapon has never been registered, so we don't have it in our system.'

'So it's a sure thing that it was the same gunman in both incidents,' Ostermann remarked.

'The one with the mother complex,' Pia added.

'Grandmother complex.' Kröger winked at her and then left the conference room.

Pia's thoughts wandered to Christoph. Yesterday before his flight took off, they had talked on the phone. By now, he must have landed in Quito. There was a six-hour time difference from Frankfurt, so it must be four in the morning there. Too early to call. But she could send him a text and tell him how much she already missed him. After their phone call yesterday, she had unpacked her bags and gone to bed early. Amazingly, she'd slept soundly for the first time in a week. Maybe it was a sign that her decision to stay here was the right one.

Andreas Neff walked into the conference room. Dark suit, white shirt, black tie. His short dark hair was perfectly combed, his black shoes polished to a high shine. He carried a cup of coffee, ostensibly from the break room at the end of the hall.

'Good morning!' he shouted energetically. His eyes looked past Kai and Pia to Kathrin. 'Ah, and who have we here?'

'Kathrin Fachinger,' she croaked. 'Don't come any closer if you don't want to catch this cold.'

'My name is Neff. I'm from State Kripo headquarters.' He briefly looked her over and lost interest. 'Are you the secretary of this department?'

Kathrin's eyes narrowed.

Kai exchanged a glance with Pia and turned away, trying hard not to laugh. Some people could really put their foot in it.

'So,' said Neff, turning to Ostermann. 'Last night, I thought of something else. Over Christmas, of course, nothing else is going to happen. Our perpetrator has strong social ties, as well as—'

'You have my cup,' Kathrin interrupted him.

'—a family, and he may have even left the area.' Neff paid no attention to her. He walked slowly round the table and took another gulp of coffee. 'The timing of the murders is a clear indication. It's significant that he struck before the Christmas period.'

Kathrin Fachinger got up, stepped in front of him, and pointed at the cup in his hand.

'That's my cup,' she repeated emphatically. 'It says so right there, see? "Kathrin's Cup."'

'Ah, yes.' Neff frowned. 'The others were dirty. You ought to wash them more carefully. A little detergent works wonders.'

'Hand over the cup,' Kathrin countered angrily. 'Next time, bring your own.'

'One should always try to get along with secretaries.' Neff smiled and handed her the porcelain mug. 'Otherwise, the coffee won't taste very good.'

'I am *not* the secretary,' Kathrin snapped. 'I am Detective Superintendent Kathrin Fachinger.'

Andreas Neff was neither embarrassed nor did he apologize.

'All right, then. Where did I leave off? Oh yes. Back to the perpetrator's profile.'

'Given the sparse information available, how did you come to such a conclusion?' Kai Ostermann asked.

'We have our methods,' said Neff superciliously. 'And naturally, a good deal of experience.'

The telephone in the middle of the table rang. Pia, who was sitting closest, leaned over and grabbed the receiver. She listened for ten seconds. 'On our way,' she said, and hung up.

'What is it?' Kathrin asked.

'Shots fired in the Main-Taunus shopping centre,' said Pia, jumping up. 'Kai, please try to reach the boss. Kathrin and I are going over there now.'

'I'll come along,' said Neff, eyes glistening.

'No, you won't.' Pia grabbed her jacket and rucksack. 'If we need you, we'll let you know.'

'What am I supposed to do here?'

'Keep working on the big picture,' Pia suggested. 'That's why we called you in.'

'I'll help you, Papa,' Sophia told him, dragging the little plastic footstool from the bathroom to the kitchen. 'I know what you need to put in chicken soup.'

She placed the stool next to him.

'Really?' Oliver von Bodenstein was somewhere else entirely in his mind and forced himself to smile. 'And what would that be?'

'Well, first water. Then salt, pepper and soup greens,' the girl ticked off on her fingers, leaning against the work surface. 'And chicken meat. But from an organic chicken, not a cheap one. Oh yeah, and mushrooms. I love mushrooms.'

'Sounds good,' said Oliver. 'That's exactly how we'll make it.'

'I want to cut up the carrots,' Sophia demanded, pulling out a drawer and taking out the biggest knife.

'Maybe you'd do better washing the mushrooms.' Oliver took the gigantic chef's knife away from her.

'That's boring. Mama always lets me cut up the carrots.' The little girl frowned and began fidgeting.

'Sorry,' said Oliver.

'But I know how to do it!'

'Mushrooms or nothing.'

'Then nothing.' Sophia jumped down from the stool and gave it a kick that sent it flying across the kitchen. She crossed her arms and sat down on the floor, sulking demonstratively.

Oliver decided to let her pout. The weekends with his younger daughter were getting more exhausting every time. From morning to night, she demanded his attention. She was intensely jealous of Rosalie and Inka, and was always acting up. Cosima apparently allowed her to do almost anything as long as she could get some sleep. Just as it was back when Lorenz and Rosalie were small. He had clearly had more to do with the children on a daily basis than she ever did, since she was always at the office or going off on business trips. Whenever she was at home for a while, it was hard for her to find her place, because the kids were used to a life without their mother. To make herself popular with them, she had spoiled both of them and allowed them to do all the things that Oliver usually prohibited. Soon the kids were taking full advantage of their mother and showing her no respect. Cosima had tried to be strict, but she was never consistent about it. During this whole period, Oliver had mediated any disputes and made sure that the rules were enforced.

These tactics had failed with Sophia, as was clearly noticeable from her behaviour. The six-year-old had never learned to go without or to follow the rules. She easily wrapped her grandparents and babysitters round her little finger, but her charm didn't cut any ice with her father. He recognized that a big problem was developing behind that pretty little face of hers, and he asked himself what he should do about it. Was it because of Sophia that Inka had still not moved in with him as they had planned? She hadn't come right out and said so, but for quite a while now, Inka had stayed away on daddy-weekends. Oliver felt left in the lurch. When he had asked her about it, she replied that she got no attention from him anyway when Sophia was there, so she might as well stay home or work at the horse clinic.

It hadn't come to any open quarrel between them – it never got that far with Inka – but the essence of the conversation was an unspoken 'her or me', which left Oliver equally disappointed and relieved because Inka had made an important decision for him. Maybe it was cowardly of him; maybe it was selfish or merely a matter of convenience. But he knew in his heart of hearts that he had neither the desire nor the energy to make compromises that would extend for years into the future by bringing up a third child.

Cosima had taken him by surprise when she waited until late in the pregnancy and presented him with a fait accompli. That was the beginning of the end. The baby hadn't been enough to satisfy her need to feel young again. She had thrown herself into an affair, taking no heed of her family. With that, she had destroyed everything. Not only her marriage, but also the opportunity for her younger daughter to grow up with both a mother and a father in the same house. Oliver asked himself over and over why he had to suffer the consequences of this situation when it was Cosima, in her boundless selfishness, who had brought it on. The relationship with the Russian adventurer had quickly crumbled. The man had been looking for a spirited lover, not an exhausted mother with a toddler.

When Oliver bought the house in Ruppertshain, he'd also been thinking of Sophia and that it would be easier for him to have her stay with him, not just on specified weekends, but also in an emergency. Yet he was not prepared to rearrange his whole life because of his daughter, or to jeopardize his relationship with Inka.

His phone rang as soon as he sat down at the table and had

eaten a bowl of soup. It was Pia, and her voice sounded strained.

'We're on our way to the Main-Taunus Centre,' she said. 'Shots have been fired, and the whole place is probably in chaos. We haven't heard yet whether there are any dead or injured.'

At these words, fear raced through Bodenstein, and he felt panic rise inside him. Rosalie had gone to the centre an hour and a half ago to shop for a few last-minute items before she left for New York.

'I'll come as soon as I can find somebody to look after the kid,' he said brusquely, and got up. 'Keep me posted.'

Then he tapped in Rosalie's number with trembling fingers. The call went through, but she didn't pick up. He tried to think clearly. On a day like today, thousands of people would go to the shopping centre. Why would anything happen to her, of all people? But didn't everyone think and hope the same thing when a tragedy struck? Somebody was injured or killed, and all those spared by fate were glad that they weren't affected.

Oliver phoned Inka, who picked up at once.

'I'm sorry, I've got to work,' he said. 'Could I bring Sophia over to the clinic?'

'I'm still with a patient,' she said after a tiny pause. 'But bring her to the clinic. Mrs Wagner can look after her until I get back.'

'I don't know what time I'll be able to pick her up.' Bodenstein turned off the stove. 'There were shots fired at the Main-Taunus Centre, and I'm worried about Rosalie. She was heading there, and now I can't reach her.'

'I'm sure all hell has broken loose over there,' Inka said.

'She wouldn't be able to hear her phone. Don't worry. And it doesn't matter if it's late.'

That was one thing he appreciated about Inka. Just like him, she calmly tackled every problem that came up, without hesitation. She was completely different from Cosima, who always had to weigh how difficult, complicated and unpleasant something might be when he made a suggestion.

'What about the soup?' Sophia piped up. She had a calculating expression on her face that Oliver did not like at all.

'Sorry.' He shook his head. 'It's too late. I have to go. Hurry and get your things, I'm taking you to Inka's.'

'But I—'

'End of discussion,' he cut her off. 'Put on your shoes and jacket. Right now.'

Sophia looked at him in bewilderment.

'But I'm hungry!'

'I'm sorry.' He picked up his own scarf and coat and held out her down jacket. 'Come on.'

'No.' The girl crossed her arms stubbornly and sat down on the floor. Bodenstein felt his nerves jangling.

'Sophia, that's enough,' he said sternly. 'I have to go to work, and I don't have time to discuss this with you. If you aren't dressed in three minutes and on the way to my car, I'm going to be very angry.'

'And then what?' she asked in Cosima's exact tone of voice.

'No Christmas presents. No watching movies. I'm not joking.'

'You're so mean!' Sophia yelled, and tears sprayed from her eyes. 'I hate you!'

*

The Main-Taunus Centre was in chaos. Not everyone had heard the shots fired in the upper floor of the shopping centre, but the rumour of an attack, of people dead and wounded, spread like wildfire. Terrified people were jamming into the already-packed shops to seek shelter. Others were trying to flee from the centre and were prevented from doing so by the teams of police who had completely locked it down shortly after the emergency call came in.

Pia and Kathrin were wearing their bulletproof Kevlar vests as they accompanied the hundreds of riot police moving along the completely deserted walkways. No one knew exactly where the shooter had been positioned, or whether he was still there or had managed to escape long before. It was better to stay under cover. The floor was strewn with shopping bags and articles of clothing that people had dropped as they fled or that had been torn from their grasp in the general panic. Several SWAT commandos from Frankfurt were combing through the entire shopping centre, looking for the gunman and his victims. Everyone thought they were hot on the sniper's heels, but for Pia, something didn't feel quite right. It didn't make sense that the killer would strike in a crowded shopping centre. Someone like that would plan in advance how he could make his escape. There was a high risk that he would be seen as he fired his gun and then got held up by the anticipated mass panic. On the other hand, the crowd provided protection, because he could simply mix in with everyone else. But he'd have to carry his weapon with him.

The Christmas music was turned off, and the silence was eerie, the only sound coming from the helicopter that was circling high above the buildings. Behind the display windows of the shops, people were packed in like terrified fish in over-crowded aquariums.

'There are a lot of injured people who need help,' the shopping centre manager said to Pia. 'Can't we at least let the ambulances through?'

The slim, tall man in his fifties was hurrying along next to Pia. She could see that he'd been through hell in the past hour. He'd had to watch helplessly as his own security team, who had been thoroughly trained for just such a worst-case scenario, got trampled by the crowds. In the passageways to the car park, there were scores of injuries as hundreds of people fearing for their lives had tried to squeeze through the doors. In the multi-storey and outside in the huge car park, cars had slammed into each other. Some people had used the chaos to loot merchandise from the shops. When the security team tried to intervene, fights erupted, resulting in even more injuries. It was supposed to have been the best day of the year for the shopping centre, but it had turned into the worst day ever.

'We have broken bones, lacerations and crush injuries,' the head of the centre told Pia. 'Children were trampled, and one woman had a heart attack. They desperately need medical attention!'

'I'm well aware of that. But there's probably a guy still running round somewhere with a gun.' Pia stopped and scrutinized the pale but determined face of the man. What should she do now? Get help for the injured and risk that somebody might be killed elsewhere? Or give the sniper the chance to get away?

You cover up this uncertainty, of which you are probably unaware, with an aggressive attitude. Andreas Neff's words were echoing in her head. Damn it!

Stay calm, Pia silently admonished herself. Bodenstein

wasn't here, and she was the highest-ranking police officer on-site. She had to set priorities and make a decision. Right now.

'Kathrin,' said Pia, turning to her colleague. 'Please tell them to let in the medics and ambulances.'

'Okay.' Kathrin nodded and grabbed her walkie-talkie.

'Thank you,' said the shopping centre manager with relief. He turned on his heel and hurried off.

Pia's walkie-talkie crackled.

'Suspect apprehended!' came the voice of the SWAT commander loud and clear, and a wave of relief flooded through Pia's body. 'On the second floor of the multi-storey by the bus station. We've also secured the weapon.'

'We're on our way,' she replied, and dashed off.

The splintering of glass, a thud and then a blood-curdling scream made her jump, sending an icy shiver down her spine.

Greta, she instantly thought. She dropped the ballpoint pen she'd been using to write the shopping list, leaped up from the dining room table and ran into the kitchen. There stood Greta, and for a second, she was relieved because nothing had happened to her daughter. But then she saw the blood on Greta's face and on the new top that she'd slipped on. Her heart seemed to miss a couple of beats. Greta had stopped screaming, but she was staring wide-eyed at the floor, and Karoline followed her gaze. What she saw shattered her world. On the worn-out black-and-cream-coloured floor tiles lay Mama, and a pool of blood had formed round her head. Blood, everywhere blood, with bright skull fragments and yellowish brain matter mixed in. The blood spread over the tiles and had sprayed over the white cupboards. She knelt down and touched

Mama's hand. Her skin was so warm. Maybe she had simply fainted and hit her head on the work surface.

'Mama,' she whispered. 'Mama, wake up!'

She touched her on the shoulder and shook her lightly. Mama's head tipped to the side, but instead of her face, there was only a bloody mass.

Karoline Albrecht shot upright in her bed. Her heart was racing so fast that it hurt. She was drenched in sweat and freezing at the same time.

Mama was dead.

It was no nightmare.

She let herself sink down onto the mattress again, closing her eyes and hoping she could fall asleep in order to delay confronting a reality that she didn't feel adult enough to face. If she could only get rid of these images! In the dream, she had seen everything so distinctly, every hideous detail, and she had relived her horror and her fear. On that evening, she had grabbed Greta, who was sobbing hysterically, and pulled her out of the kitchen. Everything that happened after that, she remembered only in fragments. At some point, Carsten had been there and also the police, and then Papa arrived . . . To see him like that, wailing in despair, was almost as terrible as the sight of Mama's missing face. Karoline sighed in torment. How was she going to carry on? How would anyone act after seeing her own mother shot down? What would other people expect of her? All her life she had dealt with problems by using logic and making rational decisions. She had always focused on finding solutions, but this time, it wasn't working. Her heart was clenched tight. *Don't cry,* she told herself. She could not give in to grief, or she would fall apart.

With an effort, she sat up. Her limbs hurt and her whole

body felt as heavy as lead. The nightmare images sloshed round in her head like water that came seeping in through tiny cracks and couldn't be stopped before it tore down walls and filled up everything to destroy it all. Her world no longer had any colours, and her life from now on would consist of a before and an after.

Karoline braced herself and got up from the edge of the bed to drag herself into the bathroom. For two days, she'd worn the same clothes, hadn't had a shower, and had eaten almost nothing. She had phoned Carsten a few times and also talked to Greta. She had worried about her father, who had spoken hardly a word, trapped in the same hell of bewilderment and horror as she was. Last night, she had driven home because she needed clean clothes, and then she fell on her bed and dropped straight off to sleep. The phone rang while she was in the shower. She didn't care who it was; she would call back later. Sometime. Right now she had to be strong. For Greta, and especially for Papa. He needed her more than ever before.

Pia was sitting at her desk, typing the final words of her report into the ComPre system on her computer. Then she saved the file. They'd been so close to catching the sniper, but then all their effort and anticipation had changed to disappointment. Three young men had just wanted to play a practical joke with the blank gun that belonged to one of their fathers. A nasty joke, as it turned out, with far-reaching consequences. Bodenstein, relieved that nothing had happened to his daughter Rosalie, had taken the three chastened wrongdoers to task and explained the seriousness of their situation. The police action was going to cost their parents a couple of thousand euros, and they might also have to pay compensation claims for damages. Thirty-four people were injured in the mass panic, some of them seriously, and the woman who had suffered a heart attack was in a critical condition. Pia got up and went to the break room, where she found Bodenstein and Nicola Engel.

'They didn't think about the repercussions at all,' Bodenstein said, shaking his head as he poured himself a cup of coffee. 'They just thought it would be great fun to fire shots in the shopping centre. Incomprehensible!'

'It doesn't surprise me.' Engel sipped at her coffee. 'Many young people these days have absolutely no concept of right and wrong. They sit at their computers and shoot people down, as blithely as we used to eliminate players from the game in Parcheesi.'

'Their parents are going to hit the roof,' Pia muttered. 'Especially the father who forgot to lock up his gun cabinet properly. Sometimes I can't believe that people haven't learned a thing from the school shootings that killed sixteen in both Winnenden and Erfurt.'

'Nobody wants to think that their kid would do anything like that,' said Bodenstein.

'All right.' Dr Nicola Engel rinsed out her cup and put it in the rack next to the sink to dry. 'At any rate, this whole incident turned out pretty well. Good work, Ms Kirchhoff.'

'I've already written up the report,' Pia hastened to say in order to avert the inevitable question from her superior.

Engel looked at her and then nodded. 'I took that for granted,' was all she said. Then she turned to Bodenstein: 'Can you spare a few minutes? I have something I want to discuss with you.'

'Of course.' Bodenstein followed her out of the break room.

Pia crossed the hall and went into the office she shared with Kai Ostermann. She was annoyed to see Andreas Neff sitting at her desk.

'What did I tell you?' He had his feet propped on the edge of the desk and was grinning, pleased with himself. 'I was sure that the incident today couldn't be the sniper. He's not going to strike again before Christmas.'

'I'd like to sit at my desk, if you don't mind.' Pia waved her hand to shoo him away. 'There's a desk free in Ms Fachinger's office at the moment.'

'There's one in here, too.' Neff pointed to the former desk of Frank Behnke, which Ostermann, as the main person in charge of case and evidence documentation, had been using as an extra space for sorting reports and case exhibits. 'So I'll take this one, if that's all right.'

'If I were you, I'd keep my hands off that desk and everything on it,' Pia advised him.

Her phone rang.

'Are you hard of hearing, or are you trying to piss me off?' she said to Neff. He made a show of taking down his feet, then got up with maddening slowness and sauntered across the room. Pia picked up the receiver and dropped into her chair.

'I have a colleague from Niederhöchstadt on the phone,' Kathrin croaked. 'He wants to talk to the boss or to you.'

'Put him through,' replied Pia.

In the meantime, Neff had begun looking through the stacks of documents that had been carefully sorted on Behnke's former desk. Kai was going to flip out when he saw that someone had messed up the order of his papers.

'Rothaus here, Eschborn police station,' the officer said. Pia knew him well. 'Today we got an anonymous letter in the post that might be of interest to your team. It's an obituary for Ingeborg Rohleder.'

Pia jumped as if she'd had an electric shock.

'An obituary?' she said to make sure.

'Yep, black border, a cross, but the text is weird,' said Police Superintendent Rothaus. 'It reads: "In memoriam Ingeborg Rohleder. Ingeborg Rohleder had to die because her daughter implicated herself in the denial of assistance and acted as an accessory to negligent manslaughter. "It's signed "The Judge." '

Pia noticed that she'd been holding her breath out of sheer tension, and now she exhaled. This was a highly interesting development. The names of the sniper's two victims had not been made public, and why would anybody from the Rohleders' circle of acquaintances want to write something like this? It clearly indicated that there was a purpose behind the perpetrator's actions. It might even offer an explanation of the motive.

Pia thanked her colleague and promised to be at the police station within half an hour.

'Any news?' Neff asked curiously.

Pia ignored his question, jumped up, and went off to look for Bodenstein. She found him outside Nicola Engel's office, about to leave.

'I'm going to rescue Inka for a change,' he said. 'You can call me if—'

'We have to drive over to Niederhöchstadt,' Pia interrupted him excitedly. 'Our colleagues received an anonymous letter in the post with an obituary for Ingeborg Rohleder. It clearly reveals that the perp knew the name of at least one of his victims and—'

She stopped talking because Neff was coming down the hall.

'Don't stop because of me,' he challenged her with a smile.

'I'm not saying anything as long as you're sneaking round, eavesdropping,' Pia replied hostilely. The smile vanished from the case analyst's face, though only briefly. Andreas Neff undoubtedly had a thick skin.

'You can't shut him out,' said Bodenstein after Neff had left. 'Engel wants us to work with him; she's made that very clear to me.'

'But he's an idiot,' Pia said stubbornly. 'And he gets on my nerves with his stupid babbling.'

Bodenstein sighed and fished his mobile out of his pocket.

'We're going to Niederhöchstadt,' he said as he tapped in a number and raised the phone to his ear. 'And we're taking Neff and Kröger with us.'

'Do we have to? Take Neff, I mean?' Pia asked, not at all pleased.

'No discussion,' Bodenstein told her. 'Try to get along with him. Please.'

Nothing in life is carved in stone, he thought. Sometimes you just had to be flexible. Even the best-laid plans could be upset if there were elements of uncertainty that could not be calculated. He'd considered another course of action, but who knew when the bakery salesgirl would be back from her holiday?

He bit into his cheese sandwich and again leaned over the table to look at the blueprints of a building and some photos. When he was at the bakery yesterday morning, he noticed that the building under construction, which he'd planned to shoot from, had been covered with exterior plasterboard over the course of a day. That was extremely irritating, because now he had to go searching for another location fast. Purely by chance, he'd found the perfect spot, and now he was looking on Google Maps to check the escape route that he'd already cased the day before.

The TV news programme was broadcasting a new report about the shots fired that morning in the Main-Taunus Centre, and the chaos that had resulted. He grabbed the remote and turned up the sound.

'According to police, it was not the sniper who had recently shot two women in Eschborn and Oberursel, but three young men who were firing blanks from a pistol . . .'

He shook his head and switched off the TV.

On the oilcloth covering the kitchen table, he had already laid out all the tools he would need to clean the rifle thoroughly. It was important to clean a rifle after each time it was fired. Any lead residue in the barrel would impair the precision of the bullet's course, and the breech had to be cleaned of powder residue and lightly oiled. Here, he could be certain that no one would disturb him while he worked. He removed the cheek piece from the stock, pressed the safety, and at the same time, pulled the bolt out of the breech housing. Then he carefully sprayed some cleaning oil through a tiny tube into the barrel and inserted the brass cleaning brush. He smiled pensively as he ran the brush through the barrel, from the breech to the muzzle. He skilfully twisted the wiper piston and the cleaning brush out of the muzzle and pulled the cleaning rod through the barrel. Then he ran a linen patch through the barrel, repeating the entire procedure until the last patch showed no more soiling. They had been two good shots. He hadn't forgotten a thing.

*

'So, this clears up everything,' said Neff as they looked at the anonymous letter in the office of the department head at Eschborn police station. 'The killer wants the attention that he feels he deserves. John Allen Muhammad in Washington, DC, called up the appropriate chief and claimed that he was God. Establishing contact with the police is absolutely symptomatic of a narcissistic personality disorder.'

Neff had been talking non-stop, almost without taking a breath, since they had left headquarters, and Pia was starting to feel like she was being brainwashed. She couldn't think clearly, and it was proving extremely hard for her to take her boss's request to heart. Christian Kröger made no secret of his dislike for the 'secret weapon'.

'A completely normal sheet of copier paper. Size A4, eighty grammes, white,' he cited, ignoring Neff. 'Who has touched it?'

'Only the officer who opened the post,' replied Police Superintendent Rothaus.

'Okay, we can easily check his fingerprints in order to rule him out.' Kröger examined the envelope; like the letter, it had been put in a plastic sleeve.

'The obit looks fairly professional,' said Bodenstein.

'These days, that's easily done,' said Kröger. 'In the notices portals of daily newspapers, you can design family notices with a couple of mouse clicks and post them online instantly.'

'I estimate that the sniper is about thirty years old,' Neff offered. 'He's comfortable with the Internet and knows how to design an obituary online and—'

'I'm forty-seven, and I know how to do it, too,' Kröger cut

him off indignantly. 'Even my parents know how, and they're over seventy.'

'Could your parents climb up on sheds in the dark and shoot somebody dead from eighty metres away even with poor visibility?' Neff countered sarcastically.

'You based your statement on the ability to design notices online,' Kröger reminded him, but Neff merely skirted that argument with a smile.

'If this notice is indeed a message from the killer to us,' Bodenstein said, thinking out loud, 'then Ingeborg Rohleder is no random victim.'

'Denial of assistance and acting as an accessory to negligent manslaughter,' Pia quoted. 'What do you think that means?'

'At least the perp has revealed something crucial,' Bodenstein said with a frown. 'Ingeborg Rohleder had to die because *her daughter* did or did not do something. And that casts a whole different light on the murder.'

'It's proof that the sniper is not shooting his victims at random,' Pia said. 'He acts deliberately, considers his actions justified, and thinks he's a judge.'

'Let's go,' said Bodenstein. 'We're going to see Renate Rohleder and confront her with this accusation.'

He thanked the officer on duty and left the station, followed by Kröger, Neff and Pia.

'A psychopath,' Neff replied unasked to Pia's last comment. 'It's obvious. He was insulted, and now he's taking revenge. Not on the guilty party herself, but on her close relatives. This is especially nefarious.'

'But yesterday you said exactly the opposite,' said Pia. 'You were one hundred per cent convinced that the sniper was killing at random.'

'Yesterday we didn't know what we know today,' Neff protested, slippery as an eel.

That was the last straw for Pia.

'You're never at a loss for an answer, are you?' She shook her head in contempt. 'Did you learn these work techniques in America, too? Taking liberties with Chancellor Adenauer's famous phrase, "What do I care what I said yesterday?" By constantly changing opinions, you're undercutting your own authority, and you shouldn't be surprised if none of us takes you seriously.'

Kröger grinned with amusement. For the first time, Neff was speechless – but unfortunately, not for long.

'At the start of an investigation, one must entertain all possible hypotheses, even if they appear abstruse at first glance,' Neff said, defending his about-turn.

'In the future, you ought to indicate that you're merely making vague conjectures,' Pia said coldly. 'Otherwise, whatever you say is intentionally misleading.'

'I did not anticipate that a dilettante like yourself would be able to follow my reasoning,' he replied. 'And no wonder. I have never experienced such a chaotic and inefficient unit as your K-11.'

Pia already had her mouth open to issue an unfriendly remark, but Christian Kröger beat her to it.

'There's only one person acting like a dilettante here, and it's you,' he pronounced from above in the truest sense of the word, for Neff reached only to his chin. 'With your half-baked theories and your obsession with profiling, you're creating chaos all by yourself. It would be best if you'd simply shut your trap and listen, then you might learn something.'

'Who do you think you are?' Outraged, Neff was about to argue, but Kröger walked right past him.

'I don't have time for this crap,' he said without deigning to give Neff another glance. 'Oh, Pia, I just thought of something. We ought to call our colleagues in Oberursel and find out whether they got a similar letter in the post.'

The metaphoric penalty card that he had shown Neff could hardly have been a darker red, and Pia had to stifle a laugh when she saw Neff's face.

Bodenstein was waiting downstairs by the security gate.

'Where were all of you?' he asked.

'The little Napoleon from State was spouting his theories left and right, and we had to have a brief discussion with him,' said Kröger. 'Listen, Oliver, I think that our colleagues in Oberursel may have received an obituary in the post, too. The gunman probably has no idea who's leading the investigation, so he's turning to the local police stations.'

'Why Oberursel?' asked Bodenstein.

'Because that's where Margarethe Rudolf lived.'

Bodenstein thought for a moment and then nodded. 'Okay, let's go.' He went into the watch room and spoke with the investigator on duty.

'So you don't doubt the authenticity of this obituary, right?' Pia asked her colleagues.

'No, I consider it genuine,' said Kröger. 'On that point, I agree with Napoleon: the perp revealed his motive to us, and it's revenge.'

'*What* did you call me?' Neff asked fiercely.

'What's so bad about "Napoleon"?' asked Kröger with an

innocent smile, and Pia had to turn away to avoid laughing in Neff's face.

'I don't have to put up with this!'

'My colleague doesn't have to put up with you calling her a dilettante either,' Kröger cut him short.

'Why can't she defend herself?' Neff countered. 'Does she need someone to be her mouthpiece? Or is there some other reason why you're standing up for her?' he said with a lewd smirk.

Bodenstein came striding out of the watch room.

'Christian, you're an ace!' he said excitedly. 'They got an obit in the post today, too! We're going to stop and see Ms Rohleder and then on to Oberursel.'

'Well, no answer is an answer, too,' said Neff. 'I thought it was something like this.'

'What are you talking about?' Bodenstein wanted to know.

'Napoleon thinks that Pia and I must have something going on with each other, because I took her side when he insulted her,' said Kröger, whereupon Neff turned red.

'What sort of crap is this?' Bodenstein's voice was sharp. 'We've got two murders to solve and no time for any sort of personal squabbles. I want a team that pulls together, not some silly wrangling about competence.'

'I'm being deliberately left out,' Neff complained. 'And then my *colleague* forbids me to speak.'

'Because you talk nothing but drivel from morning to night,' said Kröger, opening the glass door.

'Dilettantes! The whole lot of you!' Neff hissed, infuriated.

'Spiteful little troll!' Kröger mocked him.

Pia didn't say a word. She wanted to comply with her boss's request and try to get along with Neff. She gave Bodenstein a quick sidelong glance; a deep crease had formed above the bridge of his nose. She knew him well enough to see that he was just about to lose his blue-blooded composure.

'I don't have to listen to that! I'm leaving!' Neff marched past them in a huff. No one tried to stop him.

'The bus stop is just outside to the right!' Pia called after him. She couldn't help herself.

'What are you? A bunch of kindergarteners?' Bodenstein reprimanded her.

'He gets on your nerves, too. Admit it,' Pia said. 'When he's round, I can't even think.'

'Well, now he's gone.' Bodenstein didn't seem to regret it either. 'Come on, hop in. We have things to do.'

Renate Rohleder wasn't home, so Bodenstein decided to pay her a visit later and first drive to Oberursel. He was secretly relieved that Neff had gone, because the man was upsetting his team. In his initial interview with the profiler, he obviously hadn't spelled things out clearly enough. He had to tell him that his arrogant behaviour was totally counterproductive.

His mobile rang. Ms Wagner, Inka's veterinary assistant, wanted to go home, and Inka wasn't back yet. Damn.

'I'll call my father and ask him to pick up Sophia. Thanks for all your help.'

He tapped in the number to his parents' landline, hoping that they'd be able to take care of the child until he finished today. Luckily, his father had time and promised to leave right away to go and get his granddaughter at the horse clinic.

'It may be late,' Bodenstein told him.

'Then she can sleep at our house,' his father said to his

great relief. 'It wouldn't be the first time. You can pick her up in the morning.'

Bodenstein thanked him and put his phone away. He didn't like always having to leave his daughter somewhere, but what else could he do? Didn't Cosima do the same thing? After the argument in the kitchen this afternoon, he'd wanted to talk to Sophia in peace and quiet for a change, but his job took precedence. And he couldn't take the little girl along on a murder investigation.

They drove directly to the police station in Oberursel and picked up the anonymous letter. Just like the obituary for Ingeborg Rohleder, this one was also printed out on ordinary paper and stuck in a normal envelope with a computer-generated address label and a stamp. Kröger put on latex gloves before he picked up the letter and carefully examined it.

'"In memoriam Margarethe Rudolf,"' he read aloud. '"Margarethe Rudolf had to die because her husband implicated himself in a murder out of greed and vanity. The Judge."'

'I wonder what Professor Rudolf will say about this.' Bodenstein consulted his watch. A little before six. Not too late for a visit. A few minutes later, they pulled up in front of the professor's house, which was totally dark. Kröger stayed in the car while Pia and Bodenstein made their way up the short path through the light snowfall. A floodlight above the garage went on, triggered by a motion detector.

'I hope he's home.' Pia rang the doorbell.

It took a moment before the professor opened the door. His gaunt face was unshaven and pale. He looked as though he'd aged ten years in the past forty-eight hours.

'What do you want?' he asked brusquely without saying hello.

'Good evening,' Bodenstein said politely. 'We'd like to show you something. May we come in?'

The professor hesitated, then relented.

'Of course,' he said. 'Please excuse me.'

They followed him through the hall into the dining room. The parquet floor creaked under their feet. The house seemed stuffy and smelled of stale cigarette smoke and leftover food.

'Isn't your daughter still here?' Pia asked.

'Karoline has to take care of Greta. Now more than ever.' Professor Rudolf turned on the lights. 'I'm managing all right on my own. What else can I do?'

The lamp hanging above the dining room table bathed the room in a wan light that only slowly grew brighter. The professor stood in the middle of the room and made a vague gesture towards the table, which was littered with dirty plates and glasses.

No one sat down.

'Dr Rudolf,' Bodenstein began as he unfolded the copy of the obituary. 'This notice arrived in the post today at the police station in Oberursel. We presume that the killer sent it. Earlier, we had assumed that your wife's murder was a crime of opportunity, but the content of this notice now throws another light on the case.'

He handed him the sheet of paper. The professor scanned the sentence and his face turned ashen. Then he looked up.

'What . . . what's this supposed to mean?' he whispered hoarsely. 'I've worked in transplant surgery for more than twenty years. I save lives! On my trips abroad, I've been operating pro bono in hospitals in Africa!'

He pulled a chair out from the table and sat down heavily.

He read the obituary a second time and shook his head in bewilderment. His hands were trembling.

'Perhaps one of your patients died after you implanted a new organ,' Pia ventured cautiously. 'And the family members hold you responsible for the death.'

'Every patient who agrees to a transplant operation knows that the only alternative is death,' the professor replied almost inaudibly. He shoved the piece of paper away, took off his glasses and rubbed his eyes.

'Professor, we'd like to ask you to think carefully. Where could such an accusation have come from?' said Bodenstein.

The professor did not react.

'My wife, whom I loved above all else, is dead,' he whispered at last. 'My daughter and my granddaughter have been badly traumatized. We have lost our centre. Please leave me alone. I am . . . I'm in no condition to answer any questions.'

His voice broke. Slowly he raised his head as if that simple movement required enormous effort. Nothing remained of the vital, self-confident man that Pia had seen for the first time on the evening of his wife's murder. Before them sat a broken human being. And now he had to deal not only with the loss of his wife, but also with the accusation that he was to blame for her death.

'Please leave.'

'Of course. We'll find our way out,' said Bodenstein. In the doorway, Pia glanced back at the professor, who had laid his head on his arms and was sobbing.

Renate Rohleder was neither at home nor at the flower shop, so they drove back to the station. Bodenstein said goodbye to his colleagues in the car park. Kröger was going to take the two anonymous letters to the crime lab in Wiesbaden to have them examined for fingerprints and DNA traces, so Pia entered the building alone. The offices of K-11 were deserted. Kathrin had been sensible and gone home to bed, and Andreas Neff apparently had not come back. Pia went to her office and ran into Kai, who was in a bad mood.

'Neff, that blockhead, rummaged through all my case files! If I get my hands on him . . .' he complained. 'I wasted two whole hours sorting out my system all over again.'

Even though Kai Ostermann, with his ponytail, nickel glasses frames and casual clothes seemed like an unorganized computer freak, he was one of the best organized individuals Pia had ever met.

'I warned him,' she said. 'But he insisted on setting up camp in our office.'

'I dare him to show up here again,' Kai muttered angrily to himself. To help improve his mood, Pia told him about the incident at Eschborn police station, which had led Neff to leave voluntarily.

'Napoleon! He's completely out of place here,' Kai said with a grin. 'If he keeps doing this, he's going to meet his Waterloo.'

Pia told him about the two obituaries and the fruitless conversation with Professor Rudolf. She had just finished when her mobile rang.

'Hello, Henning,' she greeted her ex-husband. 'What's up?'

'I heard that I won our bet,' he said with a mocking undertone, which instantly raised Pia's hackles. 'You sent Christoph off alone on his trip to the other side of the globe.'

'What bet?' she replied coolly. 'I never shook on it.'

'You have a standing invitation. Miriam would love it if you could come over on Christmas Eve.'

That was extremely nice, but Pia felt no desire to celebrate Christmas Eve in the apartment where she had lived for years with Henning. After their separation, that was also where she had once caught him in flagrante with District Attorney Löblich on the coffee table. The apartment held too many memories, more bad ones than good.

'That's very nice of you,' she said. 'But I'm taking the opportunity to see my family. My sister and brother are both staying at our parents' place over Christmas.'

'Okay, then, have a great time and say hello to everyone from me,' said Henning.

They spoke briefly about the police action at the shopping centre, and Pia told him about the obituaries that the sniper had sent. As the leader of the Institute of Forensic Medicine, Henning was not part of the police, but he was an important component of the team. Given his astuteness and expertise, he was always able to offer helpful advice.

'It doesn't really advance your investigation, though,' he said.

'Depends on your point of view. At any rate, the obits tell us something about the sniper's motives,' Pia said. Then something else occurred to her. 'Tell me, do you happen to know a Professor Dieter Paul Rudolf? He's a transplant surgeon.'

'Hmm.' Henning thought about it for a moment. 'No, offhand, that name doesn't ring a bell. But I could find out about him. There aren't that many transplant surgeons.'

From past experience, Pia knew what excellent investigative skills her ex-husband and his wife, her best friend Miriam, possessed, so she was pleased with this suggestion.

'We're grateful for any help you can provide,' she said. 'The idiot profiler that Engel dumped on us is just causing more confusion instead of helping.'

Then they wished each other a nice weekend, and Pia hung up.

'You have a family?' Kai asked curiously.

'Naturally,' Pia replied sharply. 'Did you think I was found in a ditch?'

'Sorry, I didn't mean to pry,' said Kai. 'But ever since I've known you, you've never talked about your parents or any siblings.'

'I know. I apologize for being so touchy,' said Pia. 'Family isn't a good topic for me. It's been years since all of us spent any time together.'

As a matter of fact, Kai could hardly know anything about her family, because Pia never mentioned a word about her private life – just the opposite of Cem Altunay, who had a whole row of family photos on his desk. Pia's parents, who lived in Igstadt, a suburb of Wiesbaden, had never understood why she would abandon the security of her marriage and prefer to live alone on an old farm and return to work with the criminal police. Pia's father had worked a shift at Hoechst AG for forty years, and since his retirement, her parents' life had been restricted to church, gardening and the lawn bowling club. When Pia had told her parents about Christoph for the first time, her mother's only concern was what 'people' would say because Pia was not yet divorced. But the real rift in their relationship occurred more than twenty years in the past. Back then, Pia was stalked for months by a man she had met on holiday in France and was finally brutally raped in her own apartment. Her parents' only reaction had been embarrassed silence, and they never mentioned the incident. At her wedding to Henning a couple of years later, Pia realized that she no longer had anything to say to her parents. They lived in their bourgeois microcosm, which had become utterly foreign to Pia.

Lars, her older brother, had developed into an unspeakable smart-arse. She had deeply offended him when she turned a deaf ear to his conservative advice about investments. Instead, in the late nineties, she invested a few thousand euros in stocks in the New Market, Germany's answer to NASDAQ. When she later sold the stocks, she had enough to buy Birkenhof after she separated from Henning. Lars, who considered himself the ultimate stock market pro, had been so vexed by this turn of events that he hadn't spoken a word to her since. The only family member who had even sporadic contact with Pia was her little sister, Kim, who worked in Hamburg as a prison psychologist – a profession that in the Freitag family was almost as frowned upon as Pia's own.

'Yeah, you sure can't pick your family,' said Kai. 'I barely have any contact with my parents anymore. At Christmas and on my birthday, I always get a card on handmade paper.'

He linked his hands behind his head and laughed.

'They're such typical hippies, living on an old farm in the Rhön district with no heat or electricity and growing their own vegetables. To them, it was absolute treason that I ended up joining the police force, and in their eyes, I'm the black sheep. I still remember how ashamed I felt when I was in the riot police and was assigned to a demonstration against the transportation of nuclear waste in CASTOR containers. My parents and their activist pals had chained themselves to the railway tracks.'

Pia grinned.

'At one point, my father even told me that if I were ever kidnapped, he wouldn't pay a cent in ransom,' Kai went on. 'That's how disappointed he was in me.'

'That's pretty extreme,' Pia said. 'He didn't really mean it, did he?'

'Oh, yes, he did.' Kai shrugged. 'It made leaving much easier for me. My parents' own reality is the only one they acknowledge, and I detest people like that. They act like they're so socially conscious and enlightened, but in fact, they're the most unyielding and intolerant ignoramuses I've ever met.'

'My parents are simply bourgeois people who have never dared peek over the garden fence,' said Pia. 'They never go beyond their tiny world and are terrified of any change.' She frowned. 'In the past few days, I've been asking myself how I would react if my parents or my brother were shot by a sniper.'

'And?' Kai looked at her curiously.

'Hmm. This may sound pretty heartless, but I don't think it would affect me that much. They are strangers to me, and I have absolutely nothing to say to them.'

'Same with me.' said Kai with a nod. 'So why are you going there for Christmas?'

'Maybe for the exact same reasons,' Pia admitted. 'My own thoughts have terrified me. I want to give them one more chance. They are my family, after all.'

'But they take no interest in you,' said Kai. 'So it's your right not to take any interest in them. God knows at our age we no longer have to bend over backwards just to please our parents and siblings.'

MONDAY, DECEMBER 24, 2012

Nothing had changed in the past twenty years, neither the house nor her parents. After only ten minutes, Pia regretted her decision to spend Christmas Eve with them.

'You could have at least gone to church,' their mother had said to Pia and Kim disapprovingly. And with that, the last bit of goodwill Pia'd had when she drove to Igstadt vanished into thin air.

Feeling tense and uncomfortable, she was now sitting on the leather sofa in the living room of her parents' '70s-era house. She was squeezed in between her sister-in-law, Sylvia, and her sister, Kim, who had arrived two hours before from Hamburg and would be staying with Pia at Birkenhof.

She had done her best to start up a conversation, politely asking her parents, brother and her brother's wife how they were. That had provoked a monologue several minutes long from Sylvia, who had babbled on about pretentious trivialities. Her mother, plump and red-cheeked, paid no attention as usual because she didn't care about anything that had nothing to do with her own blood relatives. Pia's father sat silently in his easy chair and just stared into space.

'I need to go in the kitchen,' her mother said as soon as Sylvia paused to take a breath.

'Would you like some help?' asked Pia and Kim in unison.

'No, no, everything is ready,' was her reply.

Without Sylvia, the conversation would probably have come to a standstill. People simply had nothing to say. Pia sipped at her Riesling, which was so acidic that her stomach clenched painfully.

'Most people who study psychology secretly just want to analyse themselves,' Sylvia claimed, setting her wine glass on a coaster. In the five years since Pia had last seen her, she had expanded like a yeast dumpling, just like Lars, who could have taught even Napoleon Neff something about a smug attitude.

'Well, at least I have a profession and don't have to depend on a man to support me,' Kim retorted. 'I think my job is fun, and I'm good at it.'

She was the complete opposite of Sylvia: tall, slim and without a trace of make-up.

'I keep asking myself whether any man could ever put up with you,' Sylvia snapped back with an insincere smile that did nothing to ameliorate the malice in her words. 'You know, you'll be turning forty-three soon. Your biological clock must be ticking as loudly as Big Ben!' She roared with laughter at her own joke.

'I could never understand why women like you believe that a husband and children represent the very pinnacle of good fortune in the world,' Kim countered coolly. 'In my opinion, you're all kidding yourselves. I'm sure that most housewives with kids would much rather live like I do: financially independent, with a successful job, and free to sleep in on Sunday . . .'

Kim winked at Pia, who had to stifle a grin.

'It's obvious that you're trying to make your sad single life sound better than it is.' Sylvia gave a mocking laugh. But her laughter was forced, because Kim had struck a sore spot with unerring precision. 'Children are wonderful! So fulfilling for a woman. But you wouldn't know, since you don't have any.'

'A classic example of self-delusion,' Kim countered. 'Children are egotistical little monsters who destroy most relationships. And once they eventually leave home, the parents sit there and have nothing more to say to each other, because for years, they've talked about nothing but their brats.'

Pia tuned out, hoping that dinner would be over soon and they could leave. Her thoughts wandered. The incidents of the past few days had severely curtailed the retail Christmas trade in the whole region. The car parks in front of the supermarkets were empty, and the Christmas markets in Frankfurt and Wiesbaden had closed a day earlier than planned, because the crowds weren't coming. And the TV news was to blame, reporting round the clock on the sniper murders. The stations had also cut in archival footage from the States and managed to terrify people. Out of fear of being shot by a sniper, everyone stayed home. The media implied that a maniac was on the loose who shot people at random.

At first that had seemed to be true, but after receiving the obituaries, whose authenticity no one doubted, the police knew that the sniper killed only targeted individuals. At the Monday morning meeting, which Neff did not attend, Pia suggested giving the press more accurate information. But her boss and Engel considered it too risky because it might sound like an all-clear and lull the public into a false sense of security.

Fortunately, Sunday passed with no new incidents. Renate Rohleder had gone to visit a friend in Cologne, taking her dog. In the crime lab, they had managed to find fingerprints on the two obituaries only from their own colleagues who had opened the letters and potentially Professor Therbolt. The investigation had come to a standstill, and it made no sense to sit round at K-11 doing nothing. So they had all wished each other Merry Christmas round noon and gone home, hoping that Neff might be right in his prognosis.

'When are you going to introduce us to this zoo guy of yours?' said Sylvia, turning to Pia. 'It's a little strange that he would take off on holiday over Christmas without you. That would certainly make me think twice.'

'He isn't on holiday,' Pia replied. 'He's working.'

By now, the wine in her glass had turned lukewarm and tasted even more hideous than before.

'So you were looking for another workaholic like your ex?' Lars jumped in. 'But you're probably always on call, too, aren't you?'

'Actually, I am on call today,' Pia said, thinking that she wouldn't mind taking a call on Christmas Eve, as long as nobody had to die.

Neither her parents nor Lars had asked how she was doing or how her job was going. They were so indifferent that they couldn't even fake any interest out of politeness. *They take no interest in you, so it's your right not to take any interest in them,* said Kai. *So it's your right not to take any interest in them.* Kai's words rang in her ears. Somehow she would survive the evening and then call it quits with this family of hers. For good.

'It's out of the question for you to take a taxi.' Oliver took the telephone gently but firmly from his ex-mother-in-law's hand. 'I'll drive you home.'

Like Pia, he was constantly on call, so he'd limited himself to a glass of champagne before dinner and hadn't drunk anything else all evening.

'Only if it's not an inconvenience for you,' said Gabriela. 'It's already late, and you've had a long day.'

'It's not inconvenient, on the contrary,' Oliver declared.

'All right, then!' Countess Gabriela Rothkirch raised her wine glass in Rosalie's direction. 'Thank you for the fantastic Christmas and farewell dinner, my dear.'

'Yes, once again, it was top class,' Inka agreed. 'The Americans have no idea what a jewel is coming their way.'

'Thank you,' said Rosalie, moved. 'You're all so dear to me. Oh, how I'm going to miss you.' She wiped a tear from her cheek.

'We'll miss you, too,' said Oliver, making a face. 'As of tomorrow, the cooking is back in the hands of an amateur.'

'Papa! I've left you a load of recipes that are quick and easy to cook,' Rosalie reminded her father. 'And you'd better watch out if I hear you've been eating frozen pizzas.'

'Never again in my life,' Oliver promised with a smile. It had been a lovely, happy and harmonious evening. His son, Lorenz, and Inka's daughter, Thordis, came from Bad Vilbel and were going to stay at Inka's. Sophia had behaved well, considering the circumstances, although she'd been disappointed when Cosima didn't call as she'd promised.

'All right, let's go, Gabriela.' Oliver stood up. 'By the time I get back, the kids will no doubt have cleaned up the kitchen.'

'The kids?' Lorenz grinned in amusement. 'I see only one kid here, and she's out like a light on your sofa.'

'Luckily,' added Rosalie, who had often been the babysitter for her little sister.

'Even though you're all grown up, you'll always be my kids,' said Oliver.

'Oh, Papa!' Rosalie jumped up and flung her arms round his neck. 'You are really the dearest and best papa in the world. I miss you already.'

After an affectionate and tearful farewell, Oliver and

Gabriela left the house. He opened the car door for her and then got in behind the wheel. The night was icy cold and clear, and there was hardly any traffic on the streets.

'What a lovely evening,' said Gabriela. 'I'm glad that I'm still welcome in your home.'

'Why wouldn't you be?' Oliver replied. 'You're not only Cosima's mother and the grandmother of my children, you're also a magnificent woman whom I treasure in my heart.'

'Thank you, Oliver. You said that beautifully.' For a while, they drove in silence.

'I hope you know that I strongly disapprove of Cosima's way of life,' Gabriela said at last. 'Even though she's my daughter, I can't help criticizing her. Your divorce hit me hard.'

'I know, but I . . .' Oliver began, thinking that he had to justify himself somehow, but Gabriela briefly touched his hand resting on the gear stick.

'No, no, you did nothing wrong, my dear,' she said. 'In your place, I most likely would have set her suitcases at the door. Just this evening, I was thinking about how often Cosima left you alone with the kids and went traipsing round the world. And now she's doing exactly the same thing instead of taking care of Sophia. Maybe I wasn't strict enough with her when she was little.'

She gave a deep sigh.

'I'm glad that we're alone for a change,' she went on as Bodenstein drove down Ölmühlweg in Königstein. 'Because there's something I want to discuss with you. Something that's been weighing on my mind since you two divorced. A few months ago, I changed my will. Cosima will get her legal portion, but I have assigned the major portion of my assets to my grandchildren with you as my executor.'

Bodenstein couldn't believe his ears.

'But you . . .' he tried to protest. His mother-in-law refused to listen.

'I know, I know. But I've considered everything in detail and consulted with my lawyer. I'm going to give you my house as a gift,' she went on. 'I prefer to share my wealth with a warm hand rather than a cold one. And with a little luck, I'll live long enough that you'll be spared the inheritance tax.'

'But, Gabriela, I . . . I can't accept that!' Bodenstein wasn't easily unsettled, but this unexpected announcement threw him off balance. His mother-in-law's villa was located on a huge plot of land in the Hardtwald, the best location in Bad Homburg, and it was worth millions. Apart from that, she also owned apartments and houses, a significant private art collection, a charitable foundation and a considerable fortune in stock. He felt dizzy at the thought that he, a humble Kripo officer, would in the future have to deal with all this.

'Pay attention to the road!' Gabriela shouted, laughing. 'Oliver, you are the son I've always wished I'd had. You're a family man with values that you live by. You're warm-hearted, level-headed, considerate and dependable. I can't imagine anyone who would be better suited to administer my estate and protect my grandchildren. Naturally, you will receive appropriate compensation for this task, and after my demise, you can do with the fortune whatever you think is right. In addition, I would be very happy to fulfil a few of your dearest wishes in advance. You have always been much too modest. So what do you think about all this?'

She was smiling at him in the darkness.

'I . . . I don't know what to say,' Oliver stammered. 'This . . . This is . . .'

'Don't keep me in suspense,' said Gabriela, amused. 'All the documents are ready, just waiting for your signature.'

'But Cosima and her siblings. They . . . They won't put up with this.' He was gradually recovering from the initial shock.

'They'll have to put up with it,' Gabriela replied. 'It's my will, after all. Besides, Cosima, Raffaela and Laetitia have already inherited a great deal of money from their father. Your three children are my only grandchildren, and I want my property to stay in the Rothkirch family. So. Can I count on you?'

Bodenstein turned his head and smiled at her.

'Under one condition,' he said.

'And what would that be?'

'That you live for many more years.'

Countess Gabriela Rothkirch laughed.

'I can't promise you that, but I'll make my best effort,' she said, and squeezed his hand.

TUESDAY, DECEMBER 25, 2012

It had snowed again in the night. They would find his footprints, but he didn't worry about that. When he bought the shoes, he'd been extra careful to make sure they were a mass-produced brand, nothing extravagant. He didn't have to wait long; his target was as punctual on Christmas Day as on every other morning. And he hit him right where he intended. With one blow, his circulation ceased. His heart, no, her heart stopped beating. The way it should have stopped beating ten years ago, if nature hadn't been so cunningly cheated. He'd wanted so much to see the old woman's face, the shock, the painful realization that all that money had bought only ten years' postponement.

But he couldn't risk staying here, even though the temptation was great. He bent down, picked up the empty cartridge, and stuck it in his jacket pocket. Then he stowed the rifle, shouldered the bag, and stepped out of the bushes, which had provided a perfect hiding place. The darkness of night was yielding to a grey dawn as he went up the steps and disappeared. Winter had always been his favourite time of year.

The call came at ten past nine and tore Pia out of a deep sleep. Last night, she and Kim had left their parents' house right after dinner, before the animosity between Kim and her sister-in-law could escalate. Lars and Sylvia had outshone everyone else with the expensive presents they showered upon the children; even Pia's taciturn father had made a critical comment. The sisters drove to Birkenhof, enjoyed a lovely evening with two bottles of excellent red wine, and talked until the crack of dawn.

'Where to this time?' Pia mumbled into the phone.

'Fasanenstrasse 47 in Kelkheim,' the officer on duty repeated patiently. He sounded disgustingly alert. 'I'm sending the forensics guys over, and I've requested a medical examiner.'

'Could you please call Bodenstein, too?' Pia rolled out of bed and yawned. 'I'll leave at once.'

She staggered to the bathroom, brushed her teeth, and got dressed. No time for a shower.

'Hey, you're already up,' she said in amazement when she came downstairs and saw Kim sitting at the kitchen table with a cup of coffee and holding a cigarette. She had her iPad out with a keyboard attached. The dogs jumped out of their baskets to greet Pia, wagging their tails.

'Good morning,' said her sister with a grimace. 'My damn

internal clock wakes me up at seven on the dot, even at Christmas. I really wish I could sleep in.'

'Sorry there won't be any delicious breakfast,' Pia told her, patting the dogs on the head and pouring herself a cup of coffee. 'We've got another body over in Kelkheim.'

'Oh, will you take me with you?' Kim closed her iPad. 'I can be ready in two minutes.'

For years, Kim had been the acting medical director of a forensic psychiatric clinic at a prison near Hamburg, and she had an excellent reputation with the state attorney's office as an expert witness for criminal trials. Neff had taken off over Christmas and would probably not show up at the crime scene. It might be helpful to have someone present to observe the whole situation from a different angle than the criminal police.

'Sure, why not?' Pia took a gulp of coffee, which tasted terrible. It didn't bother her, because when it came to drinking coffee, it wasn't the taste but the effect of the caffeine she cared about, and that was more than sufficient.

A few minutes later, the sisters drove out of the Birkenhof gate. The estate car bumped across the train tracks.

'The shocks are in bits,' said Kim.

'The whole car is in bits,' Pia said dryly. 'Soon I'll have to start looking round for a new one, before this one breaks down under my arse.'

'You think it was the sniper again?' Kim asked. Last night, Pia had told her about the two cases she was working on at the moment.

This time, the victim wasn't an elderly woman, but a young man, and he had been shot on Christmas Day. If it was indeed the same perp, this turn of events had completely obliterated all of Neff's theories.

'Possible,' was all Pia said, turning off Carriageway B8 and speeding on. Near the turn-off to Bad Soden, a silver Mercedes SUV tore past them with a blast of its horn, in total disregard of the speed limit.

'Ah, Henning is on his way, too, I see,' she said, flashing her lights in greeting at her ex's rapidly vanishing car. She stomped on the accelerator till the pedal almost went through the floor. The old engine roared hoarsely, but the speedometer only shuddered at just over 85. The car had no more to give.

'What's it like for you when you're driving to a crime scene?' Kim asked. 'Are you excited?'

'More like tense,' Pia said. 'You never really know what to expect.'

'Do you think about where you once saw a dead body when you drive through the same area?'

'Yeah, of course. In my head, there's a sort of crime-scene map. Even years later, I remember where a house burned down or a dead body was found.'

She slowed and shifted down. At the intersection where the federal highway ended, she turned right and drove a hundred metres further along to the left.

'It's up ahead over there.' She pulled in behind a patrol car. 'And my boss is already here.'

'The victim's name is Maximilian Gehrke, and he was twenty-seven years old,' said the young police superintendent who was first on the scene with her colleagues. 'He was on his way to visit his father, as he did every morning at eight a.m. Seems to have been a firm ritual, as the neighbour who found the body told us.'

'Did she notice anything?'

'Unfortunately not. She went out with her dog and saw him lying here. She didn't hear the shot.'

'Thanks.' Bodenstein looked round. The dead man was lying on his stomach, his legs on the paved path leading to the front door of the bungalow, his upper body on the winter-yellow lawn. The shot must have killed him on the spot; he hadn't even had time to pull his hands out of his pockets in order to extend his arms to break the fall.

'Not a head shot,' Bodenstein declared. He pulled on latex gloves and touched the nape of the dead man's neck. The skin had not yet turned cold. On the left side of his back, at about chest height, there was an entry wound, round which a dark-red blotch had spread on his light grey jacket.

'A shot from behind, straight into his heart,' someone remarked behind him.

'Good morning, Henning.' Bodenstein turned round and wondered whether the medical examiner was going to wish him Merry Christmas. It seemed somehow inappropriate. 'Glad you could come so quickly. It's not that easy to get someone out on Christmas.'

'No problem. Christmas is way overrated.' Henning Kirchhoff opened his aluminium case and pulled on overalls, gloves, and booties and pulled the hood over his head. 'What do you think? The same perp as in Niederhöchstadt and Oberursel?'

'I'm not sure.' Bodenstein took a step back. 'So far, he's killed his victims with a head shot. Why should he change his MO? Though this perp obviously used a silencer, and the sniper did, too.'

Pia's old estate car turned into the street and stopped behind the patrol vehicle. Bodenstein watched as his colleague, accompanied by another woman, crossed the street and headed for the little gate through which Maximilian Gehrke must have walked before the fatal shot brought him down.

'Good morning, boss,' Pia said. 'And Merry Christmas.'

'Thanks, same to you,' Bodenstein said with a nod.

'May I introduce my little sister? She's visiting for Christmas.'

'Pleased to meet you.' Bodenstein extended his hand. 'Oliver von Bodenstein.'

'Katharina Freitag, but I prefer to be called Kim.'

A firm handshake, a searching look from grey-blue eyes wreathed by thick eyelashes. The likeness between the two sisters was astonishing: the same high cheekbones, the wide mouth with full lips, the high hairline that in the younger woman was more pronounced, because she had tightly pulled back her natural blonde hair, while Pia wore hers in a loose ponytail.

'I know it's not customary to bring relatives along to a crime scene,' Pia said. 'But Kim is a forensic psychiatrist and may be able to help us.'

'That's not up to me,' replied Bodenstein. 'But I have nothing against it if you'd like to watch, Ms Freitag.'

Across the street, a few onlookers had gathered. The news of the bloody deed early on Christmas morning had apparently already made the rounds in this genteel residential area.

'Right now, I want to speak with the father of the dead man,' Bodenstein told Pia after reporting on what he'd learned so far about the victim. Henning was almost finished examining the corpse, and greeted his ex-sister-in-law with surprise and pleasure.

The blue VW van of the evidence team drove up, and the

officers climbed out. A triumphant smile spread across Henning's lips when he caught sight of Christian Kröger.

'That makes it five to seven. I'm catching up,' he said to Pia and Kim. 'This year, Kröger beat me to the stiff seven times. If the sniper keeps this up, I might still have a real chance at a draw.'

'Give me a break, Henning.' Pia shook her head disapprovingly. 'I can't believe you two are still carrying on this stupid competition.'

'Is that why you tore past us on the B8?' Kim wanted to know.

'Hmm. Well, I guess so.' Henning seemed embarrassed to admit it.

'Let's go inside,' Bodenstein said to Pia, 'before these two start going at it again.'

Day after day in her profession, Pia encountered countless types of individuals, young and old, intelligent and stupid, pragmatic and spaced-out, gentle and aggressive, honest and hypocritical. Many of them were under great emotional duress, which meant they were often in no condition to hide their feelings. This situation – involuntarily provoked and sometimes lasting for only a few seconds – allowed her to get a glimpse into their innermost being. Her work demanded objectivity, and yet even she couldn't help regarding some people as more pleasant than others.

She felt genuinely sorry for Fritz Gehrke. The old man was devastated, yet he was trying hard to answer Bodenstein's questions. Like many people of his generation, it went against the grain to let himself go. Unlike young people, who often wept hysterically and completely broke down, he mustered all his strength to answer every question.

Since the death of his wife in 1995, the eighty-one-year-old man had lived alone in the big house, which he had built over fifty years ago as one of the first in this area. He suffered from various ailments of old age, though he did not specify them, but he managed fairly well. A housekeeper came in daily except for Sundays and bank holidays to take care of the housework. Fritz Gehrke was checked on twice a day by a mobile nursing service, and every morning, Maximilian, his only son, brought him rolls and jam and read the newspaper with him.

'I can't understand why anyone would want to kill Maximilian,' he said in a quavering voice. He had led them into the living room and sat down in an easy chair. His thin white hair was neatly parted, and he was properly dressed in a shirt and tie, slacks and a Bordeaux-red sweater. His age-spotted hand gripped the handle of his cane. The house was old but immaculately kept and well maintained. The travertine floor shone, and even the fringes of the rugs lay perfectly straight.

'Max is such a modest and kind young man.' Tears shimmered in his eyes behind his gold-framed glasses. 'He studied music pedagogy and he teaches at the music school here in Kelkheim. He also directs the church choir at St Franziskus and plays the organ.'

He knew that his son was no longer alive, but he couldn't bring himself to use the past tense when talking about him.

'Where did your son live?' Bodenstein asked.

'He has an apartment down in Kelkheim, on Frankfurter Strasse.' Fritz Gehrke blew his nose in a linen handkerchief as white as apple blossoms. 'I invited him to live here. The house has a beautiful granny flat with its own entrance, but it was important to Max to finally stand on his own two feet. He was born with a serious heart defect, spent years in clinics, and his health was never robust. He could never romp about or play football like the other boys his age. In spite of that, he always had lots of friends, because he is . . . he was . . . Please forgive me.'

His voice failed; he shook his head mutely and struggled for a moment to regain his composure.

There was a knock on the front door. Pia excused herself and went down the hall to open it.

'We're finished with the body.' Christian Kröger was still wearing his overall with the hood. 'And we found the spot where the shot was fired. Do you want to look?'

Pia nodded. She followed Kröger outside, saying hello to the men from the morgue, who put the body in a body bag for the trip to the Forensic Medicine lab in Frankfurt.

'Look, over there.' Kröger pointed to a small green area across the street, surrounded by a tall yew hedge; it lay a bit higher than Gehrke's house. 'That's where he must have stood.'

'Wouldn't that be too risky?' Pia said sceptically. 'The people in that house could have seen him.'

'No, it's ideal. I'll show you.'

Pia crossed the street behind her colleague and saw the narrow footpath with steps next to the house with the yew hedge. It led up the hill to the street above. Kröger climbed from the steps over the low chain-link fence and pushed himself through the hedge.

'Come on,' he urged her. 'But stay right behind me. This time, he left footprints. We found them in the snow.'

Pia followed him and saw that the hedge wasn't so massive as it had seemed at first glance. From here, you couldn't really

see the house further up the slope, because a huge rhododen-
dron blocked the view.

'Here.' Kröger pointed to a spot on the ground. 'This is
where he stood and waited. He cut a hole in the hedge. There
are twigs scattered everywhere.'

Pia stepped up next to him and had an unimpeded view of
Gehrke's house.

'Naturally, we'll have to do a ballistics analysis of the
bullet,' Kröger said, 'but I'm one hundred per cent sure that
the shot was fired from here. Then the shooter went back the
same way, up the steps, and he was gone. Maybe he had a car
parked up on Nachtigallenweg or further up in the development. Unfortunately, there wasn't enough snow, and we lost
the trail. From there, he could have turned onto the B8 and
been long gone.'

They climbed the steps, and Pia looked all round.

'You're right,' she agreed. 'This is the perfect escape route.'

Her mobile hummed in her jacket pocket and she pulled it
out. The number on the display was withheld, but she took the
call anyway.

'Hähnel, Kelkheim police station.' A man's voice, young
and quivering with excitement. 'A letter was just delivered here
for you.'

'For us?' Pia touched Kröger's arm and motioned for him
to stay where he was.

'Yes, it's addressed to "Homicide Division Hofheim."'

'And who dropped off the letter?'

'An elderly lady with a dog,' the officer from Kelkheim told
her. 'Some man up at the cloister handed it to her.'

'Did you get her name and address?'

'Of course!' He sounded almost offended.

'Okay. We'll come right away.' Pia cut off the call.

'What's up?' Kröger was giving her a curious look.

'That was an officer from Kelkheim police station,' Pia replied grimly. 'A woman delivered a letter addressed to us. If it's really from the sniper, he's getting really bold.'

MAXIMILIAN GEHRKE HAD TO DIE BECAUSE HIS FATHER IMPLICATED HIMSELF BY APPROVING OF SOMEONE'S DEATH AND BY BRIBERY. Pia pinned the printout of the obituary on the wallboard and wrote the name of the victim above it, with date and time of death. Little by little, a few colleagues wandered in whom the detective on duty had called, gathering in the conference room of K-11. Pia and Bodenstein had visited the woman who had delivered the letter to the police station, but she hadn't been much help as a witness. The man, who had given her quite a fright, had looked like a jogger. She couldn't see much of his face because he was wearing a cap and sunglasses, with a scarf wrapped round his neck and pulled up to his nose. He hadn't said a word.

'We know three things with some certainty,' Pia said. 'Our sniper has struck for a third time, he knows the area and he kills out of revenge.'

'But we don't have the faintest idea what he's taking revenge for,' Kai added.

'Although he does list quite concrete reasons in the obituaries,' Bodenstein said, thinking out loud. 'Does he think he's some kind of Robin Hood?'

'No,' said Kim just as Dr Nicola Engel entered the room. 'Then he would seek publicity, but he's not doing that. It's something personal.'

'Interesting,' said Engel, looking Kim over. 'And who might you be, if I may ask?'

Kim and Pia stood up simultaneously.

'My name is Dr Kim Freitag,' Pia's sister introduced herself, extending her hand to Nicola Engel, who hesitantly shook hands. 'I'm Ms Kirchhoff's sister, visiting for Christmas.'

'I see. It's unusual for family members of our colleagues to be involved in murder investigations.' The chief of Regional Criminal Investigations gave Pia a reproachful look. 'Or are we going to have mother, brother and grandparents sitting here next because they're feeling bored at home?'

Her caustic tone of voice did not bode well, and Pia, who had thought she was bringing her chief some much-needed professional expertise, lost heart.

'I . . . uh . . . I . . .' she stuttered.

'Your name sounds familiar,' said Dr Engel, ignoring Pia's embarrassed stammering. She tilted her head and scrutinized Kim.

'I'm the acting medical director of the Ochsenzoll Forensic Psychiatric Clinic in Hamburg. I appear as an expert witness all over Germany on behalf of the courts and the state attorneys' offices.' Kim magically produced a business card from the inside pocket of her jacket. 'Most recently, in the case of the autobahn killer from Karlsruhe. I'm called in mostly in cases of serial killings, rapes and sexual assault.'

'In early December, you gave a lecture at a conference in Vienna about psychobiological characteristics of violent offenders, didn't you?'

'That's right. At the Forensic Psychiatric Congress at the Palace of Justice.' Kim smiled. 'When my sister told me a little about your current case yesterday, I remembered a similar case that I worked on in the States.'

'Don't tell me it was the John Allen Muhammad case!' shouted Kai Ostermann without looking up from his laptop.

'That's right,' Kim replied in astonishment. 'Why?'

'Because our highly regarded colleague Neff from state headquarters has been jabbering away about it for days,' Ostermann said. 'To hear him talk, you'd think he solved the case all by himself when he was with the FBI.'

'Oh, really?' Kim seemed a bit surprised. 'I spent two years at Quantico, but I can't recall a German officer being involved in the investigation.'

'No surprise,' Nicola Engel interrupted the discussion. 'Let's get back to business here, and afterwards, I'd like to speak with you, Ms Freitag.'

'All right,' Kim said with a smile.

'Ms Kirchhoff, please give me a rundown of the current case,' said the commissioner, sitting down on Pia's chair.

Pia rattled off the facts they had so far as she sketched on the whiteboard the situation at the crime scene and the perp's probable escape route.

'As for ammunition, it was again a large-calibre semi-jacketed round, and once again, the shooter used a silencer,' she ended her report. 'This time, he left behind his first clue: footprints from his shoes, and he was seen by the woman he handed the letter to. Regrettably, the witness's description is quite vague.'

'I found the victim's father on Wikipedia,' Ostermann said. 'Friedrich Gehrke, born 1931 in Cologne. Studied medicine, married Marianne Seitz 1953, doctorate 1955, joined his father-in-law's firm in 1958. And so on and so forth . . . Wife deceased, company incorporated . . . blah blah blah . . . 1982 remarried. In 1998, company sold to US investor. A good number of honours and awards, including the Federal Cross of Merit First Class.'

'That "blah blah blah" might interest me,' Bodenstein interrupted him. 'What sort of company was it?'

'Originally a factory that produced stomach tablets,' Ostermann read from his screen. 'Seitz and Sons. But since the next Seitz had no sons, it was changed to Seitz and Son-in-Law. And Gehrke was a diligent partner, expanding the small company into a pharmaceutical corporation named Santex, which specialized in generic drugs. He sold the business in 1998 for two billion dollars to an American corporation. So he is not a poor man.'

'There's something else worth considering,' Kim put in. 'The sniper shot the first two victims in the head, but Maximilian Gehrke was killed with a shot to the heart. His father told us that Maximilian had heart disease.'

Bodenstein looked up.

'Until he got a donor heart a few years ago,' he said.

'Maybe the perp knew about that and wanted to destroy the transplanted heart on purpose,' Kim surmised. 'As a symbol of his omnipotence.'

For a moment, nobody said a word.

'That might be the connection between the victims.' Bodenstein jumped up and went to the whiteboard. His eyes were shining with excitement. 'Our first real clue.'

He tapped on the name MARGARETHE RUDOLF.

'Her husband is a transplant surgeon, and our last victim received a heart transplant. It can't be a coincidence.'

Ostermann's fingers were clacking on the keyboard.

'Professor Dieter Paul Rudolf, born 1950 in Marburg,' he read aloud, and then whistled. 'The guy is an eminent authority. He worked with Christiaan Barnard in Capetown, then at the University Hospital in Zürich and at the University Hospital in Hamburg-Eppendorf. He invented several new procedures and has a reputation as one of the best heart transplant specialists in Germany. In 1994, he became head surgeon at the Frankfurt Trauma Clinic. In 2004, he moved to a private clinic in Bad Homburg, and apparently, that's where he still works today. He's written a zillion books and collected a pile of awards.'

'How many hospitals in this area do heart transplants?' Bodenstein wondered out loud. 'We ought to talk to Professor Rudolf. Maybe he remembers a patient named Maximilian Gehrke.'

The grey morning had turned into a grey day with no wind. Bodenstein had got the keys to an unmarked car from the motor pool. Deep in thought, he strolled across the courtyard, towards the garages. He located the car and got in behind the wheel to wait for Pia and her sister, who were still in Nicola Engel's office.

Ever since his talk with Cosima's mother the night before, Bodenstein was feeling a bit off balance. He was honoured and flattered by Gabriela's trust in him, but it also filled him with concern. In the Bodenstein household, there had never been a lot of money. Except for the estate with the castle between Schneidhain and Fischbach, the Bodensteins possessed hardly anything of material value. He didn't have the faintest idea about the banking world or running a business, but it was something he was going to have to learn, even if he didn't agree to Gabriela's plan. After all, she had put him in her will as preliminary heir for his children, which meant the responsibility for their fortune lay on his shoulders.

Her lawyers, banking people and foundation staff, all of whom had been working for her for years, would notice in no time that he was completely clueless, and might even try to skim off money and defraud him. And there was no way he could predict Cosima's reaction to her mother's plans. He'd often thought that she wasn't that interested in money, but it was easy to act indifferent if you were as wealthy as the Rothkirchs. When her father died, Cosima had received a large sum of money from a trust fund, and with it, she financed her film projects, her trips abroad and her whole life.

His police salary, on the other hand, was laughable. True, he never could have afforded the house in one of the better residential areas of Kelkheim, which they had built twenty years ago, or the expensive private schools for the children. It wouldn't be easy for most men to be married to a woman who could afford anything she wanted, but it was not something that bothered Bodenstein, thanks to his strict upbringing to live modestly. Now everything was going to change. He wouldn't have to work as a police inspector anymore. But what would he do if he gave up his profession, which for him was far more than simply a job?

At any rate, he had decided last night before driving back to Bad Homburg that he wasn't going to mention it to anyone at first, not even to Inka. Especially not to her. She wasn't thrilled about him phoning Cosima or meeting his ex-wife whenever he picked up Sophia. It didn't matter how often he reassured Inka that his marriage to Cosima was over and done with. She didn't seem to believe it. If he took Gabriela's offer, he would be tied to the family of his ex-wife more closely than ever.

'Here we are.' Pia yanked open the passenger door and got

in, startling Bodenstein out of his musings. 'The phones are ringing off the hook, and Kai was cursing. Somehow the press has already got wind of the murder.'

'I don't think that's so bad.' Bodenstein started the engine. 'With a little luck, somebody may turn up who saw something.'

He glanced in the rear-view mirror.

'Okay, Dr Freitag? What did the big chief say?'

'She considers me competent enough to serve in a support role,' Kim said with a smile. 'Though she made it perfectly clear to me that I'm here only as a temporary guest. No salary and no responsibility for anything until the Ministry of the Interior Ministry agrees that I may be taken on as an external adviser for the case. But that's okay with me. I have plenty of leave saved up and nothing better to do right now.'

'Well, then, congratulations and welcome to the team,' Bodenstein said. 'Nicola Engel isn't easy to convince.'

He liked Kim. She was just as astute as her sister and not afraid to assert herself. She also had a good sense of humour.

'She's a pro, I'm a pro,' Kim said. 'And special cases demand special measures.'

'Hear, hear!' said Bodenstein, driving out of the courtyard onto the unusually deserted street.

Twenty minutes later, Bodenstein, Pia and Kim were facing Professor Rudolf's daughter. She was dressed all in black, and she looked as though she hadn't had any rest since Thursday evening. Her skin was pale and blotchy, her eyes swollen and red.

'Hello, Mrs Albrecht.' Bodenstein extended his hand. 'How are you doing? And how is your daughter?'

'She hasn't spoken a single word. To anyone,' replied the

woman. 'My ex-husband and his family left this morning to visit his parents at Lake Starnberg. They took Greta along.'

'That was a good decision,' said Bodenstein. 'Maybe you could use a change of scene as well?'

'No, I can't leave my father alone right now.' Karoline Albrecht pulled her knitted cardigan tighter and crossed her arms. 'Besides, I have to arrange for Mama's funeral.'

Bodenstein had seldom seen such profound despair as he now saw in her green eyes. He was not prepared for such immense pain and grief. Normally, he managed to preserve a professional distance to the victim and his or her relatives; it was something he'd learned to do in the many years he'd spent on the job. But he felt moved by this woman, who stood before him with a straight back and stony expression, mobilizing all her reserves to be strong for others.

'Don't you have a friend you could lean on?' Bodenstein asked gently.

'It's Christmas,' she reminded him. 'I could not and will not demand that of anyone. I'll manage all right. Life must go on.'

Bodenstein put his hand on her arm and gave it a squeeze. Yes, she would get through it. Karoline Albrecht was a strong woman. She would not go to pieces because of this fateful blow, even though she must feel devastated right now.

'We need to speak with your father,' Bodenstein said. 'Would you be kind enough to tell him we're here?'

'Of course. Please come in.'

They followed her into the house, which smelled better than it had on their last visit. The dining room table was cleared, the Christmas decorations put away. Karoline Albrecht left them in the dining room and then came back a few minutes later.

'My father is waiting for you in his study,' she said.

It was obvious that the professor had also suffered in the last few days. He was sitting at his desk, surrounded by bookshelves that reached to the ceiling. He looked like a grey shadow of himself and did not get up to greet them.

'Would you mind leaving us alone?' he asked his daughter, who immediately left the study, discreetly closing the door behind her. Bodenstein then told the professor about the murder that had occurred early that morning in Kelkheim.

'The victim was a young man, only twenty-seven years old,' he said. 'His father told us that he'd had heart problems since birth and was saved by a heart transplant operation.'

'Tragic.' Professor Rudolf looked at him without much interest.

'We thought that you might know him. His name was Maximilian Gehrke.'

'Gehrke? That doesn't ring a bell.' The professor shook his head wearily. 'For over twenty years, transplants have been my daily bread. I rarely recall individual cases.'

'But you must remember cases that are special or unusual,' Kim said. 'Maximilian was a young man with a congenital heart defect. Please try to think back.'

The professor took off his glasses, rubbed his reddened eyes, and carefully thought it over.

'Yes, I do recall the boy,' he said at last, looking up. 'He came into the world with a tetralogy of Fallot, and from that, he developed a right ventricular hypertrophy, with other associated unfavourable factors. After a couple of unsuccessful operations, the boy had virtually no hope of survival. His last chance was the HTX. The heart transplant.'

Bodenstein and Pia exchanged a glance. Could this be the breakthrough they'd been waiting for? Did this establish the connection between two of the killer's victims?

'Let me ask you again: does the name Ingeborg Rohleder mean anything to you?' Pia asked.

'Who would that be?' The professor put his glasses back on.

'The first victim,' said Pia. 'She was seventy-four years old, lived in Eschb . . . uh . . . Niederhöchstadt.'

'Ah yes, you did ask me that already. No, I'm sorry. I really have never heard the name before. Is that all?'

'Not quite.' Bodenstein searched for the right words to broach the sensitive topic. 'What do you think the perpetrator was referring to in his letter?'

'Believe me, I've been pondering that question night and day since you told me about it.' The man's shoulders slumped forward. 'For the life of me, I can't make any sense of it. In all the years I've worked as a GP, I've never had a problem with a patient's relatives.'

Bodenstein and Pia then said goodbye and left the house without seeing Mrs Albrecht again.

'That was great, the way you got him to remember Maximilian,' Pia said to her sister as they crossed the street to their car.

'I was thinking of that map in your head.' Kim smiled. 'The way you never forget a dead body or a murder scene. I was hoping that it might be the same for a doctor.'

'In any event, we now have a connection between two of the victims.' Pia zipped up her jacket to her chin. 'But what does it mean? It's enough to drive me crazy that there's no useful clue. The perp must have cased his targets thoroughly; he knew their habits and lifestyles and found places where he could lie in wait for them undisturbed. And afterwards he was able to vanish easily and without being seen. How is it possible that nobody ever sees him?'

'Maybe people do see him but think nothing of it,' Kim said. 'Like the man with the dog up ahead. You see him, and ten seconds later he's forgotten, so long as he doesn't do anything unusual. The perp must be a man who can adapt and move about without being noticed.'

'That thing with the letter this morning bothers me,' said Pia. 'He must feel very sure of himself to take the risk of being recognized.'

'The risk was actually quite low,' Bodenstein objected. 'I'm sure that he chose the woman carefully. She was old and fearful, and he also had the surprise factor on his side. Don't underestimate the perp. He doesn't leave anything to chance.'

'Sooner or later, he's going to make a mistake,' Pia opined.

'I'm not waiting for that to happen.' Bodenstein beeped the remote to unlock the car. 'We're getting more and more pressure by the day. People are panicking.'

'And the perp isn't going to leave it at three victims,' Kim prophesied. 'He wants attention.'

'Then he's going to get it,' Pia said. 'Let's give all the details to the press. That way we can calm down the public, when they realize that they're not in imminent danger.'

'We can't risk it.' Bodenstein shook his head and started the engine. 'It might lead to collateral damage that we'd have to answer for.'

'The only one who has to answer for any of this,' said Kim, 'is the killer.'

She opened the freezer, and all of a sudden she had tears in her eyes when she saw all those freezer bags. Mama had always been so thrifty. Rarely did she ever throw anything away. She rinsed out jam and pickle jars and saved them for canning fruit. Plastic ice cream containers had been reused for decades in the Rudolf household for freezing food, always carefully labelled. *Szeged Goulash,* Karoline read in her mother's neat handwriting on one package, *9/12/2012.*

'Oh, Mama,' she whispered, wiping away the tears. 'You know what a lousy cook I am.'

She took out the goulash, closed the lid of the freezer and went up the steep cellar stairs. Papa hadn't budged from his study since his conversation with the police officers, which was fine with her. She didn't really want him to witness her mute dialogue with Mama. He simply didn't belong here. At least not during the day. As far back as Karoline could remember, her father had left the house at seven every morning and seldom returned home in the evening before ten. Mama had never complained, and at one point, she confessed to Karoline that she was dreading the day when he retired and would be round the house all day long. She had settled into her own life, pursued numerous activities and developed interests that he had not shared. His work was the only thing he thought about, nothing else.

Like me, Karoline thought, again fighting back tears. She now couldn't understand why she had worked like a crazy woman for the past twenty years, instead of spending time with her family and friends. Everything that had always been so important seemed so banal now. She had advised top managers all over the world about values, about the reappraisal of personal deficits, about time management and strategies for improving their corporate culture and image. In doing so, she had treated with contempt all the values that had once meant something to her. In her pursuit of success and acclaim, she had not only sacrificed her marriage, but her entire social sphere had also fallen by the wayside. *Don't you have a friend you can lean on?* the police officer had asked her. No, she didn't. That was the painful truth. Her only confidante had been her mother, and now she was gone. Mama's death had left a void inside her. In other people, that area was filled with pleasant memories and experiences, with love, happiness, partners and friends, with people who meant something. In her, there was little that was memorable. Added to her grief was the shattering realization that so far, her life had been superficial and with very little substance.

Karoline forced herself to enter the kitchen. She used to love this room, which had always been the focal point of the house. Mama's domain, in which there was always something simmering on the stove or baking in the oven and sending a seductive aroma through the house. An abundance of potted herbs stood on the wide recessed windowsills, and garlic and onions occupied a wooden shelf. But now the kitchen had lost its charm and had been turned into a place of horror. The window through which the bullet had entered was temporarily patched with a piece of cardboard. That was the only thing left to remind them of what happened there Thursday evening; the crime scene cleaners had been extremely thorough.

Karoline took a saucepan from the cupboard, filled it with the frozen goulash and set it on the stove. Then she opened a package of spätzle and put on a second pot of salty water. The escape into routine chores kept her from collapsing like a house of cards and sinking into the black waters of terror. Karoline wasn't taking the sedative tablets that her doctor had prescribed, because they made her feel numb. Likewise, she had politely but firmly turned down the opportunity to speak to the psychologist from the crisis intervention centre. She didn't want to talk, because there was nothing to talk about. She would have to deal with the shock on her own. All she needed was time. She had to comprehend and accept what had happened, and then figure out how to go on.

She stared through the lattice window at the snowy garden outside. Back there behind the bare hornbeam hedge, Death had lain in wait. The police officers told her that the shooter had taken up position on the shed and had shot from there. But . . . why? The press claimed that the 'sniper' shot people at random. His first victim had been a woman out walking her dog. This morning, he had struck again, this time felling a man who was just walking through the front garden. Those two might have been victims of opportunity, people who were simply in the wrong place at the wrong time. But her mother had been in the kitchen of her own house, which stood hidden behind hedges and trees at the end of a cul-de-sac. Nobody came here by chance. The killer must have meticulously planned the shooting.

The water that she'd set on the stove for the spätzle boiled over and evaporated with a hiss. Karoline awoke from her trance, went over to the stove, and turned down the burner.

All of a sudden, the diffuse fog of grief and bewilderment that had shrouded and paralysed her over the last few days lifted: clearly her mother had not been shot at random. So why did she have to die? Was there something that Mama hadn't told them about? Was there a secret, an old wrong that she knew nothing about? She had to find out. It was essential. Otherwise, she would never find peace again.

Their colleagues from the evidence team had examined Maximilian Gehrke's apartment thoroughly and brought back several boxes containing diaries, letters and other mementos. Bodenstein again set off to visit Fritz Gehrke, while Pia, Kim and Kai went through the contents of the boxes. For a young man, Maximilian seemed to have been an unusually enthusiastic diary-keeper, but that was easy to understand. Because of his serious illness, he had spent his childhood and youth secluded from other children, and to make matters worse, his mother had died when he was ten. Not an easy life for a young person, but Maximilian did not seem embittered by it. He had always loved music and books; he had played the piano and organ and read passionately. His diaries contained book reviews and concert critiques.

'"I know that I will never grow old,"' Pia read in a diary entry from the year 2000. '"And that's why I so enjoy life, as much as I can. Papa hopes that one day a matching donor heart will be found for me, and that until then, the rest of my body will remain healthy enough to accept a transplant. I don't know whether I should hope for such an event, because it would mean that someone else would have to die first, a young person, because hearts are not transplanted from older people."'

'Pretty wise for a fifteen-year-old,' Kai thought aloud.

'No wonder,' said Kim. 'He had to deal with the topic all his life. Which makes it even more tragic that he didn't have a chance to grow old.'

With every murder case came the challenge of logically connecting things that were apparently unrelated. The police had to deal with the victim, his life story and his circle of family and friends in order to discover the motive and identity of the perpetrator. When her research was done, Pia often knew more about the victim than his best friends and closest relatives did, yet she couldn't allow herself to be swayed by his fate. Emotions such as empathy for the victim and fury at the killer could affect her objectivity. She had to thank the countless hours in the forensic institute for her ability to regard the victim as not only a human being, but mainly as an object for criminological investigation. This time it didn't work so well; that's what dawned on her with every diary page she read. Maximilian Gehrke was a victim, true, just like Ingeborg Rohleder and Margarethe Rudolf, but none of them had been the actual targets of the perpetrator. They died because the actions of a relative had awakened the urge for retribution in the killer.

'Look at this!' Kim shouted. 'I found something. On 16 September, 2002, Maximilian wrote that a suitable donor heart had been found and that he had to be at the clinic that evening.'

Kai and Pia looked up. Kim scanned the pages, turning them quickly, and read a couple of passages aloud. The seventeen-year-old was very worried about having an organ from another person inside his body. Although he was feeling much better physically just a few weeks after the operation, the origin of his new heart was bothering him a lot. What had happened to the donor? Why had that person died so young? Maximilian Gehrke had made every effort to find out the name of the donor, and eventually he was successful.

'His heart came from a woman named Kirsten Stadler,' Kim read aloud. 'He learned her identity from an employee in the Frankfurt trauma clinic, but unfortunately, he doesn't mention the person's name.'

Ostermann pulled over his laptop and entered the donor's name first in POLAS, the police search engine, then in Google.

'There are a zillion Kirsten Stadlers on the Internet, but not the one we're looking for,' he grumbled. 'On Facebook alone, there are fourteen women registered with that name.'

'Do you think that his father didn't know the donor's name?' Pia asked.

'Possibly,' Kim said with a nod. 'In Germany, the recipients of an organ are not told the identity of the donor, unlike in the USA. There, it's even common for the recipient to get in touch with the donor's family.'

'And I don't think that Maximilian told his father,' said Kai. 'He found out using illegal methods, but he didn't want to know more. He didn't intend to contact the relatives.'

Pia put the diary she'd read back in the box and grabbed her phone to call Bodenstein. The name Kirsten Stadler was a new clue, and every new clue was a promising lead, even if in the course of the investigation, it turned out to be a dead end.

He pulled down the garage door and locked it. Then he got into his car, whose motor was already running, and drove past the endless rows of garages to the street. Christmas and sniper panic had swept the streets clean. He passed only one oncoming car on the way to the autobahn. Originally, he'd planned to leave more time between each execution, but what seemed good in theory didn't always work in practice. In the meantime, the police had formed a special commission with the imaginative name

'Sniper', and he had no doubt that they would catch him sooner or later. The perfect murder did not exist, nor was he making any particular efforts to commit one. With each new dead body, there were new clues, new risks, and eventually the police would realize what it was all about. That's why he couldn't take too much time, because he still had more things to do. Unfortunately, the weather in the next two days would thwart his plans, because the forecast was for wind and rain, extremely unfavourable conditions for a shot from more than eight hundred metres. On Friday, though, the wind was predicted to calm down, which was absolutely ideal. Until then, he would go on with his life calmly and unobtrusively. Despite the hints that he had given in the obituaries, the police still seemed to be fumbling in the dark. And with any luck, they would continue to do so for a while.

THURSDAY, DECEMBER 27, 2012

All the members of K-11 were once again gathered at the morning meeting of the 'Sniper' special commission on the day after the Christmas holiday. Cem Altunay had cut short his winter getaway in Turkey, and Kathrin Fachinger had more or less recovered from her cold.

'Why wasn't I informed about the third murder on Christmas Day?' Andreas Neff complained to Bodenstein. 'How am I supposed to help out constructively when I'm being bullied here?'

'Nobody is bullying you,' said Bodenstein. 'You should have left us a number where you could be reached out of hours.'

'I did!'

'Well, I tried several times to call you,' said Ostermann.

'But your mobile was off and you don't have voice mail. I didn't want to contact you via Facebook.'

A couple of people grinned. Neff checked the call list on his phone and fell silent, looking abashed.

Dr Nicola Engel came into the conference room, and all conversation stopped. The chief stood next to the whiteboard and looked round the table.

'I hope you all had lovely holidays and are now ready to get to work,' she began. 'First I'd like to introduce a new member of our team: Dr Kim Freitag, acting director of the Ochsenzoll Forensic Psychiatric Clinic in Hamburg and an experienced expert witness. She will be assisting us in an advisory capacity.'

'How many advisers are going to be needed here?' Neff grumbled.

'You're a case analyst. Dr Freitag is a forensic psychologist,' Engel coolly reprimanded him. 'The two of you will take entirely different approaches to a case like this.'

Astounded, Bodenstein's eyebrows shot up. He had never seen his boss take such a vehement stand on behalf of an external adviser. He noticed that Nicola and Kim briefly exchanged a conspiratorial look. What was going on? Wasn't Pia's sister here purely by chance?

'We can use all the help we can get. The Ministry of the Interior and the state attorney's office are not particularly pleased that we've had a third murder and not a single hot lead.' Nicola Engel nodded at Kim. 'Dr Freitag has already worked on several cases like this one, and now I'd like to hear her thoughts.'

Kim stood up and cleared her throat.

'These three cases we are currently investigating,' she said, 'differ radically from the majority of murders you usually have to deal with. Because the perpetrator never gets close to his victims, he leaves no traces on the corpse, which would otherwise contribute to the identification of the perp. So this time, we largely have to do without concrete evidence. The motive of the perp is also unusual with regard to the three victims. His revenge is not directed at the persons he kills, but at their relatives. We have to assume that the victims did not know the perp and possibly had never had anything to do with him. The fact that the perp gives us hints about his motive reveals something about him. He is no psychopath acting out of the sheer desire to kill. Quite the opposite: he considers his actions to be justifiable and appropriate, but he does have a conscience regarding injustice. The assessment of the perp's behaviour . . .'

Her gaze fell on Andreas Neff, who was leaning against the wall, arms crossed, closing his eyes and shaking his head at each word she spoke. She stopped.

'Are you of another opinion, Inspector Neff?' she asked.

'Please go on,' Neff replied with a supercilious smile. 'I view things somewhat differently than you do.'

'Mr Neff is an internationally known expert in the field of case analysis, especially with regard to serial killings by snipers,' Ostermann volunteered. 'He was once with the FBI.'

'Ah, indeed?' Kim looked at Neff with new interest. 'When were you there and in what department?'

'That is not germane at the moment,' Neff hurried to say.

'He solved the case of the Washington sniper. Almost single-handedly,' Ostermann went on, drawing a nasty look from Neff, to which he responded with an innocent smile.

'In 2002, I worked at the Behavioral Analysis Unit in

Quantico. What about you?' Kim asked. 'I actually have a very good memory for names and faces, but I don't remember you.'

Ostermann smirked, and Pia had a hard time suppressing a grin.

'I was on the staff of the regional state attorney.' Backed into a corner, Neff turned red and then went pale.

Bodenstein looked at Nicola Engel, who was following the exchange between her two external advisers with curiosity. She made no move to intervene to save Neff from public embarrassment.

'We're getting off topic,' was all Bodenstein said. He wanted his team to have a calm setting so they could concentrate, with no arguments and definitely no rivalries. 'Thank you for your remarks, Dr Freitag. Now I'd like to report on all the facts and findings to date.'

'This afternoon, Ingeborg Rohleder will be buried,' said Neff when Bodenstein was done. He had recovered from his shock and seemed to be feeling confident again. 'I assume that the killer will show up at the funeral.'

'I don't believe he will,' Kim countered.

'Oh, he definitely will.' Neff had apparently lost his ability to smile over the Christmas break. He seemed downright grim. 'The perpetrator possesses a strong need for recognition, and he's looking for thrills and adventure. He is relatively young, agile, athletic and has pronounced narcissistic character traits. He finds satisfaction in killing.'

'I view the situation quite differently,' Kim said. 'We are dealing with a professional.'

'You mean an assassin?' Neff grinned contemptuously.

'You're not hearing me correctly,' Kim said patiently. 'I

think he's a pro. A trained sharpshooter or sniper. Maybe he was with the police or the army.'

Neff waved his hand in dismissal. 'He will definitely appear at his victim's funeral. Possibly in disguise, but he wants to enjoy his handiwork.'

'Not happening.' Kim shook her head. 'He checked off one victim as soon as she died, and now he's focusing on the next one.'

'Thank you for your assessments,' Bodenstein once more cut off the burgeoning contest between experts. 'We have to learn more about Kirsten Stadler, the donor of the heart that was transplanted into Maximilian Gehrke in September 2002. The operation was performed by Professor Rudolf, the husband of our second victim. This connection between victims Gehrke and Rudolf is at the moment our most significant lead. Pia, go and talk to Ms Rohleder again. We have to find out whether there was some link between Ingeborg Rohleder and the other two victims. Kathrin and Cem, you two drive over to the trauma clinic in Frankfurt and ask to inspect their records. They will almost certainly refuse to let you see them, so Kai will try to get a court order from the state attorney's office, just to be on the safe side. The rest of you drive to Kelkheim and canvass the residents of the neighbourhood where Gehrke lives. Oh, and one more thing. The external advisers are here to support the investigation. We're a team and need all our power and highest concentration to solve these cases as soon as possible. I want – no, I *demand* – that everyone pull together, as we normally do in this unit. I hope all of you understand.'

Bodenstein said these last sentences with a sharpness that was unusual for him, and everyone nodded.

'The meeting is adjourned. Get to work,' Bodenstein concluded, and the team broke up with much murmuring and scraping of chairs.

'And what should I do?' Andreas Neff asked, sounding disgruntled.

'I thought you wanted to attend the funeral,' Bodenstein reminded him. Then he pointed to the box containing Maximilian Gehrke's diaries on a table. 'And after that, you can get busy with the personal documents that we found in the victim's apartment. We're interested in anything that happened starting in 2002. Maybe you'll find a link between Maximilian Gehrke and our perp.'

'My mother was never in the University Clinic Frankfurt.' Renate Rohleder, already dressed in black for the funeral, stood behind the sales counter of her flower shop. She was alone with Pia and Kim. 'And I'm sure that she never donated an organ or received one. I would have known if she did.'

'Is the name Kirsten Stadler familiar to you?' Pia wanted to know.

'Yes.' Rohleder nodded, rather surprised. 'We used to be almost neighbours; the Stadlers lived three houses down the street. Until that tragic incident. Then they moved away.'

'What sort of incident?' Pia asked.

'One morning, Kirsten went out jogging in the field and she collapsed,' Rohleder said. 'She had a cerebral haemorrhage. Just like that, out of the clear blue sky. I can still remember that day; I'd left the house to walk the dog and was running late, because my dog took off, chasing a rabbit. Suddenly Helen appeared right in front of me, Kirsten's daughter. She was very upset and yelling that something had happened to her mother, and could I help her.'

Her body language disclosed much more to Pia. Renate Rohleder was nervous. She kept touching her nose, stroking her hair, and pulling at one earlobe – she obviously was not feeling well.

'And then?' Pia prodded. 'What did you do? Did you help your neighbour?'

'I . . . I didn't have my mobile with me that day,' said Rohleder. 'My dog had dashed in front of a car and was hit. I promised Helen to call an ambulance from the house, but then I . . . somehow forgot. The dog was bleeding and the driver of the car was shouting at me. I would have been too late anyway, but I probably thought that other people were on their way to the field. I . . . I couldn't have known how serious Kirsten's condition was.'

'So you failed to render assistance,' Pia said.

'Yes, yes, I suppose so.' The florist was extremely uncomfortable talking about the incident. 'I felt terrible afterwards. Kirsten was such a nice girl, I liked her a lot. Believe me, this has haunted me ever since, even in my dreams. Six months after the incident, the Stadlers moved away from Niederhöchstadt. Life simply goes on.'

'I have something to show you.' Pia took a copy of the obituary out of her rucksack and handed it to Ms Rohleder.

'What's this?' The woman hesitated.

'The perpetrator sent it to us, the one who shot your mother,' Pia said.

Ms Rohleder read the notice. All colour drained from her face. She dropped the piece of paper as if it were on fire.

'No!' she whispered in horror. 'No! That . . . that can't be true! Ms Kirchhoff, you . . . you don't think that I . . .'

She didn't dare say the words that would make her responsible for her own mother's death.

'We think it's authentic,' replied Pia sombrely. 'We've received a similar obituary for each victim.'

The bell over the door jingled as a customer came into the shop.

'Please come back later,' Ms Rohleder said. Then she took a key out of the pocket of the green apron that she wore over her black dress, went to the glass door, and locked it. Then she leaned against the door, pressed a hand to her chest, and shut her eyes for a moment.

'That's a hideous accusation. I won't stand for it. I'll sue for slander and defamation of character.' In her indignation, she was confusing two offences. 'The very thought that I would be guilty of my mother's death . . . No!'

'The only person guilty of your mother's death is the one who shot her,' Pia said. 'He has already murdered three innocent individuals, and we're afraid that he will keep going. The perpetrator could be someone who knew Kirsten Stadler. Ms Rohleder, you knew the Stadlers and may be able to help us. Who would do such a thing?'

Renate Rohleder swallowed hard. She rubbed her face.

'She was . . . so . . . so cold,' she said softly. 'She gave me the creeps, the way she stood there and said to my face that she would make sure that I'd never be happy again in my life.'

'Who was that, Ms Rohleder?' Pia prodded.

Renate Rohleder sighed.

'Helen. Kirsten's daughter,' she replied. 'A few months ago, she showed up here at the shop, together with a man. Initially I didn't even recognize her. She accused me of causing her mother's death. As if I'd done something that made Kirsten have a haemorrhage!'

'Did you know the man who accompanied her?' Pia asked.

'No,' Rohleder said, shaking her head. 'He didn't introduce himself.'

'What did he look like, and how old was he?'

'No idea, I'd guess mid- to late thirties.' She shuddered. 'He was very good-looking. But he had something . . . dark and fanatical about him. I was afraid of him, even though he didn't say a word.'

'Do you think it's possible that the perp is a woman?' Pia asked her sister after they left the flower shop and went back to the car.

'If you're thinking about the Stadlers' daughter, probably not,' said Kim, who had stayed in the background during the conversation between Pia and Ms Rohleder. 'She seems to be a rather impulsive person who has a hard time controlling her feelings. People like that tend to act emotionally, but that's not the behaviour exhibited by the sniper. The murders have a clearly masculine stamp to them. Women kill differently from men, but you know that already. In the twenty years I've been in my job, I've encountered plenty of horrific and profoundly evil acts, but never a woman who killed innocent people.'

'The exceptions prove the rule,' replied Pia. 'Just think of the female suicide bombers in the Middle East. They even accept the deaths of innocent children.'

'I still think it's out of the question. Really, Pia, forget the daughter.' Kim shook her head. 'In order to do something like this, a person has to have strong nerves and a lot of patience.'

'But who could the man be?' Pia stopped beside the car.

'You need to ask Helen Stadler,' Kim suggested. 'Come on, let's get in before I freeze my arse off.'

Pia grinned and unlocked the car. At first glance, her sister didn't seem like the type of woman who would use such expressions.

'Anyway, I'm still betting on a pro,' Kim said. 'You really ought to search for him in the army and the police.'

'What would we be searching for? We don't have enough info to ask targeted questions.'

Pia's mobile rang. It was Ostermann, who told her that he had traced the husband of the deceased Kirsten Stadler by querying with the Residents' Registration Office. His name was Dirk Stadler and he lived in Liederbach.

'You should join us,' said Kai. 'The boss is on his way, too.'

'All right, we're on our way.'

The address that Kai had given her turned out to be an older neighbourhood in which the developer had tried to combat the uniform look of the terraced houses by varying the style and wood ornamentation of the facades. Bodenstein was already waiting for them on the street corner. He had the collar of his overcoat turned up against the icy wind and his hands in his pockets. Pia parked behind his car.

'Renate Rohleder was completely shocked when I showed her the obituary,' she told her boss. 'Kirsten Stadler was a neighbour she knew well. She vividly remembers the day Kirsten died, and ever since, she's had a guilty conscience because she did nothing to help. She was in a hurry, her dog took off and was hit by a car. Most likely, she wouldn't have been able to do anything even if she had gone to her neighbour's aid or called an ambulance, because Kirsten Stadler had suffered a cerebral haemorrhage. But the daughter, Helen Stadler, seems to have blamed Renate.'

'Incidentally,' said Kim, 'she showed up a couple of months ago at the flower shop accompanied by a man and making accusations. If the perp knows things like that, then he must be from the family's closest circle of friends and acquaintances.'

'Well, let's hear what Kirsten Stadler's widower has to say to that.' Bodenstein double-checked the address, and soon afterwards rang the bell of number 58F. A thin, almost gaunt man with short grey hair and a receding hairline opened the door.

'My name is Bodenstein from Kripo Hofheim.' He showed the man his ID. 'My colleagues Ms Kirchhoff and Ms Freitag. We would like to speak with Dirk Stadler.'

'That's me.' The man regarded them with the typical mixture of suspicion and caution that almost everyone displayed when the criminal police unexpectedly showed up at the door.

'May we come in?'

'Yes, of course, please do.'

He was in his mid-fifties and wore grey corduroy trousers and an olive green V-neck sweater over a white shirt. He had to tilt his head back to look into Bodenstein's face.

'My son is here for dinner,' said Dirk Stadler apologetically. From the hall, they could see into a large, open space that was dining room, living room and kitchen combined. At the table sat a man in his late twenties who glanced up briefly from his tablet computer and nodded a greeting, but remained seated.

'My son, Erik,' Dirk Stadler introduced him. 'What's this about?'

'It's about your late wife,' said Bodenstein.

'About Kirsten?' Bewildered, the man looked from Bodenstein to Pia and Kim. 'There must be some kind of mistake. My wife died ten years ago.'

'You've probably heard about the murders committed over the past several days,' Bodenstein went on. 'In Niederhöchstadt and Oberursel, two women were shot by a sniper. Then a young man was killed in Kelkheim on Christmas morning.'

'Yes, I read about it in the paper,' Stadler said. 'And of course, it's all over the radio and television.'

Now his son got up, came closer and stood next to his father. He was only a little taller, and had the same deep-set eyes and facial features. 'The perpetrator has been in contact with us,' said Bodenstein. 'After each murder, he wrote an obituary in which he gave reasons for his action. In the diary entries of his last victim we came across the name of your late wife. The dead man, Maximilian Gehrke, was twenty-seven years old. He might not have lived even that long because he had a congenital heart defect. But ten years ago, he received a transplant, the heart of your late wife.'

Father and son both turned pale and exchanged a brief glance.

'The woman who was killed in Oberursel was the wife of the professor who performed the heart transplant back then.'

'Oh my God,' Dirk Stadler whispered in consternation.

'And the first victim of the sniper was the mother of a former neighbour of yours from Niederhöchstadt.'

'That . . . that can't be true,' Dirk Stadler stammered. 'But why? After all these years!'

'We've been asking ourselves the same question,' Boden-stein said with a nod. 'At first, there was no connection between the individual victims, but the link seems to be your late wife.'

'I . . . I have to sit down,' Stadler said. 'But please do come in and take off your coats.'

Pia noticed that the man walked with a limp that made him tilt to one side. It looked as though one of his legs was shorter than the other. Stadler sat down at the dining room table, and the officers all took a seat.

Erik Stadler gathered up the dishes and carried them over to the sink in the open kitchen. High-gloss white cabinets with dark granite counters, and lots of stainless steel. In front of the big picture window in the living room stood a small decorated Christmas tree, and on the coffee table was a plate of Christmas cookies. The house was soberly but tastefully deco-rated throughout with black, white and grey the predominant colours. In contrast to Professor Rudolf's house with all the flowers, the velvet curtains and the faded children's drawings and notes stuck to the fridge door with magnets, this house seemed devoid of a woman's touch. The only piece of furniture that didn't fit the rest of the decor was a massive antique side-board. On top stood a silver-framed photo of a blonde woman laughing happily into the camera. Dirk Stadler had noticed Pia looking at it.

'That's Kirsten, my wife,' he informed her in a hoarse voice. 'That picture was taken the summer before she died. It was our last holiday, on the Atlantic coast of France.'

His son sat down on the chair next to him.

'I . . . I can't believe that people had to die because of my wife.' Stadler cleared his throat, visibly struggling to keep his composure. 'Why? For what reason?'

'A very personal motive is crystallizing,' replied Bodenstein. 'The perpetrator seems to be focused on retribution, seeking revenge for the death of your wife. He must be someone who was once quite close to her.'

'But my wife died from a cerebral haemorrhage,' Stadler said helplessly. 'It was tragic accident, but no one was at fault. She had an aneurysm in her brain, and it burst. It could have happened anywhere at any time.'

He ate only a little, then set down his knife and fork on the plate.

'Don't you like it?' Karoline asked.

'Yes, I do. It's very good.' Her father gave her a brief smile. 'I just don't have any appetite.'

She felt the same way, but she forced herself to eat. The same way she forced herself to stay alive.

'Thanks for taking care of me, Karoline. I really appreciate your support.'

'It's my pleasure.' She also managed a brief smile.

For two days and nights, she'd been racking her brain over how to put into words what was on her mind. Why was it so difficult for her to speak about her suspicions to her father? What had happened to her confidence and courage? Since Mama died, they had barely spoken to each other, and she now realized that this was not really much of a change. They had maintained an illusion of harmony solely thanks to Mama; without her presence, silence had descended between Karoline and Papa. She had never had a close relationship with her father, perhaps because he'd played almost no role during her childhood and youth. He was brilliant, considered one of the best at his profession, and what he did was important, because he saved the lives of deathly ill patients. She had always been very proud of her father and happy to hear people speak of him with admiration, but over the years, the distance between them had grown. When she decided not to follow in his footsteps and pursue the field of medicine, she had disappointed him. After that, a gulf had opened up between them, a peculiar tension that permitted only strife or silence.

Mama's death was a chance for them to draw closer, but it seemed as though her father wasn't interested in seizing the opportunity. Every conversation devolved into trivialities, and an unpleasant undertone seemed to creep in.

'I have to ask you something, Papa,' she began at last, before he could get up and hide away in his study.

'What is it?'

'In the papers, they're claiming that Mama was a target of opportunity for this sniper.' She avoided looking at him and chose her words cautiously. 'But when I think about the circumstances, I don't believe it.'

She raised her head and saw that he was looking at her for the first time in days.

'So what do you think?' he asked.

'Nobody walks past our house by chance,' she replied, putting aside her knife and fork. 'The kitchen window faces the back garden, and behind the hedge there isn't even a path that anyone can walk along. The murderer must have checked out the house and the neighbourhood, and that's how he discovered the shed. Choosing that particular spot was no accident.'

He was giving her his full attention.

'I think he specifically targeted Mama,' said Karoline. 'But I just can't imagine why. Unless . . .'

She fell silent and shook her head.

'Unless – what?'

'Unless Mama had some kind of secret that nobody knew about. Not even you or me,' Karoline told him. 'For the life of me, I can't imagine what it could have been, but that must be the reason.'

Her father stared at her, then picked up his fork and began poking at his food without replying. Several minutes passed. Once again, this damned silence! She used to let herself be cowed by it, but this time, she wouldn't let him off so easily.

'What did the police want from you the day before yesterday?' Karoline insisted.

'They're looking for connections between the murders,' her father finally replied.

'And? Do they have any ideas? Is there a connection?' she wanted to know.

His hesitation lasted a moment too long.

'No. They're still fumbling round in the dark.' He held her gaze without flinching. The realization that he was lying struck her like a punch in the stomach.

'I don't believe you.' Her tone of voice was sharper than she'd intended, but she hated being thought stupid. 'Why are you lying to me?'

'Why do you think I'm lying?'

'Because you're evading my question,' she replied. 'I can always tell when someone isn't telling me the truth. What did the police want from you? Why did you send me out of your study like a child?'

To her surprise, he reached across the table and put his hand on hers.

'Because I wanted to protect you and keep all this from you for a little longer,' he said softly. 'I know how much you loved your mother and how much you worry about Greta.'

For a couple of seconds, she believed him, because she wanted to. But then she saw through his attempt at manipulation. Her anger surged, mixed with disappointment and the bitter realization that in the whole wide world, there was no longer anyone she could trust.

'You're not telling me something, and I ask myself what and why.' She withdrew her hand and stood up. 'But I'm going to find out.'

'Perhaps you could describe briefly the circumstances of her death,' Pia said to Dirk Stadler. 'What happened to her?'

Father and son took turns explaining what had happened on 16 September 2002. Kirsten Stadler, at that time thirty-seven years old, athletic and healthy, left on that morning to go for a walk with the dog. After that, she was going to drive the kids to school. But after an hour, their mother had still not returned, so Erik and his sister, Helen, went out looking for her. They found her lying unconscious on the path that led through the field. The dog was sitting beside her.

'The ambulance took her to A&E, and there they confirmed a cerebral haemorrhage,' Dirk Stadler concluded. 'At the time, I was on a job in the Far East and difficult to reach. My in-laws drove to the hospital to lend support to Erik and Helen.'

'It was horrible,' Erik recalled. 'Mama was in intensive care. She looked like she was just asleep, but the doctors told us that she was brain-dead. The massive haemorrhages had damaged her brain beyond repair.'

For a while, no one said a word. The wind howled in the fireplace and shook the bare branches of a pathetic-looking fruit tree that stood in the back garden on the few square metres of grass.

'When I came back from China two days later, my children were completely traumatized,' Dirk Stadler went on. 'My in-laws were not in much better shape. Under intense pressure from the doctors, they had agreed to an organ donation from their brain-dead daughter.'

He cleared his throat.

'My wife had refused to be an organ donor for various reasons; she even had a living will, which in those days was still uncommon. The doctors should have waited until I returned, but they were in a big hurry. So much so that they hadn't observed the prescribed time mandated between the two brain-death examinations. In the clinic's records, the times had been falsified. In addition, the doctors had removed more organs than they had previously indicated. Not only her heart and kidneys, but also her eyes, bones, skin and connective tissue. For this reason, I later brought legal action against the clinic.'

He stopped and looked sadly at the picture of his wife on the sideboard.

'To this day, it's some consolation to know that with the donation of her organs, Kirsten saved the lives of several individuals,' he said in a low voice. 'But my father-in-law was beside himself with grief and rage. He was firmly convinced that he'd been ambushed and betrayed, because he never signed a consent form for organ donation, merely a power-of-attorney document for the treatment of his daughter. But when anyone sues a hospital, the outcome is always the same: the UCF offered me an out-of-court settlement with payment for pain and suffering. I accepted it, because I could no longer pay the legal fees. There were enough funds left over that I could set aside money for the children's education.'

Pia was observing both men with keen attention, registering every gesture and word, but found no cause for concern. Dirk Stadler gave the impression of a man who had suffered a terrible loss and gone through hell, but he had now made his peace with the past. Erik Stadler also seemed calm and composed. He put into words what Pia had been thinking.

'We've all spent a long time getting over this,' he said. 'But Mama wouldn't have wanted us to sit round, crying. She was a happy person, and that's how we keep her in our memory. That's the only way we can live normal lives again. Time heals all wounds, even deep ones, eventually, if you let it.'

'I can't imagine who would take revenge on people who had anything to do with Kirsten's death,' Dirk Stadler added. 'I mean, back then, I could have understood it if someone blew their top in rage. But now, ten years later?'

'Excuse me, I have to go.' Erik Stadler glanced at his watch and grabbed his tablet computer. 'I have a company in Sulzbach, and we have a lot to do before year's end. Call me if you want to know anything else.' He pulled a business card out of the computer's protective cover and handed it to Bodenstein. He also gave his card to Pia and Kim.

'We don't want to disturb you any longer.' Bodenstein stood up, and Pia and Kim followed suit. 'If you think of anything else that might help us, please give us a call.'

Dirk Stadler accompanied them to the front door.

TO CATCH A KILLER

'Did you injure your leg?' Pia asked.

'Yes, I did,' Stadler replied with a smile. 'But it was fifteen years ago at a construction site in Dubai. I used to be a structural engineer and travelled all over the world. My leg has been giving me trouble lately, especially when it's cold and damp.'

'What sort of work do you do now?'

'After my wife died, I had to give up my job so I could be home for the children,' said Stadler. 'I took a year of unpaid leave and after that got a job with the Frankfurt city planning office. I fulfil their disabled quota.'

Erik slipped on his jacket and put on a knitted cap.

'Thanks for lunch, Papa.' He patted his father on the shoulder and gave him a wink. 'For once something other than bratwurst at the hot dog stand.'

'Anytime,' said his father. 'Call me about Saturday. And say hi to Lis.'

'I will. See you then.'

Dirk Stadler smiled as his son left, but the smile vanished from his face when Erik was gone.

'By the way,' he said to Bodenstein and Pia. 'My in-laws have never got over the loss of Kirsten. She was their only daughter. Since then, they've been involved in a support group for the relatives of organ donors, and there's one more thing—' He broke off and shook his head.

'What is it?' Pia prompted him.

Stadler looked sad. 'I probably shouldn't say this, but I don't want to hide anything.' He pressed his lips together, hesitated, and then took a deep breath. 'My father-in-law used to be an excellent marksman and hunter.'

*

'How horrible,' Pia said as they walked to their cars. 'From one moment to the next, everything changes forever.'

Dirk Stadler had written down the address of his in-laws in Glashütten, but first she wanted to drop off one of the unmarked cars in Hofheim before they drove up into the Taunus.

'What did you think of the two Stadlers?' Bodenstein asked Kim.

'As a husband, Dirk Stadler suffered the greatest loss,' she answered pensively. 'But I got the impression that he has processed the death of his wife and is managing well. Neither he nor his son was nervous or tense when talking with us, the way people are who have something to hide. Even their astonishment and sadness didn't seem feigned to me. At any rate, the two seem to be close.'

'Oh, damn it!' Pia stopped short. 'We completely forgot to ask about the daughter.'

'Forget about her as the perp.' Kim shook her head. 'You're looking for a man.'

'But we should at least talk to her,' Pia insisted. 'Besides, she was with a man when she went to Renate Rohleder's flower shop.'

Her mobile rang.

'Hello, Henning,' she said when she saw the number of Forensic Medicine on the display. 'I—'

'It's quarter past two,' he interrupted her coolly. 'Or fourteen hundred fifteen, if you prefer. When might the subordinate ranks from the cellar of the Institute of Forensic Medicine expect the arrival of the criminal police?'

'Why?' Pia was baffled. 'Did we have an appointment?'

'Your boss requested that we make the post-mortem of the

corpse from Christmas Day our top priority, and due to the lack of personnel, I will perform this one myself,' said Henning sarcastically. 'Why doesn't the noble Sir von Bodenstein answer his mobile? I've already tried to reach him several times.'

'We're on the way,' Pia pacified him. 'Fifteen minutes, okay?'

Henning Kirchhoff ended the call as abruptly as he'd begun.

'Damn! The post-mortem!' Bodenstein pulled his smartphone out of his coat pocket and checked it. 'I don't understand why it doesn't work. I had extra memory programmed into it. Here, see for yourself.'

He held it out to Pia.

'Maybe you shouldn't have turned off the ringtone,' she said with a grin. 'Then maybe you would have heard it.'

'Technology and I are never going to be friends,' Bodenstein grumbled as he frowned. 'We'll leave my car here and pick it up on the way back. Then we can ask Stadler about his daughter.'

They decided on the car that Pia and Kim had come in because it was a little more comfortable than the other one. Bodenstein sent a patrol to Glashütten to interview Joachim and Lydia Winkler – Dirk Stadler's in-laws.

'I found that both the Stadlers reacted appropriately when I told them about the obituary and the victims,' Pia said. She turned to her sister to explain: 'Ever since I took a seminar in observing non-verbal communication during interviews, I pay particular attention to people's body language.'

'We can't rule out anything,' Kim replied. 'There are people who can trick a lie detector. But I can hardly imagine that

Dirk Stadler with his disability could climb up on a shed or into the front garden at Gehrke's neighbour's house. Besides, his limp would make him too noticeable.'

'And that would be too simple a solution,' Bodenstein thought.

They drove along an unusually deserted autobahn in an equally deserted city. The fear of the sniper had turned the region into a collection of ghost towns.

'Take a look at that!' As they drove past, Pia pointed at a few taxis lined up at the train station waiting for fares when normally there were a hundred. 'Things can't go on like this.'

'I'm afraid he isn't done with his revenge campaign,' Bodenstein said sombrely.

'We have to do something. There's no need for panic.'

'We already discussed this,' Bodenstein said, shaking his head. 'It would be irresponsible to lull the public into a sense of security that doesn't exist.'

'As long as it's this windy, there won't be any more murders,' Kim remarked. 'The perp avoids direct contact with his victims; he shoots only from a distance. But he can do that only under ideal conditions.'

The feeling of powerlessness that was rising up inside Pia was unlike anything she'd ever experienced. They were searching for a phantom, for a clever, cold-blooded killer who left nothing to chance, made no mistakes and was always one step ahead of them. With Kirsten Stadler, they had a single dubious lead, and that was all after three murders. As Kim had said this morning, they were faced with completely new ground rules. The personalities of the victims, which normally played a significant role in police investigations, were in this case unimportant. The victims weren't the actual targets of the perp, but only means to an end. There were no traces, no evidence, no witnesses. All they had were three dead bodies, three obituaries, the impression of a shoe that had been sold in Germany by the hundreds of thousands, a description of the perp that was so vague, it could apply to one out of every three men, and the name Kirsten Stadler. What if they couldn't find this madman and stop him? How many victims would he add to his death list?

'At any rate, it wasn't the brother who went with Helen Stadler to Renate Rohleder's shop,' Kim said unexpectedly. 'The age doesn't match, and I wouldn't call him "extremely good-looking" by any stretch of the imagination.'

'Hmm,' was all Pia said, and then no one said another word until they'd reached their destination and Bodenstein turned into the car park of the forensic institute. For Pia, it was always a familiar feeling when she entered through the heavy wooden front door of the art nouveau villa on Kennedy-allee, in which the Institute of Forensic Medicine of Frankfurt University had resided since the 1940s. There had been a time in her life when she had spent more time in this building than in her own apartment. They walked along a hallway lined with dark wood wainscoting. At the end a stairway led down to the basement of the institute. In the first of the two dissection rooms the washed and naked corpse of Maximilian Gehrke was waiting for them.

'So there you are,' said Ronnie Böhme, the pathologist's assistant, as he emerged from the small office that also served as a break room. 'I'll call the boss.'

'Thanks, Ronnie.' Pia smiled and hung her jacket on the coat rack. Bodenstein and Kim left their coats on. It was always cool in the post-mortem room.

'The coffee is freshly brewed. Help yourselves.' Böhme grinned, holding the phone to his ear. At the same moment, steps were approaching, and he hung up.

'I don't want to hear any excuses.' Henning appeared in the doorway, followed by a young man who looked like a student, and State Attorney Heidenfelder. Pia recalled his first post-mortem seven years before, when he got so nauseous, he had to throw up. The corpse was Isabel Kerstner, and it was Pia's first case that she had solved together with Bodenstein.

'I wasn't planning to apologize for anything,' replied Bodenstein. 'Let's get started.'

'Thanks, but I don't need your permission to do my job,' Henning snapped.

Clearly evident in the harsh light of the operating lamp was the devastation that the Core-Lokt projectile had caused upon exiting the body. It had smashed the ribs and torn a tremendous hole in the surrounding tissue. Pia studied Maximilian Gehrke's thin face. He looked like he was sleeping peacefully. After reading his diaries, she almost felt like she knew him. Suddenly she was overwhelmed by rage at the person who believed he was justified in committing such a depraved act, setting himself up as judge and executioner.

'It's a shame that a young man who'd already been through so much had to die so violently,' she said, full of sympathy. 'At least he didn't suffer.'

'He was dead before he hit the ground,' Henning confirmed. 'His heart was literally shredded.'

'And it wasn't even his own.'

'Pardon me?' Henning gave her a quizzical look over the edge of his surgical mask.

'He had a heart transplant ten years ago,' Pia explained.

Her ex-husband dropped his hands and pulled down the mask.

'Okay. Just a minute here,' he said, looking from Pia to Bodenstein to State Attorney Heidenfelder. 'You all know that I'm a passionate advocate of post-mortems – better to do one too many rather than one too few. But I would really like to know what you hope to learn here. This is the third time I've had a cadaver whose cause of death could be easily ascertained by a first-term medical student.'

'We're grasping at straws,' Bodenstein conceded. 'At present, it appears that the female donor of the heart that Maximilian Gehrke received might be the reason for the three murders. But we have nothing tangible, no concrete evidence, not a thing.'

'We're not primarily interested in the cause of death,' Pia added. 'Perhaps some new clue will come to light.'

Henning sighed and gave a shrug.

'I wish I could help you.' He pulled his mask back up. 'But I'm afraid you're going to get the same non-committal post-mortem report as for the other two victims of the sniper.'

The feeling that her father was keeping silent about something worried Karoline Albrecht. She knew it would be a good idea to speak with the friendly detective, but she shied away from it. Her mother was dead, and she was afraid of losing her father as well, if she said anything to the police. But even worse, she feared learning a truth that might destroy the image she had of her mother. Maybe Papa was right when he said he wanted to protect her. Karoline no longer recognized herself. All her life, she had never shrunk from tackling problems and finding solutions – so why was she hesitating now, driving all round the area, unable to make a decision? Was it still the effects of the shock that she'd suffered on Thursday evening? Last night, she was on the phone to Carsten for almost an hour after she had spoken briefly to Greta, who was doing well under the circumstances. She was able to sleep through the night with no nightmares, thanks to a mild sedative.

'She'll get over it,' Carsten had said. 'You just have to give her time. And the change of scene has done her good. With Opa and Oma at the farm, the world is still in one piece.'

'Thanks to all of you for taking such good care of her,' Karoline had replied. 'Please thank your parents and Nicki, too.'

'I will. But it goes without saying.' He had hesitated briefly. 'So how are you doing? Are you managing all right?'

Out of sheer habit, she had almost answered his cautious query with a hackneyed phrase such as *Sure, I'm doing fine*, or *I'll manage*, but the lie stuck in her throat. This time it wasn't about the flu or some business deal that had slipped through her fingers. This was an existential matter, and it wasn't only about Mama's death. She was dealing with a personal identity crisis.

'I'm not doing well,' she had told her ex-husband. 'I miss Mama so much. Mostly I'd like to crawl into bed and just cry.'

She had told him about her doubts that it was a random shooting. She also mentioned that she thought Papa was lying to her.

'I have to find out what's behind this,' she'd said. 'I simply can't imagine that Mama did anything that would make someone shoot her.'

'Oh, Karoline,' Carsten sighed. 'I feel so bad for you. But

please don't do anything that might put you in danger. Will you promise me that?'

She promised.

'If you need us, we're here for you,' he'd said. 'You're welcome here anytime.'

With much effort, she managed to utter a 'thank you' before she hung up. She should have been sitting in Nicki's place with Carsten and a group of kids at her in-laws' comfortable farmhouse on Lake Starnberg. But it was too late for that.

Karoline forced her thoughts in a different direction. It had been Carsten – well aware that she wouldn't follow his advice to leave matters to the police – who had given her the idea to make contact with the relatives of the other murder victims. That was why she was now on her way to Eschborn. The first victim of the 'sniper', as the press had dubbed the insane killer, had been an elderly lady from Niederhöchstadt. Naturally, she had no idea what her name was or where to begin searching for her relatives, but the town in which she had lived seemed to be the best starting point for her detective work. The fuel light in her car started blinking as she drove through Steinbach towards Niederhöchstadt, so she stopped at the next petrol station. Although the price of fuel had dropped quite a bit, she was the only customer.

'Nothing going on here all morning,' said the assistant behind the counter, a stout woman in her mid-fifties, as she tapped her finger on the headline of the *BILD* tabloid. 'Here, have you read this? Everyone's afraid of the madman who's shooting down people at random. That's all anyone's talking about.'

'Didn't that happen pretty close to here?' Karoline found

this type of gossip disgusting, but the end certainly did justify the means in this instance. 'Did you know the woman?'

'Sure, Old Lady Rohleder. She came here often. To fill up her tank or just to buy a paper. The whole thing is really dreadful.' The cashier had nothing to do and proved to be a productive source of information. By the time Karoline paid for the petrol and returned to her car, she knew the name of the victim's dog, what make of car she drove, the fact that her daughter ran a flower shop on Unterortstrasse in Eschborn and that the funeral had taken place late that morning at Nieder-höchstadt Cemetery. In addition, and this was probably the most important piece of information, she learned where Inge-borg Rohleder and her daughter lived.

The car phone rang as Bodenstein drove past the Commerzbank stadium heading for the autobahn. Ostermann was reporting in, though he had no real news. Despite intense canvassing of the neighbourhood in Kelkheim, nobody had noticed or seen any-thing on Christmas morning. The Winklers hadn't been at their home in Glashütten, so the patrol had left a note to call K-11 in Hofheim. The techs from the crime lab had been unable to find any fingerprints or DNA traces on the envelopes or the obitu-aries, and Napoleon Neff had returned from Ingeborg Rohleder's funeral with no interesting information.

'It's a dead end,' said Ostermann. 'Unfortunately, we no longer have postmarks that reveal where a letter was sent from. Everything was printed on an inkjet printer, and the toner is mass-produced, as is the paper.'

'In the old days, we had saliva traces on envelopes and jammed keys on a typewriter,' Kröger mused in the back-ground. 'Or a type of paper that was manufactured at a specific time. Today, the perps get tips from TV police shows about what they have to do to avoid leaving any evidence.'

'Were Kathrin and Cem able to get anything at the UCF?' Bodenstein asked.

'No.' Ostermann demolished Bodenstein's last glimmer of hope. 'Supposedly there's no one in-house who's authorized to allow access to hospital records. The order from the state attorney's office hasn't arrived yet.'

They drove back in the same depressed state of silence as on the drive over. Henning Kirchhoff had been right: a post-motem in the case of Maximilian Gehrke was as unhelpful as those of Ingeborg Rohleder and Margarethe Rudolf. It was all wasted effort. Bodenstein felt like he was sitting in a car that was gradually running out of fuel.

'Your car is still parked in Liederbach,' Pia reminded him just before they reached the turn-off for the Main-Taunus Centre. He had intended to keep driving in the centre lane towards Hofheim. Just in time, he put on his indicator and veered sharply to the right.

At least Rosalie had arrived safely in New York, and her pain at leaving had given way to excitement about the city in which she was now going to live and work for a year. When could he talk to Inka about the offer from Cosima's mother? How was she going to react? So far, there hadn't been a suitable opportunity. In the daytime, they were both busy, and at night, she slept at her own place because Sophia was staying with him. He'd been pondering for days how he was going to explain everything to her without her again making the unjustified accusation that he didn't want to let Cosima go. In this tense situation, the last thing he needed was to fight with Inka.

Bodenstein stopped next to his unmarked car, undid his seat belt, and got out.

'See you soon,' he said to Pia, who had taken the wheel.

'Okay,' she said. 'Have you got your car keys?'

He patted his coat pocket and nodded before walking past the garage to the row of houses where Dirk Stadler lived. As darkness fell, the blinds had been pulled down in all the houses where somebody was already home. Here and there, faint light could be seen through the small glass panes in the front doors, but otherwise, everything was locked up tight.

The lights were off at Stadler's house. Bodenstein pressed the doorbell, waited a moment and rang again, but nobody came to the door. The gusty wind was shaking the two small box trees at either side of the front door, whirling dry leaves over the path. The temperature had dropped a few degrees, and the cold was creeping up Bodenstein's trouser legs. There was no doubt that he enjoyed his job, which he'd been doing for a good thirty years, although he was often worn out. He loved the challenges that each case brought, and he felt great satisfaction when a murderer was convicted and justice was won for the victim and his family. Bodenstein couldn't imagine working in another profession, and to be honest, he didn't have the expertise for anything else. For him, his profession had always been a calling, far more than merely a job that was over at five o'clock. And there were always recurring periods like now, when they seemed to make no headway. In his career, there had been only a few cases that had never been solved, cold cases that he retrieved from the archives from time to time to review. Modern criminological technology permitted more extensive analyses and brought more precise results, and often the networking with international police authorities helped as well.

Calm determination and patience were two important traits that a police officer needed, but at the moment, Bodenstein had the unpleasant feeling that waiting was the worst of all possible alternatives. He turned round and hurried back to his car.

Naturally, you will receive appropriate compensation for this task. Gabriela's statement kept running through his head. His officer status did not allow him to accept supplementary income just like that. Did it mean that he'd have to quit his job? And would he ever be able to meet his mother-in-law's expectations?

Bodenstein turned on the engine and set the heat on high. Icy air blew into his face. Cursing, he adjusted the fan, turned on the windscreen wipers, and drove off.

On the drive from Liederbach to Hofheim, he thought about the advantages of Gabriela's offer. He would never again have to jump out of bed in the middle of the night or on a Sunday morning because there was a dead body somewhere. He wouldn't have to worry about lack of personnel, tiffs among the colleagues, and all the regulations, restrictions and tedious paperwork. No more burned, rotting, bloated corpses; no endless questioning in which the wildest tall tales were served up; no stress, no hectic pace, no more pulling an all-nighter. Would he miss the tension that he felt each time he was called to the site where a dead body was found? The fever of the hunt, the feeling of doing something important and good, and the satisfaction of working together with his team? What sense of accomplishment would he have if all he did was worry about his mother-in-law's fortune? 'No,' he said out loud to himself. 'No, I won't do it.'

And suddenly he felt a lot better.

*

Karoline Albrecht had been sitting in her car for quite a while, wondering whether she should get out and ring the doorbell of the terraced house. She didn't really want to learn anything about this woman who had also been struck by such a cruel fate. She herself was so filled with pain and rage and grief that she didn't know whether she could stand any more. Gradually, the guests at the reception after the funeral left, and Karoline finally had to get moving before it got too late to pay a visit to a stranger.

'Yes?' Renate Rohleder scrutinized her suspiciously through a crack in the door. 'What do you want?'

'My name is Karoline Albrecht,' she said. 'Please excuse me for simply showing up at your door, but I . . . I wanted to speak to you. My mother was . . . shot last week, in Oberursel. By the same . . . murderer as your mother's.'

'Oh!' The reddened eyes of the woman widened in astonishment, and caution gave way to curiosity. She didn't ask how Karoline knew her name and address. She took off the safety chain and opened the door all the way. 'Please come in.'

The house smelled sweet and stuffy and a bit like wet dog. For a moment, the two women stood facing each other mutely in the hall, looking at each other with some embarrassment. Grief had ravaged Renate Rohleder's face. Deep furrows ran from her nose to the corners of her mouth; her eyelids were swollen, and dark circles had formed under her eyes. Although she was probably only a little older than Karoline, she looked like an old woman.

'I'm . . . so sorry about what happened to your mother,' Karoline broke the silence, and Renate Rohleder gave a sob and wrapped her in her arms. Karoline, who normally did not care much for physical contact, felt herself pressed to a soft bosom, and the ice that had covered her heart burst into a thousand pieces. She made no effort to maintain her composure but gave her tears free rein, sobbing just as hard as this other woman, whose soul had been just as damaged as her own.

Later they sat together in the living room and drank tea. They had agreed to skip the formalities and address each other in the familiar way, using each other's first names. But for a while, neither of them knew quite how to broach the subject. The old brown Lab lay in his basket and watched them out of melancholy dark eyes that were clouded over by a bluish sheen.

'Topsi hardly eats anything, now that Mama is gone,' said Renate with a sigh. 'She was there when . . . when it happened.'

Karoline had to swallow hard.

'My daughter, Greta, was standing next to my mother when she was shot through the kitchen window,' she replied, amazed at how easy it was to say these words. Until now, she and her father had chosen a multitude of euphemisms for the terrible event.

'Oh my God!' Renate's face showed her concern. 'That's even worse. How is she coping with it?'

'Well, she's with her father and his family at the moment. She seems to be doing all right.' Karoline cradled the teacup in her hands. 'I just can't believe that this guy shot my mother at random. My parents' house is at the edge of the woods, at the end of a cul-de-sac. Nobody ever walks past by chance.'

Renate straightened up and gave at Karoline a searching look.

'The murders aren't random,' she said softly. 'They're saying that in the papers only because the police aren't giving out any information.'

'What do you mean?' Karoline said in bewilderment.

'The police think it's because of Kirsten. Kirsten Stadler.' Renate's voice quavered, and her eyes swam with tears. 'They found out her name through the last victim. And through these . . . these obituaries.'

A sob caught in her throat.

'It's so terrible. We were practically next-door neighbours, Kirsten and I. I saw her often, and sometimes we went walking together. Kirsten also had a dog, a Hovawart, whose name was Spike.'

Karoline didn't have the faintest idea who this Kirsten was or what Renate was talking about.

'What obituaries?' she interrupted her.

'Wait a sec.' Renate jumped up and left the living room; she came back a little later holding a paper in her hand and gave it to Karoline. 'This is a copy of the one that was posted to the police in Eschborn.'

An obituary, printed on a sheet of paper.

INGEBORG ROHLEDER HAD TO DIE BECAUSE HER DAUGH-TER IMPLICATED HERSELF IN THE DENIAL OF ASSISTANCE AND ACTED AS AN ACCESSORY TO NEGLIGENT MANSLAUGHTER, she read.

'What's this supposed to mean?' she whispered. 'And what does it have to do with my mother?'

'I don't know.' Renate blew her nose. Then she told Karoline the story of what had happened on the morning of 16 September 2002. 'I still can't grasp that *I* am supposed to be guilty of my mother's death. What have I ever done that's so bad? I couldn't have known what was going on with Kirsten. Who would ever imagine that a young, healthy woman all of a sudden would be brain-dead? What was I supposed to do, anyway?'

For a moment, Renate just sat there, staring into space and crumpling the tissue between her fingers. Karoline understood how much courage it must have cost the woman to tell her about this. The self-recriminations must have been eating her alive.

'Am I understanding correctly?' Karoline asked. 'This so-called Judge killed your mother because you didn't help out back then?'

Renate nodded unhappily and shrugged.

'It's so inconceivable. Why didn't he shoot me? My mother was so . . . such a good person. She . . . she was so generous and so ready to help, and she would always listen to anyone's problems.'

Grief overwhelmed her, and she started sobbing again.

'It was so long ago,' Renate whimpered. 'I had stopped thinking about it, until . . . until Helen showed up in my shop, together with a man.'

'Helen?'

'Kirsten's daughter. She asked me why I didn't help her mother that day, and only then did it all come back to me.'

'When was that? What did she want from you?'

'It was a few months ago. Sometime during the summer. Helen asked me whether I was at all aware of what I'd done back then, and whether I had any regrets. The man didn't say a word the whole time, only looked at me in a funny way. It really scared me.'

What is Renate getting at? Karoline wondered.

'The police asked me about him, but at the time, I was so confused that I couldn't remember anything else. But then I had an idea.' She reached for a newspaper lying on the table and held it out to show Karoline. 'I happened to see this ad the day before yesterday, and then it dawned on me.'

She tapped on a classified ad.

'This sign was on the car that they were driving. It was parked right outside my shop window.'

The 'sign' was the company logo of a goldsmith in Hofheim.

'Do you understand, Karoline?' Renate whispered urgently. A fearful look had come into her eyes. 'I think he might be the Judge.'

Karoline stared at her as her brain desperately tried to put all the pieces of the puzzle together. Obituaries. Kirsten Stadler. Failure to render assistance. *Brain-dead*. She felt like a tightrope walker balancing above a black abyss without a net, clinging to the last remnants of a child's primal sense of trust.

'Renate, can you remember what hospital Kirsten was taken to and what happened to her there?' Her vocal cords ached with tension, her palms were sweaty and her heart was pounding as she dreaded what she might hear.

'I . . . I don't know, I have to think about it.' Renate rubbed her temples and squeezed her eyes shut. 'It was a hospital in Frankfurt – the UCF, I think. They couldn't do any more for her, her brain had gone too long without oxygen . . .'

Thoughts were racing thick and fast through Karoline's head; she no longer heard what Renate was saying. Somehow she managed to take her leave, and she found herself back outside in the fresh air. With unsteady steps, she walked along the dark street to her car.

She got in, put her hands on the steering wheel, and took a few deep breaths. Everything in her was fighting against the suspicion that her father might have had something to do with the Kirsten Stadler case. She really didn't want to know. Mama was dead, and nothing would bring her back to life.

'We couldn't have turned out more differently.' Kim had made herself comfortable on the love seat. 'Here I am, living in a loft in the middle of Hamburg, and you're on a farm.'

'It's exactly what I've always wanted.' Pia grinned and toasted her sister with a glass of white wine. 'I lived long enough in the city and had enough of wasting my time searching for a parking spot or having to park in an underground garage.'

'But you don't have any neighbours,' Kim replied. 'If anything happens to you here, nobody would know.'

'Normally, Christoph is there, and my nearest neighbour is five hundred metres away,' Pia said. 'At any rate, I feel safer here than in a city, where there's no longer any social network at all. Do you know how often we find dead bodies who have lain in their apartments for weeks and nobody misses them? What good does it do you if you live in a building with ten or twenty people and none of them takes any interest in you? Out here, people all look out for each other.'

'I don't know if I could live in such a secluded place.' Kim took a sip of wine.

'Secluded?' Pia laughed. 'Not a hundred metres from here is the busiest autobahn in all of Germany.'

'You know what I mean,' said Kim. 'I'm surprised that this solitude doesn't bother you after what you went through.'

'That happened in an apartment with neighbours on both sides,' Pia reminded her. 'And it didn't do me any good.'

After work, the sisters had gone shopping and tended to the horses. Then Pia had cooked dinner: lamb cutlets with garlic, olive oil and fresh herbs, with a polenta with Parmesan cheese and baby carrots sautéed in butter. They had enjoyed the delicious meal with a bottle of Gavi di Gavi and later opened another bottle.

'Do you cook like this every night?' Kim wanted to know.

'Yep,' said Pia. 'Actually, Christoph does most of the cooking. He's a divine chef. I was always the type who shoved a frozen pizza in the oven and gobbled gyros, bratwurst or burgers all day. But now I can cook a lot of things pretty well. Except pumpkin soup.'

'*Pretty* well? It was great.'

'Thanks.' Pia smiled and poured herself more wine. A fire was crackling in the fireplace and spreading a pleasant warmth. After the complete refurbishment of the small house three years ago, the quality of life at Birkenhof had improved dramatically: triple-glazed windows, the addition of a second storey with the new roof that was properly insulated, a modern central heating system instead of the old baseboard heaters that never really worked yet used an incredible amount of electricity. Upstairs, there was now a big bedroom with a balcony, a wonderful bathroom and another room that she and Christoph used as a walk-in wardrobe. The old bedroom downstairs had become a guest room with its own bathroom.

'I'm eager to get to know Christoph,' said Kim. 'I'm so happy that I'm here.'

'Me, too.' Pia looked at her younger sister. They used to be inseparable and had done everything together. But Pia had developed a strong yearning for freedom, and straight after secondary school she had left her parents' house, which had seemed increasingly joyless and sombre. She moved in with a girlfriend, started to study law, and always had some sort of job on the side so she could be independent from her parents. Kim, the baby of the family, had found it more comfortable to live with her parents for a longer time. She had been more soft-hearted than Pia, but also full of determination. When none of the siblings could be persuaded to do an apprenticeship at Hoechst AG, their parents had finally accepted having a bank cashier and two female college students in the family. But while Lars and Kim had consistently followed their chosen paths, Pia had abandoned her studies and joined the police force. This proved to be a humiliating decision for her parents, who had already been boasting about their daughter the lawyer at the bowling club and church choir. When she subsequently married Henning Kirchhoff – a man who cut up corpses for a living – Pia no longer figured in her parents' conversations. The same thing later happened to Kim. The younger daughter, who dealt only with hard-core criminals and psychopaths, was also quietly erased from the family history. Unlike Pia, who had burned all her bridges with a light heart, Kim was profoundly hurt by the blatant disapproval of her parents. She moved to Hamburg and for the past ten years had communicated only with impersonal Christmas cards.

'What drove you to visit our parents this year?' Pia wanted to know.

'I'm not really sure,' said Kim with a shrug. 'I feel like my time in Hamburg is over. After eleven years, my job no longer seems challenging, especially since I can't rely on becoming a medical director someday. But I have plenty of other job offers, even one here in Frankfurt.'

'Really?' Pia was astonished. 'It would be super if you came back and lived in this area again.'

'Yeah, the thought appeals to me, too,' Kim admitted as she twirled the stem of her wine glass. 'More than moving to Berlin, Munich, Stuttgart or Vienna. Frankfurt is in the middle, which I like. You can get anywhere quickly.'

'Is there any man in your life?' Pia asked.

'No,' said Kim. 'Not for quite a while now. I feel great this way. What about you and Christoph? How long have you been together?'

'For six years now.' Pia smiled.

'I didn't know that. So I guess it's serious, then.'

'I think so,' Pia said with a smile. 'We got married ten days ago.'

'What?!' Kim stared at her sister wide-eyed. 'And you tell me this sort of in passing?'

'Nobody knows yet, not even his daughters. Christoph and I wanted to do it just for us. Next summer, we're going to throw a big party here at Birkenhof.'

'Wow, that is so cool!' Kim was grinning. 'Now I'm even more curious about him.'

'You'll get to meet him soon. I'm sure you'll like him. He's a wonderful guy.' And on the other side of the globe. The second that she thought about Christoph, she was overcome by longing for him, even though she'd mostly been able to suppress that feeling during the day.

The sisters fell silent for a while. A log crackled in the fireplace with a shower of sparks. One of the dogs lay dreaming in his basket. His paws and snout twitched, and he barked and whimpered in his dream.

'I like your boss,' Kim said abruptly.

'What? Bodenstein?' Pia asked in amazement.

'No.' Kim smiled. 'Not Bodenstein. I mean Nicola. Nicola Engel.'

'Wh-what?' Pia sat up straight, her eyes wide. 'You're not serious.'

'Yes, I am.' Kim studied the wine glass in her hand. 'She has something that appeals to me.'

'Engel eats raw meat in the morning, along with a handful of nails, and if necessary, she also has one of us for breakfast,' Pia said, dazed by her little sister's surprising admission. 'She's as hard as steel and never gives an inch. What could you possibly want with *her*?'

'No idea.' Kim shrugged. 'Somehow she impressed me. And that hasn't happened to me in a very long time.'

FRIDAY, DECEMBER 28, 2012

It was the stillness that woke him. All night, the storm had raged round the house, howling in the chimney and rattling the blinds, but now it was completely still. He reached out his arm and felt for the alarm clock on the bedside table. Ten to six. A good time to begin the day. A day that would make headlines far beyond the local area. Since the first shot he'd fired, he'd been topic number one in the newspapers, and on all the television and radio broadcasts. That was not going to change. He would see to that. But he wasn't pleased that he was being described as a mad killer who was slaughtering people at random. That wasn't true, as the public would eventually learn. His idea with the obituaries was good, but the police didn't seem to want to publicize this information. So he'd found the name of a dedicated journalist, and in recent days, he had already reported several times on the murders, and he sent him copies of the obituaries.

He tossed back the covers, went to the bathroom, and took a piss. Then he took a good long shower, as hot as he could stand. This might be his last shower, just as it might have been his last night in this house. Every day, he had to count on the possibility of being caught. Every day might be his last as a free man. Because he was aware of this, he was fully enjoying even the smallest everyday things. The comfortable bed with the inner-spring mattress, the warm down quilt and the damask bed linens. The sinfully expensive shower gel, the soft towel, the underwear that smelled of fabric softener. He shaved very carefully, using lots of shaving cream. In prison, he would no longer have this luxury. And it might all end this evening. Or maybe not for three days or even two weeks. The uncertainty was exciting, a rush that he hadn't felt in a long time. And yet, that was only a residual effect from what he intended to do. There was no other option, because these people couldn't be reached any other way. They had no awareness of injustice, no guilty conscience and seemed able to get through anything. None of them had any regrets. Not one. He was going to teach them to feel regret.

He dressed calmly, checking his appearance in the mirror.

If they caught him today, he was prepared and had made all the necessary arrangements. He would deny nothing. He wouldn't need a lawyer either, because he would confess at once and without hesitation. That was part of his plan. Seven twenty-three a.m. Less than six hours until he would crook his finger and pull the trigger. He slipped on his jacket and got *going, in order to buy a loaf of bread and a pretzel stick from her one last time.*

Even Bodenstein had noticed that the wind had subsided. He stood on the balcony with a cup of coffee in his hand as he anxiously looked at the limp flags in the garden of his neighbour to the left.

Wind force zero.

Ideal conditions for the sniper.

Bodenstein shifted his gaze to peer into the distance. To his left glowed the red signal light on top of the TV tower, and next to it glittered the bank towers of central Frankfurt. In the middle lay Höchst with its industrial park, and over on the right was the airport. In between lived about 250,000 people, any of whom could be the next victim. All the police officers in the region were on heightened alert. Leave had been cancelled and reinforcements from other federal states were being requested, but it was utterly impossible to guard the entire Rhein-Main Region. The dramatically increased police presence and the public's elevated awareness might help to cut off the sniper's escape route after the next murder, but it was unlikely that the police could prevent another death. Bodenstein took a gulp of coffee.

Kirsten Stadler.

Was the death of this woman ten years ago really the reason for the sniper murders? Bodenstein didn't want to be blamed for any oversight, so as a precaution he had arranged police protection for Dirk and Erik Stadler. Not round-the-clock surveillance, since that was beyond their resources, but patrols were driving at regular intervals through the streets in Liederbach and in the North End of Frankfurt, where the father and son lived. He'd also asked to be informed if either man left his residence.

The air was cold and clear, and Bodenstein felt chilled.

The babysitter who was supposed to look after Sophia during the day didn't arrive until eight o'clock, so he couldn't leave before then. He decided to read the paper, which he normally took to the office. He went downstairs, took the paper from the mailbox, and sat down at the kitchen table with his second cup of coffee. When he looked at the paper, he almost choked. The sensational headline jumped right out at him: THE SNIPER MURDERS – WHAT THE POLICE AREN'T TELLING US. Bodenstein hastily turned to page 3 to find the article with the alleged insider information and began to read. The first paragraphs of the article consisted mainly of assumptions and speculations, but what came next made him boil with rage. The reporter, whose byline was only 'KF', revealed the first names of the victims and included the initials of their surnames. In addition, he listed the age of each one. He also claimed that the police had long known that the gunman was specifically targeting certain individuals but was keeping this information from the public, possibly for tactical investigative reasons. Where the hell did the guy get those names? Was there a mole in their own ranks supplying the press with information? Or had the perp himself got in contact with the press?

Karoline Albrecht had drunk a whole bottle of red wine and spent half the night trying to make sense of the facts that were available to her. She had to confront her father with her knowledge, even if it meant falling out of favour with him for good. She was annoyed at feeling so timid. It was affecting her judgement and leaving her petrified with fear. On the drive from

Kelkheim to Oberursel, she alternately sweated and froze, her stomach was tied in knots and her palms were damp. The last time she'd felt like this was on the morning of her driving test twenty-four years ago. As she pulled up in front of her parents' house and saw her father's car in the driveway, she was tempted to turn round on the spot and drive off.

'Pull yourself together, you wimp,' she admonished herself. She got out and took a few deep breaths, then walked to the front door. Just as she was about to put the key in the lock, the door opened.

'Hello, Karoline,' said her father. 'What brings you here so early?'

He was freshly shaven and his hair was combed. He was wearing an overcoat and holding a briefcase.

'Hello, Papa.' She was surprised to see him about to step out the door. 'Are you leaving?'

'Yes, I have to go to the clinic,' he replied. 'I feel like the walls are falling in on me, and work is still the best medicine.'

'I have to talk to you,' Karoline said before he could slip past her and get into his car.

'Can't it wait till tonight? I have an important operation at ten and have to—'

'You've always had some important operation to go to whenever I wanted to talk to you,' she interrupted him. 'But not this time.'

'Has something happened?'

Was he asking her that in all seriousness?

'I know that you're keeping something from me,' she said. 'And I ask myself why. Is it really out of pure altruism or because you've got something important to hide?'

'I have nothing to hide!' Was that a brief flicker of emotion in his eyes? Annoyance? Discomfort? Or even fear?

'Is that so? Then I don't suppose you'll mind if I ask the police whether they've received an obituary for Mama.'

His hesitation was answer enough, and the last bit of hope that she'd been mistaken went up in smoke. Her own father had lied to her, and not because he wanted to spare her, but because – exactly like Renate Rohleder – he felt guilty.

'What was in the obituary?' she insisted. 'What did the Judge write? Tell me! I have a right to know why Mama had to die and why my daughter is so badly traumatized.'

'Oh, Karoline.' He put down his briefcase and tried to put his hand on her arm, but she shrank back. 'I didn't want to keep anything secret from you, but I wanted to talk about it in peace and quiet.'

'And when had you planned to do that?' Damn, she was going to start bawling again. But tears were a sign of weakness, and she didn't need that. Not now. 'But you do know what it says, since the police were here, right?'

'Yes, I do. But I wanted to wait until you were feeling a little better. Believe me, I've been brooding over this and tormenting myself with self-recriminations.' Her father heaved a big sigh and his shoulders slumped forward, but he didn't avoid her eyes. 'The obituary said that I was to blame for your mother's death because I had *murdered* somebody. That's a completely false accusation, which is what I told the police. After all, my job is to save lives. Unfortunately, in doing so, I find myself walking a very thin line between life and death, between hope and disappointment.'

'So Mama wasn't a random victim of this . . . this sniper.'

Karoline crossed her arms. 'Does it have anything to do with Kirsten Stadler? What was that incident really all about?'

'I told you that those accusations were utter nonsense,' her father said, allowing that indignant undertone to slip into his voice, as he usually did when he grew tired of a topic and wanted to end the conversation. Karoline remembered how unpleasant Mama used to find this tone of voice. She thought it was extremely rude to reveal so clearly how much he wanted to get away from whoever he was talking to. And yet she'd always had an excuse ready for her husband, saying that he didn't mean to be discourteous, his mind was still on his patients.

Mama glossed over so many things, Karoline thought with a pang of sorrow. *Also with regard to me.*

Maybe that was the only way her mother could stand having two egocentric workaholics for a husband and a daughter.

'What happened back then?' she persisted.

'It was nothing extraordinary. A routine case,' her father declared, but Karoline didn't agree. For him, his work might be routine, but for his patients and their loved ones, the mere fact that Professor Dieter Rudolf was operating on them signified a crucial turning point. He was their last hope in a hopeless situation. Did he ever truly realize that? Was he aware of the human fates behind every medical finding?

'Papa.' Karoline lowered her voice. 'If you did something that resulted in Mama having to die, I will never forgive you.'

Her heart was hammering against her ribs. She had never said anything like this to her father. In the dim light of the porch, he seemed old and no longer the omnipotent, superior man that he had always been in her eyes. The father whose attention and affection she had desperately courted as a child.

'Who do you take me for? How could I ever wish that any-thing bad would happen to your mother?' he said gruffly. 'I can't think of any reason to feel guilty. Sadly, that case was nothing out of the ordinary. A woman was admitted to the hospital after suffering a cerebral haemorrhage, and since she had been deprived of oxygen for several hours, she was brain-dead. Help came too late. The relatives agreed to organ donation, and the required examinations were performed. The parametres were reported to Eurotransplant, which then notified the patients who were waiting for organs and whose numbers matched. The brain-dead woman underwent explantation that night. A com-pletely normal sequence of events. For the woman's family, certainly a tragedy, but for me, it was all in a day's work.'

'But something must have gone wrong,' Karoline insisted. 'Otherwise, why would someone go out ten years later and shoot innocent people out of revenge?'

'Nothing went wrong, I swear it,' replied her father vehe-mently. He picked up his briefcase and turned to leave. The floodlights over the garage door switched on, bathing the driveway in glaring light.

'Will I see you tonight?' he asked when she remained silent.

'Maybe,' Karoline replied, watching her father walk to his car. She had never before doubted anything he'd told her. And only rarely had she pondered what her father's profession actu-ally entailed. But now she suspected that he wasn't telling the truth. Something had gone wrong back then, and as a result, her mother had died.

Bodenstein was sitting alone in the empty conference room, his chin resting on his hand, feeling depressed as he stared at the whiteboard. He saw the names written on it and the photos of the crime scene and victims. The sniper was going to strike again, maybe even today, and there was no way to prevent it. No matter how he twisted and turned things, Bodenstein simply had no idea what to do, because he lacked even the slightest clue about how the gunman selected his targets.

A great injustice has been done. The guilty parties shall feel the same pain as the one who has suffered because of their indifference, greed, vanity and thoughtlessness. Those who have taken guilt upon themselves shall live in fear and terror, for I am come to judge the living and the dead.

Bodenstein folded up the copy of the letter that the Judge had sent to the editor of the *Taunus Echo*. The original was already on its way to the crime lab. A phone call from the press spokesman of the Regional Criminal Investigation this morning had sufficed to discover which reporter at the *Taunus Echo* was concealed behind the initials KF. Then it had taken a good hour before the police finally got Konstantin Faber on the line. The journalist's response was rather snotty when Bodenstein reproached him for impeding a police investigation by making hasty speculations and naming names.

'In Germany, we have freedom of the press,' Faber said. 'Besides, as a journalist, I have a duty to inform the reader.'

Bodenstein had a vehement retort on the tip of his tongue, but he decided to shift down a notch. It would do him no good to alienate the press; working together could be much more useful. Especially since Faber was the one who had received copies of the three obituaries in the post, along with a letter, all sent anonymously, of course. But there was no doubt that the so-called Judge was the person who had sent them.

On his way to the station, Bodenstein made a detour to the editorial office in Königstein to speak with Konstantin Faber. He picked up the letter from the Judge along with the envelope and obituaries as evidence, and promised exclusive information to Faber if he promised to notify the police immediately of any further communication from the Judge.

The article in the *Taunus Echo* had opened the floodgates for panicked calls to the newly added telephone hotline, but there had also been a few tips that seemed useful, and they had to be followed up ASAP. The morning meeting was brief and to the point. Bodenstein had nipped in the bud any new discussions between Neff and Kim Freitag and sent off his team with clear assignments, all of them looking for the hot lead they so urgently needed.

They had to locate Joachim Winkler, the father-in-law of Dirk Stadler, as well as the man who had accompanied Helen Stadler on her visit to Renate Rohleder's shop. Someone also had to talk to the Stadler children, Erik and Helen, and to the Stadlers' former neighbours in Niederhöchstadt. They also had to find out which staff members at the UCF had been involved in the case of Kirsten Stadler ten years ago. And they needed permission to access the records of the lawsuit between Dirk Stadler and the UCF. Who had represented the legal interests of the hospital? What was the name of the Stadlers' lawyer? Who had allegedly bribed Maximilian Gehrke's father? Was it about his son's heart transplant? Could bribery be used to acquire an organ?

Bodenstein had spent half the night researching online and found out that it was difficult to find a match donor for someone with heart disease. There were many medical parametres that had to match so that the recipient's body would not reject the donor heart. A charitable foundation called Eurotransplant based in the Netherlands coordinated the donation of organs for the patients who were on their list. Recently, there had also been some scandals about patients who had been listed under false pretences. Bodenstein had read about this in the newspaper but had never specifically dealt with the issue.

'Ah, you're still here.' Pia's voice tore him out of his thoughts. 'Am I bothering you?'

'No, come on in. And please close the door.'

Since all the insanity had started, he'd hardly exchanged more than a few words with her before someone interrupted.

Pia pulled up a chair and sat down, facing him.

'How did the Judge come upon Konstantin Faber, of all people?' she asked. 'I had a look at the website of the *Taunus Echo* and saw that he's actually responsible for the cultural and financial pages.'

'Probably by accident,' Bodenstein guessed. 'Faber is the acting editor over Christmas and New Year's, so the letter landed on his desk. As always, it couldn't have come at a worse time. At least Faber is being cooperative and not simply looking for a sensational angle.'

They were silent for a while.

'Something else is going to happen today,' Pia said. 'I have a bad feeling about it.'

'Me, too,' Bodenstein agreed.

'It's making me so fidgety, this whole mess. I can't seem to get any peace and quiet to think things over. Someone is always coming up with a new idea, or theory, or new approach, or suggesting an MO or a different perp profile.'

'I know what you mean.' Bodenstein sighed. 'At the moment, the experts who've been called in are brake pads rather than catalytic converters.'

'I couldn't have put it better myself.' Pia gave him an unhappy grin and nodded. 'I feel like I'm back at police college. Every step I take I have to explain and justify. Too much bickering and babbling.'

'So what are we going to do?' Bodenstein asked her.

'We're going to take back control,' Pia suggested. 'From Napoleon Neff and my sister, too. They're supposed to be analysing our results, not confusing us totally.'

'Agreed.'

Because of the growing public interest, the Ministry of the Interior was putting more pressure daily on Nicola Engel, and she was passing it on to Bodenstein. It wasn't the first time he'd had to coordinate and lead a big team. Until now, he'd simply been holding the reins too loosely. People like Andreas Neff, with such an inflated view of themselves, had to be kept in check or they'd drive the whole team nuts. And Pia's sister was no team player either, since she was used to being an expert witness and expressing her opinion, for which she received a great deal of respect.

'Have we heard anything about the Stadlers, father and son?' Bodenstein asked.

'Erik Stadler was working at his company yesterday and drove home at round seven. This morning, he left the house at 8:07 and went jogging,' Pia informed him. 'Dirk Stadler came out to get the newspaper but has been in the house ever since.'

'Then we'll drive over to see Erik first and after that, visit Dirk Stadler,' Bodenstein decided, getting up. 'And only the two of us.'

Many people had unbelievably steady routines. The bakery salesgirl, for instance. You could truly set your watch by her daily routine. To the exact minute. Within the past two weeks, he'd been unable to detect any deviations or irregularities. Each morning, she left her apartment at 5:45 a.m. and drove to her job at the bakery next to the REWE supermarket at Camp Phoenix Park in Eschborn. She always parked her car in the same space behind Aldi. She worked from 6 a.m. to 1 p.m., interrupted only by a breakfast break, and the time never varied. When she got off work, she went to the REWE supermarket next door to buy groceries, seldom taking more than fifteen minutes. From there, she drove to her home on Berliner Strasse in Schwalbach, where she lived with her husband, who was usually home when she arrived. He never stayed longer than till 2:30, when his lunch hour was probably over. At 4 p.m., the bakery salesgirl drove to her second job at a nail salon in Bad Soden, where she worked till 6:30 five days a week. The couple had no children; maybe they wanted to have some one day, since the woman was still young.

'Good morning.' She beamed at him when it was his turn. She was already reaching for the loaf of bread. 'The usual?'

'No, not today.' He smiled, too.

'Oh, don't you like the farmer's bread anymore?'

'I have some left over. But I would like a Flotte Henne.'

'Coming right up.' She reached her gloved right hand into the display case, picked up a roll with cheese and lettuce and slices of hard-boiled egg, and stuck it in a paper bag along with a napkin.

'And?' he asked in a conversational tone. 'Bags all packed for your holiday?'

'No, *not yet,*' *she said with a smile.* 'I'm *going to pack this* *weekend in peace and quiet. Two seventy, please.*'

He handed her a five-euro note.

'Keep the change,' *he said.* 'A little extra for your holiday.'

'Oh – thank you!' *Genuine joy flashed beneath her profes-* *sional cheerfulness.* 'Happy New Year! See you later.'

Yes, *he thought.* You will.

He wished her a Happy New Year, too, and a nice trip, *and left the bakery for the last time.*

There were only a few cars in the car park of the old factory building at the end of Wiesenstrasse in Sulzbach. The property looked neglected. The asphalt was cracked and strewn with pot-holes; old tyres were stacked against chain-link compartments filled with rubbish bags, and in a corner of the car park, a scrapped shipping container was rusting away.

'Twenty years ago, this was one of the largest middle-class employers in the area,' Bodenstein said, balancing between the craters full of meltwater. 'Until the junior director put a bullet through his head in his office. After that, the plant rapidly fell into bankruptcy. No company wanted to take over this space.'

'I can understand why.' Pia gazed up at the dreary facade. 'The building seems to have bad karma. Are we really at the right place?'

She shuddered.

'Erik Stadler doesn't seem to be bothered by the gloom.' Bodenstein nodded towards the rectangular company sign made of Plexiglas that was posted next to the entrance: SIS – STADLER INTERNET SERVICES.

The glass door was so filthy that it looked like milk glass, and very few people seemed to have bothered using the door handle, judging by the fingerprints on the glass and frame. Bodenstein and Pia entered the foyer. Worn red floor tiles, faded yellowish wallpaper, and closed doors with old-fashioned labels: OFFICE, BOOKKEEPING, WC, PRODUCTION. A laminated sign pointed the way for visitors to SIS, Inc., on the second floor. Up there, it was a whole different world, and Pia looked round in astonishment.

'Somebody sure invested a lot of money in this dump,' Pia said, impressed. 'Look at that parquet floor.'

'Vinyl,' a woman corrected her, with three document binders in her arms as she came out of the room across from the stairwell. The door said ARCHIVES. 'Optical laminate. Not cheap, but indestructible and, above all, antistatic. That's important in a company full of computers. May I help you?'

'My name is Bodenstein, Kripo Hofheim.' He showed the woman his ID and introduced Pia. 'We'd like to speak to Mr Stadler.'

'Sorry, the boss isn't here.' The friendly smile on the pretty freckled face vanished, giving way to a chilly expression. 'And, I can't tell you when he'll drop by again. Lately, he's been mostly working from home.'

'And who are you, if I may ask?' Bodenstein enquired politely.

'Franka Fellmann. Executive assistant.' She squared her shoulders, at the same time unintentionally thrusting forward her well-rounded breasts. Then she rolled her eyes and gave a theatrical sigh. 'Also bookkeeper, receptionist, secretary and cleaning woman. Whatever you wish.'

The bitter undertone could not be missed. Bodenstein knew all too well how useful it could be when someone possessed both an offended ego and a pronounced need to confide in other people. So he put on a sympathetic tone of voice.

'It sounds as though you have a lot to do,' he said in a friendly way. 'And so close to New Year's, too.'

'He left me with the entire annual report,' Franka Fellmann complained, hefting the three document binders. 'He was here briefly this morning because I urgently needed him to sign a few things. But then he disappeared, and I'm not sure I can get everything done on time.'

As the frustrated assistant was telling Bodenstein her troubles, Pia's gaze wandered over the framed photographs hanging on the walls, which were painted a mocha brown. Pictures showing a paraglider, BASE jumper, parachutist and biathlete crossing the finish line as winner.

'That's the boss in all those photos,' Ms Fellmann volunteered unasked. 'That's the sort of nonsense he lives for.'

'Erik Stadler goes BASE jumping?' Pia asked in surprise.

'That's not all. He'll do anything as long as it's life-threatening,' his assistant replied with a mixture of pride and disapproval. 'An adrenalin junkie, as they say. He even won a bronze medal in the Olympic biathlon once, when he was in the army in Bavaria.'

'Interesting,' said Bodenstein with a nod. 'In case you see or speak to your boss today, please tell him to get in touch with us.'

'What is this about?' Ms Fellmann, now once more the executive assistant, raised her carefully plucked eyebrows.

'He already knows,' Bodenstein said vaguely. 'Thank you very much.'

They turned to go when Pia thought of something.

'Oh, Ms Fellmann, could you tell us where we could find your boss's sister?'

Franka Fellmann looked first at Pia, then at Bodenstein, amazed.

'Helen is dead,' she replied. 'She committed suicide a couple of months ago. And the boss hasn't been the same since.'

Pia was the first to recover from the shock.

'We didn't know that. Thanks for telling us. Goodbye.'

In silence they went down the stairs and left the building.

'Why didn't the Stadlers tell us that?' Pia asked on the way to the car.

'We didn't ask them about Helen,' Bodenstein reminded her.

'Still.' Pia stopped. 'It's strange. They talk to us for half an hour about how the mother died, but they never mention Helen's name. And they forget to say that she killed herself.'

'Hmm,' was all Bodenstein said.

'Are you thinking what I'm thinking?' Pia asked.

'That Erik Stadler might be our man?'

'Precisely.' Pia sucked pensively on her lower lip. 'Into extreme sports. A guy who loves taking risks. And as a biathlete and former soldier, he can shoot.'

'Let's go into Frankfurt and have a talk with him,' Bodenstein suggested. 'If he's there.'

'I have a gut feeling that he isn't,' Pia replied, looking worried.

Karoline Albrecht did something that she'd never done before, and did it with a pounding heart and a guilty conscience. She rummaged through her father's study, which had always been off-limits to her. After he'd caught her thirty years ago sitting at his desk and talking on the phone to a girlfriend, the room with the bay windows, the massive safe and the bookshelves up to the ceiling had been declared a no-go zone. She never again went into the study uninvited, and to this day, it held only unpleasant memories of various moral and punitive sermons delivered to her in the holy of holies. Whenever her father left the house, he usually locked the door, ostensibly to keep out the cleaning woman. But Karoline had learned from her mother where to find another key.

For a moment she hesitated, standing in the middle of the room. Where should she start, and just what was she looking for? She finally conquered her inhibitions and began by pulling out the wastebasket, but found nothing of interest. With the meticulousness of a tax auditor, she worked systematically from the north to the south. The desk held no secrets, as anticipated, and the password of the old-fashioned computer turned out to be an insuperable obstacle for her. Checking the telephone memory, she found only a single recent call, a number with a Kelkheim area code that was called on Christmas Day. Since Thursday of last week, her father had neither placed nor received any calls, and Karoline found that odd. For almost half an hour, she thought about where her father might keep the key to the antiquated safe. She looked behind the pictures on the wall, under the carpet and in a flower vase, took one book after another out of the bookcase, and finally found the key inside a medical treatise her father had written titled *Surgery of the Thorax,* which was still a standard work for medical students. By then, her guilty conscience had evaporated. Instead, she was seized with the fever of the hunt, which forced her to concentrate and put aside her brooding. She unlocked the safe and propped open the hundred-pound door of concrete plates and steel. In addition to her parents' passports, she discovered several jewellery boxes belonging to her mother, her father's watch collection, cash, car titles, gold coins, a family genealogy, insurance documents, two manuscripts for other medical books, tax returns for recent years, and document binders with papers for property that her father had purchased as investments for his old age. What she had hoped to find was not in the safe, namely the obituary, whose exact wording she was burning to know.

Just as she was about to close the monstrous door, a telephone chirped softly. Karoline strained to listen and located the ringing inside the safe. She hurried to open one jewellery box after another and found the device, which had stopped ringing by then, among a collection of watches. It was a smartphone, a rather current model, and it was fully charged. Why did her father keep a phone in his safe? And why did he have an obsolete mobile on his desk when he owned a much more modern device?

Karoline weighed it in her hand for a moment, then pressed the Home button and ran her finger across the glass. The main menu appeared and showed two calls had come in during his absence. She bit her lip. Was her father familiar enough with this device that he would notice? Maybe he hadn't entered password protection, since he never took the smartphone with him. In the end, her curiosity was stronger than all her misgivings. First she brought up the list of all the calls that had come in and was flabbergasted. Yesterday alone, he'd had several conversations that each lasted longer than an hour. He had called a few old friends, some colleagues and companions, which in his situation was no surprise. But why had he used the old-fashioned mobile and not the landline phone sitting on his desk? She had no answer.

Purely by chance, a couple of weeks ago, his attention was drawn to the high-rise, probably because a gigantic illuminated billboard made the building stand out among all the glass and reinforced concrete facades of the office buildings in the commercial area of Eschborn South. It was approximately one kilometre as the crow flies from the Seerose Industrial Park, which on a day with no wind was not an impossible distance. He had driven there twice to look over the building in detail, which had just been renovated. Unobserved, he'd climbed up the scaffolding to the roof. The workers he encountered paid him little notice. Apparently, so many companies had been involved in the renovation that a strange face didn't attract attention. For the residents of the 312 apartments who had been living with the construction crews for months, the sight of a man on the scaffolding was nothing unusual. He had scouted how he could get onto the roof. The first time, he climbed up the scaffolding, but that would be difficult carrying the heavy case, so the second time, he went through the building. Today, he again pressed one of the many buttons on the intercom and announced himself as 'the postman.' The door buzzed and he entered the building. He knew that there were cameras in the foyer and on the way to the lifts, so he'd pulled up his hood and wore a hard hat over it.

He took the lift to the twenty-fourth floor with no problem. There he opened the glass door of the stairwell to the balcony, swung over the parapet, and stood on the scaffolding. Only a few minutes later, he was on the roof and climbing up a fixed ladder. Up there, between a forest of antennas and satellite dishes, he could be seen from the high-rise of the stock exchange, but no one would look twice at a man wearing a hard hat. He walked further along the concrete wall and then slid down into the gap between the building conduits and the side wall of the front penthouse apartment. Here he was hidden from view and could set up his rifle in comfort. And he had an unobstructed view past the wall to the Mann Mobilia building in the direction of the REWE supermarket.

It was guaranteed to be a spectacular shot, which would garner the most publicity. It was cold up here, but he'd expected that, and was wearing thermal underwear and a down jacket. He carefully assembled his rifle, chambered a round, and took up position. As camouflage, he spread a grey blanket over himself and the rifle barrel. Now he was no more noticeable than a satellite in the sky. He looked through the telescopic sight and adjusted the focus. The advertising banners of Mann Mobilia were hanging limp. No breeze. Perfect.

He observed the people, the cars, the special offer signs at Aldi. The telescopic sight was so fantastic that he could even read the registration expiration date on the number plates of the cars, from almost a kilometre away. Her car was in the car park. Everything was ready. He glanced at his watch. Eleven forty-four a.m. It had taken him eleven minutes to get here from the street door. Now he had to wait for an hour and twenty-five minutes, but that didn't matter. He had plenty of patience.

No one was home at Erik Stadler's apartment in the North End of Frankfurt, and he wasn't answering his mobile either.

'That was a useless trip,' Pia grumbled. 'Home office my foot! Who knows where he's wandering round.'

It took them a couple of minutes to get back to their car,

which she'd left in Oeder Weg. The parking situation in the North End was a disaster as always. It was especially bad in the evening, at weekends and now, between Christmas and New Year, when most people had taken days off and didn't have to go to work.

'Stadler Senior works for the City of Frankfurt, doesn't he?' Bodenstein asked, and sat down in the passenger seat.

'Yeah, but I doubt they're answering their phones,' replied Pia. 'Call Ms Fellmann instead. She liked you, and I'm sure she'll give you Dirk Stadler's mobile number.'

'What do you mean, she liked me?' Bodenstein gave her a surprised look.

With any other man, Pia would have assumed he was fishing for compliments, but not her boss. As far as women were concerned, Bodenstein was incredibly slow on the uptake; he didn't recognize the most obvious signals. In the past, this had got him into trouble several times, and he seemed to have noticed far too late what was wrong in his marriage. He simply had no defences against sly female wiles. In the down-to-earth Inka Hansen, he might have finally found the right woman. Pia rarely talked to him about personal matters, but she would have liked to ask whether he was happy with this staid and oddly emotionless vet. Pia never really knew where she stood with Inka.

'Well, she practically stuck her boobs in your face. She was seriously putting the moves on you. And then the idiotic way she was batting her eyes,' Pia now said scornfully, doing an exaggerated imitation of what the assistant had done. 'But she's head over heels in love with her boss. And as I see it, the feeling certainly isn't mutual.'

'Amazing that you can detect all that in a conversation lasting three minutes.' Bodenstein clicked his tongue, put on his reading glasses, and tapped the number from Erik Stadler's business card into his mobile. Pia was right. Franka Fellmann gladly gave him the number, and he was able to phone Erik Stadler's father.

A moment later, they heard his voice from the speaker-phone. 'Stadler.'

'Bodenstein, Kripo Hofheim. Mr Stadler, where are you at the moment?'

'At the main cemetery in Frankfurt,' Dirk Stadler replied in surprise.

'At your daughter's grave?' Bodenstein asked.

There was silence for a few seconds.

'No.' Stadler's voice sounded choked. 'My daughter is in the cemetery in Kelkheim. I'm here on business. We're examining gravestones for their stability.'

'Why didn't you tell us that your daughter had committed suicide?' Bodenstein asked.

'I didn't think it was relevant,' replied Stadler after another brief pause. He cleared his throat. 'It's still a very painful subject for me. After my wife's death, my daughter and I went through some tough times and were very close.'

Bodenstein, who'd been prepared for some flimsy lie, was disarmed by Stadler's honesty.

'Please excuse my tone of voice and my bluntness,' he said more gently. 'I was annoyed because you hadn't said a word about it yesterday.'

It was another thing that Pia admired about her boss. If he made a mistake, he had the strength of character to admit it.

Stadler accepted the apology. 'I'm sure you're under a lot of pressure at the moment.'

'We'd like to speak with you again.'

'Of course. I'll be done with work at four.'

'Then we'll see you at four thirty at your house. Many thanks.'

Bodenstein ended the call.

'Do I believe him, or do I not believe him?' he said more to himself than to Pia.

'Why would he not want to tell us about his daughter's suicide?'

'That's exactly what I'm asking myself.' Bodenstein leaned back against the headrest, closed his eyes, and sank into a meditative silence.

Celina Hoffmann uttered a curse. She drove down the row of parking spaces for the third time, but there wasn't a vacant spot anywhere. It was already one minute to one, and if she didn't find a parking space soon, she'd be late for her shift. And she would miss Hürmet. She wanted to pay her colleague back the fifty euros she'd borrowed from her two weeks ago, and she had to do it before the end of the year. Celina didn't have a whole lot of personal rules, but she was superstitious, and her grandmother had always preached that you shouldn't start the new year with any debts, because that would draw bad luck and even more debts would follow.

'Well, all right,' she muttered as she saw an Opel reversing out of a parking spot right in front of her. She put on her indicator and backed up a little. The old guy was turning the wheel this way and that, while his wife was trying to direct him, standing helplessly next to the car. This might take a while.

Damn! Today was another one of those days when everything, absolutely everything, was going wrong. First she had

overslept, and then she discovered that there was hardly a drop
of fuel left in the tank. She barely made it to the petrol station,
and after she'd filled the tank, she noticed that she'd left her
wallet at home. Fortunately, she knew the young guy who
worked at the station. He advanced her some money, and then
she drove back home and had to trudge up to the eighth floor,
because the lift was broken again. No, this was definitely not
her day.

At last, the old guy got the car out of the space. His wife
climbed into the passenger seat, and Celina could finally park
her car. She ran across the car park, and even from a distance
could see the queue in front of the bakery counter. Old
Asunovic was working her shift. Another piece of bad luck.
She would naturally tattle to the boss that Celina had come in
late. She pushed her way through the waiting customers and
opened the door in front of the counter that led into the tiny
break room and the storeroom.

'Did Hürmet already leave?' she called breathlessly, flinging
her jacket and bag onto a chair and slipping into her smock.

'Late again?' bleated her older colleague, who was sliding a
tray of pretzel sticks out of the convection oven. 'Of course
Hürmet has left. It's five past one.'

'Ah, shit. I couldn't find a parking space.' Celina squeezed
past her colleague into the salesroom.

'Finally,' said Özlem, her other colleague on the midday shift,
who was equally pissed off. 'All hell has broken loose in here.'

'Hey, if you happen to see Hürmet coming out of REWE,
let me know, okay?' Celina said. 'I have to give her that fifty
euros. For that, I'll be cleaning up tonight, too.'

'Okay.' Özlem nodded and served the next customer.

*

Fourteen minutes ago, she left the bakery and as usual disappeared into the supermarket. He waited patiently. It was just as crowded as usual. Although not all the office workers from the high-rise office buildings were on the job in the last week of the year, the car parks were jammed, and there was hustle and bustle everywhere. People went into the shops and came back out, some looking frantic, others calm and relaxed. From this position, they looked like ants. There still was almost no wind, though up here there was a light breeze, but he'd added that into his calculations. At this great distance, even with a precision rifle like his, some deviation in the trajectory was unavoidable. This time he was going without the silencer, because it would lower the speed of the bullet. At shorter distances, this was negligible, but from six hundred metres, he didn't need anything slowing it down. He checked his breathing, concentrating completely on the exit door of the supermarket. And there she was. With the shopping basket on her arm, she headed straight past the boutique and the shoe shop towards Aldi, where her car was parked. Inhale. Exhale. He had her head precisely in the crosshairs and curled his finger. Stop! Damn, she stopped and turned round. Apparently, someone had called her name. Didn't matter, he wouldn't get her lined up like this in the field of fire again. He squeezed the trigger, the shot cracked, and the recoil slammed the rifle against his collarbone.

Karoline was sitting at the table in the kitchen of her apartment, frowning as she looked at the PowerPoint presentation that she'd opened on her laptop, trying to grasp the correlations. So far, the information at her disposal was pretty skimpy, but at least she'd found out who the third victim was. The newspaper and Internet gave only the first names and the first letter of the last names of those affected, but from that and an item on her father's secret mobile phone, she had come to a conclusion that seemed logical. But it still wasn't clear what Renate Rohleder and her father had to do with Friedrich Gehrke. Karoline knew Gehrke slightly; he belonged to her parents' larger social circle and had to be round eighty years old by now.

'Maximilian has been shot,' the old man said in a trembling voice when he left a message on her father's voice mail. 'Please call me.'

That's all he said. The relationship between Gehrke and her father didn't seem to be so superficial as she'd thought. He did have her father's secret mobile phone number, after all, while she did not.

Karoline had called Renate to hear from her about the advertising display with the company logo that she had seen on the delivery van belonging to the man who accompanied Helen Stadler. She had also Googled 'Hartig', the goldsmith's in Hofheim. The owner of the business was Jens-Uwe Hartig. He had a shop and workshop in Hofheim on the main street, but the website told her nothing. A few pictures of objects he had made himself; otherwise, only information about opening hours, telephone number and tax number. Not even a photo of the boss at work, and no vita either. What did this Jens-Uwe Hartig have to do with the daughter of the deceased Kirsten Stadler? Was it possible that he and the daughter were behind the murders?

Karoline massaged the back of her neck and bit absent-mindedly into the salami sandwich that was both her breakfast and lunch. Something didn't fit, but she simply didn't have enough information. She closed her laptop and instead took out the list of her father's contacts that she had written down from his smartphone before she put it back in the box of watches, closed the safe, and returned the key to its hiding place. Then she had closed and locked the study, but kept the door key. Just in case. A feverish impatience had replaced her paralysing sadness, and she couldn't stand to be in her parents' house any longer, since it was filled with memories of Mama. From her car she phoned Greta, who to her relief seemed to be feeling a little better. At least she wasn't crying anymore. Greta even told her mother that she had gone with her cousin Dana to the riding stables and now she wanted her own horse. After New Year, it was a tradition for Carsten to take the whole family on a skiing trip to Austria, and Greta was looking forward to that.

As she ate her sandwich, Karoline studied the contact list and was again stopped by a name that meant nothing to her. Peter Riegelhoff, with a Frankfurt area code and a long telephone number that obviously belonged to an extension, because a search in the Internet reverse phone book produced no hits. In the past few days, her father had called this Riegelhoff several times. Karoline consulted the Internet and found that there were several men in Frankfurt with this name: an importer of organic wines, an advertising man, a dentist and a lawyer. To find out which was the right man, she would probably have to try calling them willy-nilly. She wasn't keen on doing that, sniffing round in her father's affairs, but he'd left her no choice.

'Hürmet! Wait!' Celina stormed out the side door of the bakery and ran after her colleague. Hürmet stopped. She turned round with a smile.

'I don't want to start the new year owing any money.'

Celina grinned and waved the fifty-euro note that she'd stuck in the pocket of her smock earlier. As she reached out her hand, Hürmet's head exploded. Just like that. A pink fountain of blood and brain matter sprayed into the air. At the same time, there was a loud bang, and the shop window next to her shook. Time froze. Celina opened her mouth and wanted to scream, but no sound came from her lips. She simply stood there, looking on in disbelief as Hürmet fell to the ground not a metre away. Silently she collapsed into herself, as if her body were made of jelly. Celina still held the money in her hand as she stared in bewilderment at her colleague, who suddenly had no face. All round her, panic broke out. People were screaming; parents pulled their children to the ground; many people just took off running; others sought cover behind parked cars. Celina didn't notice that cars were crashing into each other and people were running into other people and knocking them down. She stared uncomprehending at the bloody mass that had once been Hürmet's head and heard a shrill, hysterical shriek. Somebody grabbed her hard by the arm. She tried to pull away, but she couldn't take her eyes off the horrendous sight. Not until a man gave her a slap did she come to her senses.

Celina's throat hurt. The screaming had come from her. What had just happened?

'Where . . . where is Hürmet?' she stammered in confusion. 'I . . . I have to pay her back the fifty euros.'

Her knees gave way, she staggered, and all at once, everything went black.

The emergency call reached them at the exact moment they were leaving the A66 at the exit to Hofheim.

'Where exactly?' Bodenstein asked.

'Eschborn, Seerose shopping centre,' said the officer on duty over the radio. Pia reacted in an instant. She hit the left indicator, did a U-turn, and stepped on it. Seconds later, they were on the autobahn going back in the opposite direction.

Bodenstein asked for more details.

'A woman was shot in front of a supermarket,' said the watch detective. 'That's all I know. The whole shopping centre has been sealed off, and a chopper's in the air.'

'When did you get the call?'

'At one thirty-seven p.m.'

Three minutes ago. The police could hardly move much faster than that, yet Bodenstein had a hunch they'd arrive too late. The gunman would have taken off. Or maybe he was still there, blending into the crowd, and could make his escape that way.

Bodenstein knew the shopping centre. There were supermarkets and furniture stores, two fast food restaurants and a host of other shops and businesses. The car park had an exit directly towards the A66 and another that led to the L3005, where you could turn left towards the Taunus, or stay on towards the A5 heading north. There were also footpaths and bike paths and a tractor track in the direction of Schwalbach that would offer ideal escape routes. The best camouflage, though, was definitely the crowds of people that came to a shopping centre like this at noon on a Friday between Christmas and New Year.

'You think it was the sniper?' Pia was watching the road intently, passing a line of cars on the right at a hellish pace and ignoring the honking of incensed drivers.

'Yep, I'm sure of it,' Bodenstein said grimly.

'But it sounds exactly like last week at the Main-Taunus Centre.' In Pia's voice, there was a note of quiet hope that it might be another false alarm, but Bodenstein feared the worst.

'No, nobody mentioned a dead body at that one, only shots fired,' he countered. 'It was him, that shitface. And he picked the perfect spot and the perfect time.'

Who was the victim this time? Another person targeted by this ice-cold killer who struck in broad daylight and vanished into thin air? What sort of sicko would execute innocent people to get back at their relatives? Why was he seeking revenge at all? What did he want to achieve, what was his goal? And how the hell was it possible that after ten days they hadn't progressed one step further? It was devastating for the morale of his team. In addition to the lack of results and the wearisome waiting game, they were under constant pressure from the Ministry of the Interior, the press and the public. Under these circumstances, even the most experienced police officer might not be able to remain calm and rational at all times. Mistakes could result from jumping to the wrong conclusion or from making hasty decisions, merely because the team was anxious to do anything at all.

Pia turned off the autobahn and braked sharply. The traffic was jammed beneath the overpass.

'We need the blue light, or we won't get any further,' she said. Bodenstein fished out the police light with the magnetic foot from behind his seat, opened his window, and slapped it onto the roof.

'Up ahead everything is blocked,' said Pia. 'Maybe we'll catch him this time.'

The whole of Sossenheimer Strasse, which served as the exit route for the business district, was blocked by patrol cars angled across the road with blue lights flashing. An officer moved a car back a bit so that Pia and Bodenstein could get past. Pia rolled down her window.

'Which way?' she asked.

'Left at the traffic lights, then straight ahead and turn left at KFC into the car park!' The uniformed officer had to shout to be heard over the hammering of the low-flying helicopter.

'Thanks.' Pia drove on but had to stop after a few metres because hundreds of people were trying to flee from the shopping centre, most of them in their cars, but also a good number on foot.

Finally she pulled the steering wheel hard to the right, drove halfway up onto the pavement, turned into the car park by Mann Mobilia, and circled round the furniture shop.

'Let's walk from here,' she said, snapping off her seat belt. 'We can't get through with the car.'

Bodenstein nodded in agreement. They crossed the hopelessly jammed street. Even the entrance ramp to the L3005 was closed off. The officers, in Kevlar vests and with weapons drawn, were checking each car before letting any past the checkpoint.

'Completely insane,' Bodenstein said to Pia. 'The guy is probably in Switzerland by now.'

The huge parking lot of the REWE supermarket was mostly empty after being blocked off. Paramedics were giving first aid to a few people who had suffered a shock or had been injured by shards of breaking glass. The police chopper circled overhead in the overcast sky, and blue lights were flashing everywhere.

For the victim, help had come much too late. The bullet had burst the head of the young woman and then shattered the display window of the shoe shop behind her. Just like Ingeborg Rohleder, Margarethe Rudolf and Maximilian Gehrke, she was dead before she hit the ground. A young life, snuffed out from one second to the next. Because a madman wished it so.

'Do we know the identity of the victim?' Pia asked her colleagues, who had been on the scene only a few minutes after the fatal shot was fired.

'She worked over there in the bakery and was on the way to her car,' replied a detective superintendent. 'One of her colleagues was standing right nearby when she was shot. She's in shock and is being treated by a paramedic.'

The officer handed Pia the victim's handbag, a cheap knockoff of a designer brand. Besides a wallet, it contained a mobile phone, a key ring, and all sorts of odds and ends. Pia thanked her for the information, then took a pair of latex gloves out of her pocket and pulled them on. In the wallet, she found a driving licence.

'Hürmet Schwarzer,' she read, looking at the photo. 'What a lovely young woman, only twenty-seven years old. Lived in Schwalbach.'

'Why?' Bodenstein asked himself. 'Why would he kill a twenty-seven-year-old bakery sales assistant?'

'If it was the sniper, we'll know soon enough,' said Pia. 'He's getting bolder and bolder each time.'

'Because he wants attention,' Bodenstein suggested. 'He doesn't kill for the simple thrill of it. There's a lot more behind this.'

'One thing is for sure,' said Pia. 'He's playing us for fools and carrying out his intentions with ice-cold precision.'

Bodenstein looked round. Where had the sniper taken up position? Diagonally, across the street, he saw a building under construction. Did the sniper lie in wait on the roof of the unfinished building? If so, how did he get up there? Did the furniture shop have surveillance cameras in its car park that may have caught the perp on video?

Bodenstein had seldom felt so powerless. He felt like somebody who wanted to open a treasure chest with a crowbar but couldn't find anywhere to insert the lever.

Karoline Albrecht left the editorial office of the *Taunus Echo* in Königstein and walked up Limburger Strasse to the pedestrian zone, which was usually swarming with shoppers in the days after Christmas. This time, many of the shops were closed. Somebody had accomplished this simply by firing three shots. But at least the pub, which had been mentioned to her at the editorial office, was open. Karoline entered, pushing aside the curtain meant to keep out the wind. A couple of men were sitting in the semi-darkness at the bar, drinking coffee. Neither of them matched the photo of Konstantin Faber that she'd found on the website of the *Taunus Echo*. She didn't want to ask about him, so she decided to wait for a while. The woman at the reception desk of the editorial office had told her that he went to this pub almost every morning. So she ordered a cup of coffee and sat down at one of the few tables, receiving curious looks from the men at the bar.

Just as she was about to pay and leave, the door opened. The curtain parted, and a bitterly cold draught blew in. Karoline recognized the man at once, although he was considerably more rotund than in the photo, and he had less hair on his head.

'I hope everyone had a merry Christmas!' Konstantin Faber

TO CATCH A KILLER

said to the other customers, and sat down next to them at the bar.

'Shut the hell up,' replied one of the men. 'I had the worst sales ever before Christmas.'

'Me, too,' the other chimed in. 'All year, we were looking forward to the Christmas business, and then this goddamn killer ruined it all.'

Both men nodded, looking depressed. Apparently, they were chefs, because they talked about cancelled reservations and about staff calling in sick with the flimsiest of excuses. Karoline pretended she was busy with her mobile as she listened intently to their conversation.

'People ordered their last-minute gifts online,' said the second man dejectedly. 'I'll have to let two people go in January, that's for sure.'

'I'm closing till all this crap is over,' said one chef. 'We're leaving for Italy tomorrow. Whether it's ten days earlier or late doesn't really matter.'

One man had heard that since yesterday the bus drivers and train engineers were refusing to go to work. In Frankfurt, the S-trains were going nowhere, and the taxi drivers were staying home.

'I hope they catch this nutcase soon,' said the proprietor, shoving another cup of coffee over to Faber. 'The infrastructure in the whole Rhein-Main region is going to collapse if this keeps up.'

'We've got problems, too,' said the journalist. The office had been getting complaints from numerous subscribers that their daily paper wasn't being delivered. Many of the delivery boys had called in sick, and you couldn't really blame them.

The men at the bar continued to discuss what the police

could and should be doing. Karoline would have liked to tell them that there was no need for panic, because the sniper wasn't interested in shooting paper boys or bus drivers. The police probably hadn't thought about this aspect, but obviously, the Judge was causing major headaches for many businesses and shop owners in the region.

Karoline got up and went over to the bar.

'Excuse me for bothering you,' she said to the journalist. 'Are you Mr Faber from the *Taunus Echo*?'

'Who wants to know?' Faber looked at her impatiently. 'Are you from the police?'

'No. One of your colleagues told me that I might find you here,' she replied. 'I'd like to talk to you. But perhaps somewhere more private.'

'Oho, Faber, somebody wants to drag you off,' teased one of his pals, and the others laughed, but he didn't pay them any mind. He was no longer looking annoyed.

'Okay.' He got up from his barstool and grabbed his jacket. 'Put it on my tab, all right, Willi?'

'No problem,' replied the proprietor.

Karoline paid for her coffee and followed Konstantin Faber out to the street.

For Pia, it was unusual to work under the eyes of the public. Mostly dead bodies were found in a residence, in the woods or somewhere else hidden away. She then had to deal with one or two witnesses and with those who had discovered the body. But this time, there were dozens of people who had seen Hürmet Schwarzer get shot. In a country where firearms were a rarity and generally not part of everyday life, this experience was even more traumatic. It was particularly bad for a seven-year-old boy who had been with his parents and siblings in the shoe shop when the plate-glass window was shattered by the bullet. His older siblings were trying on some shoes, but he was bored and had been looking out the window when the horrible event took place right in front of him. The little boy had had some good luck with the bad, because the bullet that killed Hürmet Schwarzer flew past him only millimetres away and slammed into some shelving.

The boy now lay inside an ambulance and was being treated by a paramedic. Bodenstein talked to his parents while Pia looked for the young woman who had stood next to the victim.

'May I speak to her?' she asked the doctor.

'You can try,' he said. 'She is suffering from shock. She hasn't said a word to us yet.'

Celina Hoffmann, a blonde woman in her early twenties, sat slumped on the running board of the second ambulance, staring at her hands. She was wearing her bakery smock, and someone had put a foil blanket round her shoulders. At first, Pia thought the woman had freckles, but then she realized that her face, hair, smock and hands were covered with blood spatter.

'Hello, Ms Hoffmann,' said Pia. 'I'm Pia Kirchhoff from Kripo in Hofheim. May I sit with you for a moment?'

The young woman raised her head, looked at Pia with an empty gaze and shrugged her shoulders. She was trembling all over, and her face was grey. Even if the shock eventually receded, she would never forget what she had experienced today. Some people were more robust than others and could cope with processing such a horrendous experience; for others, it would leave behind lifelong scars on their souls.

'I . . . I wanted to pay back the fifty euros to Hürmet before she went on holiday,' whispered Celina Hoffmann, holding out a crumpled banknote to Pia. A tear ran down her cheek. 'She loaned it to me before Christmas, and I didn't want . . . I . . . It's bad luck if you go into the new year with debts.'

'You and Hürmet were colleagues, weren't you?' Pia asked.

'Yes. We . . . We both work at the bakery,' Celina replied in a quavering voice as she stared at her hands covered with spots of blood. 'She always works the early shift, and I usually don't come in until midday. And today . . . Today I came a little late, because . . . my car ran out of petrol. Hürmet had already left, but she always goes shopping after work, so I looked to see if she was still round. Then she came out of REWE. I . . . I ran out and called to her. She stopped and . . . and . . . turned round to face me and then . . . then . . .'

She fell silent and broke into tears. But talking about it seemed to have done her good, lessening the shock. Celina Hoffmann sobbed in despair. Pia handed her a pack of tissues and waited patiently until the young woman regained her composure and spoke again.

'I . . . I couldn't even understand what happened,' she went on after a moment. 'Hürmet lay there in front of me, and I was screaming like a crazy woman until a guy slapped me and took me away from there.'

'Did you see the direction the shot came from?' Pia wanted to know.

'No. I . . . I was only looking at Hürmet.' She stopped and glanced up. 'But it was definitely from behind me to the right, up high. Because . . . because she was standing with her back half turned to the car park, and . . . and . . . her face . . . it just exploded somehow.'

The young woman covered her face with her hands as she relived the horror of the last half hour – a scene that her mind so wanted to eradicate. Pia was impressed. It was extremely seldom that an eyewitness could remember something in such detail. Often, it seemed heartless to question a person immediately after they had lived through or seen something terrible. But the sooner a witness could be questioned, the greater the chance of getting an unexpurgated and thus fairly factual statement. If the witness first had a chance to think everything over and talk to other people, then what they saw could be mixed up with all sorts of conclusions and emotions. The human brain was designed to protect the person by erasing the memory of terrible events or breaking them into fragments. For this reason, people often failed to remember accidents they had seen or even experienced, and this type of amnesia was generally permanent.

'I know that it's not easy for you,' Pia said sympathetically. 'But you'll need to talk to my colleague from the evidence team.'

Celina Hoffmann nodded. Pia jotted down her name, address and phone number, then made sure that her colleagues from the bakery were allowed to see her. In the meantime, Christian Kröger and his team had arrived and begun to examine the crime scene.

'According to the witness, the shot came from the right, behind and above,' Pia reported to Kröger and Bodenstein. 'So if she was standing here, the bullet came from somewhere over there.'

She pointed towards the furniture shop.

'Hmm, I reckoned more like from the roof of the building under construction,' Bodenstein said.

'No, the angle of the shot doesn't match.' Kröger looked round and shook his head. 'I concur with the witness. The bullet entered above the left ear and passed through the skull. I'm guessing the shooter was on the roof of Mann Mobilia. We'll go up there and do a trajectory analysis.'

'Her phone is ringing!' called one of Kröger's people, and held out Hürmet Schwarzer's handbag to Pia. She exchanged a look with Bodenstein, then stuck her hand in the bag and pulled out the phone.

The display said PATRICK CALLING. Whoever that was, it must be a close friend, if Hürmet Schwarzer had stored him under his first name. Pia took the call.

'Hürmet, where the hell are you?' the man shouted. 'Why don't you pick up?'

'This is Pia Kirchhoff from the criminal police, Hofheim,' she said. 'With whom am I speaking, please?'

'Where's my wife?' the man asked after a brief pause. That explained his relationship to the dead woman. 'What's going on? Why doesn't she answer her phone?'

'Mr Schwarzer, where are you now?' Pia countered with another question. No telling what the news of his wife's death might trigger if the man was possibly at the wheel of a forty-ton truck.

'I . . . I'm at home,' said Patrick Schwarzer, giving his address. His voice sounded shaky, losing its self-confidence. 'Please tell me, what has happened to my wife?'

'We'll be over there right away,' replied Pia, terminating the call, and handed the phone to her colleague, who slipped it into an exhibit bag.

She felt a great reluctance to confront the bewilderment

and grief of a relative for a fourth time in a week. She would rather delegate the task to someone else.

'Come on,' said Bodenstein, who knew exactly what was going through her mind. 'Let's get it over with.'

'What does the victim's husband say?' Dr Nicola Engel wanted to know an hour later at the improvised meeting being held in Pia and Ostermann's office. 'Is there a connection between his wife and the other victims? Did he know Kirsten Stadler?'

'We didn't have a chance to question him.' Bodenstein waved aside her query. 'He works in customer service at a bank in Hattersheim and had come home for lunch as usual. Because he hadn't listened to the radio, he didn't know what was going on in Eschborn. He was completely unprepared.'

'How certain is it that this perp is the sniper?' Nicola Engel asked.

'One hundred per cent. It's the same ammunition he used for the other three victims,' said Pia.

'Why do you think he decided to make contact with the press?' The commissioner hadn't been at the morning meeting when Bodenstein presented the letter from the Judge to the journalist Konstantin Faber. 'What's your opinion of his message?'

' "A great injustice has been done. The guilty parties shall feel the same pain as the one who has suffered because of their indifference, greed, vanity and thoughtlessness. Those who have taken guilt upon themselves shall live in fear and terror, for I am come to judge the living and the dead." ' Andreas Neff, leaning on shelves for document binders, read the message aloud.

231

'A psychopath,' he then pronounced judgement. 'A megalomaniac who sets himself up as the Judge over life and death. With this message, the perpetrator reveals quite a bit about himself. For example, he is religious. The last sentence of his message is taken from the Catholic profession of faith. He has a mission and at the same time wants to challenge his pursuers. For him, it's a game. Our killer is an adventurer.'

He looked round the room, inviting confirmation.

'Do you believe me now? Was my profile right?'

The question was directed at Kim, who was standing next to him.

'To believe means not to know,' she replied without even looking at Neff. He, on the other hand, scrutinized her with unconcealed interest. It was clear to everyone that he liked her. But it was equally clear to everyone except himself that Kim was not the slightest bit interested in him. She didn't deign to respond to his theory, as she bit her lower lip, obviously thinking about something else.

'Has anyone talked to Helen Stadler yet?' she suddenly broke her silence. 'Why was she at Renate Rohleder's?'

Bodenstein and Pia exchanged a quick glance. In the hectic rush of the past few hours, they had completely forgotten to inform the team what they had discovered earlier in the day.

'Helen Stadler, the daughter of Kirsten Stadler, committed suicide a few months ago,' Bodenstein said. 'One of Erik Stadler's colleagues told us that today, and his father confirmed it.'

'Erik Stadler was once a biathlete. He does stuff like BASE jumping and other extreme sports,' Pia added reluctantly, because it seemed to support Neff's theory. 'He even won a bronze medal at the Olympics. In addition, he was in the army.

That means he knows how to shoot. He may even be an expert marksman. And today at noon, he was not at work or at home.'

'There you have it.' Andreas Neff nodded with satisfaction. 'He's the one. As the son of Kirsten Stadler, he also has a suitable motive.'

'How do you see it, Oliver?' Nicola Engel asked.

'Erik Stadler does seem to meet all the conditions,' Bodenstein admitted, rubbing his unshaven chin.

'Then you should put him on the wanted list,' Engel advised.

'Officers from Frankfurt are already staking out his apartment,' said Kai Ostermann. 'I'm sending another patrol over to his office. He's bound to turn up sooner or later.'

'Kirsten Stadler's parents haven't called in either,' Cem told them. 'They have at least as strong a motive as the widower and the son.'

Engel thought for a moment, then got up from her chair.

'We're going to the media,' she announced. 'We're going to give them everything we know to date. Four victims in ten days! This case is upsetting the whole region. We've been ordered to ask for assistance from the public, so that means all crime scenes and times will be published. Someone must have seen something. For both the print media and television, I want detailed reconstructions of the crimes, including the possible escape routes used by the perpetrator.'

'I'm worried about that,' said Ostermann.

'The press will also point out that the killer must have had a sports bag or large shopping bag with him,' Cem Altunay added. 'That's what he used to transport the stripped-down rifle.'

'I want results,' Engel said emphatically. All that was miss-ing was for her to clap her hands. 'So, get to work!'

'The motive of the perp seems to be retaliation, not mere revenge,' Kim remarked.

'What's the difference?' asked Kathrin Fachinger scepti-cally. 'It boils down to the same thing – lynch law.'

'Retaliation is the reciprocation of an injustice inflicted as vengeance and requires a punishment qualitatively correspond-ing to the deed,' replied Kim. 'What you did to me, I will do to you – in the negative as well as in the positive, because it's also possible to retaliate with goodness. In the ethical sense, retaliation is the basis for the social principle of justice. Ven-geance is an extreme form of retaliation, for example, blood vengeance. The avenger ignores legal means of reparations because he considers them inappropriate.'

'I don't see any difference,' said Ostermann. 'According to Section 211 StGb, revenge is a classic characteristic of murder.'

'That's true,' Kim agreed. 'The final outcome and its effect are the same. The difference lies in the motivation. In my opinion, we're dealing with a very rare type of murderer. He is anything but a psychopath, nor is he megalomaniacal. This is no game he's playing with us; he's not like somebody who's after kicks or a challenge. He seeks out his sniping positions purely from the aspect of usefulness, not as provocation. I still believe that we're looking for a pro.'

*

MARGARETHE RUDOLF HAD TO DIE BECAUSE HER HUSBAND IMPLICATED HIMSELF IN MURDER OUT OF GREED AND VANITY.

Karoline Albrecht struggled with all her might against the tears and was grateful that Faber was tactfully allowing her the moment she needed to compose herself. He stood at the window of the conference room on the second floor of the newspaper's editorial offices with his back turned to her.

'Why did he decide to send this to you in particular?' she asked, her voice breaking.

'To tell you the truth, I have no idea.' Faber turned round. 'Maybe he reads our paper. Maybe he knows me personally.'

He pulled out a chair and took a seat facing her. There wasn't much going on in the editorial office; most of the desks in the city room were empty.

'It could also be a coincidence,' he said. 'Most of my colleagues are on leave over Christmas and New Year. I voluntarily took over the post of editor-in-charge, especially since the week between the years is usually slim pickings when it comes to hot news stories.'

Karoline Albrecht looked at him. He had immediately believed her when she said she was the daughter of the second sniper victim. He didn't even ask to see her ID, which listed her birth name. Probably everyone could see what a shitty time she was having.

'What do you know about the case?' she asked.

'Not a thing,' Faber said with a shrug. 'That's the point. My article is a compilation of speculations. The police were pretty angry about it, but I think the public needs to be kept informed.'

His reply disappointed her. The journalist knew less than she did.

'Why don't you go to the police?' he asked her. 'You're related to the victim, so they'll talk to you.'

Karoline Albrecht said nothing for a moment.

'My father is a very respected surgeon,' she replied. 'He's one of the best in the world in his field. For many people, he's the last hope, and he has saved countless lives. But now somebody is accusing him of a murder, and my mother was killed because of it. I can't believe it.'

'So you want to find out if your father is really guilty.'

'Precisely,' she said. 'I want to know why my mother had to die. That's of only marginal interest to the police. They just want to catch the killer. For me, that's not enough.'

'And how would I be able to help you? I'm only the local editor of a regional newspaper, responsible for business and culture. Not some investigative reporter who uncovers conspiracies.'

Karoline Albrecht noticed his discomfort and nodded. He was a short, overweight man with thin hair and wearing a grey cardigan. He seemed like a disillusioned teacher waiting for retirement, not some Bob Woodward or Carl Bernstein. Maybe he was too old and too comfortable to recognize the journalistic chance that had been offered to him because the sniper had chosen to contact him, and no one else. Konstantin Faber was no dynamo, and he'd be no help to her.

'May I have a copy of the obituary and the letter?' she asked.

'Yes, of course,' he hastened to reply. They got up. Karoline grabbed her handbag and the four pages and followed him down the carpeted hall to the photocopier.

'In case you have any more questions, please call me,' he told her as they said goodbye. His face clearly showed the relief he felt because she didn't insist on his assistance.

'Thank you.' Karoline handed him a business card. 'And perhaps you can let me know if you learn anything new.'

'I will,' he assured her, avoiding her gaze. No doubt he was promising anything just to get rid of her as fast as possible.

Dirk Stadler arrived at the same second as Bodenstein and Pia. He greeted them with a nod, drove into one of the many garages, and came limping towards them a minute later.

'I apologize for being a little late,' he said, extending his hand first to Pia, then to Bodenstein.

'We're late, too,' said Bodenstein. 'You may have heard that we have another dead body.'

'Yes, the news was on the radio,' Stadler confirmed. 'Come on, let's go in the house. It's much warmer inside.'

Just before they reached the front door, they were stopped by a neighbour who had accepted a package for Stadler and now handed it to him.

'I have really nice neighbours,' Stadler said with a smile. 'I've been lucky. In a housing estate like this, we live pretty close to each other.'

He asked Pia to hold the package so he could unlock the front door.

'For the time being, I'm buying almost everything online,' Stadler explained as he opened the door. 'It's not good for shop owners, but easier if you're not so steady on your feet.'

They entered the house, and he turned on the light and took off his coat. Pia put the package on the small sideboard in the hall; then she followed Stadler and her boss into the large dining room. Stadler offered them something to drink, but they politely declined.

'How did you decide that these murders might have something to do with my late wife?' Dirk Stadler wanted to know as they took seats at the dining room table.

'Renate Rohleder, the daughter of the first victim, happened to be one of your neighbours when you were still living in Niederhöchstadt. On the day your wife died, your daughter asked Renate for help, but she refused,' Bodenstein began.

'I remember her,' said Stadler with a nod. 'She has a flower shop in Eschborn, doesn't she? And she also had a dog. My wife went for walks with her occasionally.'

'Right,' said Bodenstein. 'The husband of the second victim was head surgeon in transplantation at the clinic where your wife died and where her organs were later processed. The third victim was the recipient of the heart of your late wife. A young man who had a congenital heart ailment.'

'Oh my God,' Stadler whispered, visibly moved.

'And now,' Bodenstein went on, 'we have a fourth victim. A young woman, twenty-seven years old. We don't know the connection yet, but I'm afraid it will turn out that her husband was also involved in the events of 16 September 2002.'

He didn't mention the obituaries or the letter.

'Why didn't you tell us the other day that Helen was dead?' Pia asked.

'How could I know that her death played any relevant role?' Stadler was clearly wrestling with his self-control. 'And it . . . It's still so fresh. For years, I worried a lot about Helen, but during the past year, I firmly believed that she was stable and had finally overcome her feelings of guilt and depression. She was almost done with her studies and had a nice boyfriend. They got engaged last summer, and were planning to get married in October. The wedding invitations were already sent out. And then . . . then . . . she threw herself in front of the S-train. Without any warning.'

'Where did that happen?' Pia asked. 'And when?'

'In Kelsterbach,' Stadler answered in a choked voice. 'On 16 September, the tenth anniversary of her mother's death.'

'Why was your daughter depressed?' Pia dug deeper. 'Why did she feel guilty?'

Stadler didn't answer at once. He struggled for a moment. His grief was so obvious that Pia almost felt an urge to console him.

'My wife went jogging with the dog every morning,' he said at last. 'No matter the weather. She was very fit, and she was training for the New York City Marathon. America had always been her great dream, and she would have preferred to live there. Helen often went running with her, but on that morning, she didn't feel like it. She wanted to stay in bed a little longer. She had just turned fourteen. But after an hour, Kirsten still hadn't returned to get Erik ready for school and go to work herself. The children were worried. They couldn't reach her on her mobile, so they went out looking for her. They knew the routes she liked to run. And then . . . then they found her. She hadn't got very far, so she must have lain there for at least an hour. Erik phoned for an ambulance from Kirsten's mobile and tried to revive her, while Helen took off to get help. Later at the hospital, the doctors established that Kirsten had suffered a cerebral haemorrhage, which would not have been fatal in and of itself. If they had found her sooner and given her CPR, they could have operated and she wouldn't have had to die.'

He looked up. His eyes glistened, and then a tear rolled down his cheek.

'All her life, my daughter blamed herself, because on that morning she didn't bother to go running with her mother.' Stadler's voice threatened to break. His jaw muscles were working, his nostrils quivering. 'Do you understand? Helen was firmly convinced that she could have saved her mother if she'd been with her.'

'What a nightmare,' Pia said on the way back to the station. 'First his wife dies, then the daughter kills herself after being tormented by feelings of guilt for ten long years. Some people really get a full dose of fate.'

It had started to rain. Rain mixed with snow.

Bodenstein had put on his reading glasses and in the dim dome light was paging through the trial documents that Dirk Stadler had agreed to let them take along. 'It's really a tragedy.'

He was hoping to find in the files the names of additional people who'd had anything to do with Kirsten Stadler at the Frankfurt trauma clinic ten years ago. Maybe this way, they could identify potential victims and warn them.

'We have to talk to Helen Stadler's fiancé right away,' Pia said, thinking out loud as she pressed the switch for the windscreen wipers. The spray kicked up by the cars in front was mixed with road salt and kept smearing the windscreen. 'Good thing that her father is so cooperative. Otherwise, we wouldn't have made any progress at all today.'

Bodenstein grumbled something. His back was bent, and his nose almost touched the page he was reading.

'We'll be back at the station in ten minutes.' Pia said. 'Then you can read more comfortably than you can here in the car.'

'You're right.' He flopped the document binder closed. Then he heaved a sigh and stared through the windscreen at the street wet with rain. His fingers were drumming on the cardboard cover of the binder, and he had pursed his lips in thought. Pia recognized that tense expression. Something was bothering her boss, but he hadn't processed it enough to share it with her. She took the exit off the autobahn, and two kilometres further on she turned into the parking garage of the Regional Criminal Unit. Right past the security gate, Ostermann intercepted them.

'Engel has called a team meeting,' he told them, nodding in the direction of the break room. 'There's a big press conference tonight at seven at the town hall.'

'It's about time.' Pia took off her wet jacket.

'Nothing from Erik Stadler yet, but the Winklers called back,' Ostermann went on.

Bodenstein nodded and handed him the binder that Stadler had let him borrow.

'The trial documents for *Stadler v. the UCF*,' he said. 'Maybe we'll find some names that we don't know yet.'

'I'll check it right away,' Ostermann promised.

'After the press conference, we'll drive to Glashütten to talk to the Winklers,' Bodenstein decided. 'Is that okay with you, Pia?'

'Sure. But wouldn't it make more sense if I went to see Helen Stadler's fiancé? You don't need me at the town hall. I could also have another talk with the husband of today's victim.'

'Dr Engel will make that decision,' said Bodenstein, seeing his boss coming down the hallway. Her high heels hammered an aggressive staccato on the tiles.

'Already in battle uniform with knives whetted,' Ostermann remarked.

'I heard that.' Dr Engel rushed past them, leaving behind a cloud of verbena and lemon scent. 'What are you all standing round for? Go, go, get in there!'

After last evening's conversation with Kim, Pia puzzled over what her sister could find so fascinating about Dr Nicola Engel. Even after a long, exhausting day, this woman never seemed to run out of energy. As always, she looked perfectly turned out from head to toe: meticulously varnished nails, discreet make-up, and her hairdo looked immaculate, as if she'd just come from the hairdresser. She wore a bright green suit with a single strand of pearls, a multicoloured scarf and five-inch patent leather heels. Although Pia knew that Engel and Bodenstein had been a couple aeons ago and at one time were even engaged, she secretly imagined that Nicola Engel had no bed at home; at most, she had some sort of electronic recliner to sit on, and she would arise fully charged the next morning and ready to carry on. It was impossible to picture this woman ever wearing worn-out jogging pants or a faded T-shirt as she sprawled comfortably on the sofa with no make-up on. Bodenstein seemed to have a weakness for high-maintenance women who raced through life full-speed ahead. Cosima von Bodenstein was the same type, and Inka Hansen was also essentially a cool, determined workaholic.

'Ladies and gentlemen, please take your seats,' the commissioner said to the team. 'In half an hour, the press conference will begin at the town hall, and I don't want to be late.'

Present were Bodenstein, Ostermann, Altunay, Fachinger, Kim Freitag, Andreas Neff and a few officers from other units who were working on the special commission. Bodenstein and Pia took turns reporting on what happened and what was learned that day.

Nicola Engel had agreed that immediately after the meeting, Pia, Cem and Kim would go to see Helen Stadler's fiancé, who ran a goldsmith's shop on the main street in Hofheim.

'So, here we go,' she said with a look at her watch. She was ready for action. 'Ostermann, where is the statement for the press?'

'Here it is, fifteen copies.' Kai handed her a thick stack of papers in a folder, which she promptly handed to Bodenstein.

'I've also compiled the most important points in my profile of the perpetrator,' said Andreas Neff eagerly, straightening his tie. 'I think it best if I speak after you and—'

'You will not be speaking at all. At least not to the media,' Engel told him firmly as she slipped on her coat.

'But I have the necessary expertise to—'

'We've got plenty of expertise for the moment.' Dr Engel didn't even look at him. 'Joining me on the podium will be Bodenstein as lead investigator, the head of the police force, the press spokesman and someone from the state attorney's office.'

'Then I might as well go home,' moaned Neff, visibly disappointed. 'Obviously, nobody here appreciates my abilities.'

'I appreciate it when someone takes their proper place on the team and does the job for which he was brought in,' Engel snapped, giving him a sharp look as they stood at the security gate. 'To my knowledge, you are a case analyst. Your task is to deduce from crime-scene evidence the sequence of events of the crime and correlate them with the other crimes, supplementing the work of my investigators. You are not qualified to make conjectures about the psyche of the perpetrator. That's a matter for the forensic psychiatrist.'

'I've never heard that there's some quota of women that has

to be met,' Neff fired back, insulted. 'But everything here seems to be firmly in female hands.'

'Let's go, ladies and gentlemen. I don't want to keep the press waiting.' Nicola Engel signalled to the officer at the gate to release the lock. She strode outside and then noticed the rain. 'Bodenstein, do you have an umbrella?'

'Red-haired biddy,' Neff sniped behind her. 'She really needs a man.'

'And it would do you good to have your balls in a woman's hand once in a while,' Kim said to him in passing.

Neff turned bright red. Nicola Engel, who had heard the comment, turned round and grinned.

'Wait a minute! Stop! I have something important to tell you.' Christian Kröger came storming down the corridor excitedly.

'We're running late, Kröger,' said Nicola Engel. 'What is it?'

'We know where the sniper fired the shot that killed Hürmet Schwarzer!' he shouted, almost out of breath. 'With the data we gathered, we were able to reconstruct the crime. Body size of the victim, angle of the shot, et cetera.'

'We know how it works,' Nicola Engel interrupted him impatiently. 'Get to the point.'

'We're not dealing with just a good or a very good shooter . . .' Kröger refused to be rushed. He even took time for a dramatic pause. 'This guy is an *extraordinarily* good marksman, undoubtedly a trained sharpshooter or precision shooter, because he is able to do what nobody could do if shooting were just a hobby. He actually fired from the roof of a high-rise on Bremer Strasse in Eschborn. From a distance of almost a kilometre.'

'Are you sure that's correct?' Nicola Engel was sceptical.

'Oh yes. A hundred per cent. No doubt at all.' Kröger nodded emphatically. 'There's no other building that's high enough to create such an angle. We were on the roof and did a laser measurement: 882.9 metres – it's crazy!'

'We should check with all the shooting clubs in the area,' Ostermann suggested. 'An expert like that would have a reputation in those circles. And check the army and our own people: active and former reservists.'

'Good.' Engel nodded curtly. 'Get it done, Ostermann.'

'And send people to the high-rise,' Bodenstein added, having already popped open his umbrella. 'Ring every doorbell, talk to all the residents. And find out if there are any surveillance cameras.'

'Will do.' Ostermann saluted and nodded.

The police car pulled up at the foot of the stairs.

'Well done, Kröger,' said Nicola Engel. Then she turned away and under the protection of Bodenstein's umbrella hurried down the steps into the rain.

'Fantastic woman,' Kim murmured with a wink to Pia.

'Come on, we're leaving, too,' she replied. 'Maybe we can still catch this Mr Hartig.'

Bodenstein had never seen such a crowd at a press conference. In front of the town hall stood satellite trucks from all the TV networks in Germany, and the reporters were pushing their way to the accreditation counter in the foyer. Uniformed officers ushered Dr Engel, Bodenstein, the head of the police force and the press spokesman past the crowd. In a smaller room, State Attorney Rosenthal was already waiting to be updated on the latest developments.

'We have listed all the crime scenes with date and time in the handouts,' Dr Engel said after Bodenstein had finished his brief report. 'Since we're looking for help from the public, we have to give out detailed information; otherwise, it makes no sense.'

'I agree completely,' said the state attorney.

Bodenstein's mobile rang. Cosima. She had always had a talent for calling him at the least convenient moments.

'Excuse me,' he said, retreating to a corner of the room to take the call.

'Hello, Oliver!' his ex-wife shouted after he picked up. 'I just wanted to say that I'm on the train to Königstein. There weren't any taxi drivers at the airport who would take me to the Taunus.'

'I thought you were on your way to Siberia,' Bodenstein replied in amazement.

'It was just too cold for me.' Cosima laughed, but it didn't sound genuine. 'My team is still working, but I've pretty much lost interest. Shall I pick up Sophia later at your place?'

'Okay, if you like. She's with Inka. I'm stuck working on a tough case. And I have to go to a press conference right now.'

'Is it that sniper? People are completely hysterical about it.'

'I have to go, d—' He stopped himself. He'd almost let the word 'dear' slip out. After four years. Good God, he hoped she hadn't noticed.

'No problem,' said Cosima. 'I'll pick her up from Inka, if I can get from Königstein to Ruppertshain somehow.'

'Okay, I'll let Inka know that you're coming,' he said.

'Thanks. See you tomorrow.' And she ended the call.

In twenty-five years, Bodenstein had never seen Cosima leave a film expedition early – no matter what the external circumstances might be. Something didn't add up. Had she heard that her mother changed her will? Was that why she was coming back? He quickly sent a text to Inka. She would certainly not be sad if Sophia went back to her mother three weeks earlier than planned. The thought gave him a slight pang of regret.

His phone rang again, and this time it was Ostermann.

'Erik Stadler just came home,' he said. 'What should we do?'

'Just a sec.' Bodenstein went over to talk to Engel and the state attorney.

'Do you have enough circumstantial evidence for an arrest warrant?' Rosenthal wanted to know.

'Nothing really concrete,' Bodenstein admitted. 'I'm afraid it wouldn't be enough for the magistrate.'

'But enough for a temporary detention order, at any rate,' said Dr Engel.

'Okay, then bring him in and interview him,' agreed the state attorney, consulting his watch. 'We have to go.'

'Kai,' Bodenstein said to Ostermann, 'keep surveillance on Stadler's house in case he tries to take off. When I'm done here, I'll drive to Frankfurt and bring him in.'

On the way to the stage, where a table and five chairs had been set up, he texted Pia again and then turned off his smartphone.

'Closed at six thirty. What crap!'

Pia peered inside the dark window of the goldsmith's shop and tapped on the glass door. Maybe Jens-Uwe Hartig, the fiancé of the late Helen Stadler, was in a back room. But nothing moved, and the place remained dark.

'Goes home right on time,' said Cem. 'Have we got a private address for Mr Hartig?'

'Unfortunately, no.' Pia pulled out one of her last business cards and sat in the car to write a note on the back. The long day, the relentless tension and the damp cold were taking their toll. She was feeling irritated, her whole body ached and she wanted nothing more than to go home and curl up on the sofa. Just as she was climbing out of the car, an elderly man appeared. He came over and planted himself right in front of her.

'Can't you read the signs over there? This is a pedestrian zone!' he snapped at her. Pia's quota of courtesy and forbearance was all used up for the day.

'Go and buy yourself some new glasses,' she responded. 'Vehicles aren't allowed from nine a.m. to six p.m., but it's six thirty now.'

She left him standing there and went over to drop her card through the shop's letter box.

'Let's drive up to the Winklers in Glashütten,' she said to Cem and Kim. 'That's more important.'

In the meantime, the old man had fished a mobile phone out of his jacket pocket and was standing in front of the car to take a picture of the number plate. Pia paid no attention to him and handed the keys to Cem.

'Can you drive? I've had it for today.'

'Sure.' Her colleague took the keys and got in behind the wheel. Pia got in the passenger seat, and Kim sat in the back. During the trip, no one spoke, and Pia was grateful for the peace and quiet. The roads were deserted, and when they reached Königstein, the rain turned into a heavy snowfall. Pia finally noticed the text from Bodenstein.

Erik Stadler has turned up. After the press conference I'll go see him.

Erik Stadler. Was he close to his sister? What was it like for him to look on as she suffered all those years? Was his sister's suicide the cause of the murders? Erik Stadler and his father had a double reason to hate Renate Rohleder, Dieter Rudolf and Fritz Gehrke. Pia yawned. It was so hot in the car that it made her tired. Right now, she could have been on a ship with Christoph, sitting in the sun, without a care in the world. Instead, she was driving through the snowy dark, making no progress on the investigation. It was terrible having to react instead of being able to act. Four dead! And they were still fumbling in the dark.

'Here we are,' Cem said suddenly, startling Pia. 'The light's on, looks like they're home.'

Kim closed her iPad and they got out, trudging through ankle-deep snow to the Winklers' front door. Pia rang the bell.

Lydia Winkler, the mother of Kirsten Stadler, was a slight woman with short hennaed hair and a worn-out face full of wrinkles.

'Please come in,' she welcomed them. 'I'm sorry you had to drive up here in such terrible weather.'

'No problem.' Pia forced a smile. 'Fortunately, the state of Hessen allocates winter tyres for our official cars.'

The house was bigger than it looked from outside. It was built in typical seventies style, with dark wooden ceilings, Persian rugs on dark-brown tiles, old-fashioned curtains and huge windows with metal frames. It resembled Fritz Gehrke's place. Mrs Winkler led them into the living room, which was as big as the entire ground floor of Pia's house at Birkenhof, though it looked smaller because of the dark ceiling beams.

'Just a minute, and I'll get my husband.' The woman vanished without inviting them to sit down. Pia, Cem and Kim exchanged glances, then looked round the room. On a sideboard stood dozens of framed photos, and Pia examined them curiously. Most of them showed Kirsten Stadler or her children at various ages; the son-in-law was nowhere to be seen. Photos of their dead daughter also hung on the walls. Kirsten Stadler had been a pretty girl and later an attractive woman with a warm smile.

It took quite a while before Mrs Winkler reappeared, her spouse in tow. He was a good bit taller than his wife, with a sinewy bald head and thin face, bitter lines etched round his mouth. In his light blue eyes lurked an irritability just waiting to surface at the slightest provocation. Pia thought he was disagreeable at first sight.

'Ah, the police. I don't suppose you could have thought to come later,' said Joachim Winkler sullenly, shoving his hands demonstratively in his trouser pockets. Pia didn't reply, and for a moment, there was an uncomfortable silence. It was very warm in the house, and she felt herself sweating. Her mouth was as dry as dust, and she had developed an instant headache.

'What do you want from us?' Winkler asked brusquely.

'You may have already heard from your son-in-law, Dirk Stadler, that the sniper murders in recent days are most probably linked to the death of your daughter,' Pia began without preface. Winkler's hostile expression darkened when she mentioned the name of his son-in-law.

'No, we didn't know that,' Winkler replied gruffly. 'We don't keep in contact with our daughter's husband.'

Neither he nor his wife asked what the link might be. They

seemed tense, but not particularly surprised or even interested. A disconcerting reaction.

'The murder victims are relatives of people who might have been connected with the death of your daughter,' Pia went on. 'Mr Stadler mentioned that he thought you might also have something to do with it.'

She noticed Cem's dumbfounded look but caught her mistake too late.

'What the—?!' Joachim Winkler exploded, his face crimson with indignation. 'How dare that man claim something like that?'

The conversation was clearly off on the wrong foot before it had really begun. Pia's clumsy misstatement, which had made Winkler see red, was due to fatigue or maybe because of her instinctive dislike of Stadler's father-in-law. But exhausted or not, as a professional, she should not have made such a mistake. It was best to turn over the interview to Cem, who was much more diplomatic than she was.

'Don't get excited, Jochen.' His wife reached out, tried to pat her husband's arm, but he roughly shook it off.

'I refuse to listen to this nonsense,' Winkler snorted in rage. 'I have nothing to say.'

He turned round abruptly and left the room with stiff strides. A moment later, somewhere in the house, a TV was turned on full blast.

'Please excuse me.' Pia shrugged regretfully. 'I expressed myself poorly, but we've been under enormous pressure for several days.'

'That's all right.' Lydia Winkler managed a strained smile. 'My husband is very sensitive when it comes to Kirsten. He still blames himself for everything that happened.'

Helen Stadler had felt guilty about her mother's death. And now her grandfather seemed to be blaming himself?

'But your daughter died of a cerebral haemorrhage,' said Pia. 'No one is to blame for that.'

'We've all been through some very difficult times. Our family was devastated by Kirsten's death. It's always hard to deal with a sudden, unexpected death, but when such circumstances are added, then it's even worse.'

'What circumstances do you mean?' Cem asked.

'It's a long story.' Lydia Winkler sighed and pointed to the sofa. 'Please have a seat.'

Karoline Albrecht had been to a few press conferences before, but she'd always been seated on the podium. Now she was standing in the crowd, among the reporters hungry for sensationalism, the camera people and the photographers, all of them waiting for what the police were going to announce. Konstantin Faber had sent her an e-mail telling her about the press conference to be held on short notice, but then added that he would not be attending. The turnout was large, and no one was actually checking accreditation or press cards, so it had been no problem for her to get into the hall.

It was a little past 7:00 p.m. when the police officers and the state attorney finally mounted the stage and sat down at the long table in front of a forest of microphones. Floodlights flared and cameras flashed. The chief of the Hofheim police, an energetic redhead named Nicola Engel in a bottle green suit, was first to take the floor. To Karoline's surprise, Engel laid all the facts on the table. She had assumed that the police would continue to keep things secret and cover up their lack of success in the investigation, not come out with such candour, no holds barred.

'You don't have to write everything down,' said Dr Nicola Engel to the reporters. 'We've prepared an extensive press release packet containing all the data and facts. Thank you for your attention. You may now ask questions.'

A veritable storm broke loose, everyone jumping up and shouting at the same time. The two young women in charge of holding microphones were overwhelmed until the red-haired woman stepped in and let one reporter after another take the floor.

'Do you have any hot leads?' someone asked.

The hall fell silent, the shutters clicked and the cameras flashed.

'Unfortunately, no,' replied Chief Detective Inspector von Bodenstein in a calm voice. 'This evening, we have presented all the facts that we have. We will inform you immediately when we learn anything that will help calm the public. But regrettably, we have nothing yet. For this reason, we would like to ask everyone in the Rhein-Main area to be on high alert. The only thing we can say with certainty at this time is that the perpetrator does not pick his victims at random. We cannot tell you any more today.'

At a quarter to eight, the press conference was over. The hall emptied quickly, and only a few TV people remained, packing up their gear. Karoline asked herself why she had come here at all. To her it felt as though the memory of her mother, who was referred to only as 'Victim No. 2', had been somehow sullied. She found herself wanting to grab one of the microphones and yell at this mob of sensation-seekers so they would finally show some respect. But then they probably would have pounced on her, on the daughter of 'Victim No. 2', and try to get background information or photos from her. Or – even worse – make a sob story out of her mother's death.

As Karoline crossed the foyer of the Stadthalle, she saw Inspector von Bodenstein, who was being badgered by a reporter with the words *Taunus Echo* on his shoulder bag. That made her curious. Faber, that coward, had sent one of his flunkies instead of coming himself. She slowed her pace and pricked up her ears.

'Do you think we just sit round, twiddling our thumbs?' Chief Inspector von Bodenstein was saying, and from his expression, she couldn't tell whether he was annoyed or furious. 'We have a dozen officers answering the hotline, and thanks to your colleagues' articles, they are flooded with calls.

'As of this afternoon, the perp was allegedly seen by about two hundred people, in every likely or unlikely location. Each of these tips has to be checked out. Perhaps you can imagine how much of our manpower that ties up and how much time and money are required.'

'But this way, you might get a tip that results in a real lead,' replied the reporter almost a little truculently.

'No, it's nothing but a waste of time.' Chief Inspector von Bodenstein looked at his mobile phone and frowned. 'Believe me, this isn't the first time in my life I've investigated a murder. I know when vital information should be made public and when it should be withheld. Freedom of the press notwithstanding. Tell Mr Faber that he ought to let me know when he finds out anything more, and preferably before he publishes it in your paper.'

'I do have some information of interest for you,' Karoline Albrecht heard Faber's colleague say as the inspector was about to leave. 'We've learned the identity of a lawyer who represented the clinic against the Stadler family back then. His name is Dr Peter Riegelhoff. Maybe he knows more about what happened.'

Stunned, Karoline gulped for air. That was something she had told Faber earlier in the day, after he assured her that she could speak to him in confidence. What a devious shithead! A bad feeling crept over her. What else had she told that journalist? Had she mentioned any other names? What if that caused problems for the police?

'I hope that you and Mr Faber do not try to investigate on your own,' the inspector said to the reporter. 'That could have fatal consequences. And it's dangerous. Tell Mr Faber that he must honour our agreement. Good evening.'

With that, he turned away and strode off.

Karoline watched him go. Should she stop him and tell him that she'd talked to Faber? But what could she say that he didn't already know? All her information came from Renate Rohleder, who had got it from the police. She stepped outside into the fresh air, pulled up the hood of her coat, and watched Bodenstein and his red-haired boss get into a black car.

No. It was way too soon to bother the harried inspector with some vague theory of hers.

Relieved, Pia sat down between Cem and her sister on the sofa. Lydia sat down across from them in an easy chair. In a calm voice, she told them what had happened on 16 September 2002 – how she had got the desperate phone call from her grandson, Erik, who sobbed that his mama had collapsed and wouldn't wake up.

'My husband and I drove to Niederhöchstadt at once to

pick up the children,' she said. 'And then we drove to the hospital where Kirsten was taken. Erik and Helen were completely out of it, Dirk was abroad and couldn't be reached by telephone. At the hospital, they informed us that Kirsten had suffered a cerebral haemorrhage and had been without sufficient oxygen for too long. She was brain-dead. We were completely in shock and couldn't comprehend what the doctors were saying. Kirsten was in the ICU and looked as if she were asleep. She was on a respirator, but her skin was warm. She was even sweating and . . . and her digestion was functioning.'

Lydia Winkler paused briefly and swallowed hard. Then she took a deep breath and went on.

'The doctors told us frankly that the haemorrhage had irreparably damaged large parts of her brain stem and the cerebrum. They began to pressure us to make the decision to release her organs for donation. It . . . it seemed like murder to us to cut her up and let her organs be removed, because she . . . she seemed so alive.'

The woman's voice broke again, and she fought back tears. The pain was deep-seated; what had happened was still so present, as if it had occurred only a short time ago. Dirk Stadler had been on the other side of the world and couldn't be reached, and the Winklers were completely overwhelmed as the doctors at University Clinic Frankfurt pressured them to make a decision. They had never spoken with their daughter about organ donation and didn't know whether she possessed an organ donor card or had made a provision in her will.

'We begged them to wait for Dirk, but the doctors pressured us even more. They wanted us to feel a moral obligation, telling us about patients who could be helped. They were relentless.' Lydia twirled her reading glasses between her fingers and forced herself to continue her story. To make matters worse, Erik, then seventeen, had overheard a conversation between two doctors and understood that they had given up on saving his mother's life. The measures taken in intensive care were aimed only at keeping her organs functional.

'The boy went crazy,' Lydia recalled. 'He threw a fit, yelling and screaming. We couldn't calm him down. At some point, they sent us all home. And when my husband and I arrived at the hospital the next morning, we learned that the doctors had taken matters into their own hands. During the night, they had taken out everything from our child that could be taken out, even . . . even her eyes and bones! She had been literally eviscerated.'

She paused briefly and grimaced. It was clearly proving very hard for her to maintain her composure.

'The way she looked as she lay in the morgue, nothing but an empty shell; it was horrendous. They had sealed up her empty eye sockets,' she said in a trembling voice. 'And she looked as though she'd suffered tremendous pain. We had wished a peaceful death for Kirsten, going to sleep surrounded by family after the life-support systems were turned off, but that was not to be.'

Dirk Stadler returned the next day from the Far East, and they presented him with the authorization to remove organs, signed by his father-in-law. Joachim Winkler had protested again and again that he never signed such an authorization, merely a power of attorney for the treatment, because at the time she was admitted, Kirsten Stadler was no longer able to make any decisions for herself.

'But there was his signature in black-and-white,' Lydia

continued. 'They had deceived us, but in the end, it was our word against theirs. Later they claimed that because of the extreme emotions of the situation in which we found ourselves, my husband probably hadn't listened properly. That made him terribly bitter, because he couldn't prove they were wrong.'

'Is that why your son-in-law sued the UCF?' Cem asked.

'Yes, that was one of the reasons,' said Lydia. 'But we were most concerned about how Kirsten was treated there. She stopped being a human being in the eyes of the doctors when it was clear that she would die. They were like vultures. It was simply revolting the way they dug everything out of her body. It was so . . . so disrespectful!'

'How was the lawsuit resolved?' asked Cem.

'Dirk and the clinic later reached an agreement out of court. He received a payment for damages, and the clinic paid his legal fees. For me, that's the same as an admission of guilt.'

Pia secretly revised her overhasty judgement about Joachim Winkler. At the same time, she recognized that the man had the perfect motive for the murders. The only question was whether a seventy-year-old would be physically capable of committing those murders.

'Your son-in-law told us that you and your husband are active in a type of support group,' Pia now said.

'Yes, that's right,' said Lydia Winkler. 'After Kirsten's death, we felt like we'd been turned to stone. There was no one we could talk to about our doubts and our guilt feelings. Our granddaughter found the group on the Web. HRMO is an association of relatives who have had similar experiences to ours. Parents whose minor child has been released for organ donation after an accident, spouses, parents of grown children.

No one is prepared for a situation in which they have to make a decision of such consequence. To see your loved one no longer as a human being, as a dying person, but merely as . . . as inventory, as a warehouse for replacement parts, that's the worst thing anyone can experience. Death is bad enough; when it's handled with such a lack of dignity, then it's something you can never forget. Even today, ten years later, I still dream about what happened almost every night, and it doesn't make me feel any better that Kirsten helped some other people to live. Her life was not saved, and as a consequence, Helen was also destroyed.'

His fourth victim was finally deemed worthy of a special report by the television stations. They reported live from the press conference held by the police. The press was now calling him the 'Taunus Sniper'. Who had come up with such a histrionic name? He listened to the broadcast and it confirmed his suspicion that the police investigators were clever.

'At the moment, we are assuming that the crimes are related,' said the lead investigator, a good-looking man with a striking face and a sonorous baritone voice. He would have fit in well with the cast of one of those American TV series like Criminal Minds *or* Cold Case. *'The motive of the perpetrator is revenge, but his victims are not the actual targets. Their relatives are the real targets.'*

'Congratulations, Mr von Bodenstein. You're on the right track.' With a mocking smile, he raised his beer bottle in a toast to the inspector on the screen. Then he took a big swig and bit into his cheese sandwich.

Finally the police were doing what he'd long expected them to do: they were asking the public for help, looking for witnesses and presenting an astounding number of facts about the four victims. They had now revealed the precise circumstances of the murders as well as dates, times and locations. They even showed portions from Google Maps, just as they did on the TV programme Germany's Most Wanted.

He leaned back and thought it over. His pursuers were coming closer, yet they were fairly clueless, and that was good. They wouldn't catch him too soon, although the air was growing thinner for him each day, and in the future, he would have to be even more careful. He should have allowed himself more time. Something he hadn't thought about was the panic that had been stirred up. In the introduction to the show, the TV people had interviewed a waitress, a retailer, the director of a shopping centre, and a bus driver. Everyone feared being the madman's next victim, so almost no taxis or buses were running, taverns had closed because their patrons were staying home, and parcels were stacking up at delivery services because the drivers refused to work. The whole thing had assumed proportions that he hadn't foreseen, but it left him just as cold as the descriptions they had given of him. He didn't give a damn if they considered him a lunatic, a maniac, a psychopath or an ice-cold killer. One day, he would explain his motives, even if he had to wait until a courtroom appearance. He grabbed the remote and turned off the TV. In the sudden silence, he heard the rain drumming against the windowpanes. He would see the whole thing through to the end. He had given his word.

Joachim Winkler had the perfect motive; there was no doubt about that. The more his wife told them about her husband and his deep despair, the more obvious it was to Pia that he could be their perp. Consumed by self-reproach, pain and impotent rage, he'd been living under a tormenting, irrational guilt. There was no proof that he had been deceived by the doctors at the clinic when he had signed a putative power of attorney for Kirsten's treatment. For a know-it-all, self-righteous person like Winkler, this had probably been the bitterest defeat that he could suffer. And he knew all the people who had been involved with his daughter's death. Lydia Winkler stated that her husband had pursued the suit against the UCF with true obsession. From that point on, his whole life had been shaped by his wish for retaliation.

'Thank you for your candour,' said Cem kindly and sympathetically, as was his way. 'I can imagine how difficult it must be for you to speak about all this.'

'I hope it will help you make some progress in the case,' replied Lydia Winkler with a sad smile.

She got up from the sofa. The TV in the next room was turned off, but Joachim Winkler did not reappear.

'Does your husband happen to own a gun?' asked Pia, following a hunch.

'Yes, several,' Lydia said with a hesitant nod. 'He used to be a good sharpshooter and passionate hunter. But that was a long time ago.'

'Could we take a look at the weapons?'

'Of course.'

They followed her through the kitchen into a large double garage, occupied only by an older-model white Mercedes. Next to a workbench and a deep freeze stood a metal gun cabinet. Mrs Winkler took a key from a drawer in the workbench and opened the cabinet. Five rifles. Four repeating rifles and an air rifle. Pia pulled on latex gloves and took out one weapon after another, looked in the barrels and the magazines, and sniffed them. Mrs Winkler watched her do this with growing distress.

'Do you think that my husband had something to do with these murders?' she asked, upset, as Pia put the last rifle back in the cabinet and shook her head. None of these guns had been used recently.

'We're not drawing any conclusions,' Cem hastened to say. 'But we are duty bound to follow up on every lead.'

Mrs Winkler closed the gun cabinet and glared at Pia.

'My husband has Parkinson's. Without his pills, he can't even shave himself.' She pressed a switch, and the garage door rattled open. 'I'm sure you can find the way to your car. Goodbye.'

'Goodbye,' replied Cem. 'And once again, many thanks.'

Lydia Winkler nodded mutely, her hand on the switch. The garage door instantly closed behind them.

'She was pissed off,' said Kim as they trudged through the snow along the driveway, which had not been shovelled.

'I couldn't care less,' said Pia. 'The old man has a motive and is boiling with hatred. It wouldn't surprise me if he's involved somehow.'

'He has Parkinson's,' Cem reminded her.

'So what? That simply means that he couldn't do the shooting himself. But he could certainly do the planning and surveillance.'

They reached the car. Cem took a short broom out of the boot and swept the snow off the windscreen and rear window as Pia and Kim got in the car.

'The perp *must* be closely associated with Kirsten Stadler,' said Pia after Cem got in and started the engine. 'Widower, son, parents. They all have a motive, and maybe even two motives because of Helen's suicide. We have to check the alibis of all of them.'

'He's been there since seven fourteen p.m. and hasn't left the apartment,' reported one of the two officers who had been staking out the building on Adlerflychtstrasse in the North End, where Erik Stadler lived.

'Is he alone?' Bodenstein asked.

'No idea,' replied the uniformed officer. 'There are ten apartments in the building, so there's constant coming and going.'

'How did he arrive? In a car, on foot?'

'On foot. He was wearing jogging clothes.'

'Okay.' Bodenstein looked up at the brightly lit penthouse. 'Then let's go in.'

They crossed the road and went to the street door. Bodenstein didn't want to warn Stadler and possibly give him a chance to escape, so he pressed one of the lower buttons and hoped that the nameplates were arranged according to the location of the apartments. A woman who lived on the ground floor opened the door. After she had seen Bodenstein's ID and the uniformed officer, she merely nodded and then closed her door. They took the lift to the eighth floor and then walked up a couple of steps to the penthouse. They could hear loud techno music through the closed door to the apartment. Bodenstein rang the bell. The music stopped, footsteps approached and the door opened. Erik Stadler was wearing only boxer shorts and a white vest, which revealed his buff torso. There was an artistic tattoo on Stadler's left shoulder. He raised his eyebrows when he saw the police.

'Did the stodgy bastards downstairs complain about the

noise again, eh?' he said. Then he recognized Bodenstein. An anxious expression came into his eyes, and his smile suddenly seemed forced. 'Is that why the Kripo is here?'

'Good evening, Mr Stadler,' replied Bodenstein. 'We're not here because of the music. May we come in?'

'Yes, please do.' He stepped aside and let them in.

Like his father, Erik Stadler also seemed to have a penchant for extravagance. Most of the load-bearing walls had been replaced by support columns, so as to create a very spacious room. Floor-to-ceiling windows allowed a view over the roofs of the financial district. At the far end was an open kitchen, and next to it, stairs led up to a gallery. A lovely apartment, and certainly not cheap in this part of Frankfurt.

'What's this about?' Erik Stadler wanted to know. He was trying to act relaxed, but he was not. Uneasiness was oozing out of every pore of his body.

'Where were you today at round one p.m.?' Bodenstein asked him.

'Right here,' Stadler said. 'I was working here at home, as I often do. I can concentrate better here than at the office.'

'Do you have any witnesses?' In his career, Bodenstein had looked into the faces of many individuals who tried to lie to him. They all thought they could fool him, but very few succeeded.

'No, why?' Erik Stadler was an amateur liar with a guilty conscience. He was having trouble maintaining eye contact with Bodenstein.

'Where were you on Wednesday, December nineteenth, round eight in the morning?' Bodenstein asked without answering Stadler's question. 'On Thursday, December twentieth, at seven in the evening, and on Tuesday, December twenty-fifth, round eight in the morning?'

Stadler pretended not to understand.

'On the twenty-fifth? That was Christmas.' He scratched his head, tugged on his earlobe and his nose, and crossed his arms. 'I was out running early that morning. I exercise a lot, to balance out all the hours I spend sitting at a computer.'

'Where were you running, and between what times exactly? Did anyone see you? Did you speak to anyone?'

'I can't remember. I run every day. Why is this important?'

Bodenstein didn't let Stadler's questions throw him off track. He noticed the sweat on the man's forehead, the nervous fidgeting of his hands, the evasive gaze. Nobody remained calm when being questioned by the criminal police. Bodenstein knew that. But Stadler's nervousness exceeded the norm.

'You're a biathlete?' he asked. 'Unusual for someone from this neighbourhood.'

'During my stint in the army, I was in the alpine division,' replied Stadler, and this time he was telling the truth. 'That's how I got into the biathlon. Nowadays, I seldom have time for skiing.'

'But you do have time for other unusual extreme sports.'

'Now and then. What are you getting at?'

'Are you a good shot?'

'Yes. In the past, I was pretty good, at least. But that was several years ago.'

Bodenstein mentioned the names of the sniper's victims, but Stadler apparently knew only Ingeborg Rohleder, the mother of his former neighbour, and Professor Rudolf. He claimed he'd never heard the names Maximilian Gehrke or Hürmet Schwarzer.

'Mr Stadler, you don't seem to have sufficient alibis for the times I asked you about,' Bodenstein said. 'I must advise you that you are under suspicion of having committed four murders. Because of that, I need to ask you to come with us to police headquarters.'

'You can't be serious!' Stadler protested. 'I'm no murderer!'

'Then tell me what you were doing during the times when the murders were committed.'

'I . . . I can't.' Stadler again ran his hands over his hair. 'I'll have to think about it.'

'You'll have plenty of time to do that down at the station,' Bodenstein said. 'Please get dressed and pack a few things. My colleague will accompany you.'

'Am I under arrest?'

'Temporarily detained,' replied Bodenstein, and read him his rights.

'You're making a big mistake. I have nothing to do with this,' Stadler declared.

'I hope so, for your sake.' Bodenstein turned away. 'Please hurry.'

Ten minutes later, they took the lift down to the ground floor. A woman approached them in the foyer. She had short black hair and was wearing sports garb under a light-coloured trench coat.

'Erik!' she exclaimed when she recognized the man walking between the two police officers. 'What . . . What's going on?'

'Lis, I . . .' Stadler began, and wanted to stop, but the officers hurried him along.

'What's going on?' The woman dropped her sports bag. 'I

want to speak to my boyfriend. Why are you taking him away? Where are you taking him?'

Bodenstein barred her way.

'To Hofheim,' he said. 'We have to speak with him.'

'Yes, but ... what ... ?' She broke off, staring at him wide-eyed. 'But you're ... I saw you before on the TV, didn't I?'

He nodded and saw the horror in her eyes as she put two and two together and understood. Her shoulders slumped. She turned away, sat down on the stairs, and began to cry.

It was eleven o'clock when they got home. Bodenstein had treated everyone at the office to another round of pizzas, so neither of them was hungry. Kim had already disappeared into her room with a yawn. That gave Pia a chance to Skype with Christoph, who had Wi-Fi on board the cruise ship. For a few minutes, she could forget the whole unpleasant day and laugh with him as he comically described the other guests.

'You look exhausted,' he told her.

'I had a tough day. We now have a fourth dead body, and we're still pretty much fishing in the dark. For some reason, the case isn't making any progress. Sometimes I wish I could just beam myself over to you.'

'Me, too.' He smiled sympathetically, then turned serious. 'I'm glad you're not staying alone at Birkenhof.'

'Yeah, I'm happy to have Kim with me,' Pia admitted.

It was comforting to talk to Christoph. Even though there were thousands of kilometres between them, she felt that he was very close.

'I wish you were here,' he said finally. 'Nothing seems right without you.'

His words warmed her heart. Tears filled her eyes. When his image was gone, she closed her laptop and stared for a while into space. Had she ever loved a man as much as Christoph? With Henning, it had been completely different. Even when he was out driving round and she didn't know exactly where he was, she had never missed him as much as she missed Christoph. Sometimes she'd actually been glad when Henning wasn't round.

Her thoughts wandered to Dirk Stadler. Christoph had lost his first wife, the mother of his three daughters, in a similar way. A stroke. Out of the blue. He had told Pia how it happened, and how full of despair he'd been, abruptly left alone with three little kids. All his dreams about living in Africa with his wife had gone to the grave with her. But his kids had forced him to keep going. Thanks to them, he had been able to cope with the loss of his wife and find his way back to life, just like Dirk Stadler. But Stadler had also lost his daughter ten years later. How would he react if it turned out that his son was a quadruple murderer? Did he know what Erik had done? All the facts were pointing to Erik Stadler as the perp. Bodenstein was fairly convinced that with the detention of Erik Stadler he had caught the sniper, but Pia wasn't so sure. Was it a sign of his innocence that he had not demanded to see his lawyer? Maybe tomorrow they would know more.

Kai had assiduously ploughed through the thick file that Dirk Stadler had lent him. To his disappointment, he found only the names of Professor Rudolf and the leader of the clinic, Professor Ulrich Hausmann. There was no mention of Patrick Schwarzer. Kathrin had spoken again this evening with the husband of the dead bakery saleswoman, but he couldn't remember ever having heard of a Kirsten Stadler. He'd been on strong sedatives and hadn't been able to give them any useful answers.

Pia's phone buzzed. She grabbed it and read the text that Kai had sent her.

> Are you still up? Just finished researching HRMO. Some creepy shit.

Attached was a link to a website. After talking with Christoph, she was wide awake, so she turned on her laptop and copied the link into her browser. It took her to the HRMO website – which was an acronym for Help for Relatives of Murder Victims of the Organ Mafia.

'Good God,' she murmured, and began to read.

HRMO was founded in 1998 by several people who under great duress had been pressured to donate their children's organs and signed a release only later to discover that their children, although declared brain-dead by the doctors, were not dead, but dying. Pia clicked on the button 'About Us' and learned that HRMO now had 392 members, including family members and other people who had been confronted with the topic professionally or were opposed to transplant procedures for other reasons. On the Web pages, individuals from all walks of life recounted the loss of their children, and hospital workers described the process of organ transplant. Pia was shaken by what she read. She had never known much about the topic of organ donation, and a few years earlier had cluelessly filled out an organ donor card. She dialled Kai's mobile number and he picked up at once.

'This is outrageous,' she said.

'Lydia Winkler also wrote an account,' said Kai.

'I've seen it.' Pia scrolled down. 'It's horrible! I'm going to cancel my donor card.'

'I don't think organ donation is bad – on the contrary,' said Kai. 'If as an adult you've been informed in detail and accepted the fact that you're not going to die in the presence of your loved ones, then it's all right. At least you can save lives that way.'

'Would you want to die like that?' Pia was horrified. 'Just imagine, you're not really dead, like that woman in the States who woke up on the way to the operating theatre.'

'There are precise guidelines for the establishment of brain death,' said Kai. 'The doctors have to establish proof of the clinical symptoms, and also the irreversibility of the patient's condition.'

'Do you think they can be relied on to do that?' Pia shuddered.

Kai didn't reply. Instead he said, 'I find it interesting to see what people in this forum are concerned about. Their biggest complaint is that while in a state of emotional crisis, they are morally pressured to agree to an organ donation.'

'Like Kirsten Stadler's parents were,' Pia said. 'The doctors told them about patients who would die if they didn't get a new heart or a new kidney immediately. Mrs Winkler told us that the doctors really put on the pressure, asking her whether she wanted to be responsible for another person's death because she was taking so long to decide. That's so absurd!'

'And then there's the fact that someone who is brain-dead doesn't even look dead,' Kai added. Pia heard the clacking of his keyboard. 'Given the state of shock that they're in, people don't realize that their loved one is going to die. Naturally, they hope that he'll regain consciousness. On the other hand, the doctors can't wait forever, because organs can be removed only from a living person, not a dead body. According to the definition, someone who's brain-dead is dead. I was looking at a linked article about a conference of the German Ethical Board, which posed the question, "In practice, what is the protocol regarding morality and human dignity associated with the definition of brain death?" And the conclusion is: "The brain-dead individual is physical existence on the cellular level, but without any capacity for understanding or social interaction – signifying a vegetative state and not life." In the definition of brain death, the interests of transplant medicine have always played a role.'

As he spoke, Pia clicked on the masthead of the website.

'Joachim Winkler is deputy chairman, Lydia Winkler is secretary,' she interrupted her colleague. 'The chairman is a Mark Thomsen who lives in Eppstein, which is also the official seat of the organization. There's even an emergency hotline. The HRMO people are on call round the clock to offer assistance to anyone in a crisis situation.'

'Are Erik Stadler and his father members?' Kai asked.

'They're not listed on the board, at least,' said Pia. 'There is no communication between Dirk Stadler and his in-laws, and he has spoken disparagingly about HRMO. I don't think he's involved. I suspect that he decided long ago not to think any more about that topic. If someone continues to dwell on a particular problem, he won't be able to get over it eventually. And I got the impression that Dirk Stadler has successfully dealt with the loss of his wife. In any case, he's no lone wolf sociopath. He has good relations with his neighbours, for example.'

'Hmm,' was all Kai said.

'I've thought over the fact that the murders of Hürmet Schwarzer and Maximilian Gehrke don't really fit into the pattern,' Pia said, changing the topic. 'Why did Gehrke have to die? Because he received Kirsten Stadler's donor heart?'

'No, because the perp wanted to punish his father,' Kai countered.

'For what?' asked Pia. 'What had his father done?'

'He's influential and has a lot of money,' said Kai. 'He may have bribed someone so that his son could get a new heart sooner.'

'But that doesn't make sense at all.' Pia shook her head. 'Eurotransplant decides who gets an organ. And they have to match the parametres. Not everyone can tolerate every organ.'

'Don't you read the newspapers?' Kai asked with a mocking undertone. 'Right now, there's a juicy scandal in the news because cheating has been going on at the clinics, and patients who really shouldn't have been allowed to get a new liver got one anyway.'

'I know.' Pia had to yawn. 'We're going to have to ask an expert exactly what the procedure is. I'm just afraid they're all going to stonewall us if we ask them that sort of question.'

'Then ask your ex,' Kai suggested, yawning, too. 'Maybe he knows. Well, I think I'm hanging up work for tonight. Tomorrow is another day.'

They said good night, but Pia was still too wound up despite her fatigue to think about going to bed. She surfed the Net till far past midnight and learned things that made her understand why so many people preferred not to fill out an organ donor card.

SATURDAY, DECEMBER 29, 2012

In the night, the snow had stopped, and the temperature had climbed a few degrees. Bodenstein drove through the dim early morning light along the winding road from Ruppertshain to Fischbach. Late last night, Ostermann had sent him the address of Jens-Uwe Hartig in Kelkheim-Münster. Hartig's house was on the way to the station in Hofheim, so he decided to drop in and visit the fiancé of the late Helen Stadler before he talked to the man's brother.

Cosima had come to get Sophia last night, but Inka didn't stay the night with him. She was going to have to get up several times during the night to check on a horse that had been operated on for colic, so it was more practical for her to stay at home. At first, he thought of proposing that he go to her house – maybe she had secretly even counted on it – but after such a strenuous day, he felt like being alone and not doing any more talking. Down the hill in Kelkheim there was thick fog, and it was a couple of degrees colder than in Ruppertshain because of an inversion layer, which was common after a few winter days with no wind.

Bodenstein found the address without using the satnav. He got out and rang Hartig's doorbell, but there was no answer. Just as he was about to return to his car, the front door of the apartment building opened and a woman with a pushchair and a dog on a lead came towards him.

'Let me help you,' he said. He held the door open for her until she had manoeuvered the dog and buggy outside. Then he showed her his ID and asked for Jens-Uwe Hartig.

'He just drove off a minute ago,' said the woman. 'No

doubt headed for the cemetery. Since it happened, he goes there every morning before work.'

'Since what happened?' Bodenstein asked.

'Well, since his girlfriend killed herself. Two weeks before the wedding. It's really been hard on him.'

The dog was jumping round impatiently, getting the lead tangled up in a wheel of the pushchair.

'Did you know his girlfriend?' Bodenstein bent down to untangle the lead.

'Thanks.' The woman smiled. 'Yes, I did know Helen. She stayed with him now and then.'

'But she didn't live here permanently?'

'No. After the wedding, they were going to move to Hofheim. He has a house there. But now he doesn't want to live there without her.'

'I see. Do you happen to know which cemetery Helen is buried in?'

'At the Main Cemetery.' The woman took a step towards him and lowered her voice. 'Her father lives in Liederbach, but Jens-Uwe wanted her to be buried in Kelkheim. So that he can "take care" of her. Sounds a little freaky, don't you think?'

Bodenstein thought so, too. He thanked the informative neighbour and headed off to the Main Cemetery.

'What was it like ten years ago?' Pia wanted to know. 'Were the procedures as strictly administered back then as they are today?'

She and Kim were sitting across from Henning at his desk in the Institute for Forensic Medicine. They had been listening to him explain how an organ transplant was conducted and what prerequisites an organ recipient had to meet. He also described the regulations, which were under strict oversight by the German Foundation for Organ Transplantation, in particular after the scandals in recent years, which had drastically reduced the willingness of the German public to become organ donors.

'Yes, even then, the regulations were very strict,' said Henning. 'Maybe not quite so much as they are today, but we learn from each instance of inappropriate behaviour and error, and then new regulations are adopted.'

'Would it be possible for someone to buy himself or a relative preferential treatment?' Pia asked.

'What are you getting at?' Henning took off his glasses, polished them, and looked at Pia with a frown.

'We're wondering why the sniper shot Maximilian Gehrke,' Pia replied. 'He was the recipient of Kirsten Stadler's heart. His father is rich. Maybe he pulled some strings with the doctors at the UCF.'

Henning put his glasses back on and thought about it.

'A patient on the Eurotransplant list can, of course, be registered as an especially urgent case,' he said at last. 'Although only high-urgency patients are considered anyway. If the histological and immunological conditions are a match and the patient happens to be nearby when there is a donor heart, then it might be possible.'

'Do you know of any cases when that has happened?' Kim asked.

'Not in the case of heart transplants. But these days, there's a lot of media coverage of donor livers,' Henning replied. 'For a heart, the body size and weight cannot deviate more than fifteen per cent. And naturally, the blood type must match. It's impossible to do a transplant across blood-type boundaries. In the past, attempts were made in the USA and in Switzerland.

In 1997, there was a successful transplant in Bern, but in 2004, a female patient died because the doctors apparently had confused the blood types of the donor heart and the recipient.'

'What do you mean, confused?' Kim asked in astonishment.

'If a donor heart has the universal type O, then it will match with all other blood types,' Henning explained in his best professorial tone. 'Conversely, however, a donor heart of blood types A, B or AB will not match with a recipient of blood type O. It's also unusual for anyone to pay to get an organ.'

Pia was disappointed, because she had believed she'd found the sniper's motive with regard to Maximilian Gehrke's father.

'Reasonably unusual, but not impossible,' Henning went on. 'In Germany, hundreds of people are waiting for a donor organ, but the willingness to donate is rather small compared to all the other European countries. That means that many patients have to spend months on a waiting list and in the meantime have to be treated with drugs. At the hospitals, the doctors who do the procedures are very familiar with these patients and their medical histories. If a potential donor is delivered to this clinic, the information is sent to Eurotransplant, which then sends back the names of several potential waiting high-urgency patients. But if the clinic says they have a possible recipient right there on-site, then that patient might receive preferential treatment. A heart must be transplanted within four hours of removal from the body of the donor; otherwise, it will no longer function.'

'How do you know all this?' Kim wondered.

'Just like you, I often serve as an expert witness for the

state attorney's office and clinics.' Henning smiled. 'If you like, I can try to find out more about this particular case.'

'That would be great.' Pia finished her coffee, looked at the clock, and got up. 'The UCF has stonewalled us completely. As if they have something to hide.'

'And they may well have,' said Henning with a nod. 'Something must have happened and they want to keep it quiet.'

'Kirsten Stadler's family sued the UCF back then, but the lawsuit ended in an out-of-court settlement and payment of damages,' Pia told him.

'Punitive investigations against doctors who are alleged to have acted negligently are often settled out of the public eye, and the lawsuits are dismissed,' Henning said, also standing up. 'But I do have to come to the defence of my fellow physicians. It's actually surprising that more things don't go wrong in hospitals, because the doctors and other personnel work under incredible pressure. It's common knowledge that after ten or twelve hours, no one is in any shape to concentrate anymore. And a surgeon and anaesthetist can't afford to make mistakes by not being able to concentrate. A car paint-sprayer can always paint over a bad spot, but the surgeon doesn't get a second chance. The pressure is intense, and the responsibility huge.'

They had reached the hallway when Pia thought of something else.

'Could you have a look and see whether a post-mortem was performed here last September on a Helen Stadler who committed suicide?' she asked her ex-husband, who seemed especially kindly disposed today. 'She threw herself in front of a commuter train on September sixteenth, 2012, in Kelsterbach.'

'Sure.' Henning nodded. 'I'll let you know.'

*

In the car park of the Kelkheim Main Cemetery, there was only one car at this early hour, a dark Volvo with a company name painted on the side: GOLDSMITH HARTIG IN HOFHEIM. Bodenstein parked next to it, climbed out, and walked through the foggy dimness up the steps to the entrance gate. The last time he'd been here was a couple of years ago, on a radiantly beautiful summer day, when the murdered teacher Hans-Ulrich Pauly was buried. Before the chapel of remembrance, he turned left and followed the main path. He liked the peace and quiet of cemeteries. Wherever he went with his family on holiday, he would make a point of visiting churches and taking long walks through the cemeteries. He liked to read the inscriptions on gravestones, wondering who these people were who had found their last resting place there. Old cemeteries in particular suited his slightly melancholy nature, and even Cosima's mocking criticism had never broken him of this habit.

Cosima. What could have happened? Why had she broken off the long-planned trip so suddenly? Did it have something to do with a man, a disappointment? Although they'd been divorced a long time now, he was not completely indifferent to his ex-wife's feelings, and he felt anger at whoever might have hurt her. As he slowly walked along the rows of graves through the fog, among the bare winter trees with rain dripping from their branches, he thought about how strange and unpredictable the human psyche was. No one had ever hurt and disappointed him so deeply as the mother of his three children, and yet here he was, feeling sympathy for her.

In the grey light of morning, Bodenstein became aware of a movement up ahead to his left. In a row of apparently new graves, some of which still had no gravestones but only a temporary wooden cross, he saw a man standing with bowed head and hands clasped. Bodenstein stopped at a respectful distance, but the man seemed to sense his presence. He looked up, turned round and came slowly towards him.

'Jens-Uwe Hartig?' Bodenstein addressed him.

The man nodded. He was in his late thirties or early forties and looked dazed. Red eyes, unshaven, his dark hair dishevelled. Bodenstein introduced himself.

'I visit her every morning,' Hartig said. His voice sounded hoarse. 'We were going to get married. The invitations had been sent out. Everything was ready, even the menu for the wedding breakfast. The honeymoon was booked. Three weeks in California, that was Helen's big dream. But in the end, they killed her.'

'Who killed your fiancée?'

Hartig stopped and rubbed his hand over his eyes.

'Her demons,' he replied softly. 'Her demons were stronger than my love. They hunted her down, and that's something I have to live with. But my life no longer has any meaning without Helen.'

'Joachim Winkler was previously a chemist; he worked for forty years for the former Hoechst AG.' Kai Ostermann had done careful research. 'Later he was with one of the subsidiaries of the group. He never ran foul of the law, but he's a registered gun owner and owns several hunting rifles.'

'We've seen them,' said Pia. 'But they haven't been used in years. How can we find out whether he really has Parkinson's?'

'I can take care of that,' Andreas Neff offered.

After her verbal exchange with Neff before the press conference last night, Pia hadn't expected him to show up, but he was right on time and seemed to have had a change of heart.

For the first time, he wasn't wearing a suit. Like the rest of them, he had on jeans and a jumper. Gone were his tie and his arrogant attitude, and he even apologized for his behaviour.

'Okay.' Pia wasn't an unforgiving person, and she was ready to give Neff a second chance. He was an experienced policeman, and in this situation, she needed every team member she could get.

She began the meeting without waiting for Bodenstein, because he had texted her to say that his conversation with Jens-Uwe Hartig might last a while. Cem reported on the visit to the Winklers; Pia and Kim then related what they had learned from Henning.

'What blood type was Kirsten Stadler?' Pia asked.

'I'm afraid I don't remember off the top of my head,' replied Kai, looking embarrassed.

'Give me the file,' said Kim. 'I'll see what I can find.'

Kai shoved over the file that Dirk Stadler had given Bodenstein.

'I've tried to reach this Professor Hausmann,' he said. 'He's still the medical director of the UCF. He's away over Christmas, supposedly somewhere far away, and he can't be reached by phone or e-mail. The clinic administrative staff at the UCF is still not cooperating. So far, we haven't received the staff list from 2002.'

'Then we'll have to work on some other angle. I propose that we form two groups, focusing on two different approaches.' Pia looked over at Nicola Engel standing in the doorway listening, but the chief nodded for her to keep talking. 'One covering the search for the sniper and the other the search for potential future victims.'

'Why don't we put them all under surveillance?' asked

Cem. 'The Winklers, Dirk Stadler, his son? We're fairly certain that the perp has to come from Kirsten Stadler's family circle.'

'That's not feasible, just from a personnel and cost perspective,' Dr Engel said from the doorway. 'Besides, our suspicions aren't solid enough. No judge in the world would approve that type of surveillance.'

'Then we'll send out beefed-up patrols,' Pia said. 'That's all we can do.'

They divided up the tasks, and then Pia adjourned the meeting.

'I'm going to interview Erik Stadler,' she announced. 'Kim, I'd like you to listen from the next room.'

'I'll go with you,' Nicola Engel offered, and Pia nodded, surprised. 'You do the questioning and I'll listen in.'

It was extremely rare for the chief to participate personally when a suspect was interviewed. But this case was also extremely tricky.

'All right, then,' Pia said. 'Let's go downstairs.'

Bodenstein was looking at the jewellery in the display cases of the small shop. Rings, brooches, chains, watches and clasps made of silver, gold and platinum, adorned with pearls, diamonds and gemstones, some simple, some artistic, with intricate filigree.

'You made all these yourself?' he asked, impressed.

'Sure. It's my profession.' Jens-Uwe Hartig smiled. 'Naturally, I do repairs, too, but it's much more fun to design my own jewellery.'

'And where do you work?' Bodenstein looked round.

'Come on, I'll show you the studio.' Hartig disappeared behind a curtain, and Bodenstein followed him down the hall to a surprisingly large room. There he saw four workbenches, shelves full of casting forms, chemicals, vices, plastic boxes of tools, and propane bottles.

'We make everything here ourselves,' Hartig declared, stroking the worn wooden top of one of the workbenches. 'Special commissions, reworking and refurbishing of old jewellery, as well as cleaning and repairs. But we also galvanize, forge, roll and solder.'

'We?' Bodenstein asked, looking at the tongs, files, saws and hammers hanging neatly at each workplace.

'I have two employees and one apprentice,' Hartig explained. 'The art of the goldsmith is one of the oldest types of metalworking in the world, and a truly fascinating profession. It requires creativity, but also patience and good motor skills. Naturally, we use laser welding tools and work with CAD technology, but I particularly love the traditional methods. This, for example, is a blowpipe.'

'Interesting. And the material that you work with? Where do you store that? It's pretty valuable, isn't it?'

'At night, we put everything in the safe,' replied Hartig. 'Filings are separated after alloying and recycled.'

He led the way from the workshop and stepped into a small room that obviously served as kitchenette, break room and office.

'Coffee?' asked Hartig, switching on the coffeemaker.

'Please,' Bodenstein sat down. 'Black.'

The grinder began to clatter as Bodenstein looked round. On the wall hung a large black-and-white photo of a beautiful young woman.

'That was Helen,' said Hartig, who had followed Bodenstein's eyes. 'My great love. My soul mate.'

'You miss her a lot, don't you?'

'Since her death, I feel like I'm only half a person,' Hartig admitted, setting down a cup of coffee for Bodenstein. 'Sometimes I ask myself whether I'll ever feel whole again.'

Bodenstein refrained from offering any pat phrases of sympathy or any pseudo-psychological advice. Instead he told the goldsmith the reason for his visit and his suspicion that the sniper might be someone the Stadlers knew, someone who was retaliating against those who had caused the family such suffering and pain.

Hartig leaned on the sink, coffee mug in hand, and listened attentively but without saying a word.

'When and where did you meet Helen?' Bodenstein asked.

'It was about four years ago. I gave a speech at a support group that her grandparents regularly attended. And Helen frequently came with them.'

His reply caught Bodenstein's attention.

'And why were *you* there? Have you also lost a relative?'

Hartig heaved a sigh and sat down at the table across from Bodenstein. He shoved a stack of notes aside and set down his coffee mug.

'Even worse,' he said bitterly. 'I am someone who has killed.'

'What do you mean?' Bodenstein asked, startled.

'I was a doctor.' Hartig leaned back. 'I come from a true dynasty of physicians. Great-grandfather, grandfather, father, uncle, cousins – all doctors. Not simple country doctors, but geniuses of medicine. Pioneers in their fields. Highly respected. That's the world I grew up in, and for me, there was nothing else. And God blessed me with the attributes that a good surgeon needs. Medical study was easy for me, and my name opened doors that remained closed to others. But I lacked the mental toughness and cold-bloodedness that are needed to become really good. I began to have doubts about what I was doing. I was too soft, too sympathetic.'

'And so you quit and became . . . a goldsmith?'

'The dexterity required in this profession is the same skill that a surgeon needs.' Hartig smiled but turned serious at once. 'But I no longer have to see the suffering that people go through, all the torment and pain, the despair of the patients and their relatives when they're told there is no more hope. And I didn't like the work atmosphere. In many clinics today, there is still a leadership culture reminiscent of the army. Dissent and independent thinking are forbidden. Maybe it would have turned out differently if my father hadn't felt compelled to make a cardiac surgeon out of me. He sent me to work with a friend who was a transplant surgeon. When I witnessed my first multivisceral transplant, I suffered a trauma. Do you know what the procedure is like?'

Bodenstein shook his head.

'From one moment to the next, the person is transformed from an intensive-care patient into a warehouse for replacement organs. Heart, lungs, liver, kidneys, pancreas, portions of the intestines, the bones, the tissues, the eyes – all of them are used. And it has to happen fast. In a multi-organ explantation, a team of surgeons comes from all over Germany and descends upon the body and tears it to pieces. Explantation of organs always takes place at night so that they don't disturb the hospital drainage system. The patient is brought in and is cut open. Iced water is poured into the opening in the body to cool the organs; then he is bled out. It's a totally hectic scene, with people running round in the operating theatre and yelling into phones. You stand up to your ankles in blood. There is always an anaesthesiologist present, because brain-dead patients still react – their blood pressure rises, they twitch, they sweat, like any living human being in sleep. And then it's over. Everyone suddenly disappears. I stood there alone with this empty shell of a human being, who only an hour earlier was still breathing. No one cared about him anymore. I ran through the hospital, trying to find someone who would at least sew up that bloodless, cold corpse.'

'What clinic did you work at?' Bodenstein asked.

'At the Dortmund Heart Center,' Hartig replied, rubbing his chin. 'There was such inhuman contempt for the dead body of the donor, and the staff showed no respect or sensitivity. I found it intolerable. It's not that I'm against organ donation per se. It can save lives, and I know that it has to be done fast at the crucial moment. What bothers me is *how* it's done. It's . . . without dignity. Most doctors have no respect for a person who has declared a willingness to help other individuals by donating his organs, and who thus relinquishes the opportunity to die surrounded by his loved ones. The current practice is simply unethical. There is no humility. The surgeons try to be faster and more efficient each time. And that's how mistakes are made. Organs are damaged, rendered unusable, and there are arguments and wrangling among competing surgeons. It's disgusting.'

'And that's why you left the medical profession?' Bodenstein asked. 'You could have chosen another branch of medicine.'

'That option never entered my mind,' said Hartig as he got up. 'Instead, I picked a fight with the system, because I really believed that I could change things. Would you like more coffee?'

'No thanks.'

'There are strict regulations to follow before an individual can be declared brain-dead,' Hartig continued after he'd poured himself another cup of coffee and sat back down. 'Regulations that are stipulated by the Federal Association of Physicians and by the German Foundation for Organ Donation. Every action must be precisely documented, because the definition of brain death is still being debated. Over the course of twelve hours, two independent doctors who have nothing to do with explantation must examine the patient. It must be twice determined that irreversible brain damage exists and the patient can no longer breathe independently. Only then is he declared brain-dead. Before that, of course, tests are done to determine possible suitability as an organ donor: these include identifying blood type, ruling out infectious diseases and so forth. A hospital is a business, however, and specialized clinics place great value on their reputations. Doctors want to be showcased, and use operating theatres on their CVs. Organ transplantation is and will remain the king of surgical disciplines. And unfortunately, that's why adherence to the regulations is often lax – something that receives the tacit consent of the hospital's administration and management. Many times, I witnessed how senior physicians of intensive-care medicine, neurosurgery and transplant surgery curtailed the prescribed examination times, though this was not officially documented. I reported this to my boss and got royally chewed out. I reported it to clinic management and was promptly muzzled. But I could no longer reconcile what was happening with my conscience. These regulations exist for a reason. That's why I reported another violation direct to the Federal Association of Physicians. I was personally threatened, but I didn't care. At that time, I was twenty-six and foolish enough to pick a fight with an all-powerful system in the name of justice and morality. But in the end, not a single one of those doctors suffered any repercussions. They just kept doing things the way they always had. I was out anyway, and my father was through with me. In his eyes, I had besmirched the family name, repudiating the unwritten rules of the brotherhood of physicians. I was a traitor.'

'What do you know about the case of Kirsten Stadler?' Bodenstein asked, drinking the last of his coffee, which was now tepid.

'Something similar must have happened,' said Hartig. 'Mistakes were hushed up, reports falsified, documents vanished. The anaesthesiologist's records disappeared into thin air. Or there may not have been any record at all, because with explantations there is technically no anaesthesia involved, since a brain-dead patient is officially regarded as dead. Other documents from the operating theatre may have been missing because they referred to external teams.'

Bodenstein studied the man, trying to assess him. His words carried a certain sense of resignation, but he didn't seem at all bitter or vindictive. Instead he seemed happy to have escaped a situation that he hadn't been able to cope with. The sadness in his eyes could be due to the loss of his great love rather than the fact that he had failed so colossally in his profession at such a young age. On the other hand, there might be a connection that shouldn't be overlooked. How deeply had Hartig been involved in the Stadlers' drama? How much had he made their tragedy his own? Hartig was not officially a member of the family, but he was quite close to being one. Did he know the name of the hospital staff member they were so urgently seeking? Were they finally nearing a breakthrough in this case?

For a moment, neither of them spoke.

'At HRMO, I've met a lot of people whose lives were destroyed by just such events,' Hartig said. 'I decided to go to bat for these people.'

'Against organ donation?' Bodenstein asked.

'No, not against organ donation as such,' Hartig replied. 'But against the procedures in the clinics. Against exerting moral pressure on relatives who are overwhelmed when confronting such a crucial decision regarding their child or partner who has been in an accident. I have seen more than once how relatives who are in shock succumb to the pressure inherent in the doctor's request for an organ donation. In the end, they acquiesced against their will because they didn't want to be responsible for the death of another person. And after that, their lives were destroyed. Hospitals and doctors must adhere to the guidelines and act according to ethical and moral principles. They must allow relatives more time. They must provide better and more comprehensive information, also mentioning how a decision against organ donation may have an effect. The lack of available organs is already proving fatal for many who are urgently waiting for a donor organ. Because of such scandals, there is a steady decrease in the number of people willing to become organ donors.'

'Did Helen share your opinion?'

'No,' said Hartig with a shake of his head, his gaze shifting to the photo on the wall. 'Helen was not in a position to hold an objective opinion. She took an extreme view, believing that organ donation was contrary to nature. She never got over the circumstances of her mother's death. It tore her up inside. I could not heal her.'

Karoline Albrecht parked in front of Fritz Gehrke's house in Kelkheim and got out of the car. The fog was hovering low between the houses, and it was getting colder. She went through the front gate and followed the path of concrete slabs that led to the house. She walked past an evergreen arbor vitae and the lawn with patches of snow, strewn with brown leaves. She shuddered when she saw the dark spot on the concrete slabs. This was how far Maximilian got before the fatal shot struck him down. Mama had died on the spot, but how fast was life extinguished when a rifle bullet exploded inside a body and shredded the heart? Did Maximilian have enough time to feel anything, think anything? One last thought that raced through his mind – or simply a rip in the film, then blackout?

The closer she got to the front door, the more she doubted her decision. Why did she have to disturb an old man grieving over the loss of his only son? In order to tell him that he was to blame? What Fritz Gehrke may have done ten years ago was understandable. What father wouldn't give his sick child an advantage if he could afford it and had the opportunity? She would have done the same for Greta. She stood at the front door for a full minute. Should she have phoned to announce her visit? Or was it better to have the element of surprise?

Karoline took a deep breath and pressed the doorbell. It took a moment before the door opened. She hardly recognized the man she hadn't seen in so long and remembered as full of energy. Only a sad shadow remained of that Friedrich Gehrke, who was once an important business leader in Germany and a member of dozens of boards of directors. This man was stooped and ashen-faced, with watery eyes.

'What do you want?' he asked. 'Who are you?'

'I'm Karoline Albrecht, the daughter of Professor Dieter Rudolf,' she said. 'Perhaps you remember me.'

The old man scrutinized her, and then an expression of recognition flitted across his lined face.

'Of course. Little Karoline.' Gehrke smiled briefly and held out a thin, age-spotted hand. 'It's been a long time.'

He opened the front door a little wider and gestured for her to come in.

'Well over twenty years,' said Karoline.

'Come in and take off your coat,' he said kindly. She removed her coat and hung it on one of the coat hooks, then followed him down the hall into a small living room.

'This isn't exactly a courtesy call,' she said after sitting down on an uncomfortable armchair. 'My mother was murdered. By the same person who killed your son.'

'I know.' Gehrke sat down, too, leaning his cane against the arm of his chair. 'I know. I'm so sorry. She was a wonderful woman.'

Karoline swallowed hard.

'I . . . I don't understand any of this,' she managed to say. 'And I want to find out why my mother had to die.'

'Unfortunately, there are often no explanations,' replied Gehrke. 'Sometimes we just have to accept things the way they are, as hard as that may be. Believe me, I'm also suffering terribly. Max was the only person I still cared about. He was just in the wrong place at the wrong time.'

Karoline looked at the old man in amazement. Didn't he read the papers? Hadn't the police told him anything about the background of the murders? Or was Gehrke possibly a bit demented?

'But that's not true,' she contradicted him. 'This killer isn't shooting people at random. The police think that the murders are connected to the death of a woman named Kirsten Stadler ten years ago. My father told me that back then she came into the UCF with an acute cerebral haemorrhage and became an organ donor after she was declared brain-dead. After every murder, the killer has sent the police an obituary in which he has offered an explanation. He accused my father of having killed out of greed and vanity. That's why Mama had to die.'

Fritz Gehrke stared at her in stunned silence.

'Please, Mr Gehrke, tell me what happened ten years ago, if you know,' Karoline pleaded. 'My father claims that it was all purely routine, but I can't believe it.'

She looked on in shock as tears filled the old man's eyes. Gehrke was clearly struggling to keep his composure and to find the right words.

'Was there also an . . . obituary for Maximilian?' the old man said hoarsely. There was a look of alarm in his eyes.

'Yes.' Karoline hesitated a moment, but then opened her handbag and took out the copy of the article and held it out to him. Gehrke hesitated before taking the piece of paper and reading the article.

Maximilian Gehrke had to die because his father implicated himself by approving of someone's death and by bribery.

The colour drained from his face and he uttered a tormented sound. His hand began shaking badly.

'May I keep this?' he whispered.

Karoline nodded uneasily.

Gehrke took a moment to regain his composure.

'Maximilian received the heart of this Ms Stadler,' he said huskily, and Karoline couldn't believe her ears. How could her father keep quiet about this detail? 'It was hard for him to cope with the fact that someone had to die so that he could stay alive. I . . . I was just so happy that he could be healed.'

'Yes, but . . . why was he then shot?' This piece of news thoroughly confused her.

'We did things that we thought were acceptable. All of us,' said Gehrke in a brittle voice. 'And now we have to pay for them.'

'My mother had to pay for something she knew nothing about,' Karoline contradicted him. 'Just like your son. I'm sure you can understand, Mr Gehrke, that I'd like to believe my father had nothing to do with my mother's murder. But if he did, then . . . then . . . I'll never be able to forgive him.'

Her voice failed her, and for a moment, she pressed her lips together and shook her head.

Gehrke grabbed his cane and laboriously stood up. He went to the window and looked out into the foggy twilight.

'I think it's better that you go now,' he said softly.

Karoline picked up her purse. 'I'm so sorry. I didn't want you to—'

'There's nothing for you to be sorry about,' the old man interrupted her, and raised his hand. 'I'm very grateful. Now at least I'm no longer tormented by wondering why my son had to die in such a manner.'

She looked at him and understood what he meant. As bitter as the truth might be, she, too, had been relieved when Faber showed her the obituary. But there was a difference between her and Fritz Gehrke, and she fervently hoped that it wouldn't make the old man fall apart: the killer's accusation was directed at him, just as it was at Renate Rohleder and at her father. Gehrke must know whether there was any truth to the claims made by the killer or whether the murders were only the crazy actions of a psychopath.

Spending a night in a solitary cell in police custody does something to a person who isn't used to being locked up and alone. The isolation and the feeling of impotence when the cell door shuts with a metallic clank are things that seldom pass without leaving a mark. Even Erik Stadler was nervous; he hadn't slept well.

Pia often conducted interviews in her office in order to create an atmosphere as relaxed and conversational as possible, so that the suspect might eventually confide in her. At the police college and in seminars, she had learned all types of interview techniques, and she knew which methods to use to get the suspect to talk, because it was important for the suspect to talk. Suspects often lied, but the more they talked, the more they got tangled up in their lies, especially under stress. Yet she decided not to have Erik Stadler brought to her office. Instead, he was taken to one of the windowless interrogation rooms. The tiny space had only a table with a recorder, three chairs, two cameras on the ceiling and a one-way mirror, through which witnesses could observe the questioning from the next room without being seen.

'Why are you holding me here?' Erik Stadler wanted to know after Pia had turned on the recorder and given the prescribed statements for the transcript.

'You know why,' she replied. 'Have you finally remembered what you were doing at the time of the crimes?'

'I told you that yesterday. I was out jogging.' Stadler was making a big effort, but he was too nervous to sit still. He was under a lot of stress. Was that a sign of his guilt? 'I didn't shoot anybody! For me, this whole thing was over long ago. Life must go on, and I want to live. As a free man.'

'Who doesn't?' Pia countered. 'Sometimes people do things without considering the consequences, and suddenly they're stuck and can't go back.'

'I – didn't – shoot – anybody!' Stadler repeated with emphasis. 'I was out jogging. I jog a lot. I do sport because I want to stay fit.'

'Where did you go jogging? Did anyone see you, did you speak to anyone?'

'No, I already told you that,' the man said. 'I always run alone. Most people can't keep up with me.'

'How was your relationship with your sister?'

'My sister?'

'Yes.' Pia nodded. 'Your sister, Helen, who committed suicide in September.'

'Helen and I always got along well,' Stadler replied. 'Our mother's death was a terrible blow to her psyche, and she convinced herself that she was to blame. In the past few years, we weren't as close as before. I had my company and Helen her studies and her boyfriend. I had the impression that she was coping all right.'

'Why did she kill herself?'

'I don't know. Maybe she was more troubled inside than she appeared.'

'Do you know your sister's fiancé well?'

'What do you mean by "well"?' Stadler said with a shrug. 'I know him. He was always with Helen in the last years, hardly ever left her side. Wherever she went, he went, too.'

'Do you like him?'

'Yeah. He's all right. He took care of my sister, mothered her. She needed that. Before, that was my father's role. Then Jens-Uwe took over.'

Pia's mobile phone vibrated. She glanced at the display. Henning had e-mailed her the post-mortem report on Helen Stadler.

'Okay,' she said, and got up. 'I'm going to send in a colleague, and you can show him your jogging route on the map. We'll talk again later.'

She nodded to Nicola Engel, who hadn't said a word, and both went to the door. Pia knocked to be let out.

'Just a moment!' Stadler jumped up. 'When are you going to let me go?'

'When I'm convinced that you're not the person who shot four people to death in the last ten days,' replied Pia as she left the room.

It wasn't the first post-mortem report of an apparent suicide that Pia had read, but she still didn't understand the selfishness of suicides. She felt a deep sympathy for the train driver and the members of the volunteer fire department who had been forced to gather up scattered body parts. Helen Stadler had been inconsiderate enough to jump off a bridge over an open stretch of track and right into the path of a commuter train. Her petite, 50 kilo body was ripped apart, though her torso and arms remained relatively intact.

Pia had just finished reading the report on the screen when Bodenstein stuck his head in the door.

'Hello, boss. What did the fiancé say?' Pia asked.

'Plenty,' said Bodenstein. 'I think we've made a big step forward. Please call everyone together and then come to my office.'

'I'll go get Engel.' Pia jumped up from her chair, and Kai grabbed his phone to call Cem and Kathrin. A few minutes later, they were all jammed into Bodenstein's office, listening to the account of his conversation with Jens-Uwe Hartig.

'He was a doctor, but he had to hang up his profession after he reported his boss and his colleagues to the Federal Association of Physicians. He said that they had repeatedly violated the regulations within the framework of organ explantation.'

'What?' Pia was astounded. 'Hartig was a transplant surgeon? Isn't that a strange coincidence?'

'No, not at all,' Bodenstein replied. 'He got involved with HRMO, the support group, because he was unhappy with the unethical way many doctors treat organ donors. That was where the Winklers and Helen Stadler first met him.'

'What clinic did he work for?' Pia asked.

'A heart centre in Dortmund,' replied Bodenstein. 'Kai, please check this out ASAP. And find out where he studied.'

'Right away.' Kai nodded and jotted down a note. 'If, as we suspect, Kirsten Stadler died in the hospital after her family was pressured to donate her organs, then we have the motive for all the murders. We only need to find out the names of everyone who was involved. I assume that it was not the entire staff; a handful of people at most.'

'Did you ask Hartig for names?' Nicola Engel asked.

'Of course,' said Bodenstein with a nod. 'Evidently, after ten years, he can no longer remember any except for Rudolf and Hausmann, but we already knew about them.'

'Then let's ask Erik Stadler,' Pia suggested.

There was a knock at the door, and an officer from the watch room came in.

'The post was delivered,' she said, holding out an envelope that had already been opened. 'And this came with it.'

'Thank you. Put it on the table.' Bodenstein put on his reading glasses and a pair of latex gloves and pulled the letter out of the envelope. It was an obituary with a simple cross like the previous three.

There was tense silence round the table.

'"In memoriam Hürmet Schwarzer,"' Bodenstein read aloud. '"Hürmet Schwarzer had to die because her husband implicated himself by driving drunk and negligently hitting two individuals, which led to the condoned death of two people."'

'He obviously knows that we're responsible for the investigation, so he's speaking to us directly,' Cem remarked.

'Why two people?' asked Kim.

'Good question.' Bodenstein laid the letter on the table. 'I assume that he's referring to Kirsten Stadler and her daughter, Helen. So we have to ask the question, to whom did they mean so much that he would kill for them?'

'The father and the brother,' said Pia.

'And Hartig,' Bodenstein added. 'In his office, there's a big photo of her, and every morning before work, he visits the cemetery.'

'We ought to confront Erik Stadler with the obituaries,' Pia suggested.

'Let's do that now,' Bodenstein agreed, and got up. Pia went to her office, printed out the post-mortem report, and stuck it in the case file.

'What sort of impression did you get of Hartig?' she asked Bodenstein on the way downstairs. 'What sort of guy is he?'

'A sensitive man. A sort of Good Samaritan.' Bodenstein held open the glass door to the stairway for her. 'He was in love with Helen in an almost obsessive way. Her death has really thrown him for a loop.'

'So much that he would shoot people?'

Bodenstein thought about that for a moment.

'He seems to be a man who consistently finishes whatever he starts. And even though I called him a Good Samaritan, I think he's a fighter and not the type to suffer in silence. He'll put up a fight for anyone or anything close to his heart.'

'He knows all the connections at the clinic and I'm sure every name as well,' Pia said. 'We need to consider him as a potential suspect, which means we have to ask him about his alibis for the crucial times when the murders were committed.'

'And we have to learn more about Helen,' said Bodenstein. 'Where did she live? Where are all her personal possessions?'

'Let's ask her brother.' Pia nodded to the officer who was waiting near the door of the interrogation room and now let them in.

Erik Stadler was lying, and Bodenstein asked himself why. What did he have to hide? Was he the sniper? It was time to raise the stakes and apply more pressure. They couldn't allow him another opportunity to think things through.

'We're getting nowhere,' said Bodenstein. 'Let's start again from the beginning. What exactly happened back then, with your mother?'

'You already know that,' Stadler replied, looking irritated. 'My father and I told you everything the other day.'

He massaged his wrists, tugged on his fingers, and grew more and more nervous.

'There are reasons why we doubt your story,' Bodenstein said. 'So? What was your mother's condition when you and your sister found her? What exactly did you do? And what happened when she was taken to the UCF?'

'What the hell does it matter?' Anger flared in Stadler's eyes, as if he was afraid of being led into a trap. Anyone who had given a truthful account of a past event he had experienced wouldn't be afraid.

'We think it's very important.'

Stadler thought about it, then shrugged. His eyes darted here and there, and he began to sweat. Finally he rubbed his hands on his thighs, a clear sign of how much stress he was under.

'My mother went jogging and didn't come back. Helen and I went out looking for her, since we knew the route she always took. When we found her, she was lying next to the path with the dog sitting next to her. I rang for an ambulance on her phone, then I knelt down and tried to help her.'

'Can you be more precise?' Bodenstein made his voice a bit sharper. 'What form did your concern take? Did you hold her hand?'

'No, I tried to resuscitate her. I had recently taken a first-aid course for my driving licence, and knew what to do.'

'Was your mother at this point breathing on her own?' Pia asked.

'No,' Stadler said after a tiny pause. 'But I kept on giving her CPR. Until the ambulance arrived.'

'During this time, did your mother ever regain consciousness, even briefly?' Bodenstein asked.

They were taking turns firing off the questions, giving Stadler no time to focus on either one of them.

'No,' he said, and this time Bodenstein continued the questioning as he fixed his eyes on Stadler.

'And then?'

'Then the paramedics took over. They loaded her in the ambulance and drove away.'

'Why didn't you go with them?'

'I . . . I had the dog. And Helen was completely hysterical. I called my grandfather and he came down with Grandma. Then Helen and I drove with them to the hospital.' Erik Stadler was relaxing a bit, Bodenstein thought, because now he was actually telling the truth.

'What happened there?'

'We didn't see my mother for quite a while, not until later in intensive care. She was hooked up to a zillion tubes and a respirator. Nobody would tell us what was going on with her. My grandpa was throwing a fit.'

'Where was your father?'

'Out of the country. We couldn't reach him on the phone.'

'Then what happened?'

'Listen,' Stadler said, leaning forward. 'I don't remember it all very well anymore. It was ten years ago. My mother was declared brain-dead because she had been deprived of oxygen for too long.'

'Did your mother collapse at the beginning or the end of her jogging route?' Pia asked, digging deeper.

'What difference does that make?' Stadler gave her an annoyed look.

'Maybe she collapsed only a few minutes before you and your sister found her. And maybe she wasn't unconscious at first. Which would mean that her brain hadn't been without oxygen for as long as you stated.'

'I don't understand what you're getting at.'

'Here's the thing: was her brain really irreparably damaged because of lack of oxygen or not?' Pia explained. 'You say that you started CPR right away, then the paramedics took over. At the hospital, she was also hooked up to a respirator.'

Erik Stadler shrugged. 'That's what I already told you. It was like this,' he said. 'The doctors confirmed brain death. The cerebral haemorrhage had damaged the brainstem irrevocably. She never woke up again.'

'Your grandmother told us that you blew your top when you found out the doctors were no longer interested in saving your mother's life. At that point, they viewed her simply as a possible organ donor.'

'I was seventeen years old!' Stadler protested vehemently. 'I was in total shock. My mother died right before my eyes! And I don't understand what this is all about at this late date. It's been ten years. She's dead.'

'I'll tell you why this is important,' said Pia. 'Outside, someone is running round shooting innocent people in order to punish their relatives for what happened to your mother back then. Somebody who knows what *really* happened. Someone who believes that your mother's life could have been saved. If she had really lain in the field for two hours and was already brain-dead when she was taken to the hospital, it would have been a terrible stroke of fate. No one could be blamed. But that's not what happened!'

Stadler flipped out. Under the increasing pressure of the questioning, which had been hitting him for fifteen minutes like machine-gun fire, he cracked.

'And what if I told you that they let my mother die because they desperately wanted her organs?' he yelled. 'You'd take me for a nutcase who hasn't been able to accept his mother's death, even after ten years. Someone who's spreading horror stories.'

'No, we wouldn't do that,' said Bodenstein calmly. 'And we would track down the people who permitted this to happen and call them to account. We think that's a lot better than shooting people's wives and children.'

'You could save lives,' said Pia.

'I've heard that line before,' Stadler said with a cynical laugh. 'That's exactly what they told my grandfather. Just sign here so that we can remove the organs. Your daughter may be dead, but she can still save lives. They really leaned on my grandparents hard. They cited examples: the little boy can live if he gets a new liver in the next fourteen days; this young mother of three will die if she doesn't get a new kidney within a week. And on and on.'

Beads of sweat glistened on his forehead. His breathing was laboured.

'Please calm down,' Bodenstein said soothingly. 'We're not trying to open old wounds.'

'But that's what you're doing,' said Stadler. 'I've been trying for ten years to forget this horror. My sister is dead because she could no longer live with her guilty conscience, but she was never to blame for anything.'

He fell silent, shook his head, and briefly closed his eyes.

'When can I go?'

'Not yet.'

'When? You can't hold me for more than twenty-four hours without a reason.'

Bodenstein stood up and Pia grabbed the file.

'We do have a reason,' Bodenstein said. 'As long as you have no alibi for the times of the murders, we consider you a suspect. I told you that last night. You have the right to remain silent, to avoid incriminating yourself, and you can call a lawyer at any time.'

'You've got to be kidding!' Stadler was getting worked up again. 'I didn't shoot anybody! I don't need a lawyer!'

'On the contrary. I think you do. Or four alibis.'

'We're not really making any progress,' said Pia to her colleagues in the corridor after Erik Stadler had walked past. She was disappointed because she'd been hoping for more from the interview. Something substantial. Some indication that Stadler was the Judge.

'You never get over something like this,' replied Kim, who along with Dr Engel, Kathrin, Kai and Cem had observed the questioning from the next room. 'At any rate, he's not telling the truth about his mother's death. His behaviour indicates that he's lying. Based on his profile, he could be the perp. He had the motive and the opportunity.'

Pia didn't want to hear any more of this profile shit. She almost regretted involving her sister in the investigation. They were overlooking something. But what?

'There's something he's not telling us,' said Kim. 'I wonder why?'

'Maybe because the clinic made them agree to the official version of what happened,' Bodenstein guessed. 'That's why they got the hush money.'

'But they never told Helen anything about that,' Kai added. 'She believed that she was to blame for her mother's death.'

'Careful,' Bodenstein warned. 'That's speculation. All we know is that something's fishy about the whole story. A powerful pressure has been building up round someone connected to the family or their circle of friends, and now it has exploded.'

'And maybe there's a reason behind this that's much more mundane than we suspect.' Pia gnawed on her lower lip as she tried to piece together the thoughts running through her head.

'Stadler is a good shot, at any rate,' Kathrin remarked.

'Biathletes shoot at a disc several metres away,' Cem said dubiously. 'Our man shot a person from a distance of almost a kilometre. That's something totally different.'

'What do you intend to do now?' Nicola Engel asked. 'Let him go?'

'Reluctantly,' Bodenstein admitted. 'But we can't hold him much longer without new evidence.'

'Then dig some up.'

'One telling piece of evidence is that there haven't been any more dead bodies since he's been sitting in that cell,' said Kathrin.

'That's not enough.' Bodenstein shook his head. 'We'll let him go, but only under certain conditions. Kai, arrange to have him watched. And he has to relinquish his passport and report to our colleagues in Niederhöchstadt once a day. Cem and Kathrin, you go talk to Stadler's girlfriend. I want to know how Stadler's been behaving recently, whether he's changed in any way . . . You know what I mean.'

'Yeah, we know,' said Cem.

Everyone could feel the pressure that was growing by the hour. Secretly, they were all waiting for an emergency call to come in and a fifth obituary to appear in the paper. An officer of the watch came down the hall.

'A Ms Wenning is waiting downstairs. She wants to speak to you,' he told Bodenstein. 'She has a lawyer with her.'

'Thanks. We'll be right down.' Bodenstein nodded, then turned to Cem and Kathrin. 'Your visit to Stadler's girlfriend will have to wait. Drive into Frankfurt and talk to Stadler's neighbours. But first pay a visit to Patrick Schwarzer. Maybe today he'll be in the mood to talk to you. Show him the obituary. We need to establish a link between him and Kirsten Stadler.'

The group broke up. Only Pia stayed behind.

'What is it?' Bodenstein asked.

'We're asking the wrong questions,' said Pia.

'How do you mean?'

'Just what I said.' She looked at her boss. 'Stadler is hiding something, but it doesn't necessarily have to be about the murders. Remember the Kaltensee case? Marcus Nowak and Elard Kaltensee, the professor?'

'Yes, of course.' Bodenstein gave her a quizzical look. 'What have they got to do with this?'

'We thought they were both suspects because they'd obviously been lying and were hiding something from us,' Pia said. 'It turned out they weren't clamming up about the murders as we thought; but they didn't want to tell us about their secret connection. Erik Stadler also has some secret that he doesn't want to reveal at any cost, but he isn't the Judge.'

'What makes you so sure?'

'Hmm.' Pia shrugged. 'It's only a hunch. But he was telling the truth when he said that he'd been trying for ten years to forget the whole thing and simply wanted to lead a normal life again. But I also think that he was forced to stick to the official version of the events – a version that had been explicitly spelled out. His nervousness was due to the fact that he wasn't allowed to speak candidly.'

Bodenstein frowned as he thought about what she'd said.

'You may be right,' he admitted. 'But why is he willing to risk becoming a suspect and continue sitting here in custody?'

'There could be several reasons for that. Either the secret he's hiding seems worse to him than being suspected of the murders. Or – and this I consider more plausible – he's trying to protect someone.'

They looked at each other for a moment.

'Stadler first or his girlfriend?' Pia asked.

'First the girlfriend,' Bodenstein said.

Lis Wenning, pale and visibly anxious, was waiting in the lobby at the security checkpoint. Next to her stood a tall man sporting a moustache and dressed in a suit and tie. Everyone in the criminal police in the Frankfurt region probably knew who he was. Hiring Dr Anders as a lawyer was tantamount to a confession of guilt, because the defence lawyer almost exclusively took on cases of individuals accused in particularly spectacular murder cases that would get his name in the papers. Naturally, he couldn't pass up the Taunus Sniper case.

'I'd like to speak with my client,' he demanded at once.

'You may as soon as we've spoken with Ms Wenning,' Bodenstein replied. 'Please wait here.'

The lawyer objected while Lis Wenning apologized for the

inconvenience. Pia noticed that she was on a first name basis with him.

As they walked along the corridor, Pia asked the dark-haired woman curiously, 'How do you happen to know Dr Anders?' They entered the interview room where Erik Stadler had recently been sitting.

Bodenstein closed the door and asked Ms Wenning to take a seat. She sat down on the edge of the chair, holding the straps of her handbag tightly. Her big brown eyes looked anxious.

'He's a member of my fitness club,' she replied. 'I don't know any other lawyers. When your colleague took Erik away last night, I knew that it must be about something serious. Where is Erik now? What are you accusing him of?'

Pia studied the woman and decided not to go easy on her.

'We suspect Mr Stadler of having shot four individuals,' she said.

'You can't be serious!' Lis Wenning turned even paler and pressed her hand to her throat. 'Why would he do something like that?'

'To avenge the deaths of his mother and sister,' said Pia. 'He hasn't been very cooperative so far. He has no alibis for the times of the murders and claims he was out jogging. Maybe you could help him – and us.'

Stadler's girlfriend was trying to process the shock of what she'd just heard. She shook her head in bewilderment.

'Where was Mr Stadler on December nineteenth between eight and ten in the morning?' Bodenstein asked. 'On December twentieth round seven in the evening? And on Christmas Day at eight a.m.? And yesterday round noon?'

'I . . . I don't know,' Ms Wenning stammered. 'On the nineteenth and twentieth of December, he was probably in his office. And on Christmas Day, he was already gone when I woke up. He didn't come back until the afternoon.'

She hesitated.

'He didn't tell me where he'd been. And I didn't ask. Yesterday, he also planned to go into the office. They're in the middle of compiling their annual figures, and his bookkeeper called.'

'He wasn't at the office. They told us he was working from home.'

Lis Wenning looked helplessly from Pia to Bodenstein.

'Ms Wenning, has Mr Stadler been behaving differently over the past few weeks?' Bodenstein spoke in a quiet, insistent voice. 'Have you noticed any change in him?'

She struggled for a moment with her loyalty, but then she nodded.

'He has changed,' she said honestly. 'Quite a bit. Ever since Helen's death. Her suicide affected him tremendously. He and Helen were always very close. Sometimes I was even a little jealous.'

She forced a joyless smile that vanished from her face at once.

'How has he changed? What seems different about him?' Pia asked

'He stopped laughing,' said Lis Wenning. 'He retreated into himself and seemed far away, lost in his own thoughts. And he started devoting an excessive amount of time to sports. Erik . . . is addicted to danger and thrills. I don't go with him anymore when he does these crazy things, I can't stand it.'

Lis Wenning fell silent. She pressed her lips together and looked upset.

'Lately he seems worried all the time,' she whispered, looking down. 'I've had the feeling he might be hiding something from me. He was always late and he hid his mobile from me.'

'Can you guess what could have been occupying his attention so much?' Bodenstein asked.

'I . . . I . . . thought . . . he might have another woman.' A tear rolled down her cheek. 'A couple of times I asked him about it, but . . . but he refused to talk about it. He really isn't like that and . . . only recently he told me that . . . that he loves me.'

That was really all she knew. If she could have given him an alibi, she would have. She might even have tried to lie for him, but she didn't.

'Does Mr Stadler own a gun?'

'Yes, several. He keeps them in a cabinet at his office.'

'I wonder if you'd be kind enough to turn them over to one of our colleagues today,' Bodenstein concluded the conversation. 'We will check the weapons and hope that Mr Stadler will talk to us on Monday. He'll have to remain in custody until then.'

Lis Wenning nodded and got up.

Bodenstein and Pia accompanied her back to the lawyer, who was waiting impatiently to see his client. But first Bodenstein wanted to speak with Mr Stadler again. He asked Cem to drive Ms Wenning back to Sulzbach and confiscate the weapons.

Erik Stadler was sitting with his eyes closed on the narrow bed in his cell, his head tilted back against the wall.

'Mr Stadler,' Bodenstein began while Pia stood by the door. 'Why don't you tell us the truth? Why would you risk being charged with murder if you're innocent? Are you trying to protect somebody?'

No answer.

'Today we're going to remand you to the investigating prison for people awaiting trial. You might be there for quite a while, depending on the circumstances.'

Erik Stadler opened his eyes, and for a few seconds, Pia hoped that he would start talking and tell them the truth. But she was disappointed.

'Do whatever you like,' Stadler replied. 'I'm not saying another word without my lawyer.'

As Bodenstein and Pia turned into the cul-de-sac to Dirk Stadler's house, they almost ran into a woman who came dashing round the corner, her head down. In the glow of the streetlight Pia recognized, to her surprise, Erik Stadler's bookkeeper.

'Ms Fellmann?'

The woman turned round in fright and then stopped. Her eyes were swollen and her face wet with tears.

'I . . . was just at Mr Stadler's to give him the keys to the office after I tried all day long to reach Erik,' she explained. 'Yesterday was my last day at work, but he promised me that today we'd have a glass of champagne together. I finished up the year-end bookkeeping – all by myself because my boss left me in the lurch. He didn't even call.' She broke into tears.

'How long have you worked for Mr Stadler?' Pia asked.

'Since the very beginning,' Franka Fellmann sobbed. 'Since October 2009. At first only part-time, but business was really good, and then Erik needed a full-time bookkeeper.'

She rummaged in her handbag, took out a pack of tissues and blew her nose loudly. 'Mainly I was responsible for getting the clients to pay on time. These computer geniuses don't like to deal with such mundane matters.'

She gave a bitter laugh, then sobbed again.

'Erik was always a great boss, and I had a lot of fun building the company up with him, but now . . . it's no longer working. I have a son who needs me, and I've had to take care of everything at the office for the past couple of months. Ever since the boss's sister died.'

'Did you know his sister?' Bodenstein asked.

A tiny expression of disapproval flitted across her face.

'Yes, of course. It's a very casual office. We had a lot of parties, and Helen was often invited.'

'What sort of person was she?'

Franka Fellmann thought about it for a moment and then started crying again.

'I know you're not supposed to speak ill of the dead,' she told them. 'But Helen was an odd duck. Everybody treated her with velvet gloves. A slap in the face probably would have helped her more, instead of all the tiptoeing round. If you ask me, Helen destroyed her family with her obsession about her mother.'

Bodenstein and Pia exchanged a quick glance but took care not to interrupt Fellmann's outpouring of words.

'As soon as a celebration or a barbecue really got going, she would mention her mother and bum everybody out. She always had to be the centre of attention. It was a totally pathological thing with her, this craving for attention. Sometimes I got the feeling that she enjoyed this role and the way she could manipulate everyone round her. Once I told her she ought to get counselling, and she tore into me like a fury. After that, she never spoke to me again. She would look right through me as if I were made of glass.'

'What sort of work did Helen do? Did she work in her brother's company, too?' Pia wanted to know.

'She might have wanted to, but she had absolutely zero skills,' replied Fellmann. 'For a while, the boss had her answering the phone, but she couldn't even do that right. She showed up whenever she felt like it, made personal phone calls and was totally unreliable. Eventually, I said it was either her or me. Of course, that meant that she and Jens-Uwe didn't want anything to do with me, but afterwards, the company ran smoothly again, and that was the most important thing to me.'

Fellmann had been jealous of Helen Stadler; she had even hated her. But when Helen died, things did not improve for Franka. Her boss's sister had reached from beyond the grave to destroy everything that had meant anything to Ms Fellmann.

'So what did she do after that?'

'I think she applied to university. To study sociology and psychology, or something like that. But she never graduated.'

'Where did she live?'

'Here, with her father.' Fellmann cocked her head towards the house. 'She didn't want to move out, although Jens-Uwe has a pretty big apartment.'

'So you know her boyfriend, Jens-Uwe Hartig?'

'Yeah, sure. A funny guy.' She dabbed her eyes with the tissue. 'With a high-level need to take care of somebody. He only had eyes for Helen. He was always hanging round her, mothering her and doing favours for her, just like the boss and his father. But what I found strange was how those two were always talking about the past. Like two people in an old folks' home. They seemed to live only in the past. Instead of getting Helen back on track, Jens-Uwe may have reinforced her craziness instead.'

'They were planning to get married, weren't they?'

'Yes. In early October. In church and at the register office in Kiedrich. That's where Jens-Uwe is from. I had the invitations printed, that's how I know. I think secretly Erik, his girlfriend and his father were all happy, because then they would finally be rid of the responsibility for messed-up Helen.'

She sobbed again.

'I have a feeling that I'm letting Erik and the others down, but I just can't keep on like this. For weeks, he's rarely been at the office, doesn't tell me where he is, doesn't answer his mobile. The job got to be too much for me. And now he doesn't even show up on my last day, even though yesterday he swore he would.'

'Was he at the office yesterday?' Pia asked.

'No. I haven't seen him since before Christmas,' Fellmann replied.

'Did he tell you where he was? Was he abroad, by any chance?'

'No idea. He didn't tell me a thing.'

The mobile in her pocket rang. She took it out and looked at it.

'My son,' she said apologetically, wiping away the tears. 'I have to pick him up at a friend's place.'

'Just one more question,' Pia said. 'Do you happen to know whether Jens-Uwe Hartig is a marksman?'

'A marksman?' Fellmann looked puzzled for a moment. 'No, sorry, I have no idea.'

'Why did you tell us such a tall tale last time?' Pia asked Dirk Stadler as they stood facing him a little later. He had taken the decorations off the Christmas tree and moved it to the patio. He was busy vacuuming when they arrived.

'What tall tale?' Stadler gave them a baffled look. He limped over to a stool, sat down and massaged his leg.

'About the day your wife died. It didn't happen the way you told us.'

'Of course it did. Why would I make up a story about that?'

'Because someone paid you to keep your mouth shut,' said Pia. 'So that you would give up and keep quiet and not tell anybody that your wife was still conscious when your son administered CPR and brought her back to life. How much did they pay you?'

That was a risky interpretation of what Erik Stadler had told them, but Pia dared take the gamble, anticipating a vehement denial. But Stadler merely sighed.

'Fifty thousand euros. But what you're saying is nonsense. Erik couldn't do anything to save Kirsten. She was unconscious and no longer responsive.'

'How would you know? You weren't there.'

'Erik told me himself,' Stadler claimed.

'So truth and justice were worth fifty thousand euros to you?'

'I don't think you understand,' Stadler said with a shrug. 'Nobody did anything wrong. But my father-in-law wouldn't agree to say that he was the one who had given permission to remove her organs. He was the one who wanted to file a complaint, but I was convinced that doing so would be fruitless. The opposing side had his signature on the consent form, so I was sure to lose in a trial. They offered me money if I would retract my complaint, and I accepted. Put yourself in my place.

I had simply run out of energy. A pointless lawsuit against a hospital, which might drag on for years and probably bankrupt me. And it wouldn't have brought Kirsten back. I would have to look for a new job so I could take care of my children, especially Helen, who at the time was only fifteen. I agreed to the settlement and took the money. That way I could at least provide some starting capital for their lives.'

'What was the basis for your suit?' asked Bodenstein. 'How did you find out that the procedures weren't properly followed?'

'I gave you the documents,' replied Stadler.

'I'd prefer to hear the details from you,' Bodenstein persisted.

'I didn't want to sue.' Stadler cautiously stretched out his leg with a grimace. 'For the sake of my children, I wanted to push the whole topic aside. I wanted to grieve with them for their mother, and try to accept her death. But my father-in-law gave me no peace. He was obsessed, coming up with all sorts of abstruse conspiracy theories. And what Jens-Uwe told him was naturally grist for his mill.'

'Just a moment,' Bodenstein interrupted him. 'Mr Hartig told us that he met Helen for the first time four years ago. So how could he have already told your father-in-law anything back then?'

Stadler looked up, bewildered.

'It could be that he didn't meet Helen until later. But he'd known my in-laws longer, through the support group that they discovered shortly after Kirsten's death. He told them that he'd already learned that some examinations were not being done within the prescribed time frame, and that operating theatre protocols were sometimes missing or falsified on purpose by the doctors. He was very persuasive, and finally I let them talk me into filing the lawsuit. After that, the topic dominated our family – for years. The wounds would never heal. No one but me noticed how much Helen was suffering because of all this. She was a teenage girl, extremely sensitive and vulnerable, but also radical in her views, the way young people often are at that age. She was firmly convinced that her mother had been deliberately allowed to die so the doctors could transplant her organs.'

'And was that the truth of the situation?' Bodenstein enquired.

Dirk Stadler slumped forward and uttered a sigh.

'What I'm trying to tell you is that there is no deception or twisting of the truth. My wife suffered a cerebral haemorrhage while jogging and died. Helen couldn't have changed that fact, even if she'd been standing right next to Kirsten. Maybe my wife could have vegetated for another few days or weeks in the ICU, kept alive by machines, but she was never going to wake up. Her brain was dead. The EEG showed a flatline. Helen didn't want to hear that. She was desperate, unable to escape the idea that she was somehow to blame. In the past ten years, Helen tried to kill herself six times. Sometimes she would disappear for several days. I didn't know where she was, and each time the phone rang, I was afraid they'd found her body. But she always showed up again, saying only that she'd been at a friend's house. Then a few years ago, she fell in love with Jens-Uwe. Everything seemed to be going better. Helen calmed down and began to take an interest in other things. Her suicide struck us like a bolt from the blue. She had finally regained her footing in life, and she was looking forward to her wedding . . .'

Dirk Stadler stopped and rubbed his eyes.

'I still can't comprehend it. She had just tried on her wedding dress in Frankfurt, and the same night, she took her life.'

'Why in Kelsterbach? What was she doing there?'

'That's something else I don't understand. To this day, it's a riddle why she went there and how she got there.'

'Did she leave a suicide note?'

'No, I'm afraid not.'

Pia thought about the letter that the Judge had sent to the editor of the *Taunus Echo*: *For I am come to judge the living and the dead.* The sentence came from the Apostles' Creed.

'Are you a religious man?' Pia asked.

'No.' Dirk Stadler shook his head. 'I stopped believing in a just God many years ago.'

'May we take a look at Helen's personal effects?'

'If you like. I've left everything the way it was in her room upstairs.'

'Do you know where your son has been in the past few days?' Bodenstein asked.

'No.' The sudden change of subject seemed to surprise Stadler. 'I last saw him on Christmas Eve, when he and Lis came to visit me. Just before you arrived, his bookkeeper brought me the keys to his office, because she couldn't reach him. Is something going on with him?'

'We took him into police custody yesterday,' said Bodenstein. 'We've issued a preliminary indictment against him.'

'Against Erik?' Dirk Stadler was astonished. 'You . . . you believe that my son would be capable of shooting people?'

'Well, he is a good shot. He definitely has a motive. And he has no alibi for the times when the murders were committed.'

'But Erik? He would never . . . do anything like that!'

Neither Bodenstein nor Pia missed the tiny hesitation. Was Dirk Stadler not entirely convinced of his son's innocence?

With an effort, Stadler got up from the stool and limped towards the living room. His accommodating attitude had evaporated.

'If you would like to see Helen's room, it's upstairs, the second door on the right. Please pardon me if I stay down here, my leg is bothering me quite a bit today.'

'Of course,' said Bodenstein.

Stadler bent towards the vacuum cleaner, but then something seemed to occur to him.

'If I were you, I'd talk with Jens-Uwe. Or with Mark Thomsen.'

'Mark – who?'

'The chairman of HRMO,' said Stadler with a bitter smile. 'Helen's . . . surrogate father. As if she needed one.'

There was a lot of activity at the Seerose Shopping Centre in Eschborn. All the sensation-seekers were out in force. People had come from near and far, not to shop, but to see and take pictures of the spot where Hürmet Schwarzer had died. The shoe shop's display window with the bullet hole had already been replaced, and the bakery where the victim had worked was again open for business. As if nothing had happened.

'Unbelievable,' said Pia in disgust as they drove past, seeing the crowd trying to get a look at the bloodstain. 'Why do people do stuff like this?'

'I'll never understand it,' said Bodenstein, shaking his head. 'But right now, I'm starving. Want to get something to eat?'

'Good idea,' Pia agreed. 'How about that Burger King up ahead?'

'If you must.'

Bodenstein was no fan of fast food, but Pia felt a need for some calories, meat, and mayo. The alternative was KFC, but that wasn't her favourite. A few minutes later, they were in the queue at the counter of cash registers.

Bodenstein was studying the menu on the wall with a sceptical look. He seemed completely out of his element.

'May I help you?' The young man behind the counter slapped down a tray and took Pia's order.

'Have you found something you'd like?' she asked her boss.

'Not yet.' Bodenstein thought about it, then turned to the cashier. 'What can you recommend today?'

'Uh, what do you like to eat?' replied the young man, putting on a polite expression after a moment of irritation. 'Are you a vegetarian?'

'No. Do you still have that Filet-O-Fish on your menu?' Bodenstein asked.

'No, we don't. This is Burger King.'

Pia had to stifle her laughter as Bodenstein listened to descriptions of the various burgers and condiments available, then asked for more information. The people standing beside and behind him were gawking in astonishment. Finally he decided on a Big King XXL with fries and a mineral water. Pia let him pay, grabbed her tray, and headed for an empty table.

'Why is everyone staring at me?' Bodenstein asked as he sat down across from her.

'I've never seen anything like that,' Pia snorted, and then laughed until tears came to her eyes. ' "What can you recommend today?" Who asks that in a fast-food joint?'

'I'm not familiar with their selections,' Bodenstein replied with dignity, but then even he had to grin. 'So the Filet-O-Fish isn't offered here?'

'No!' Pia shook her head and wiped away her tears with a paper napkin. 'Oh man, the look that guy gave you, I'll never forget it for the rest of my life!'

With a smile, Bodenstein unwrapped his burger, examined it critically, and then bit into it.

'Hmm, not bad,' he said. 'But it doesn't look anything like the one in the advertising photo.'

Pia shook her head as she chewed. They had spent almost an hour in Helen Stadler's room and found nothing helpful. Plenty of books and clothes, photo albums, cosmetics and textbooks. There were old stuffed animals in a box in the wardrobe; mementos in her desk drawers: used concert tickets, postcards, old photos of her mother and all sorts of things that Helen had kept because she couldn't bear to throw them out. There was absolutely nothing out of the ordinary, except they didn't find the one thing that every young person had in her room, namely a computer or laptop.

Dirk Stadler told them that Helen had owned a laptop. On the day of her death, she'd taken it with her in her rucksack, as usual, and he'd never seen it again. After the investigation, the police had returned the rucksack and all its contents to him, but there was no laptop. Strange. Stadler suspected that she might have left it at Jens-Uwe's on that day.

Pia was just finishing her fries when Kai called. She'd asked him to find out about a Mark Thomsen, the chairman of HRMO.

'Dead end,' he said. 'There's no one in the area by that name.'

'But he's listed on the masthead of HRMO's website,' Pia

recalled, holding her phone clamped between her shoulder and ear.

'Correct. His name is there. And the town of Eppstein. But that's all,' said Kai. 'According to the residential Registration Office, there's no Thomsen living in Eppstein. I can't find him in our computer either.'

'Well, that's interesting.' Pia wiped her greasy fingers on a fresh napkin. 'You could call Lydia Winkler. Maybe she knows something.'

'Will do. Oh, and there's news about Patrick Schwarzer. Get this: he used to do community service work, driving an ambulance.'

'Let me guess,' said Pia. 'He was on duty on September sixteenth, 2002.'

'You got it,' Kai confirmed. 'His birthday was the day before, and apparently he partied hard, so the next day, he still had quite a bit of residual alcohol in his bloodstream. When he tried to turn the ambulance round with Kirsten Stadler on board, he went into a ditch. And that resulted in a delay of a good forty-five minutes.'

Cem and Kathrin had confronted Patrick, the widower of Hürmet Schwarzer, with the message from the Judge, and that jogged his memory. He'd completely forgotten the episode from ten years before, since the patient had no personal connection to him. And it was the only blunder he'd made in two and a half years. When he realized that this mistake, so insignificant to him, had eventually cost his wife her life, he broke down and announced he was going to kill himself. Cem called a psychologist and waited until Schwarzer's father and brother arrived.

' "The guilty parties shall feel the same pain as the one who has suffered because of their indifference, greed, vanity and thoughtlessness. Those who have taken guilt upon themselves shall live in fear and terror, for I am come to judge the living and the dead." '

Pia quoted from the letter that the Judge had sent to the newspaper editor.

'The killer has evidently achieved his goal,' Kai said dryly. 'The guy is completely devastated.'

On the way to the car, Pia related to her boss what Kai had told her about Patrick Schwarzer's past.

'Another strike against Erik Stadler,' Bodenstein said, thinking out loud. 'He must have been aware of the long delay back then.'

'What if we're dealing with a professional hit man that one of the Stadlers hired?' said Pia with a shiver. It would be nearly impossible to catch a pro who may even have come in from another country and would vanish the same way.

'If so, we're looking for his client.' Bodenstein peered out into the fog that was growing thicker.

'Then all our thoughts about profiling are no longer relevant,' Pia replied. 'The murder contract could have been arranged by the elder Winkler, or Stadler with his gammy leg.'

'Damn it,' Bodenstein cursed. 'We're no further along than we were last week, and we're running out of time!'

'At least we've found out what it's all about,' Pia argued. On a full stomach, she was again thinking effectively. 'The deaths of Kirsten Stadler and her daughter are the reasons for the murders.'

'And why do you think that?'

'Helen's suicide was probably the trigger,' Pia suspected. She raised her hand and checked off the suspects on her fingers. 'Erik Stadler. Dirk Stadler. Joachim Winkler. Jens-Uwe Hartig. Those are our main suspects, and we need to watch them closely. Even more important, we need to find any other potential victims. So we're going to have to put more pressure on Stadler Junior, Hartig and the UCF.'

'Let's do it,' Bodenstein agreed with a nod. 'We need to get this motherfucker.'

SUNDAY, DECEMBER 30, 2012

The dim light of dawn filtered through the slats of the blinds as Bodenstein opened his eyes and waited for his mind to disengage from the remnants of a confusingly realistic dream. It was rare for the cases he worked on during the day to bother him at night. Yet this time, some of the people who'd been baffling him and his team with riddles had slipped into his dreams, as if they wanted to tell him something. He turned over on his back, savouring the utter silence in the house. No child calling for him, no dog who wanted to be taken for a walk. And no Inka either. The other side of the bed was untouched. She'd sent him a text in the late afternoon saying that she had to go to Limburg on an emergency case and had no idea how late she would be. Since she didn't want to wake him, she would sleep at home. The flimsiness of her excuse made Bodenstein feel depressed. In the past, she had often come to his place in the middle of the night, and she had a key to the front door. Why was she doing this? What had happened?

On Christmas Day, everything had seemed fine, but now she was suddenly retreating from him. Did she feel that he wasn't paying enough attention to her? Or did she have doubts about a future together with him? He realized that she had a problem with Sophia, but he'd hoped that their relationship was strong enough to solve it. When he'd been married to Cosima, there were often minor fights and arguments, but with Inka, he had never had any clashes. She simply clammed up whenever something displeased her. What he'd at first taken as harmony now appeared to be more a result of her inability to resolve conflict, and even worse: her lack of interest. Inka was proud and independent. She had never had a long-term partnership and apparently hadn't missed it, so why would she change now, in her early fifties? Had she grown too close to him? Did things seem confining? Was he too boring for her?

Bodenstein glanced at the digital display on his alarm clock. Eight o'clock. Today he wanted to pay a visit to Fritz Gehrke and try to talk with him about the Judge's accusations from the obituary. He sat up, swung his legs over the edge of the bed and went to the bathroom for a shower.

Why hadn't Inka answered his good-night text?

What exactly did he feel about her? It was hardly love; at any rate, not that deep, warm, heart-pounding feeling he had felt for so long with Cosima, even if it wasn't necessarily recip-rocated. His relationship with Inka had not developed out of stormy infatuation and passion. It was an old affection that had been rekindled through the marriage of their children. They both had their own work and their own lives, and they had never made a deliberate decision to become a couple. Inka had drawn closer gradually, and he had accepted the fact that she never took the step to rent out her house as a way of making their partnership official. After Oliver's divorce from Cosima and his brief affair with Annika Sommerfeld, Inka had been a willing confidante. They had talked for hours on the phone and in person. At some point, they had landed in bed together. That had been good. Familiar. Unfortunately, no more than that, he now had to admit to himself.

As he shaved, he thought about the fact that he hardly knew Inka. There was a boundary that she wouldn't let him cross. Always this caution, a locked room inside her to which he was denied entry. He could talk with her about all sorts of things, but she never talked about herself. To this day, she wouldn't tell him who Thordis's father was. She didn't talk about her time in America and never mentioned any acquaintances or friends.

It bothered him that he had thoughts like this. Just because they hadn't slept together in two nights and she hadn't texted him. Why should he immediately question their relationship? She'd simply had too much to do at her horse clinic, and he was busy, too. Still, doubt gnawed at him. Was he convincing himself that everything was fine because he was too afraid to face the truth? Was he really satisfied with a relationship that was so casual?

Bodenstein got dressed and went downstairs to the kitchen, absent-mindedly pressing the button on the coffeemaker and shoving two slices of bread into the toaster. No message from Inka on his phone. He spread cream cheese and strawberry jam on the toast and ate it standing up as he drank his coffee. Out the window, another overcast, sunless day was dawning. In the newspaper, he'd read recently that December of 2012 was about to become the darkest month since 1951, when weather records were first kept. Maybe it was just the lack of light along with the difficult case that was oppressing his psyche and making everything seem so bleak.

Then he remembered the offer from Cosima's mother,

which he still hadn't discussed with Inka and had almost repressed. The longer he waited to mention it, the harder it would be. On the other hand, he didn't want to bring up something so important without having time to discuss it in detail, especially since she reacted so sensitively to anything that had to do with Cosima's family.

He decided simply to wait. Tomorrow was New Year's Eve, and the next day was the start of a new year with new opportunities. Right now, he had a murderer to catch.

It was cold in the house, so cold that he could see his breath like a whitish cloud. Under the two blankets, it was nice and warm, although his bladder was full. Otherwise, nothing was pressing him. The days had turned into nothing but waiting for the weather to pass. He hoped the fog at least would lift soon. Last night, he'd been reading a mystery until his eyes almost fell closed. It had been one of his favourite books, and it was certainly written in a suspenseful way, but he found the description of the violence of this psychopath against women revolting.

His gaze moved over the ugly, faded wallpaper to the window with the paint peeling off the sill.

He threw off the covers, grabbed his fleece jacket, which was hanging over a chair next to the bed, and slipped into his lined boots. In the bathroom and living room, it was just as cold as in the bedroom, and the woodbox next to the stove was empty. He went to the toilet, then put on his scarf and jacket, grabbed the basket and stepped outside to chop some firewood. The wooden steps of the porch creaked under his weight, and a crow cawed as it flew out of a stand of three trees. The fog had settled over the houses, enveloping everything in a damp cold. He went round the house, picked up a couple of logs, and pulled the axe out of the chopping block. A bit of exercise in the early morning suited him fine. After ten minutes, he had enough firewood for two days, so he lugged the basket back into the house. A little later, a fire was crackling in the stove and radiating a pleasant warmth. He filled the cheap coffeemaker with water, spooned ground coffee into the filter, and turned on the machine. Last summer, he had thought about fixing up the house, but other, more important things intervened. Now it was no longer worth the trouble. The police would get wise to him sooner or later. They'd catch him and put him on trial. The public would hate him and think he was sick. They'd call him a crazy psychopath, and he couldn't really blame them, considering what he had done and was going to do. In the eyes of the public, nothing could justify his actions, but he couldn't care less. The people who had to die had been sentenced to death by their own fathers, husbands and children – he was merely the executioner. He had documented everything meticulously. The living would receive their punishment and the dead would get justice. All of them.

It was nine o'clock on the dot when Bodenstein parked in front of Fritz Gehrke's house and got out of the car. He opened the garden gate, went up the steps and along the path to the front door. No one answered when he rang the doorbell. The blinds were closed all over the house, and Bodenstein had a bad feeling. As he was thinking whom he could call to check on Gehrke, a small white car with the name NURSE HILDEGARD painted on the side pulled up. A stout woman with bobbed hair dyed cherry red got out with a black bag over her shoulder and strode up the steps. Under a thick down jacket, she wore some sort of white uniform, and she had on white shoes to match.

'Isn't even the Sabbath sacred to you damned reporters?' she admonished him before he could say a word. 'Get out of here or I'll call the police!'

'I'm not from the newspaper. I'm from Kripo,' said Bodenstein, showing her his ID. 'And you are?'

'Oh, I'm sorry, I didn't know. I'm Karin. Karin Michel.' The expression on her red-cheeked face changed to remorse.

'Not Nurse Hildegard?' Bodenstein said with a smile.

'We're all Nurse Hildegard.' Ms Michel gave him a mischievous smile. 'There are seven of us. Most of us used to work in nursing homes, but working somewhere like that is pretty frustrating in the long run. Sure, the work is still stressful, but this way, we have more time for the oldsters. And they appreciate it.'

She fished out a thick ring of keys from her jacket.

'The blinds are all drawn,' Bodenstein said. 'No one reacted when I rang.'

'Oh, that's normal,' replied Karin Michel. 'Sorry I yelled at you. But for the past few days, there have been reporters constantly hanging round, and it was a real bother for poor Mr Gehrke. As if he hasn't suffered enough.'

She put on her glasses, which were hanging round her neck on a cord, and searched for the right key. Bodenstein respected people like Karin Michel. It wasn't easy to take care of old or sick people and stay cheerful, warm-hearted and sympathetic.

'No need to apologize,' he said. 'How often do you visit Mr Gehrke?'

'Morning and evening. It's not good for the old man to be alone so much,' she went on. 'Max used to visit his father every day and was always helping out. Terrible what happened. Just horrible.'

Finally she found the right key and opened the front door. The house was warm, and it smelled stuffy and smoky. Bodenstein's premonition grew stronger, but Karin Michel didn't seem to notice anything unusual.

'Hello, Mr Gehrke, it's me, Karin!' she shouted. 'Oh, he's sitting here in the dark again. He does that a lot. Forgets to turn on the light and open the blinds. He fell once, but luckily didn't hurt himself.' She pressed a switch, and the electric blinds in the whole house rolled up. 'I told Max he ought to get motion detectors installed in the house, but Mr Gehrke wouldn't hear of it. It would use too much electricity. He was born in 1931, the war generation. They're always thrifty. I've got lots of clients like Mr Gehrke.'

The woman was talkative but not nosy. She didn't try to find out anything from Bodenstein.

'Could you wait a moment? I'll go and find him and tell him that you want to talk to him.'

'All right,' Bodenstein said with a nod. 'Thank you.'

'Be right back.' The nurse marched off, calling loudly for the old man.

Bodenstein paced restlessly. Suddenly he heard a scream. He took off after the nurse and found her in the hallway, her face chalk-white.

'Oh God, oh God!' she cried. 'Mr Gehrke! Over there.'

Bodenstein pushed her gently aside and entered the study. His sense of foreboding had proved correct. Fritz Gehrke was dead. He sat slumped at his desk, his chin on his chest. At first glance, he looked as if he'd dozed off and departed this life in his sleep, but then Bodenstein noticed the syringe the dead man still held in his hand. Bodenstein put his arm round the nurse's shoulders and led the trembling woman into the kitchen.

'Sit down,' he said. He searched the cupboards until he found a glass, filled it with water and handed it to her. 'When was the last time you saw Mr Gehrke alive?'

'Yesterday. Last night round six in the evening,' she murmured in a daze before taking a gulp of water. Her hand was shaking. 'He was the same as ever, and wished me a good evening when I left.'

'Was he diabetic?' Bodenstein asked.

'Yes, type 2. But he dealt with it well. He's . . . He was a very disciplined man.'

She began to cry.

'This isn't the first dead person I've encountered.' She wiped the tears away with her hand. 'But Mr Gehrke was such a dear man. So brave. What happened to his son simply broke his heart.'

Bodenstein had a completely different suspicion, but he didn't want to take away the woman's illusion, and so he didn't comment.

Karoline Albrecht drove onto the A3 autobahn at Niedernhausen. She put on her indicator and stepped on the gas. The black Porsche 911S accelerated like an aeroplane, the 400 horsepower at her back roared, and the speedometer read 150 km/h after a few seconds. She had always loved driving fast. Her first car, which she received right after she got her driver's license, had been a VW Golf GTI. Now she drove a Porsche. As a partner, she was entitled to a company car in that price range, but it was really just as superfluous as her luxurious house. Greta had given up horse riding when she went to boarding school, but if she was going to start riding again, Karoline could buy her a horse. In that case, a robust four-wheel-drive vehicle with a towbar would be more practical than a pricey sports car. For a couple of minutes, Karoline indulged in fantasies about her future and pictured the house she would buy for Greta: an old farmhouse in a lovely garden with tall old trees and rosebushes and perhaps a pond by a weeping willow, its branches hanging down to the water. With the money that she could get for her luxury abode in Kelkheim, she wouldn't have to work for a couple of years, and she would also inherit something from Mama. The thought of her mother snatched Karoline right back to reality. At Montabaur, she had to slow the Porsche down to 100 km/h. Carsten had called last night and invited her to spend New Year's Eve with them at his parents' house on Lake Starnberg in Bavaria. She was still welcome at her former in-laws' house, thanks to Nicki, Carsten's second wife, who had accepted Karoline into her family without resentment since she was Greta's mother. But Karoline had politely declined the invitation. She couldn't simply drive off, not now. There was Mama's funeral to arrange. And she needed to find out what happened ten years ago, or the uncertainty would torment her till her dying day.

She glanced at herself in the rear-view mirror and glimpsed the chaos that was raging inside her – sorrow, grief, rage and pain, all the feelings that felt so burdensome because she was afraid of losing control. How long could she hold on before she collapsed like a house of cards? When would her strength run out, this iron self-control of hers?

She'd always been good at focusing on one thing to the exclusion of everything else, and this was a skill she needed right now. According to her satnav, she would arrive round 11:26 at the home of Dr Hans Furtwängler, who was one of the people her father had phoned in the past few days. Her conversations with Gehrke and Arthur yesterday had not been very instructive. She was haunted by a gloomy certainty that something was there – an old debt that connected her father with his friends and colleagues. Karoline didn't have much hope of learning more from Furtwängler, but each tiny bit of information was a piece of the puzzle. With a little luck and using her powers of deduction, she might eventually see the whole picture.

Karin Michel sobbed, utterly undone, twisting a wet tissue between her fingers. 'Max's death upset him so much that he no longer wanted to live.'

Bodenstein and Pia exchanged a glance. The stack of empty document binders and the ashes still warm in the living room fireplace spoke of something different. The labels on the spines of the binders had been carefully removed and also burned, so that there was no longer any hint of what had been in them. Fritz Gehrke had disposed of all the documents, and then he took his life with an overdose of insulin. He hadn't left a suicide note, but on his desk lay the copy of the obituary that the sniper had sent. Bodenstein had deliberately not told him about it; he had wanted to proceed cautiously and not show it to the old man until today. Somebody had beaten him to it – but who? It could only have been Faber, that journalist, who had probably done his own research. The content of the obituary was doubtless the trigger for Gehrke's suicide. Later today, Bodenstein was going to give Faber hell.

'Does Mr Gehrke have relatives we should inform?' Pia asked. She had already put on latex gloves and bright blue booties over her shoes.

'As far as I know, there's a sister somewhere,' replied Karin Michel, now somewhat more composed. 'But she lives abroad and she must be round eighty.'

'Thank you, I'm sure we can locate her.' Pia jotted this down. 'You may go now, Ms Michel. Thank you for your help.'

The nurse got up from the kitchen chair, and Pia accompanied her to the front door. Before she left, she took the front door key off her key ring and handed it to Pia.

'I won't be needing this anymore,' she said sadly, and left.

In the meantime, Kröger's team had photographed the body and the study and done a careful examination of the rest of the house. Dr Frederick Lemmer, who'd arrived shortly after Pia, had earned a lot of bonus points from Kröger by waiting respectfully until the evidence team finished working. Just as Pia returned to the study, two men carefully lifted the body of the old man from the chair and laid him on the rug.

'May we take a look round now?' Bodenstein asked Kröger.

'Sure, we're done in here,' said the head of the evidence team.

They searched the desk, not too surprised to find very little on the desktop or in the drawers. Fritz Gehrke had made a thorough job of it.

Lemmer measured the temperature of the corpse, found the typical greyish-purple lividity on the buttocks, back, bottom of the thighs and in the lower part of the calves, because the blood drained by gravity into the lower extremities as soon as it stopped circulating.

'Rigor mortis has not yet dissipated,' he told Bodenstein and Pia. 'I estimate that death occurred between ten p.m. and one a.m. No external influences are evident at first glance.'

Pia pressed her gloved finger on the telephone's memory button. The last number was dialled at 8:48 P.M. and had an Oberursel area code. Before that, Gehrke had phoned someone in Cologne.

'I bet this is Professor Rudolf's number, the husband of our victim number two,' said Pia.

'What makes you think that?' Bodenstein wanted to know, astounded.

'Just a hunch,' said Pia.

The phone rang. Pia wanted to pick up at once, but Bodenstein signalled for her to wait. A number with a Frankfurt area code. After the third ring, the voice mail kicked in.

'Fritz, it's me,' said a man's voice after the beep. 'I just heard the news. Fritz? Are you there? All right, I'll try you again later.'

'Why didn't you want me to take the call?' Pia was baffled.

'So that no one else burns any documents,' said Bodenstein, turning to Christian Kröger.

'Could your team check all the phone numbers from the phone's memory? Incoming and outgoing calls?'

'No problem,' Kröger said with a nod. 'It's best we take it with us.'

'Can we keep the line working and redirect any incoming calls?' Bodenstein asked. 'As long as no one knows that Gehrke is dead, he might get some calls that would be informative for us.'

'Sure, we can do that. I'll take care of it.'

'Please do it ASAP. And give Kai the list of calls so he can check them out.'

'Okay, okay,' said Kröger indignantly. 'Everything has to go so fast. You know I'm doing the best I can.'

'Christian, you're our best man. We all know that.' Bodenstein patted his colleague on the shoulder.

'Oh sure. No need to go overboard,' grumbled the head of
the evidence team, and walked off, shaking his head.

Pia's phone rang.

'It's Kai,' she told her boss, switching to speaker so that
Bodenstein could listen in.

'I found Thomsen,' said Kai even before she could say good
morning. Kai was not easily riled, but he sounded excited.
'Actually, his first name is Markus and his surname is Brecht-
Thomsen – at least, that's how he's listed. No wonder I couldn't
find him yesterday when I checked the resident's register.'

'Where does he live?' Pia asked.

'Lärchenweg 12 in Eppstein-Vockenhausen,' Kai replied.

'Thanks,' said Bodenstein. 'We'll go pay him a visit right
now.'

'Hold on!' Kai shouted. 'I've got more. Mark Thomsen
used to be one of our colleagues! He was with the Federal
Border Patrol, in GSG-9, the anti-terror unit. So we can
assume that he's probably an excellent shot.'

Bodenstein and Pia left Gehrke's house, since there was
nothing more for them to do there. Cem and Kathrin could
talk to the neighbours later and find out whether Gehrke had
had any visitors recently, especially last night.

'Isn't is weird that everybody involved in this case is good
with guns?' Pia said as she got in the car with Bodenstein.
She'd parked her own car up the street; she would come back
for it later.

'Depends on your point of view,' said Bodenstein, and
moved the car back so that the hearse could park. 'There are
plenty of people in Germany who are familiar with guns. As

hunters, target shooters or police officers. Not so many as in America, of course, but enough. In other investigations, we never asked about marksmanship, because it wasn't important to the case.'

'Sounds reasonable.' Pia leaned forward and entered the address that Kai had given them into the satnav. 'Now I'm anxious to meet Helen Stadler's surrogate father and hear what he has to say.'

The house at Lärchenweg 12 in Vockenhausen was a bungalow that must have looked quite nice at one time. Now it seemed dilapidated. The plaster was peeling, the roof had moss on it, and the front garden gave an impression of neglect.

Bodenstein rang the bell. No one opened the door, but in the driveway in front of the garage stood a dirty black SUV, and they could hear the sound of an axe in the Sunday stillness.

'Somebody's chopping wood. Come on, let's go round back,' Pia suggested. They went round the garage into the garden, which hardly deserved to be called that because it didn't look much better than the front. The lawn wasn't being mowed as winter approached, and a variety of junk and refuse was stacked along the side wall of the house and behind the garage. By the back steps stood a man chopping wood, dressed only in jeans and T-shirt despite the cold. He was good at it, splitting the thick logs and tossing the firewood into a basket on the back porch steps. Next to him lay a rottweiler, who now turned his head and jumped up.

'Oh great!' Bodenstein yelled, ducking behind Pia for cover.

'What kind of brave knight are you?' Pia chided. She stood calmly as the dog, a muscular colossus, ran towards her, barking ominously. The man slammed the axe into the chopping block and turned round.

'Enough, Arko!' he commanded in a sharp voice. The dog froze and stood as if rooted to the spot.

'Mr Thomsen?' Bodenstein ventured forward, still behind Pia. 'Excuse us for bothering you on a Sunday, but . . .'

He took out his ID, but Mark Thomsen waved it off.

'You're cops,' he said. 'I don't need IDs. I can tell by looking at you. I used to be part of that club. What's up?'

He was in his late forties, wiry and in superb condition. Thick dark hair, a precisely trimmed moustache and a couple of tattoos on his muscular biceps.

'We're investigating the sniper case,' Bodenstein said.

'Aha,' said Thomsen without much interest. 'And what do I have to do with it?'

'In our investigation, we've come across HRMO and learned that you were the first president. Can you spare a moment?'

'If it'll help.' Thomsen shrugged, grabbed the basket, and whistled to the dog, who walked close by his side without taking his eyes off the strangers. 'Let's go inside.'

They followed him across the back porch into the house. It was cold inside.

'That's the drawback with a woodstove,' said Thomsen. 'It'll warm up soon. Go on in the kitchen.'

He fired up the stove, which was in the living room. The inside of the house was in no better shape than the exterior. Doors and doorframes were scratched, the floor tiles were filthy, the windows almost black with dirt. On the other hand, the kitchen was spick and span, clean and orderly. On the wall hung a framed photo of a boy about fourteen in a football strip, grinning happily at the camera.

'How can I help you?' Mark Thomsen said as he entered the kitchen. 'Coffee?'

Bodenstein and Pia declined.

'What is HRMO exactly, and what does the acronym stand for?' Pia asked.

'We're an association with common interests,' Thomsen explained, pouring himself some coffee and adding a spoonful of sugar. 'The acronym stands for Help for Relatives of Murder Victims of the Organ Mafia.'

'Murder Victims of the Organ Mafia?' Bodenstein repeated. 'What does that mean?'

'Transplant doctors are absolute vultures. If they sniff out an opportunity somewhere to obtain an organ, then to them, nothing is sacred anymore. And what takes place when organs are removed is nothing but murder,' Thomsen said earnestly as he leaned against the counter. 'One person has no chance against all of them, but together we can make some noise and warn people who have ended up in the same situation that we were once in.'

'What situation?' Pia asked.

'Losing a loved one in an accident is bad enough, but if you're then put under pressure in the hospital, it's pure hell,' replied Thomsen. 'You never get over it.'

'Have you experienced this yourself?'

'Yes. It was fifteen years ago. My son was in a bicycle accident. At the hospital, they determined he was brain-dead. My wife suffered a nervous breakdown, so the doctors latched on to me. They applied massive pressure to make me agree to have my son's organs removed.' Thomsen glanced at the photo on the wall. 'I didn't want to do it. Benni didn't look dead to me. I didn't want to admit that he wouldn't wake up. But they played on my emotions, using all the tricks in the book. Benni's death was terrible, they said, but there was absolutely nothing more they could do for him. But with his organs, he could help save other sick people. I wanted to think it over and discuss it in peace and quiet with my wife, but they kept pressuring me. They couldn't keep Benni stable for very long, and time was of the essence. At some point, I couldn't stand it any longer; my nerves were shot and I consented. And I still regret it to this day.'

Thomsen heaved a sigh.

'They wouldn't let me be with my son when he died. They took him from the ICU to the operating theatre, and when we saw him the next day in the morgue, he was no longer our son. Only a grey shell, his facial features contorted, his eyes glued shut, because they'd even taken his retinas.' His voice sounded calm, but the pain was still there. Fifteen years hadn't been enough to alleviate it. 'My son died without dignity, on an operating table. At the age of fifteen. If you have children, then maybe you can comprehend how I felt then and still feel today.'

'Yes, I can understand it,' Bodenstein said with a nod. 'I have three children myself.'

'My marriage couldn't *survive* what happened. My wife left me two years later, and I lost my job.'

'What sort of work do you do now?' Pia asked.

'I work for a private security service.' Thomsen gave a laugh that sounded forced. 'I wasn't qualified to do anything else.'

'You were in the GSG-9,' said Bodenstein.

'A long time ago. I've been out for twelve years.'

'You never forget how to shoot.'

'That's true,' Thomsen replied, and his eyes took on an sardonic glint. 'It's like riding a bike.'

He said it so dryly and soberly that Pia was reminded who this man was, standing there before her in jeans and T-shirt. Not any old cop could get into the GSG-9. Along with extremely hard physical training, members of this elite unit learned to push themselves to the limit, also mentally, and during missions often far beyond that. They were trained to be highly efficient fighting machines who knew no hesitation or pangs of conscience. The perfect killers.

'Did you know Helen Stadler?' she asked.

Thomsen's expression was once again inscrutable, but for a fraction of a second, there was a twitch at the corner of his mouth.

'Sure,' he said. 'Her grandparents are active in HRMO. What about Helen?'

'You must know that she's dead.'

'Of course. I was at her funeral. Why are you asking about her?'

'We suspect that the sniper is killing people because of her and her mother,' said Bodenstein. 'That's why we're starting from the assumption that the perp must be among Helen Stadler's closest friends or acquaintances.'

'I see. And so you thought that a washed-up ex-sharpshooter from the border patrol might do such a thing.' Thomsen snorted in contempt and set his coffee mug in the sink.

Pia turned her head and saw the rottweiler lying in the hall and staring at her attentively with his amber-coloured eyes. A dog as dangerous as a loaded weapon. Just like his master.

'Dirk Stadler called you Helen's "surrogate father",' she said. 'So you must have been pretty close to her.'

Thomsen crossed his arms and shot her an appraising look, which sent shivers down her back. The man was creepy, and her intuition told her that something wasn't quite right with him.

'Joachim Winkler is a hunter,' he said. 'He's a pretty good shot. Just like Helen's friend Hartig. And her brother was a biathlete. They were all much closer to Helen than I was.'

'Winkler has Parkinson's,' Pia replied. 'Without taking pills, he can hardly hold a glass of water, not to mention make a precision shot from a distance of almost a kilometre.'

Somewhere in the house, a telephone began to ring. Thomsen gave a start and stood up straight.

'Pardon me a moment,' he said brusquely, and left before Bodenstein could stop him. The dog had got up and was now blocking their way. When Pia took a step towards the doorway to listen in on what Thomsen was saying on the phone, a dull rumble came from the throat of the rottweiler.

'It's okay,' she said to the dog. 'Stay cool.'

Mark Thomsen came back a little later. He patted the dog on the head in passing and ordered him to lie down.

'Do you own a gun, Mr Thomsen?' Bodenstein asked.

'Why?'

'Please answer my question.'

'I have a gun permit. But I've sold off all my weapons over the past few years because I needed the money.'

'Do you have receipts?'

'Of course.'

'What's the name of your employer?'

'TopSecure.' Thomsen glanced briefly at his watch. He seemed nervous.

'Where were you on December nineteenth between eight and ten in the morning, on December twentieth round seven in the evening, on Christmas Day at eight in the morning, and round noon on December twenty-eighth?'

Thomsen's eyes narrowed.

'What's the point of this nonsense?' he asked grimly. 'I have no idea where I was. Probably here. When I work the night shift, I sleep during the day.'

'On December nineteenth, did you work the night or day shift?'

'Night shift.'

'So that means you have no alibis for these times,' Bodenstein concluded. 'And that makes you a suspect. Motive, means, opportunity – you know all that, naturally, as a former police officer. I would like to ask you to come with us.'

Thomsen didn't answer. His eyes flickered quickly round the small kitchen before he looked back at Bodenstein.

'No,' he said then.

'What's that supposed to mean?'

Thomsen turned round and pulled open a drawer. Before Pia knew it or could react, he was holding a pistol to her head. She could feel the cold muzzle of the gun on her temple.

'Put your service weapons and mobile phones on the kitchen table.' His tone of command was unmistakable. 'Now!'

'What's this about, Mr Thomsen? You're only going to make it worse on yourself,' Bodenstein protested. But Pia took her weapon out of the holster and placed it with her phone on the table. Her hands were trembling, and her pulse was racing.

Thomsen didn't give the impression that he would hesitate even a second before firing.

'Put down the weapon,' said Bodenstein, amazingly calm. 'Nothing has happened yet, and if you give me your gun and come with us, we'll forget about this whole thing.'

'As an ex-policeman, I know that's not true,' Thomsen countered. 'And all that de-escalation shit won't work on me. So get moving.'

Bodenstein glanced at Pia; then he, too, laid down his service weapon and phone.

'Nothing will happen to you if you don't try anything stupid,' Thomsen assured them. 'Now, walk ahead of me to the hall and then down to the basement.'

Each task gave her joy. What was more beautiful than having her own house? For months, she had planned, chosen flooring, wallpaper, bathroom tiles, the banister, the flagstones for the patio. At first, there had been only blueprints and an open field, but then things finally got going, and day by day, what she had imagined was turning into reality. Bettina Kaspar-Hesse went to the construction site daily, documenting in photographs how the project gradually took shape: the concrete foundation for the basement, the floor slab, the walls, the ground floor, the second storey and the attic. She had waded through mud in rubber boots, had spoken to the construction foreman and the architect, made small and somewhat larger alterations, and longed for the day when she could finally move in and take possession of her dream. The old apartment on Sterngasse had become much too small; the children urgently needed more room than the couple of square feet that had sufficed until now. In the new house, there was plenty of space. Large rooms, a playroom in the basement and their own back garden with a swing, a pool and a huge trampoline. Bettina enjoyed the luxury of driving her car straight into the garage and entering the kitchen directly from there. She no longer had to struggle with her groceries across the car park and up to the fourth floor. She smiled and ran her hand along the oak counter. That morning, she had woken with a feeling of deep satisfaction, gazing from the bed out the floor-to-ceiling windows to the woods. She thanked her lucky stars for the way her life had changed over the past ten years. Back then, she never would have thought that everything would be so wonderful one day. Overwhelming despair had finally driven her to free herself from her terrible first marriage, and then she happened to meet Ralf, her childhood sweetheart, again. He had supported her, instead of trying to hold her back as her ex had done. Her first husband had never succeeded at anything. He started drinking out of frustration and then began beating her. The shadows of the past had faded long ago. With Ralf, peace and quiet had returned to her life, and he had given her two wonderful children, even though she had given up hope of ever becoming a mother. The house was now the crowning jewel of her happiness. Her own house. Her own furniture. Everything had turned out exactly as she and Ralf had planned as they sat together in the evenings poring over the blueprints, fantasizing, laughing and calculating. One day, all their debts would be paid off and they would grow old together in this house. Old and grey and full of love for each other.

Bettina smiled and turned her attention to the quiche lorraine pastry that she had taken out of the fridge. She still had a lot to do for the New Year's Eve party tomorrow night. On the stove, the *Tafelspitz* – boiled rump fillet, an Austrian speciality – was simmering away in a big pot. She had pondered quite a while what to serve, and *Tafelspitz* was easy to prepare and tasted even better each time it was reheated.

'We'll be celebrating Christmas in our new house,' Ralf had insisted last summer, when nothing seemed to be moving at the construction site. She had secretly had her doubts. But he had been right. They moved in on November 24 and unpacked the boxes in no time, hanging up their clothes in the wardrobes and putting all their books on the shelves.

She heard the key turn in the front door.

'We're home!' shouted Ralf, and then the children came running into the kitchen with shining eyes and red cheeks, elated about the trip to the pheasant run that Ralf had taken them to so Bettina could work in peace and quiet. They tore open the fridge, took out a bottle of multivitamin juice, and climbed up on the stools at the breakfast counter in the open-plan kitchen.

'Hey, sweetie.' Ralf came into the kitchen in his stockinged feet, put his arm round her waist, and kissed her. 'Mmm, something smells delicious.'

'That's for tomorrow.' Bettina's heart pounded as always when she saw her husband come in the room. 'But I've got a surprise in the oven for the hungry mob.'

'I smelled it already.' Ralf looked through the glass in the oven door. 'Pizza!'

'Pizza, pizza!' the children shouted with joy. 'What's on it, Mama?'

'Everything you like,' said Bettina with a smile. 'Hurry and set the table and wash your hands so we can eat.'

She looked at her husband and he gazed back at her.

'I love this house,' she said. 'But I love you a whole lot more.'

He took her in his arms and tenderly rubbed his cold cheek against hers.

'I love you, too,' he whispered. 'And I always will, until the end of my days.'

'Damn it!' Bodenstein swore. 'This is unbelievable. He locked us in!'

Thomsen had herded them into the basement furnace room. The fireproof safety door had closed behind them with a dull thud, and then the guy had turned the key in the lock. They were trapped. And the heat was turned off. It was cold in the small room, cold and dark.

Pia tried to get her shivering under control. Fear had surged into all her limbs. Thomsen had appeared to be a threat, but she had no idea they'd end up in a situation like this.

'Ostermann knows where we were going,' Bodenstein tried to reassure her as he felt along the wall for a light switch. In vain. It was probably on the outside. A little light seeped in through a small window in a barred air shaft.

Pia didn't want to think about what might happen. What if the guy set fire to the house to get rid of all the evidence? Maybe he'd even flood the basement, like crazy Daniela Lauterbach had done that time in the Snow White case.

Pia took a deep breath and forced herself to calm down. He'd said that nothing would happen to them. So she just had to believe him.

'Do you think this is our guy?' she asked. By now, her eyes had adjusted to the dim light. She found an empty bucket and turned it over to sit down on.

'He might be,' said Bodenstein. 'He's a good enough shot, anyway.'

'And he's got nothing to lose,' Pia added. 'Oh, crap!'

'What is it?' Bodenstein asked in annoyance.

'If only I'd had a chance to go to the loo one more time. I really have to pee.'

'Then use the bucket,' Bodenstein suggested. 'I won't look.'

'Nah, I can hold it.' She tried to pull the sleeves of her jacket down over her freezing hands. 'Thomsen really loved Helen Stadler. When I asked him about her, his face twitched.'

'Erik Stadler also liked his sister a lot,' Bodenstein argued.

'Sure, but that was brotherly love,' said Pia. 'He suffered all those years because the family had been broken up. But he still managed to build up a successful company, and he has a girl-friend, hobbies, friends.'

'And the profile that Neff came up with fits him like a glove.'

'The profile is bullshit,' said Pia. 'Besides, Stadler is much too frenetic and impatient. This Thomsen character seems more the type. He's ice-cold. And a pro.'

'We shouldn't forget about Jens-Uwe Hartig.' With his hands stuffed in his coat pockets, Bodenstein began pacing from one side of the room to the other, five metres forward, five metres back. Pia turned her head to watch him like a spectator at a tennis match. 'He has basically given up everything in his life. Both professionally and privately. The desire for revenge must be boiling inside him. And if what Thomsen said is true, he knows how to shoot. For years, he and Helen talked about nothing but the past. In my opinion, that's pathological. Normal people eventually look to the future after processing what has happened to them. Helen Stadler seems to have been incapable of doing that. And the same goes for Hartig.'

'Helen turned her purported guilt over the death of her

mother into a lifelong obsession.' Pia nodded. 'Almost as if she had wanted to take the blame.'

'She made it into something uniquely her own, like a terminal disease.' Bodenstein leaned against the wall. 'There are plenty of people who constantly have some sort of disease in order to get attention.'

'I simply can't understand how someone could immerse themselves in something like that – and for years.' Pia shook her head and pressed her knees together. Gradually her shivering diminished. Thomsen had locked them up so he could make his escape, not to do them any harm.

'The reality is,' Bodenstein replied, 'that everyone else managed to cope with all these strokes of fate and learned to live with them, but Helen did not. We have to investigate Hartig more closely. Perhaps he sees it as his duty to take revenge on those who drove Helen to commit suicide.'

'And the grandparents, the Winklers,' Pia said, thinking out loud. 'They blame themselves for turning their dead daughter over for organ donation. Their decision and its consequences eventually drove Thomsen completely over the edge.'

Her bladder was almost bursting. If she hadn't been locked in here with Bodenstein, but with Kai or Christian, she would have had considerably fewer inhibitions about peeing in the bucket. In front of her boss, it would be extremely unpleasant.

'So, four suspects: Jens-Uwe Hartig, Mark Thomsen, Joachim Winkler and Erik Stadler,' Bodenstein summed up. 'The last three, at any rate, are familiar with firearms. That remains to be seen in Hartig's case. All four have a relatively strong motive, probably the means, and possibly also the opportunity. Hartig and Stadler are single, so they can dispose of their time freely. Winkler is retired, and Thomsen works shifts.'

'But it would take some time to study the victims and their day-to-day habits, and to find the right location for the strike.' Pia rubbed her palms together and stretched out her left leg, which was about to go to sleep. 'And we shouldn't forget about Stadler Senior. He was the hardest hit. Oh man, I can't stand it any longer. Boss, please turn round.'

She stood up, flipped over the bucket, and pulled down her trousers.

The team came to let them out at 4:40 in the afternoon, four and a half hours after Thomsen had locked them in the furnace room. Cem Altunay had brought along four uniformed officers. He was grinning when he shoved back the bolt and opened the door.

'Where the hell have you been?' Bodenstein acted as if Cem hadn't shown up for an appointment.

'Unfortunately, we had to wait until we got a phone call telling us your whereabouts,' Cem replied. 'Kai thought you were just having a leisurely lunch somewhere.'

'Pardon me?' Pia stared at her colleague, flabbergasted.

'Yeah, Thomsen called the station half an hour ago and told us that he'd locked you in the furnace room,' Cem went on. 'He said the back door was open and the key was in it. Then he hung up.'

'I wonder why he did that?' Pia said, stretching her aching limbs.

'He noticed that the situation was getting dicey for him, and needed some time to collect himself,' Bodenstein guessed. 'Let's search the house. Cem, please inform the evidence team.

I want them to turn this place upside down. And tell Kai to put out an APW on Thomsen right away.'

'He already has,' Cem said.

Upstairs on the kitchen table, they found their service weapons and mobile phones right where they'd put them. The woodstove in the living room was putting out heat like a sauna, and Pia, who was chilled to the bone, quickly thawed out. Then she went through the house with Oliver and Cem. After separating from his wife, Thomsen had arranged the house to suit himself. In the living room were several weight machines and a treadmill instead of a sofa and easy chairs; in another room were an empty desk, a rumpled bed and a wardrobe with the doors standing open.

'He took stuff with him,' said Pia. 'And clothes, too.'

'Thomsen is on the run,' said Bodenstein with a grim expression.

'Detectives?' called an officer from upstairs. 'Come up here and take a look at this!'

The three rooms and bathroom on the second floor seemed unused; theywere stuffy and unheated. The young female officer led Pia and Bodenstein to the room next to the bathroom, which had probably belonged to Thomsen's son, Benni. A single bed stood under the sloping ceiling, and above it hung yellowed posters from the 1997–98 season of Frankfurt United. On the wall next to the desk were six empty corkboards. Someone had obviously torn off in great haste the sheets of paper that had been posted on them, because here and therewere pins with scraps of paper clinging to them, and the carpet underneath was also strewn with pins.

'This was on the floor behind the desk.' The officer was

smiling excitedly as she handed Bodenstein the piece of paper. 'Looks like he missed this one.'

'Take a look at this,' Bodenstein said after scanning the items and giving a low whistle. 'It looks like a record of his shadowing activity.'

He handed it to Pia.

'It sure is.' She nodded. 'A handwritten dossier on Maximilian Gehrke. His complete daily routine from May through to August 2012. Somebody was watching him regularly, and for weeks at a time.'

'Thomsen is our man,' said Bodenstein with conviction.

'But look at the handwriting. It doesn't look like a man wrote this. More like a young girl.'

'What's that got to do with anything?' Bodenstein examined the six corkboards more closely. 'They're full of holes.'

'There are six of them,' Cem observed, deep in thought. 'I wonder if that might mean something.'

'What do you think?' Pia wanted to know.

'Maybe one board for each victim,' her colleague replied sombrely. 'If so, then the sniper has two more people in his sights.'

Finally, the case was starting to move.

After twelve days with no leads, no clues and not a scrap of success, the team now plunged into their work with feverish activity, newly motivated and driven by cautious excitement. Feeling tense but focused, they compiled the tiniest details, eliminated any contradictory modes of thinking, and recapped the facts. Even so, the picture that was emerging, from all the pieces of the puzzle they had so far, remained rather vague.

'By the way, the editor of the *Taunus Echo* denies having

been in contact with Gehrke,' Bodenstein informed the rest of the team. 'He claims that Karoline Albrecht, the daughter of victim number two, showed up at his office and demanded to see the obituary for her mother. Besides that one, he also showed her the other two that he had. And he made copies of them for her.'

'And what does Ms Albrecht say to that?' Pia enquired. 'Why would she go visit Gehrke?'

'Maybe she knew him.' Bodenstein shrugged. 'He was an acquaintance of her father's, after all.'

'I still haven't been able to reach her. We don't have her mobile number.'

Outside the window, darkness had fallen long ago, but no one had any intention of going home. Not now, not when they were on the verge of a possible breakthrough. Somebody ordered pizza for everyone from the Italian place over on Elisabethenstrasse. They ate standing up or sitting at the tables in the operations room of the special commission, while Kai Ostermann summed up what they knew so far.

In the attic of Mark Thomsen's house, two rifles and ammunition had been found, neatly stowed in a weapons cabinet. According to the documentation, one rifle and a handgun were missing. In addition, they confiscated a couple of document binders, but Bodenstein had no great hope of finding any decisive new revelations in them, because Thomsen seemed to have taken everything with him that was important. He'd certainly had enough time. The search for him and his dog was ongoing, and his photo had been given to the press. They had questioned his ex-wife, and what she told them confirmed not only his motivation, but also the profile that Kim had drawn of the perp. After the death of his son, the main thing Thomsen had on his mind was to denounce the unethical actions of the surgeons, and it had infuriated him that he couldn't find anyone to agree with his concerns. In addition, he was an excellent sharpshooter who remained cold-blooded and calm even in high-stress situations. When they talked with his ex-wife, the real reason why he was no longer a police officer came to light. An incident, which she did not go into further, had led to his suspension, trial and dishonourable discharge.

In the vague hope that Thomsen might make a mistake and seek shelter with the Winklers in Glashütten, they staked out the family's house. They also phoned all the members of HRMO they could find through the website. But no one knew a thing. Mark Thomsen seemed to have vanished without a trace.

Although every indication seemed to point to him as the perp, Bodenstein didn't forget about the other suspects. Erik Stadler had confirmed Patrick Schwarzer's story, as well as the fact that there were not many people who knew about his mistake. The A&E doctor and the paramedics, for instance, had been mad as hell when the drunken Schwarzer drove the ambulance into the ditch.

In the meantime, Ostermann was busy researching Jens-Uwe Hartig.

Inquiries with the army and the police had produced a few new names, none of which had any connection to Kirsten Stadler – except for Mark Thomsen.

Nothing had been found in Fritz Gehrke's house that was of any interest. The old man had cleaned things out thoroughly before his suicide. He left no suicide note, but did refer to his will, which he had changed two days after his son's death to make the German Foundation for Organ Transplantation his sole heir.

'It's an irony of fate that he, as a doctor of medicine and director of a pharmaceutical firm, was unable to help his own son,' remarked Neff, who had casually taken a seat next to Kim at the desk. 'So his millions were of no use to him.'

'But he did manage to help him,' Kim contradicted Neff. 'He succeeded in getting a new heart for his son.'

Pia looked at her sister. A fleeting thought ran through her head.

'Where did Gehrke study medicine?' she asked.

'In Cologne,' replied Neff.

'Tell me, Kai, have you already checked all the numbers from Gehrke's phone?'

'Yes. Fortunately, he didn't like to use a mobile phone. He preferred the landline, which made checking them easier.' Kai pulled out the list and shoved it over to Pia.

'The last call before his death was, in fact, to Professor Dieter Rudolf,' she said. 'And before that, he called a Dr Hans Furtwängler in Cologne. Who's that?'

Kai typed the name into his computer. While he searched, Pia went on.

'The call this morning with the Frankfurt area code was placed from the landline of a Peter Riegelhoff.'

'That name sounds familiar,' said Bodenstein.

'A lawyer,' said Ostermann. 'I already checked it.'

'Yes, that's it,' said Bodenstein. 'The guy from the *Taunus Echo,* who buttonholed me after the press conference at the Stadthalle, mentioned him. Riegelhoff was the lawyer for the UCF who worked out the deal with the Stadler family. What does he have to do with Fritz Gehrke?'

'That's what we have to find out,' said Pia, leaning over the printout of the phone calls. 'Gehrke spoke to Dr Hans Furtwängler for fourteen minutes, then he dialled the landline of a Dr Simon Burmeister in Bad Homburg, and that call lasted only twelve seconds.'

'Answering machine,' Kai guessed. 'Okay, I found Furtwängler. Born 1934, professor emeritus, previously internist and oncologist, speciality haematology.'

'And Dr Simon Burmeister,' announced Neff, who had been Googling at the same time, 'is the head of transplant surgery at the UCF.'

What had Fritz Gehrke wanted from those four men? What did he have to do with them? He was on a first-name basis with the lawyer, so they must have had some sort of trust relationship, because a man like Gehrke would not switch to a first name basis with younger men very quickly.

'Are there any similarities?' Pia asked. 'Were they perhaps all in Rotary or Lions or some other organization?'

'Simon Burmeister was also at the UCF as early as 2002,' said Kim, who was looking at the UCF website. 'Burmeister is probably Professor Rudolf's successor. According to his CV, he's been at UCF since 1999.'

'So he could be a future target of the sniper.' Bodenstein grabbed his phone. 'Please give me his number, Pia.'

Pia read it out to him, but Bodenstein only got Burmeister's voice mail. He left an urgent message for him to call back, and then dialled the number of the lawyer, Riegelhoff. He was able to reach only his wife, who didn't seem miffed at the late call on a Saturday night. Her husband was at the office, she said, and gave Bodenstein both his landline and mobile numbers.

Riegelhoff didn't answer, so Bodenstein left a message on the office answering machine and on the voicemail of his mobile.

It was just after ten in the evening when Dr Nicola Engel entered the conference room and announced that the judge responsible for authorizing the wiretap on the Winklers had approved the warrant, as well as search warrants for the residences of Erik Stadler and Jens-Uwe Hartig.

'Very good.' Bodenstein was satisfied. He stood up and looked round at the team. 'Stadler is no rush, but Hartig will be getting a visit from us at five o'clock tomorrow morning. First at his residence, then in his shop. That's all for today. It was a strenuous day for all of us, and tomorrow we'll be at it early.'

They turned off their computers and closed their laptops. Pia stretched and yawned. She noticed Kim looking at the commissioner, and she also saw Neff's gaze following Kim's. Their colleague from state police headquarters seemed to be trying to cosy up to her sister, even bringing her coffee and treats like chocolate croissants. The more Kim gave him the cold shoulder, the greater were his efforts to win her favour. Neff may have thought he was unobserved, but she could read his face like a book. And what Pia read there filled her with disquiet. Neff was a conceited arsehole, and she distrusted the change in him. What was he up to?

Karoline Albrecht massaged the back of her neck, which was stiff from sitting too long at the computer. She was searching for information on Dr Hans Furtwängler, whom she had visited in Cologne today, but she couldn't find anything conspicuous. Furtwängler seemed not to have accomplished anything especially remarkable or reprehensible in the forty years he was active as a doctor. He had been head of oncology and haematology at a large hospital in Cologne; later, when he reached retirement age, he went into private practice. He had introduced a few new therapeutic methods that were standard nowadays for the treatment of leukaemia. Besides the Federal Cross of Merit, he had received numerous other honours; he was a member of various medical associations, the Lions Club and a couple of professional groups. No scandals, no legal proceedings. Nothing. Then she had repeated the procedure with Dr Arthur Janning, once her father's best friend, but the search yielded nothing more of interest. Janning, head of Intensive Care Medicine at the UCF, was just as above suspicion as Furtwängler.

In vain she had looked for something in the CVs of the two men that could have explained the veiled intimations that Furtwängler and Janning had made. Her conversation with Furtwängler, an agile octogenarian with a fresh Caribbean suntan, had proceeded quite informally after he had first expressed his condolences with the appropriate sorrow. Karoline had claimed that she just happened to be in Cologne and had recalled her visits to his lovely garden from her childhood, but as soon as she mentioned the name Kirsten Stadler, the man's jovial demeanour abruptly vanished. she ran into a wall of silence and the conversation soon came to a standstill.

Karoline glanced at the clock on the stove. Almost midnight.

Disheartened and disappointed by the lack of progress she'd made, she wanted to give up and crawl into bed, but then an idea came to her. Greta had been longing for her thirteenth birthday more than any other, because then she'd finally be old enough to have a Facebook account. Since then, she seemed to spend half her life on social networks, uploading photos, posting daily trivialities and defining her degree of popularity by the number of 'Likes' she received. Karoline had already seen Greta sulk for a whole weekend because she'd been 'unfriended' by someone on Facebook, which was tantamount to not being invited to a birthday party in the old days. Greta had declared that she almost wouldn't exist in the world if she weren't on Facebook.

So Karoline had set up a user account for herself and learned the basic concepts. To her amazement, she had received friend requests from all sorts of acquaintances and former schoolmates. She poured herself another glass of white wine and logged on to Facebook. Via the search box, she instantly found Helen Stadler. She was astonished to see that the account was still active; apparently, no one had thought to shut it down. She could hardly believe her good fortune, and clicked on Helen Stadler's friend list, which at fifty-four persons was quite manageable. Since she hadn't been friended by her, she could see only a few photos and postings, but she jotted down the names of those who had commented on Helen's postings or 'Liked' them. One name popped up more often than others: Vivien Stern. Karoline went to her page and wrote her a brief note. She doubted whether the young woman would answer, but there was always a chance.

MONDAY, DECEMBER 31, 2012

Today was the last day of the old year, a special day. For many people, it was the perfect moment to look back on the old year and to take stock. What was good, and what was bad? What would I want to change? Where would I like to be at this time next year? As far as he was concerned, everything was clear. Nobody would ever understand why he had to do all this, so he would either be sitting in prison or roasting in hell. It pretty much boiled down to the same thing.

Most people would be celebrating the new year, and not alone. They would eat, drink, act as though it were a special night, but it was a night like any other. In other cultures, 31 December was an utterly normal day. He no longer had any interest in celebrating, with the fireworks, the bottle rockets and all that New Year's Eve hysteria. Not anymore. In the old days, it had been different. Back then, he had drunk champagne with his colleagues and later celebrated at home with his family. They always had raclette or fondue, to go with the wine. But that was long ago. Today he was alone. And tonight he was going to kill someone. There were plenty of people who looked forward to the new year but would not live to experience it. On New Year's Eve, there were more accidents than usual, and old people died as always. But one person would die who was not yet on the list. Or was he? Was this person already fated by birth to be killed on 31 December 2012, by a semi-jacketed .308 Winchester round fired from a Steyr SSG 69 rifle? Or was his death merely a result of the various decisions that he'd made in his life, leading him to that moment tonight when he would perish?

He felt no sympathy. No one had ever had any sympathy for him. He, too, had had to accept what happened and learn from it in order to keep living. He, too, had been left behind, unable to change a thing. Fate struck out of the blue, mercilessly and without warning. And then you sat there and had to deal with it. For the rest of your miserable life.

*

Pia had not slept well. Something kept churning inside her head, and it was driving her crazy because she simply couldn't grasp what it was. At quarter to four in the morning, she got up and dressed, then went down to the kitchen to make herself some coffee. Last night, she had Skyped with Christoph but very wisely neglected to mention the incident with Thomsen and the cocked pistol pressed to her temple. He was already worried about her, afraid that she wasn't eating right or getting enough sleep, so she didn't want to cause him even more concern. She missed him with every fibre of her being. In the daytime, she managed to forget how much she missed him because she was so busy working on the case. But at night, she lay awake in bed and longed for his familiar presence, for the smell of his skin and the sound of his breathing in the dark. She'd never realized before how much she'd got used to him being close, and how much it hurt when he was away.

Fortunately, it was only temporary. How would it feel to lose someone you loved through death, gone from one second to the next? How would it be to get the news that your partner or daughter, mother or son had died, without having the chance to say goodbye? Pia thought about Dirk Stadler, who'd had to cope with two such traumas, first when he'd lost his wife and then his daughter. And about Jens-Uwe Hartig, who'd had to bury his fiancée shortly before their wedding. And Mark Thomsen, who had lost his son and then his wife and finally his job.

Pia recalled the horror that Renate Rohleder and Professor Rudolf felt when they realized their mistakes had caused the dearest people in their lives to be killed. The sniper had robbed Fritz Gehrke, that old, sick man, of the most important person he still had in his life. And Patrick Schwarzer, who in his view had made a minor error, was then punished for it ten years later.

A fate worse than death – the saying contained a real kernel of truth. The loss alone was enough to tear open wounds that would never heal, but knowing that you were to blame for the death was a truly devilish punishment. Was that why Gehrke had killed himself?

Just as Pia was making herself two slices of toast with salted butter and Nutella, Kim showed up.

'Good morning,' she murmured, shuffling over to the coffeemaker. 'How do you manage to be so disgustingly awake?'

'Good morning.' Pia grinned. 'It's the early-bird gene. I'm the lark and you're more of an owl. Would you like some breakfast before we get going?'

She slapped the warm pieces of toast together and bit into them.

'I can't stomach anything this early in the morning.' Kim shook her head in disgust and sipped her coffee.

'Mark Thomsen doesn't have a real motive,' said Pia with her mouth full. 'Unless there's something connecting him to the Stadlers that we don't know about.'

'I've been wondering about that, too,' replied Kim. 'Stadler got a payoff from the UCF back then. What if he hired somebody?'

'A contract killer, you mean?'

'Yeah, exactly. A pro.'

'I thought about that, too,' Pia admitted. 'You've been convinced the whole time that the perp is a pro. Dirk Stadler has the same motives as his in-laws and his son. And anyone who has the right connections can find somebody to do the dirty work. Lithuanians, Russians, Kosovo Albanians – they'll do that sort of stuff for cheap.'

'We don't have to go that far.' Kim was gradually waking up. 'What about this? Maybe Thomsen was paid by the Stadlers to carry out their revenge.'

Pia thought it over as she ate her toast. Was Mark Thomsen a man who would kill for hire? What good would blood money do him if he was caught and had to spend his life behind bars? No, a guy like him acted out of conviction or not at all. He wasn't the type to let himself be harnessed to someone else's cart.

'Let's wait and see what the house searches turn up.' She glanced at the clock, cleared the dishes from the table and put them in the dishwasher. 'I'm going to take the dogs out and feed the horses. See you later at the station?'

'Of course,' said Kim with another yawn. 'I'll be there at nine. And before that, I'm going to do some shopping.'

'You're a sweetheart,' said Pia with a grin. 'Not that we couldn't celebrate New Year's tonight without our traditional meat fondue.'

'Should I also buy a few fireworks?' Kim called after her as she went into the hall and slipped on her wooden clogs.

'Don't bother,' Pia said cheerfully. 'From here we can see the fireworks in Frankfurt and all along the Taunus slope. It would just be a waste of money.'

Bodenstein knew at once that the search of Jens-Uwe Hartig's residence would turn up nothing. At five in the morning, Hartig was already fully dressed. Or maybe he'd never gone to bed. Unshaven, he opened the front door and refused to take the search warrant when Bodenstein tried to hand it to him.

'All right, then,' he said calmly. 'Okay if I make some coffee?'

'Please do.' Bodenstein and Pia followed the man into the kitchen. 'Haven't you slept at all?'

'A little.' Hartig watched without emotion as an officer carrying laundry baskets walked past him and switched on the lights in all three rooms. Then Hartig turned to the coffeemaker, picked up the glass pot, and filled it with water. 'I don't sleep well anymore, not since Helen died. Mostly I watch documentaries on TV, or go over to the shop. Work takes my mind off her.'

'Were you there last night? Your car's engine is still warm.'

'Yes. I got home half an hour ago.' The hint of a smile passed over his exhausted face. He opened a cupboard. 'As if I knew you were coming. Would you like a cup?'

'No thanks,' the two detectives both replied. The coffee machine began to chuff. The stuffy odour of sweat and cigarette smoke was replaced by the aroma of coffee.

'Do you know Mark Thomsen?' Pia enquired.

'Yes.' Hartig nodded. 'Kind of an idiot.'

'Were you jealous of him?'

'Why would I be jealous?' Hartig countered.

'Because your fiancée had a pretty close relationship with him,' said Pia. 'Dirk Stadler described Thomsen as her "father surrogate".'

'That's bullshit. Mark seemed to latch on to her from the first time she went to a HRMO meeting with her grandparents. At first she liked the attention, but with time it became . . . unpleasant.'

'In what way?'

'He was patronizing and condescending, and he kept giving

her unwanted advice.' Hartig shook his head as if to dismiss an unwelcome memory. 'He even fixed up a room in his house for her.'

'Do you think he was interested in her sexually?'

'You've seen Helen's picture,' replied Hartig with a hint of bitterness. 'She was very beautiful and always made a needy impression. Crude macho types like Thomsen love that sort of person. It makes them feel big and strong, even though they're nothing but failures. Thomsen is a poor soul, who revels in fantasies of revenge. He kept pestering her with his ideas, blatantly trying to incite her.'

'What sort of revenge fantasies?' Bodenstein enquired.

'He wanted to punish the people who in his opinion were to blame for his misery.'

'Do you believe that Thomsen would actually shoot someone?' Pia asked. 'There's a big difference between talking about it and doing it.'

'I certainly do.' Hartig poured himself more coffee and grimaced. 'There's not much holding him back. He shot people when he was with the GSG-9. And more than once, he's said that it would be no big deal for him to take somebody out from a couple of hundred metres. It's like a video game, nothing more.'

Pia didn't reply. She didn't believe that Thomsen would have really killed her or Bodenstein yesterday, but he wouldn't have hesitated to shoot her, maybe in the leg, to underscore his demands.

'Do you know how to shoot, Mr Hartig?' Bodenstein asked.

'I used to. My father was a fanatical hunter and was always dragging my brother and me into the forest, even when we were kids. The first time he put a rifle in our hands, we were still in nursery school.' Hartig laughed unhappily. 'That was his idea of how to make little bed wetters into tough guys.'

'Shooting is like riding a bike, you never forget how,' Pia paraphrased what Thomsen had told her yesterday.

Hartig looked at her face and shrugged.

'I wouldn't even remember how to load a rifle,' he claimed.

That brief glance from his dark eyes had been enough to tell Pia he was lying. His apparent indifference, his lack of expression, the way he was neglecting his appearance – it was all carefully contrived in order to deceive them. Jens-Uwe Hartig was a very intelligent man for whom any sort of failure was equivalent to a personal insult, a man who took action and moved things along if they were important to him. He had already shown how far he was prepared to go when he revolted against the methods used by his medical colleagues. With his eyes wide open, he had destroyed his own promising career in medicine.

Pia regarded the man with the greasy, scruffy hair who was trying to play the part of a grieving man with a broken heart. She had to admit he did it well. Pia might have been duped by him if that strange look hadn't flared up in his eyes, a look that in no way matched the rest of his manner. There was something calculating and cryptic about his expression that evoked a vague unease in Pia.

While their colleagues packed up everything that seemed worthy of examination, Bodenstein got a call. Lis Wenning wanted to speak to him, so he decided that Pia should stay to supervise the search of Hartig's shop. In the meantime, Bodenstein would drive over to Erik Stadler's office, which opened at seven thirty, in order to bring Stadler's girlfriend to the station for an interview.

'Where exactly were you when the murders occurred?' Pia asked Hartig when they were alone in the kitchen.

'If you tell me what the times were, I can give you an answer,' Hartig said. 'By the way, do you mind if I smoke?'

'No, go ahead. It's your house,' said Pia. She told him the times and dates of the four murders.

Hartig listened intently, then lit a cigarette and took a deep drag. He had thin wrists and lovely, slender fingers. Surgeon's hands. Jens-Uwe Hartig was, in general, a handsome man.

'I can't remember exactly,' he admitted, squeezing his eyes tight for a moment. 'And I don't really have any alibis. That must be one reason why you're having my home searched. I'm a suspect, aren't I?'

Again, the strangely furtive glance.

'Maybe,' said Pia. 'We hope to find information in your house that we urgently need, but that you have refused to share with us.'

That wasn't quite the whole truth, but it was certainly one of the reasons why the search warrant had been approved.

'What information?'

'About employees of the UCF who dealt with Kirsten Stadler. Do you happen to recall any names?'

'No, I'm afraid not,' Hartig apologized. 'I remember only Professor Rudolf and Dr Hausmann.'

'Stop this charade!' Pia felt the same helplessness that she'd felt thousands of times before when questioning suspects who were lying or simply refusing to answer. 'You and Helen hardly talked about anything except what happened to her mother. So I'm sure names must have been mentioned. Why won't you help us? Don't you care if more innocent people die?'

'You're desperate, aren't you?' Hartig said with a contemptuous smirk. 'You don't even know these people. Why do their deaths bother you so much?'

Pia stared at him in amazement. Was he serious, or did he just have a sick sense of humour? Why couldn't she figure out what it was about Hartig that upset her so much?

'I seldom know the people I have to deal with in my job,' she replied. 'But that doesn't change the fact that I don't like it when someone sets himself up as judge over life and death. We live in a nation governed by law, which I represent. If everyone did whatever came into their head, we'd be living in anarchy.'

'The rule of law is a farce.' Hartig's expression was contemptuous. 'For me, my concern with the Stadlers ended on the day I lost Helen. After that, I broke off all contact with her family and turned my sights towards a future that has nothing more to do with Helen or her demons. Can't you understand that?'

'Yes, I can,' said Pia. 'But I still don't believe you. Why do you keep going to the cemetery each morning?'

Hartig sighed.

'I loved Helen more than anyone else in my life,' he replied. 'The fact that she preferred death to a life with me affected me deeply, and to this day, I don't understand it. Maybe that's why I visit her grave every morning.'

Pia surveyed him sceptically, but waited in vain for some telltale gesture, a compromising twitch of his lips, or any other sign that he was lying. She decided to take off the kid gloves.

'How do you get along with Erik Stadler and his girlfriend?' she began innocently.

'Since Helen died, I've had no contact with them. But before, we always got along fine.'

'And with Helen's father?'

'Dirk was very grateful to me for everything I did for Helen.'

Not a real answer to her question.

'And what was it you did for her?'

Hartig hesitated briefly before he replied.

'I protected her. As best I could, and as much as she'd allow me to do. Helen was a woman full of contradictions.' He gazed pensively at the glowing tip of his cigarette. 'On the one hand, she was courageous and self-confident, but on the other, she was full of fears and doubts. She never got over the loss of her mother and the circumstances of her death. She held on to every person who meant something to her with an obsessiveness that for many was hard to bear. The fear of being abandoned again became deeply rooted in her soul.'

He stubbed out his cigarette and rubbed his face. Pia was reminded of what Franka Fellmann had told her about Helen Stadler.

'We've heard that Helen had serious mental problems, yet she refused to see a therapist.'

'She suffered from post-traumatic stress disorder. She didn't need therapy, just love and security. The feeling of being safe. And that's what I gave her.'

'It apparently wasn't enough. Otherwise, she wouldn't have taken her own life.' Pia was eager to see how Hartig would react to this provocation. She was expecting an angry outburst, a fierce protest, but she got the opposite response.

'Yes,' said Hartig calmly. 'It obviously wasn't enough for her. That's the worst thing about it. I failed her.'

'People have told us that Helen never tried to work through

the trauma; instead she wallowed in it. And you supported her choice. Last summer, you and Helen visited the flower shop owned by Renate Rohleder, whose mother was the first victim of the sniper. What were you looking for there?'

'I did not encourage Helen to dwell on the trauma. I helped her to work it out.'

'By threatening people?'

'No one threatened anybody,' said Hartig, shaking his head. 'Helen was totally beside herself when she stood there, facing that woman. Until we walked into that flower shop, I had no idea who Renate was.'

Pia asked him a few more questions about Helen, Dirk and Erik Stadler, Mark Thomsen and Helen's grandparents. Hartig answered calmly and without hesitation. Everything he said sounded absolutely credible and sincere. His expression matched his tone of voice, and he didn't try to gloss over or conceal anything. No contradictions, no exaggerations. The perfect surviving relative who was still wrestling with the loss, but who wanted to regain his footing in life. A little *too* perfect. Pia was amazed that Bodenstein, who was an extraordinarily good judge of character, had been fooled by Hartig. He had called him a Good Samaritan who'd been utterly derailed by Helen's death. The man who stood before her seemed in no way devastated. Either he was making a gigantic effort to process the loss of his beloved fiancée and his failure to save her or he was an ice-cold, calculating psychopath who was leading them all down the garden path.

Lis Wenning showed up without a lawyer. She made a bleary-eyed but composed impression. Bodenstein took her into his office and offered her a seat in one of the visitors' chairs.

'I would walk through fire for Erik,' she began. 'We've been together for six years now, and have weathered both highs and lows in our relationship, especially since Helen's suicide. Erik loved his sister very much, and her death hit him hard. But he also viewed her shortcomings realistically. Helen suffered a psychological trauma because of her mother's death, but above all, because of the break-up of her family. She clung to her father, and he in turn found comfort in being with his daughter. She was truly sick: she had anxiety attacks, an extreme fear of loss and she could not cope with even the slightest change.'

Lis Wenning shook her head.

'When her father wanted to buy a new car, she had a fit; she locked herself in the old car and cried like a little girl. New furniture scared her. If something was simply moved in the house, she was frightened. Dirk humoured her and changed nothing. He idolized her. And she could be extremely lovable sometimes.'

'Your boyfriend's bookkeeper told us quite different stories about Helen,' Bodenstein remarked.

'Franka? Yes, I bet she did. Erik had Helen working for him for a while, when his father was extremely busy. Franka was insanely jealous. She would rather work a twelve-hour day than have assistance from anyone else. She took over everything in the company, and Erik let that happen because it was convenient for him. But then she started treating him like a child. And she would snap at clients on the phone because she was completely swamped and could no longer attend to her own work. So finally, he decided to fire her.'

'Oh, she told us that she had quit,' Bodenstein remarked.

'Yes, this time she did,' Lis Wenning agreed. 'When Erik

tried to fire her two years ago, she promised to improve, so he changed his mind and hired a receptionist.'

'Back to Helen.' Bodenstein stretched out his legs. 'How was her relationship with Mark Thomsen?'

'She liked him a lot,' Wenning recalled. 'I'd almost say she worshipped him. For a long time, he was the only person she confided in. When girls reach a certain age, they no longer tell their fathers everything.'

She smiled, but then turned serious again.

'But then Jens-Uwe came along, and she lost interest in everyone else. She had known him for a while before that, but he paid her little attention while he was still married.'

'I had no idea about that.' Bodenstein was surprised and jotted down a note.

'None of us ever met his wife, but she apparently left him. He was very upset when his marriage ended, which made him attractive to Helen. Then he fell in love with her. It was the real thing. For a while.'

'What do you mean? I thought they were going to get married,' Bodenstein said in surprise.

'*He* wanted to get married, but she didn't. She always acted happy, but she wasn't. I think she was afraid of him.'

'Why would she be afraid of him? Her father told us that the relationship with Jens-Uwe had done her good, and she'd calmed down a lot.'

'He gave her pills. He was a doctor and could write prescriptions. I don't know much about it, but once I saw one of the prescriptions and Googled the drug. Lorazepam is a benzodiazepine, and is used to treat anxiety, epilepsy and sleep disorders. And it's very addictive. I told Erik about it, and he talked to Helen, but she denied everything. But I'm convinced that she was taking the pills, because she had totally changed. She often seemed far away, tired and lethargic.'

'Why would Hartig want to give her those pills?' Bodenstein asked.

'So he could control her better,' replied Wenning. 'Jens-Uwe was a control freak. He kept calling her and texting her, and he expected answers instantly. And Helen obeyed. Until Mark heard about it. He got her to stop taking the pills. She had terrible withdrawal symptoms that tormented her. And she probably realized that Jens-Uwe wasn't good for her. Instead of persuading her to begin psychotherapy, he sedated her. Helen tried to break out of the relationship, but he wouldn't let her go. All she could do was decide not to move in with him. She was very unhappy.'

'A neighbour told me that he bought a house to move into with Helen after the wedding,' said Bodenstein.

'He'd already owned the house for a few years. He used to live there with his ex. That's why Helen didn't want to move there.'

'Do you think Hartig is capable of killing someone?' Bodenstein asked after a brief pause.

Lis Wenning considered his question.

'There's something strange about him,' she admitted. 'Something obsessive, like a lone wolf. But whether he could kill someone? I don't know.'

'What about Mark Thomsen?'

'He's killed people on the job,' she replied. 'As an officer in the Federal Border Patrol. Mark was really fond of Helen. Like a daughter, I would say. Her suicide hit him hard. Yes, I think he could do it. After all, he doesn't have much left to lose.'

'Apparently, he and Helen concocted plans for revenge,' Bodenstein said. 'Do you know anything about that?'

'No.' Wenning shook her head. 'Helen never talked to me about the sad incident with her mother. All I know about it is what Erik and Dirk told me.'

'How about an alibi for your boyfriend? Why won't he tell us where he was at those specific times?' Bodenstein wanted to know.

'Maybe because he really can't tell you,' said Lis. 'When he's running, he tunes out everything. And he doesn't just run a lap of the park, like other people do. When he's into it, he can run thirty or forty kilometres.'

'Do you consider him capable of shooting anyone to death?'

'Never!' Wenning said with conviction. 'Erik might be a little crazy when it comes to his daredevil hobbies, but he loves his freedom more than anything else. For that reason alone, he would never do anything that might land him in prison. And for that matter, he's . . . selfish. As sad as Helen's suicide made him feel, he would never put his own life in jeopardy because of her.'

Henning phoned Pia just as she drove into the courtyard at headquarters in Hofheim.

'Sorry I didn't call earlier,' he said. 'But I still don't have any results worth mentioning. The people I'm expecting information from either went away over Christmas and New Year's, or they're stonewalling. But I've done some research and spoken with a few people who worked at the UCF back when Rudolf was there.'

Pia parked in the back by the garages where the service vehicles were kept, and turned off the engine.

'Rudolf probably did circumvent certain regulations in order to help a friend's son. The young man suffered from a cardiac disease that could only be cured by a transplant.'

'Let me guess,' Pia interrupted him. 'Maximilian Gehrke.'

'No names were mentioned,' replied Henning. 'The incident took place in the summer or autumn of 2002. A patient was brought in. And she happened to have blood type—'

'O,' said Pia, finishing the sentence. 'Possibly Kirsten Stadler. What happened then?'

'My informant refuses to testify and will deny that he ever discussed this matter with me,' Henning emphasized, 'but he swears that the patient was left to die even though they still could have helped her. And he also knew that the woman's family received a significant amount of money after the fact.'

'Is fifty thousand euros a significant amount?' Pia asked.

'I heard talk of a million,' Henning countered.

How many hearts had been transplanted during the summer or autumn of 2002 at the UCF anyway? And how many brain-dead women of blood type O had been brought in during this time? She couldn't automatically assume that it was Kirsten Stadler they were talking about, but it was highly likely.

A silver BMW drove into the courtyard and parked a few metres away. Pia watched as Andreas Neff got out and stood next to the car talking on the phone before he grabbed his briefcase and sauntered over.

'At the moment, we're firmly convinced that the perp is retaliating against relatives of the people he holds responsible for the deaths of Kirsten and Helen Stadler,' Pia said to Henning. 'If your informant was actively involved in the Kirsten

Stadler case, then he or his closest relatives are in great danger. If you tell us who he is, we can protect him.'

'I'll tell him that,' Henning promised. 'If we don't hear anything else today, I wish you a Happy New Year. And if you don't have anything better to do – we're having a few people over to celebrate at Ralf and Tina's place, and you're most welcome.'

It gave Pia a little jealous pang to hear that Henning was going to celebrate the New Year with Miriam, his second wife and Pia's former best friend, in exactly the way she'd always wanted to: on the roof terrace of Henning's brother's penthouse apartment, which had a fantastic view of the financial district and the fireworks. But back when they were married, Henning hadn't had either the desire or the time. Pia had usually welcomed the New Year in one of the two post-mortem rooms at the Institute of Forensic Medicine. Or she had spent the evening alone at home on the sofa. A lot of things hadn't changed for her. Tonight she'd be sitting on the sofa at home, too, but at least not entirely alone.

'Thanks for your help, Henning,' she said, opening the car door. 'I hope you guys have a nice party.'

She headed across the car park to the entrance of the Regional Criminal Unit. It was a mystery to her why everyone associated with the Frankfurt Trauma Clinic was so taciturn. There must be a reason for this collective refusal to testify, just as there had to be an explanation for Rudolf's move from the renowned hospital with all its medical and financial means to a rather insignificant private clinic. What had really happened back then? It couldn't solely be related to the Kirsten Stadler case. Something else must be involved. And it made Pia angry that as far as the UCF was concerned, she kept running into walls of silence.

'I'm talking to you only because Helen would have wanted it that way,' Vivien Stern began the conversation. Karoline Albrecht sat across from her at a little table in the corner of Cafe Laumer. Last night, Vivien had left a message on Karoline's Facebook page, agreeing to meet for coffee, much to her surprise. Since it was Karoline's treat, the young woman boldly ordered the most expensive breakfast with a glass of prosecco. For the first time in days, Karoline had a little appetite, and decided on a brioche and a cafe au lait.

'Anyway, she wanted to go to the media with what she'd found out. But she was murdered before she could do that.'

'Excuse me?' Karoline stared at the young woman in astonishment. Vivien Stern was twenty-five years old and had spent a year at the University of Williamstown in Massachusetts, where she'd been studying earth sciences and biology. Yet if she'd claimed she was only graduating from secondary school next spring, Karoline would have believed her. She was very slim, with straight, ash-blonde hair and a pretty face. 'I thought Helen committed suicide?'

'No way!' replied Vivien in a tone of utter conviction. 'She was on the track of a huge news story and totally committed to seeing it through. She would never have jumped in front of a train.'

'What sort of news story?' Karoline asked. It almost turned her stomach to watch the way Vivien put a slice of smoked salmon on a croissant and bit into it.

'Helen was obsessed with the thought that the doctors had let her mother die so they could get at her organs,' she told

Karoline with her mouth full. 'I always found it a tad absurd, but she was collecting evidence, and eventually I was convinced that she was right. She wanted to bring to light everything that happened back then. Everybody had lied to her, and she was going to flip out if she couldn't uncover the truth. Besides, she suspected that her friend was trying to poison her.'

'Did you and Helen know each other well?'

'Yes, we did. We'd been best friends in school and later studied together here in Frankfurt.' Vivien followed the smoked salmon croissant with a soft-boiled egg. She seemed to be starving.

'I see.' Karoline looked at her notebook. She'd jotted down a few questions that she wanted to ask the young woman, but Vivien spoke first, telling her that Helen had been bossed round by her boyfriend, who had numbed her with drugs.

Karoline Albrecht put down her pen and sighed. Vivien was turning out to be a chatterbox with a penchant for dwelling on melodramatic details and a predilection for exaggeration. Karoline was wasting her time. She was also having to strain to hear her conspiratorial whispering, because of all the background noise in the cafe. At the next table, a couple of middle-aged women kept bursting into cackling laughter.

'Helen was so mentally exhausted; it was really a shame.' Vivien shook her head and took a deep breath. 'I told her she ought to take a year off and come to America with me to study. A new life with new friends. Leave all this shit behind. She thought it sounded awesome, and we started to make plans. We didn't tell anyone, but somehow Jens-Uwe got wind of it. Maybe he was hacking her mobile or her laptop. Anyway, one evening he showed up at my door. He told me I'd regret it if I kept filling Helen's head with such bullshit ideas. She loved him and didn't want to go to the States. I told him to fuck off, and then he had a fit and beat me up. When I told Helen about it, she got very quiet. Her mobile kept ringing. It was him. He always wanted to know where she was and who she was with. That scared her, especially after she found out that he'd done the same thing to his ex-wife. He stalked her until she had to get a restraining order from the court. When she told me that, I put even more pressure on her to come with me. And I wanted her to tell her father and Mark all about Jens-Uwe.'

'Mark?' Karoline was starting to lose track of all the people whose names she'd never heard before and who meant nothing to her.

'A kind of fatherly friend. I think she knew him from the support group that she often went to with her grandparents. But she didn't want to tell him anything. She said Mark would kill Jens-Uwe if he heard what was going on. The best thing would be to just disappear, from one day to the next.' Vivien sighed and took a sip of prosecco, which brought a grimace to her face. She chased it with some freshly squeezed orange juice. 'So I arranged everything in secret. Student visa, apartment, application to the university in Connecticut and plane tickets. We were supposed to leave on October first. All this time, Helen had been playing the role of the happy fiancée to keep Jens-Uwe calm. She even bought a wedding dress! At the same time, she secretly talked to all sorts of people and was convinced that she could file some kind of lawsuit against the doctor who was responsible for her mother's death.'

Now it's getting interesting, Karoline thought, feeling her stomach start to flutter with excitement. *Has my patience finally paid off?*

'Have you got any names?' That was the crucial question.

TO CATCH A KILLER

Vivien hesitated.

'Unfortunately, no.'

Karoline's hopes were dashed.

'Well, then, let me thank you for your time.' She forced a smile and took out her wallet to pay the bill. 'Maybe what you told me will help somehow.'

'Why don't you let the police find out who shot your mother?' Vivien asked.

'That's exactly what I'm going to do,' replied Karoline. 'And I'm sure they'll find him. But there's something else I'm interested in.'

'What's that?'

Karoline hesitated. There was no morbid curiosity in the young woman's eyes. Instead she saw a glimmer of mistrust. Vivien Stern didn't want all the gruesome details; she wanted to know why Karoline had contacted her, and why she was interested in Helen's story. She felt like she was being tested, even though that was completely ridiculous.

'After every murder, the sniper has sent an obituary to the police,' Karoline told her. 'Each one gave a reason for killing that particular person. He doesn't kill those who are actually guilty. He murders their closest relatives. Mothers, sons, wives.'

'And why is that?' Vivien seemed honestly shaken.

'So that those left behind will feel the same pain that they had caused out of indifference or greed. That's what he wrote in an anonymous letter to the police.'

'Oh God.'

'My mother apparently had to die because my father had incriminated himself in murder out of greed and vanity.' Karoline found it easier than she'd feared to speak these words. 'My father is a transplant surgeon. He was the one who removed the organs from Helen's mother.'

Vivien stared at her, open-mouthed.

'I want to find out the truth, because my father never told me anything,' Karoline went on. 'I have to know what really happened back then, what my father and his doctor colleagues did. My thirteen-year-old daughter was standing next to my mother in the kitchen when the sniper shot her. You can imagine what a shock that was.'

The young woman nodded, obviously moved.

'If I find out that what the sniper wrote is true,' said Karoline, now lowering her voice, 'I will never be able to forgive my father. I'll see to it that he ends up in prison.'

She took a deep breath. Vivien stared at her with a steadfast gaze, then grabbed her handbag and took out a worn black notebook.

'This is Helen's notebook. Everything she found out is in here. She always left it with me because she didn't trust anyone else. Maybe I should have given it to the police, but I was afraid.' Suddenly there were tears in her eyes. 'I . . . I think that the sniper is Jens-Uwe. He . . . he used to be a doctor, and he was somehow mixed up in the whole thing.' Vivien rummaged in her purse until she found a pack of tissues. Karoline waited until she'd blown her nose. 'I'm deathly afraid of him after he attacked me that one time. The guy is capable of anything. In three days, I'll be back in the States, and I'll be safe there. But until then, you have to promise me that you'll keep my name out of all this. Okay?'

Karoline could tell her fear was genuine. There was no reason for her to mention Vivien Stern's name. Or was there?

Wouldn't the police inspector want to know where she got the notebook?

'I want to be honest,' she replied. 'If the notebook is important for the case, I'll have to give it to the head of the investigation and tell him where I got it.'

Vivien looked at her and swallowed. Then she nodded slowly.

'At least you're not lying to me,' she said. 'Everyone else would have promised me anything, swear to God.'

She shoved the black notebook across the table.

'Take it. I hope it helps.' The young woman gave her a serious look. 'Maybe then the police will catch the bastard who killed Helen.'

Pia opened the glass door and nodded to her colleague in the watch room who had let her through the security gate. The team meeting in the special commission room on the ground floor had already begun. Pia took the empty chair next to Kai. Bodenstein was just reporting on his conversation with Lis Wenning. It was her turn next.

'I'm sure that Hartig is lying when he claims he couldn't remember any more names,' she said.

'In my opinion, there's only one explanation for why he doesn't want to help us: he's the sniper and wants to finish what he started,' Kathrin replied. 'Why don't we bring him in?'

'Because we don't have any evidence against him,' said Bodenstein.

Pia wished she were as convinced as Kathrin that Hartig was the perp, but she wasn't.

'I just spoke to Henning on the phone, and he spoke again with a doctor who was working at the UCF at the time,' she went on. 'He stated that in the case of Kirsten Stadler there was definitely something fishy going on, but he didn't want his name to be mentioned. We seem to be uncovering nothing but contradictions, and I'm getting the feeling that no one is telling us the truth. But why?'

'The sniper seems to be harbouring a deep-rooted hatred that's been festering for a long time,' Kim suggested. 'Helen's suicide could have been the trigger – the spark that set off the powder keg.'

'I agree with you.' Andreas Neff nodded and pulled a sheet of paper from his briefcase. He gave the impression that he'd unearthed a lot of news and was just waiting for the right moment to give his report. 'I've also been looking into Dirk Stadler some more. By the way, all resources are available to us at State Criminal HQ.'

'Show-off,' Kai muttered.

'Stadler was born in Rostock, in the former East Germany, but he has lived in the West since he fled in 1982. Civil engineer. He was a project leader with the Hochtief firm here and also abroad. No priors, currently four points on his licence. A car is registered in his name, a silver Toyota Yaris, number plate MTK-XX 342. Since 2004, he's been employed by the City of Frankfurt. He has a valid disabled badge.'

'Very good.' Bodenstein nodded his approval. 'Have you double-checked all this?'

'Of course. I also ran a check on Mark Thomsen. It was a little harder to pull the info on him, but I have my connections.'

He paused briefly to look round the table, but when he received no applause for his efforts, he continued.

'The official version is that Thomsen had to leave the

Border Patrol in 2000 because of an unfavourable psychological report after he shot two individuals to death even though there was no tangible threat in the situation. In reality, he was suspended and then given a less than honourable discharge from the police force. During his time with the Border Patrol, he fatally shot a total of seventeen people.'

This fact alone was the basis for ranking him number one on the list of suspects.

'I also thought it might be very interesting to have a look at the bank accounts of Hartig, Stadler and Winkler. As well as their e-mails.'

'For that we need a court-approved warrant.' Bodenstein shook his head.

'Not in a volatile situation like this.' Neff smiled innocently. 'As I mentioned, I have a few good connections and just went ahead and did it.'

'Without discussing it with me first?'

'You have enough on your plate. I didn't want to bother you,' replied Neff. 'You should be glad that someone on your team shows some initiative.'

'Well, I'm not!' Bodenstein said sharply. 'There's a huge difference between showing initiative and taking steps without proper authorization! That is a gross violation of civil rights and will not hold up in court.'

'Don't worry.' Neff grinned. 'We can always get a warrant after the fact.'

For a moment, Bodenstein wrestled with himself. He knew that Neff was right, but he didn't like this sort of disregard for regulations. As head of the investigation, he was responsible for everything that his team did. On the other hand, he reluctantly had to admit that information via e-mails and phone calls could be a valuable asset in their currently desperate situation. In the end, he decided to take the risk and include Neff's results in their investigation.

'All right, then, what did you find out?' he asked.

Smiling confidently, Neff pulled a fat pile of computer printouts out of his briefcase.

'Thomsen made very few calls in recent weeks,' he began. 'We have checked out all the calls. He phoned the Winklers a couple of times on the landline. Otherwise, I think he used a pay-as-you-go mobile, which can't be traced. Yesterday at twelve forty-four p.m., he received the first call in a long time on his landline.'

'That's correct,' Pia confirmed. 'He got a call while we were at his house. And afterwards, he suddenly started acting nervous.'

'Were you able to trace the number?' Bodenstein asked.

'Not yet.' Neff shook his head. 'It was a mobile number in the Netherlands. Thomsen was also sparing about the e-mails he sent. Because he used to be a police officer, he knows all the things we're able to do, so he has been very careful. He has only one bank account at a savings bank with a balance of €2,644.15. His salary goes into that account, and payments are regularly deducted for telephone, electricity, mortgage, a newspaper subscription, a private supplementary medical insurance and a credit card. He has a MasterCard that he apparently uses to pay for everything: booze, groceries, sundries. All pretty much unremarkable.'

Although Bodenstein knew only too well how much surveillance was actually possible these days, he was again amazed at the detail the government could find out about every single citizen. And in almost no time, with very little effort.

'It gets more interesting with Jens-Uwe Hartig.' Neff was visibly enjoying the undivided attention of the rest of the team. 'He has a number of accounts, but he's also deep in debt. The apartment in Kelkheim and the house in Hofheim have large mortgages outstanding. His business is in a rented shop. He pays maintenance to his ex-wife in Bremen. And listen to this: up until September, Dirk Stadler transferred a thousand euros to him every month with the reference code 'Helen'. Shortly after Helen's suicide, Stadler and Hartig spoke on the phone often, and several times a day. Hartig also frequently called Erik Stadler. In November, these calls stopped abruptly, as though they had broken off contact.'

Pia and her boss exchanged glances. This confirmed what Hartig had previously told her.

'However, three days ago, on December twenty-eighth,' said Neff, his eyes gleaming, 'Stadler and Hartig spoke on the phone from seven forty-five p.m. to nine minutes past nine p.m. I have no idea what they talked about, because we have no wiretap on their lines.'

'Then we'll just ask Stadler what they were talking about for an hour and a half,' Pia suggested, and Bodenstein nodded.

'I doubt that Helen would commit suicide without leaving a note,' said Pia. 'Maybe Stadler and Hartig withheld it because there's something in it they didn't like. I think we'll have to start with her. Helen seems to be at the centre of the whole case.'

No one contradicted her. Kai began to analyse the tips that had come in on the telephone hotline. After all the details of the murders had been revealed at the press conference, a veritable flood of leads came in. The police gave each one an internal tracking number and then followed up on the information, if only to identify the lead as false and rule it out. Eight officers from the search, burglary and fraud divisions were employed full-time to connect either by phone or in person with all those who had called in.

'No hot leads yet,' Kai ended his report.

Cem and Kathrin had spoken with the director of the security company that Thomsen worked for. He had nothing unfavourable to say about his employee. Thomsen was punctual and reliable. He got along well with his colleagues, and he was a favourite of the firm's clients. Wherever he was assigned, they had no more break-ins. At Cem's request, the director printed out a copy of Thomsen's time sheet, which listed each assignment, what time he'd come to work and when he'd left. Several times per shift, the employees were required to check in, giving the time and location. This data was stored in the computer. In addition, the entire vehicle fleet was equipped with GPS by TopSecure, so that the location of each vehicle could be tracked at any time.

'Interesting to see Thomsen's assignments,' said Cem. 'For example, the Seerose commercial park in Eschborn. That's where Hürmet Schwarzer was shot. Otherwise, he was off on all the other days when murders occurred.'

'The dog you saw yesterday with Thomsen belongs to his boss,' Kathrin added. 'TopSecure owns five trained dogs. Thomsen often took Arko home with him, and no one seemed to mind.'

'Where is the dog now?' Pia asked.

'He was apparently returned to the kennel sometime yesterday,' replied Kathrin. 'No one knows exactly when that was done, but this morning the dog was back.'

'That might mean that Thomsen is still in the area, hiding out somewhere,' said Pia.

'Did you have a good look at the post-mortem report on Helen Stadler?' Bodenstein asked Pia.

'Not really,' she said. 'Kathrin handled that.'

'The impact from the train didn't leave much of her body,' Kathrin put in. 'But at the time of death, she had a large concentration of barbiturates in her blood.'

'That's very interesting,' Bodenstein said. 'Erik Stadler's girlfriend just told us that Helen had undergone withdrawal treatment after Jens-Uwe had almost poisoned her with antidepressants and sedatives.'

His gaze fell on Peter Ehrenberg from the burglary squad, who was leaning against the doorframe, listening with his arms crossed.

'What's up?' he asked.

'We've got something,' replied Ehrenberg, who had always got on Bodenstein's nerves with his apathetic attitude. 'From the high-rise in Eschborn. A woman claims she saw the perp on the scaffolding.'

'What? When did you get the tip?' Bodenstein seemed electrified.

'I think it was Saturday.'

Silence fell over the big room, and everyone stared mutely at the man who was in charge of evaluating the calls on the tip hotline.

'On *Saturday*?' Bodenstein asked in bafflement. 'Today is Monday! How come you're just mentioning it now?'

'Do you know how many leads we have to check out?' Ehrenberg fired back, insulted. 'The phone has been ringing off the hook.'

'Didn't anybody look at the security tapes yet either? That was a direct order!'

'Of course we did, on Friday,' Ehrenberg defended his team. 'But there are three hundred and twelve apartments in that building, with hundreds of people living there. And there are construction workers going in and out all day long. If you don't know exactly what you're looking for, you're not going to find a thing.'

With a great effort, Bodenstein brought his rising anger under control. He wanted to grab the fat little man by the shoulders and shake him, but then Ehrenberg would instantly go on sick leave. He grabbed the phone to inform Dr Nicola Engel.

'Here.' With a sullen expression that gave little evidence of a guilty conscience, Ehrenberg handed Kai a USB stick. 'Start at 11:33 a.m.'

Without a word, Ostermann took the stick from him and stuck it into his laptop. The others gathered round his desk and stared tensely at his monitor, which now showed the glass entrance doors of the high-rise.

'What exactly did the man see?' Bodenstein enquired.

'It was a female witness,' replied Ehrenberg. 'She lives on the ninth floor and saw him outside her window on the construction scaffolding. He was probably on his way down. Because the facade had been under construction for months, the sight of workers is nothing unusual for the residents. The woman noticed him only because he had a bag slung over his shoulder.'

Footsteps came down the hall, and Nicola Engel entered the room.

'A witness observed something at the high-rise in Eschborn

and called it in on Saturday,' Bodenstein told her, giving Ehrenberg a withering glance. 'Unfortunately, our colleagues didn't find out about it until today.'

Nicola Engel had no comment, but Ehrenberg's face flushed. 'What's on the video?' she asked brusquely.

'Just a moment.' Kai rewound a little way. The video was in black-and-white and rather grainy. At 11:33 a.m., a man entered the foyer, resolutely turned right, and strode towards the lifts. He was wearing a white hard hat over a hood, and he was careful to keep his face turned away from the camera. Over his shoulder, he carried a dark-coloured sports bag.

'I don't believe it,' Bodenstein snapped through clenched teeth. Nicola Engel admonished him with a glance.

'Her description was quite accurate, but it's not much help,' Ehrenberg continued. 'Height between five-eleven and six-one. The woman couldn't see his hair because the man had pulled his collar up to his nose and wore a hood under the hard hat. Gloves, jeans, black jacket, white hard hat. He looked athletic and wore trainers instead of work boots.'

This description would fit Erik Stadler as well as Mark Thomsen or Jens-Uwe Hartig.

Kai tried to improve the sharpness of the image.

'How did the man get into the building?' Nicola Engel wanted to know.

'He simply rang the bell.' Ehrenberg gave a shrug. 'Apparently, he was pretending to be a delivery guy. They'd been working in the building for months. The front doors are often left open, and nobody looks very closely at strangers and construction workers anymore. He must have been there a couple of times before, or he wouldn't have known the way to the roof. Then he found a spot where he could wait undisturbed to take his shot.'

'Good, thank you, Officer Ehrenberg,' said the commissioner. 'You may resume your work.'

'I've been answering the phone for the past three days,' he said. 'When are we going to be relieved?'

'Never.' Nicola Engel fixed her gaze on him sharply. 'Every available officer in the station will remain on duty until we catch this perp.'

'But I—' Ehrenberg began.

'You'll be paid the standard surcharge for Sundays and holidays, as well as overtime. What else do you want?' she cut him off. 'I expect more careful work in the future. No more lapses will be permitted.'

Ehrenberg turned away without comment, though not without casting a dirty look at Bodenstein, as if he were to blame for the whole thing.

'With this video footage, we can now narrow down our search,' Pia remarked after he'd gone. 'During the Mermaid case, we also received a decisive tip when the investigation was featured on *Germany's Most Wanted*. Maybe somebody saw the guy getting into a car. A photo always sparks people's memory.'

'Okay,' Engel agreed. 'I'll see what we can arrange. Put together all the info you have. And, Bodenstein, we have to release Erik Stadler from investigative custody if we have no new evidence against him.'

'But since he's been in custody, there haven't been any more shootings,' Bodenstein remarked.

'No judge in the world is going to accept that reasoning,' said Dr Engel, shaking her head.

'Then at least I want him kept under surveillance,' Bodenstein demanded. 'We do have other possible suspects, but we
haven't ruled him out completely.'

'I'll get it approved,' the commissioner promised, and
turned to go. 'Order his release, and keep me in the loop.'

Dr Peter Riegelhoff still hadn't called back. The lawyer was
neither at his office or at home, and his mobile was turned off.

'When somebody so obviously goes out of his way to avoid
us, it means he's got something to hide.' Bodenstein was more
furious than he'd ever been before. It was bad enough that the
information from the witness in the high-rise hadn't been
checked out until now. Even worse was Ehrenberg's reaction.
Everyone on the special commission team was working full-tilt
and with total concentration, and a single unmotivated slow-
coach like Ehrenberg negated all their efforts. Valuable time
had been wasted, time that could cost a person his life. Ostermann had given clear instructions to the officers who were
taking and evaluating the hotline calls: every tip, no matter
how unlikely its connection to any of the crime scenes, had top
priority.

'Maybe Riegelhoff is on holiday,' Pia said. 'Lots of people
were always over Christmas, and—'

'Let's go out to Liederbach,' Bodenstein interrupted her as
they drove along the A 66. 'I want to speak to Stadler Senior
one more time.'

Pia put on her indicator and took the next exit off the autobahn. A couple of minutes later, they found Stadler loading a
suitcase into the boot of his car.

'Going somewhere?' Pia asked.

'Yes. I'm going to visit my sister in Southern Bavaria,'

replied Stadler. 'Nobody should have to spend New Year's Eve alone. I'll be back on Wednesday. Got to get back to work then.'

'Please give us your sister's address and a mobile number where we can reach you,' Pia requested.

'Of course. Come in, I'll write it down for you.'

Stadler closed the boot with a bang, then limped off towards the house. Pia and Bodenstein followed him. It was dark inside the house; all the blinds had been rolled down. Stadler pulled out the drawer in the sideboard in the hall, took out a pad and pen, and jotted down an address and several phone numbers.

'What's going on with my son?' he asked Pia as he handed her the piece of paper.

'He should be coming home today,' replied Bodenstein. 'Mr Stadler, we have a question for you. Do you know how to shoot?'

'Me? No way.' Dirk Stadler shook his head with a hint of a smile. 'I disapprove of firearms. I'm a confirmed pacifist.'

'Did you serve in the army?'

'No.'

'One more thing,' said Pia. 'When was the last time you spoke to Mark Thomsen?'

'That was a long time ago.' Stadler frowned and thought about it. 'Two or three weeks after Helen's funeral.'

'He hasn't tried to get in touch with you recently?'

'No, he hasn't.'

'And how about Jens-Uwe Hartig? Have you spoken to him recently?'

'No. Jens-Uwe broke off contact completely after Helen's death. And I can understand that. Helen was our connection.'

'Why were you making payments to Mr Hartig once a month?' Bodenstein asked.

'That was my contribution to household expenses and for Helen's studies,' Stadler replied. 'Officially, she was still living here, but in reality, she was almost always at his place. She had no income of her own, and I didn't want Jens-Uwe to have to pay her bills as long as they weren't married.'

That sounded logical, since Stadler had stopped making payments after Helen died.

'Thank you very much, Mr Stadler. That'll be all for today,' Bodenstein said with a nod. 'Have a nice trip and a Happy New Year.'

'Thank you, and I wish you both the same,' Stadler said with a smile. 'I hope you will have a quiet night tonight. And if you have any further questions, just give me a call.'

It was rush hour at the supermarket. People were carrying bottle rockets and fireworks to their cars, stocking up on groceries and booze as if there were no tomorrow. Even at the bakery next door, business was as brisk as usual, Hürmet Schwarzer already forgotten. Management didn't think the tragic death of a shop assistant was worth even a photo with a black ribbon. It was only three days ago, and the bloodstain in front of the shoe shop was still clearly visible. In her place, other pretty young women were selling loaves of bread, rolls and pastries smiling just as insincerely as lovely Hürmet had. That's how people were. Repress and forget.

He carried his shopping bags to the car, which was at the far end of the car park, and glanced over at the high-rise, as almost everyone had done since last Friday, giving an involuntary shudder. People were still talking about what happened, and they avoided stepping on the bloodstain. A few candles and flowers had been left there, and some people were even taking pictures of it. But the incident didn't particularly affect them; it had nothing to do with their miserable little world. They soothed their guilty conscience with stupid clichés like 'Life must go on' while deep inside, they knew that their lack of empathy, their selfishness and their hunger for sensationalism were disgusting. He looked into people's faces and saw heedless animals who thought only about themselves, gobbling their food and propagating as if their genes were worth it. He was having a harder and harder time tolerating other people. He was glad that he could escape because he had no ties to any of them.

He stowed the shopping bags and the case of mineral water in the boot; then he drove under the autobahn towards Sossenheim, the district with the ugly apartment buildings. His garage was one of 250 others that had been built in long rows. Twenty metal doors on the left and twenty on the right. No one gave a rat's arse about anyone else here. He stopped in front of the door marked 117 in the fourth row, climbed out, opened the door, and pulled on his gloves before he backed out the other car. He left the engine running so the heater would warm up. Then he drove his car inside, transferred his purchases, and closed the garage door. This procedure was always a bit laborious, but it was a matter of security. Since the police had turned to the public for help, the newspapers, radio and television were running daily reports about him. He had to be more careful than ever, because he still had a lot to do. He had discarded the idea of turning to the public via the reporter in order to divulge his motives. All the evidence against him would probably come out during his trial, but until then, he'd arranged everything. It was good that he had this house, this place of refuge. He drove on the A66 autobahn and glanced at the clock on the dashboard as he turned onto the B8 at the Main-Taunus Centre. Ten more hours. Then number five would die.

'I wasn't jogging, but I . . . I couldn't tell you what I was doing. Lis would have left me instantly.' After three days of investigative custody, Erik Stadler looked much the worse for wear.

'Were you with another woman?' Pia asked.

'No!' Stadler hung his head. 'I . . . I went climbing with a friend on the construction site of the European Central Park and . . . jumped off.'

Bodenstein and Pia stared at him, speechless.

'Why in God's name didn't you tell us that sooner?' Bodenstein was the first to regain his composure. 'We suspected you of being a murderer. Even worse, we wasted a lot of time on you. Time we could have spent tracking down the killer.'

He was extremely pissed off.

'I'm sorry,' replied Stadler, ashamed of himself. 'I was thinking only of myself. We'd been planning the jump for months.'

'You could get killed doing stuff like that.' Pia still couldn't believe it.

'I'm not afraid to die,' said Stadler. Now that he'd been released, he seemed relieved. 'A boring life would be much worse for me.'

Bodenstein sighed with fatigue and rubbed his face. He'd never experienced anything like this before. This man would rather let his business suffer and be accused of murder than admit to a misdemeanour that, in comparison, was truly ludicrous. Pia's intuition had been right after all. As had been the case with Professor Kaltensee and Markus Nowak's previous cases, Erik Stadler's suspicious behaviour was based on entirely different motives.

'You may go,' said Bodenstein, now feeling depressed.

'You mean you're not going to charge me with anything?'

'No.' He shoved a notepad and pen across the table. 'Please give us the name of your . . . friend who's also willing to risk his life. And then get the hell out of here before I change my mind.'

'Oh, one more thing,' said Pia. 'What did you talk about with Jens-Uwe Hartig on Friday?'

'With Jens-Uwe?' Stadler looked up from the notepad.

'Yes. With your sister's fiancé.'

'I haven't heard a word from him in months,' said Stadler. 'Here's my friend's number.'

'Last Friday from seven forty-five p.m. till nine oh nine, you spoke with Hartig on the phone,' Pia persisted. 'What about?'

'I swear to you, I didn't,' Stadler argued. 'The last time I talked to him was at Helen's funeral.'

Something began to dawn on Bodenstein. He got up abruptly, tore open the door, and went out in the corridor. Pia grabbed the notepad from the table, nodded to Stadler and ran after her boss. She caught up with him on the stairs leading to the second floor.

'What is it?' she asked him, out of breath.

Bodenstein said nothing. With a grim expression, he turned left and strode into the conference room. Ostermann, Neff, Kim and Kathrin looked up in astonishment.

'Neff!' Bodenstein barked. 'Whom did Jens-Uwe Hartig talk to on the phone last Friday evening?'

'Uh . . . just a moment . . .' Napoleon was rummaging frantically through his documents. 'I'll find it in a second.'

'Hurry up,' Bodenstein grumbled. A deep crease had formed between his eyebrows, a sign that he was really angry.

'Here it is. Aha,' Neff said with an uncertain smile. 'From seven forty-five to nine past nine, Mr Hartig was on the phone to Dirk Stadler.'

'To *Dirk* Stadler?' Bodenstein asked to make sure.

'Yes, that's what I just said.'

'That's not what you said earlier today.' Bodenstein was just about to lose control. 'Pack up your things and get out of here, Neff. I've had enough of your sloppy work methods!'

'But . . .' Neff began, and that word was the straw that broke the camel's back.

'Don't give me any goddamned excuses. When I say something, I mean it!' Bodenstein shouted at him. 'Get out at once! And turn in your visitor's ID downstairs in the watch room. I don't want to see you here again.'

He turned on his heel and left, slamming the door behind him and leaving the whole team baffled. Bright red with his lips pressed together, Neff grabbed his briefcase, got up, took his jacket, and left the room without another word.

'Bye-bye, Napoleon,' muttered Kai. 'And don't ever show your face here again.'

'Wow, I've never seen the boss that furious before,' Kathrin whispered; then she grinned. 'People, this booting-out is worth a whole case of champagne! I'm sure glad we're finally rid of that slimy bastard.'

Karoline's father wasn't home when she returned to the house in Oberursel in the early afternoon. Ever since their argument, he seemed to be avoiding her, and that was okay with her. At four, Karoline had a meeting with Irina, her mother's Russian cleaning lady. The woman wanted to discuss how things would be arranged from now on. She used to come twice a week to take care of the brunt of the cleaning, while Mama had done all the rest. But now her father needed someone to do his laundry and cook for him, too. As she waited for Irina, she looked through the post that her father, as was his habit, had tossed in the silver bowl on the sideboard in the hall. He'd taken what interested him into his study, leaving behind all the letters of condolence stacked up in the bowl unopened. Among them was also an opened envelope with a notice from the Oberursel register office, saying that Mama's body had been released for burial. Her father hadn't even considered that worth giving her a call, she thought in annoyance. As usual, he couldn't be bothered taking care of practical matters. She rummaged through the silver bowl and found the card from the mortuary that had transported Mama's body to the forensics lab. She also found the inspector's business card, which her father had likewise tossed in the bowl. Karoline called the mortuary and asked them to take care of her mother's funeral and all the formalities. She promised to fax the register office and let them know. As soon as she hung up, Irina called and burst into tears before Karoline could even say hello. Half an hour later, she'd finished everything. She wrote her father a note to tell him that Irina would be coming in every other day between nine and noon. If that didn't suit him, he would have to call her and arrange his own schedule.

Karoline sat down at the dining room table, where she'd sat so often with her mother, and opened the condolence cards. As soon as the date was set for the funeral, she would have to make a list of addresses to send out the notices, which the mortuary would design for her. She had to decide on a fitting quotation and also have a talk with the vicar about renting a venue for the funeral reception. Then she had to notify all the associations and organizations that Mama had joined. Her eyes were burning and her back hurt, but she didn't allow herself to take a break. For days, she'd been handling one task after another; it was the only thing keeping her going. There was nothing desperate about her search for the truth in her father's past, but she was convinced that it might be the only reason why she hadn't lost her mind or simply collapsed.

Outside the windows, darkness had already fallen. In a few hours, the new year would arrive. She still had time to get in her car and drive over to see Greta. It wouldn't take more than four hours at most. She remembered the notebook that Vivien Stern had given her that morning. Karoline got up and turned on the light. She took the notebook out of her pocket and began leafing through it curiously. It seemed to be a diary that Helen Stadler had kept day by day, jotting down every triviality that passed through her head. Karoline had viewed Vivien Stern as a rather flipped-out young woman, yet her anxiety had been genuine. She didn't know what to make of Vivien's claim that Helen Stadler was murdered.

In March, the style of the diary entries changed. Karoline attempted to decipher the meaning of the dates, figures, names and cryptic squiggles that seemed to make no sense. But then she began finding names that she recognized, and she felt a fluttering sense of excitement. Was Helen after the same thing that she was looking for? The young woman had not shied away from speaking directly to the men whom she blamed for the death of her mother. Professor Ulrich Hausmann, Dr Hans Furtwängler, Fritz Gehrke – even Professor Dieter Rudolf.

Karoline swallowed hard. Helen had met with him on 7 June. Why? What did she want to ask him? Had he given her an answer? She quickly leafed ahead, just skimming the pages, but then she stopped short.

'Oh my God,' she murmured when she understood what all these names meant, the ones that Helen had written down.

Suddenly she realized how late it was. Her father might come home at any minute, and he was the last person she wanted to see this evening. She would call the police inspector when she got home. She hurriedly stuck the notebook back in her pocket, placed the note she had written to her father on the table, turned off the light, and left the house.

Bodenstein had to stop at the level crossing in Kelkheim, and he used the time to look at his smartphone, which had been beeping for a while now. Inka had sent him a text, and he also had a new e-mail. He gave a start when he read the sender's name: The.Judge@gmail.com. Was this some nasty joke, or was the sniper contacting him directly? After the press conference, his name had been all over the media as the leader of the investigation, so it was a simple matter to find his e-mail address. Damn! The message had come in half an hour ago, and in his anger at Neff's negligence, he hadn't noticed. After he'd blown his top and thrown that guy out, he'd tried at once to call Dirk Stadler, but his mobile was turned off, and no one had answered his sister's phone either. After twelve days of high tension, Bodenstein's nerves were just about shot. Quickly, he opened the e-mail and the file attached.

'Good God!' he exclaimed. Adrenalin shot through his body. He didn't notice that the barriers had lifted until the car behind him beeped. He swiftly put on his indicator and pulled into the car park of Kelkheim police station, which was only fifty metres ahead on the left side of the road. From there, he called Pia. New Year's fireworks were already going off here and there. The whole world would be boisterously celebrating, but somewhere a person was about to die on this last night of the year if he didn't prevent it.

'The Judge got in touch with me, this time by e-mail. Listen to this,' he said when Pia called. ' "Tonight Number Five will die. It won't be long now before the whole truth will be revealed to you." '

'We have to find Riegelhoff straight away,' Pia said. Not a word of complaint that she'd have to keep working. 'Maybe we should bring him in for a chat. He's probably the only person who knows all those involved back then.'

'And Professor Rudolf,' Bodenstein replied. 'I am at the station in Kelkheim. I'll send a cruiser over to get him. By the way, I couldn't reach Dirk Stadler, either on his mobile or at his sister's.'

'It's New Year's Eve,' Pia told him. 'And I don't think Rudolf is going to reveal something tonight, of all nights.'

'If he doesn't, I'll bring him into the station.' Bodenstein was standing in front of the station door. 'We have to talk to him. I'll come and pick you up.'

He broke the connection and read the text from Inka.

Sorry, she wrote, *Emergency in Usingen. Be there later!*

Emergency here too, he wrote back. *I'll be in touch. In case I don't see you – Happy New Year!*

Then he put away the phone and went inside the station.

After Bodenstein's call, Pia ran round, feeding the horses and dogs, and tried to call Kim. Her sister didn't answer, so she sent her a text. Then she walked in the dark along the track between the paddock and the riding area, thinking about Christoph. Over in the Galápagos, it was only eleven thirty in the morning.

She wished she could put a tail on all the suspects and tap their phones, but they didn't have enough manpower for that, and the Frankfurt judges were known for their reticence when it came to signing warrants for wiretaps. On that topic, Bodenstein always went strictly by the book, while she would have taken a more flexible approach, especially when there was a chance of learning something significant. When Neff had admitted today that he'd done research on his own that was only semi-legal, her boss had not been happy. Yet it was the first truly useful action that conceited little snot had taken. Then he'd ruined it all by being just as slipshod and inattentive to detail as Ehrenberg, who had overlooked what was probably the most important piece of information to surface since the start of the investigation. No wonder Bodenstein had lost his cool. They were all on edge.

Pia opened the big gate and shut it behind her. Above her droned the traffic on the autobahn. It was pitch dark and cold as hell. She understood her boss's reaction. The sense of powerlessness they all felt had stripped them of any remaining scraps of patience. But the most unpleasant thing was the way the administration of the UCF was stonewalling. Even after four deaths, they still didn't seem to comprehend the gravity and the urgency of the situation. Or – and this seemed more likely to her – they were afraid that something might come out that had previously been so carefully hushed up.

A car emerged from under the autobahn flyover. The glare from the headlights approached swiftly, and the car reached her a few seconds later.

'Riegelhoff is at home and is waiting for us.' Bodenstein shifted into reverse and backed into the dirt road to turn round. 'But just to be safe, I sent some officers over so he won't change his mind.'

'Why didn't he call and tell us to come over?' asked Pia, fastening her seat belt.

'We'll have to ask him that.' Bodenstein was irritable and tense. The car bumped over the railway tracks.

'Why is the Judge now announcing his attacks?' Pia asked. 'What's the point of that?'

'No idea,' replied Bodenstein as he got onto the A66 heading for Frankfurt. 'Maybe he wants to piss us off, play cat and mouse in order to show us what idiots we are. What really bothers me is that Faber has obviously been doing some investigating of his own behind our backs, even though I asked him several times not to do that. I'm really pissed off at him!'

Pia said nothing. In all the years they'd been working together, she'd never seen him in such a thunderous mood. Obviously something else was bothering him, too, something personal that was adding to the strain and making him touchy.

Here, of course, everything was less comfortable than it was at home, but that didn't bother him. There was no dishwasher, so he washed the two saucepans, the plate and the cutlery by hand. He liked washing up. It was a satisfying task, like cleaning windows and mowing the lawn. You saw the result at once, and it was conducive to relaxing and thinking things over. He liked the small house with its simplicity and bare-bones furnishings. He fully enjoyed the time he was able to spend here. Soon he would have to exchange this place for a prison cell, and not a second went by that he wasn't aware of that. He put away the clean crockery and cutlery, wiping down the scratched sink with a microfibre cloth. The stove was making noise; it was so hot that he could walk round in a T-shirt. Here it was peaceful; there were no neighbours to bother him, no one who wanted anything from him. And above all, he had Helen's papers here. Whenever he had the slightest doubt about the reason for his actions, he needed only to reread everything, and then his anger was reawakened and fierce, along with the thirst for revenge, for punishment and retribution. The way she had suffered, they would have to suffer, too. Death would have been too merciful for any of them. They had to endure what Helen had endured, the same helplessness and despair; they had to be damned until the end of their lives and even beyond. He glanced at the clock. It was 7:42 p.m. He had to see about getting ready. He got dressed carefully because the night was cold, and he didn't know how long he would have to wait. Long underwear, black jeans, over those the thermal trousers, also black and with no reflectors. Then the black polar fleece pullover and the black hoodie. Three pair of socks with the cheap trainers, which he had bought a size bigger so they would fit. Gloves, cap. He had no real concern that the police might work out who his next victim would be. How could they guess what names were on the list? His e-mail was purely intended as a provocation. They had got a bit closer to him, but he still had a safe head start.

The rifle was already in the car. It would take him about half an hour to drive there; he'd already timed it a couple of times. The petrol tank was full. Tonight the weather was supposed to be calm. Maybe a slight drizzle, but no wind. All over Europe, people would be celebrating the New Year in a few hours, shooting millions of euros worth of fireworks into the night sky. And that suited him just fine.

She turned left onto Oberhöchstädter Strasse as her smartphone beeped. With one hand on the steering wheel, Karoline opened the e-mail that had just arrived. It was from Konstantin Faber and was exceedingly unfriendly.

> *Hello, Ms Albrecht, why did you feel justified in passing along to third parties the information that I entrusted to you? The police called me today and accused me of forwarding one of the obituaries, because Friedrich Gehrke, the father of Victim No. 3, has committed suicide, and the obituary was found at the scene.*

She heard a loud honking and saw that she had drifted over the line into the oncoming traffic. She whipped the wheel to the right, then put on her left indicator so she could turn off onto Füllerstrasse at the traffic lights. A wave of nausea came over her. What had she done now? Fritz Gehrke had killed himself? That couldn't be true! And she was to blame because she'd given him that obituary. But he'd seemed so level-headed. He even seemed grateful to her because now he understood why his son had had to die. The left-turn signal turned green, and Karoline put her foot down. Her thoughts were racing. She drove along the road that led to the B455, wondering whether to bother the inspector at eight o'clock on New Year's Eve. What had she done with his business card? She rummaged through her handbag on the passenger seat, then dumped everything out and flicked on the interior light. There it was. No, that was the card from the mortuary. But she did have . . . Something rushed through the beam of the headlights, and Karoline was shocked to see that she was driving too fast, way too fast. She hit the brakes hard, and the Porsche went into a skid on the rainy road. Tyres squealing, the car went into a curve and she whipped the wheel sharply to the right. The rear end skidded out and she felt a dull thud as the rear axle struck the kerb of Waldparkplatz.

'Shit!' The steering wheel was torn from her hands in the collision, and her temple whacked against the side window. For a second, she felt weightless. Then the car flipped onto its side on the wet tarmac, spun round like a top, and kept sliding over the embankment. There it ploughed a furrow into the underbrush of the woods. The sound of ripping metal vibrated through her bones, wood splintered under the weight of the car, until the vehicle finally came to rest. Now it was pitch dark and utterly still, except for the soft clicking of the engine cooling down. Karoline hung dazed from the seat belt, feeling something warm dripping down her face. Then she blacked out.

Riegelhoff's house, a charming little single-family dwelling, was located on Waldfriedstrasse, right next to the city woods. A police car was parked on the pavement out front. Police officers from Frankfurt were already on-site.

'It's outrageous to keep us here!' complained the lawyer, a robust man in his mid-fifties with grey hair and a reddened, knobbly nose. He was wearing a tux with a bow tie under a cashmere coat; his wife had on a floor-length gown with a fur-trimmed cape over her shoulders. 'We have a dinner invitation and we need to leave.'

Bodenstein quickly stepped forward to reply.

'If you'd called me back, you could have saved us all this trouble, and we would be celebrating somewhere, too,' he replied coolly, omitting any form of greeting. 'More important, maybe we would have known whom the sniper was going to shoot tonight and could protect him.'

'I don't know what you're getting at, but—' Riegelhoff began.

Bodenstein cut him off. 'We'll explain it to you,' he said. 'And if we don't get any useful information from you, then you can spend the night in a cell, I can promise you that.'

Riegelhoff's eyes were shooting daggers at Bodenstein, but he seemed to understand the seriousness of the situation and relented.

'Ten minutes, darling,' he said to his wife, who merely shrugged. Then he nodded to Bodenstein and Pia. 'Please come with me.'

He took off his coat, tossed it over the banister, and led them into his study. Pia briefly explained what they'd learned from the sniper and the assumption that he was taking revenge on people whom he believed had caused the death of Kirsten Stadler or condoned what happened.

'How can I help you?' asked Riegelhoff, probably still hoping to get the matter over with rapidly and be off to his party.

'Ten years ago, you represented the UCF in a lawsuit filed by Dirk Stadler,' Bodenstein now took over. 'So you know the people involved in the Kirsten Stadler case; you know their names. The sniper has announced that tonight he will shoot a fifth victim. And it will very probably be someone who was not involved.'

'Perhaps you yourself are on his list,' Pia added. 'So your wife could be shot. Or your children.'

'A bad joke.' Riegelhoff gave a thin-lipped smile.

'It's no joke,' Bodenstein replied, dead serious. 'He shot the mother of a woman who had refused to help Kirsten Stadler's children when they found her lying unconscious in a field. And the wife of an ambulance driver because on that day he still had residual alcohol in his bloodstream and drove the ambulance into a ditch. Further victims were the wife of Professor Rudolf and the son of Friedrich Gehrke, who had received a heart transplant from Mrs Stadler. You knew Mr Gehrke, and on Saturday, you attempted to return his call.'

Riegelhoff turned pale. His fingers fiddled nervously with one of his cuff links.

'What do you mean, I *knew* him?' he asked uneasily.

'The day before yesterday, he took his own life,' said Pia.

'Oh . . I . . . I didn't know that.' Riegelhoff seemed concerned, but Pia did not miss the tiny flicker in his eyes. Was that relief? How odd.

'What could Fritz Gehrke have wanted from you? Why did he burn documents before he killed himself?'

'I'm afraid I don't know,' Riegelhoff answered. 'He only left his name and phone number on the answering machine and asked me to call him back. I was rather amazed, because I hadn't heard from him in eight years.'

'Then it was probably about the case from back then,' Bodenstein suspected. 'What did Gehrke have to do with it?'

Riegelhoff hesitated. In front of the house there was a loud bang, and the lawyer flinched. He tried to cover up his nervousness with an offhand remark.

'Your horror story is making me jumpy,' he said with an uneasy laugh.

That was enough for Pia. She had no more time for tactics and evasive manoeuvres.

'Dr Riegelhoff, this matter is deadly serious,' she said emphatically. 'We're trying to protect the individuals who might be the next victims on the sniper's list. You could help us. Give us the names of doctors and responsible administrators who worked at the UCF in 2002. We don't care what they had to do with the case, but tonight someone is going to die, and *you* might be able to prevent it. Do you understand? Would you want to be responsible for someone's death?'

Riegelhoff thought a moment, then decided to make an effort.

'I have the documents in the archive at my office,' he said. 'We could drive over there.'

'Okay, let's go,' said Bodenstein with a decisive nod. 'Your wife should come with us. We can't guarantee that the sniper doesn't have you or your family in his sights.'

It was dark. And cold. A dull, throbbing pain in her body, but much worse was the terrible pressure in her head. She didn't know what was going on. Where was she? What had happened? Why was there such a stench of petrol? A light was blinding her, and she shut her eyes again.

'Hello? Hello!' A strange voice. Brightness. 'Hello! Can you hear me? The ambulance is on the way.'

Ambulance?

'Hello! Stay awake!' Somebody was roughly patting her cheek.

This must be a dream.

'Go away,' she murmured, in a daze.

'She's coming to,' said a man's voice.

Karoline heard a siren, then another one. She opened her eyes with difficulty. Blue lights were flashing. It was as bright as day. But it was evening. New Year's Eve! She wanted to call Greta and wish her a Happy New Year. Greta. Mama.

A metallic crash right next to her ear, cold air.

'I'm cold,' she said.

'We're almost done,' replied the man's voice. 'We're getting you out. Does anything hurt?'

'My head. And my arm. What happened?' Karoline blinked into the bright light, recognized a police uniform.

'You had an accident.' The officer was young, no more than mid-twenties. 'Can't you remember?'

'Yeah. There was . . . an animal on the road. I . . . I had to brake,' Karoline whispered. Other men arrived. Orange jackets, dark blue overalls. Paramedics. Firemen.

They got her out of the seat belt, which had protected her from worse injuries, and lifted her carefully from the wreck of the Porsche on a stretcher.

'I can walk by myself,' she protested weakly.

'Sure, sure,' was all they said. They put a neck brace on her, and Karoline caught a glimpse of the area before they loaded her into the ambulance. The road was blocked. Police. Fire department. A bright-yellow tow truck arrived just then. It was bright inside the ambulance, they strapped her in and started an IV drip to prevent shock. The doctor asked for her name and address, today's date and the day of the week. He seemed satisfied when she gave the right answers without hesitation.

Why had she seen the animal so late? Why was she driving so fast? Then she remembered. She'd been looking for the inspector's business card. But why?

'I need my bag and my mobile phone,' she told the younger of the paramedics, who seemed more approachable than his older colleague. 'They must be in my car.'

'I'll have a look and see if I can find them,' he promised her, and vanished from sight. A few minutes later, he returned, and she was relieved to see him holding up her brown Bottega Veneta handbag.

'I found the mobile and put it inside,' he said, settling on the jump seat next to her. The doors slammed shut and the ambulance began to move.

'Thank you. And the wallet and key ring?'

The young man felt in her bag and nodded. 'Both there,' he confirmed, and she closed her eyes. 'Now we're going to the hospital in Bad Homburg. Is there someone you want us to call?'

'No, thank you.' Karoline tried to smile. 'I'll do it later myself.'

She surrendered to the shaking of the vehicle, listened to the siren, and tried to work out in her mind the route they were taking. Luckily, she didn't seem to be badly injured. And now it didn't matter that she'd forgotten to go shopping.

There was nothing better than careful planning. The shell of the building was a perfect site for an ambush, with an ideal escape route; he had meticulously checked it out twice. He had parked his car at the HEM petrol station, right next to the roundabout, and from there, it was only a couple of minutes to the A5 autobahn. If things got dicey, he could also drive across the fields to Weiterstadt or through the industrial zone to Büttelborn and over to the A67. All round were only meadows and farmland, except for the three newly constructed houses. He had found a comfortable position, and instead of the bipod, he was using two sacks of mortar, which also provided something to hide behind. It was only quarter past nine. Plenty of time. As he lay there, he screwed the Kahles scope onto the rifle and looked through it. Wonderful optics. He looked into the brightly lit house, saw the man standing in the open kitchen with a different woman. They were talking and laughing. In front of the house stood a car with number plates from Gross-Gerau; that's why he'd assumed that they'd invited guests tonight. But it didn't matter. The children were sitting in the living room in front of the TV, one on the floor, the other sprawled on the black leather sofa. Cute kids. A boy and a girl. He saw the homeowner upstairs now with another man. He was no doubt proudly showing off his new house. They had just moved in a couple of weeks ago. Luckily. If they'd been in their old apartment in a multi-family dwelling, he would have had much greater problems finding a suitable shooting position. Of course, he could have dealt with the man somewhere else – in his car, on his way to work, in the car park – but he wanted to do it exactly like this. Right before their eyes. Before the eyes of his children. They should see the way their father died, they should feel as helpless, shocked and desperate as Helen had. And they must never forget the sight for the rest of their lives.

It was a little past nine by the time they reached the lawyer's office on the west side of the Frankfurt North End. They got out of the car. The patrol officers from the other car went inside with them. It took Riegelhoff a few moments to find his card key and run it through the card reader at the glass front entrance, his hands were shaking so hard. He gave a start at each fireworks blast. Bodenstein and Pia exchanged a meaningful glance.

The renowned law firm of HR&F Partners, at which Riegelhoff was one of the senior partners, was located on the top four floors of a modern office building on Eschersheimer Landstrasse. The archive took up half of one floor. Riegelhoff was clearly not familiar with the filing system, because it took him all of forty-five minutes to find the twenty-three document binders pertaining to Stadler's suit against the UCF.

In his office, a sort of penthouse with a glass roof that was surrounded by a terrace, Riegelhoff set to work. Meanwhile, his wife showed the two inspectors where to find the toilets and the kitchen. Then she sat down behind her husband's desk.

'Please go outside if you want to smoke,' said the lawyer without looking up when he heard the click of a lighter.

'Oh,' said his wife, and stood up. The taffeta of her gown rustled as she shoved open one of the floor-to-ceiling French doors, and an icy gust of wind swirled inside. Pia saw Mrs Riegelhoff pacing back and forth outside the windows, smoking and talking on the phone. She was a good-looking woman who couldn't have cared less what her husband was working on. Her only concern was the party that they seemed about to miss.

'Why did Mr Stadler have only one binder of documents for the whole case?' Bodenstein asked.

'His lawyer probably had a few more,' replied Riegelhoff, 'but as a matter of fact, the plaintiff side did not receive all the documents. There were certain internal protocols that the Stadlers never saw.'

'Why not?' Pia was amazed.

'Because something actually did go wrong,' Riegelhoff admitted. 'There was faulty behaviour on the part of the doctors. That's why the hospital was so interested in reaching an out-of-court settlement with the plaintiff. A trial would have led to a scandal, which would have resulted in a massive loss of confidence and great financial losses for the UCF.'

'Why didn't you tell us that earlier?' Bodenstein angrily raised his eyebrows. Everyone he talked to during this investigation seemed to dole out information one scrap at a time.

'Because the UCF is our client, and one of the most important,' said Riegelhoff. 'I may get in a lot of hot water for showing you the files, but I refuse to take the blame for anyone's death.'

Had he suddenly discovered his conscience, or was he simply accepting the inevitable, now that he found himself between a rock and a hard place?

'How much money did the Stadlers receive in the out-of-court settlement?' Pia wanted to know.

'Fifty thousand euros,' said the lawyer. 'But as far as I know, the Stadler family got even more money from Mr Gehrke.'

'What do you mean?' asked Bodenstein and Pia in tandem.

'I have no direct knowledge of their agreement. But they were satisfied with the sum we offered and withdrew their suit,' said Riegelhoff as he flicked through another binder. 'The rest was no longer of any importance to me.'

The ringing of Bodenstein's mobile cut through the silence. He handed the pages to Pia and took the call.

'Bodenstein,' he snapped.

'This . . . this is Karoline Albrecht,' a woman's voice said, to his surprise. 'I'm the daughter of . . . of Professor Rudolf. Please excuse me for calling so late.'

'I know who you are,' said Bodenstein. 'It's good that you called. I have a bone to pick with you.'

'About Mr Gehrke. I know. I'm sorry. I had no idea that something like that would happen,' said Ms Albrecht. She was mumbling as if she'd already had a couple of glasses of champagne. 'But I'm calling about another matter. I have Helen Stadler's diary, and I think there's something in it that may be important to you. A death list.'

'A "death list"?' Bodenstein enquired. 'What's that supposed to mean?'

'A list of names. It starts with Ingeborg Rohleder. Then comes my mother's name, then Fritz Gehrke's son, and a couple more names that don't mean a thing to me. Oh yes, Dr Burmeister and Dr Janning are on it, too.'

Bodenstein was speechless for a moment.

'Also, I've heard that Helen didn't commit suicide,' said Ms Albrecht. 'She was murdered, and by a friend, at that.'

'Where is this diary now?'

'I don't know.'

'I thought you had it.'

For a couple of seconds, it was deathly still on the other end, and Bodenstein was afraid that Karoline Albrecht had broken the connection.

'There's a small problem. I had an accident, and now I'm in the hospital in Bad Homburg. The diary is probably still in my car, and I don't know where they took it.'

'Where did the accident take place?' Bodenstein had quickly recovered. The station could find out everything else. She told him the site of the accident, her registration number and make of car, and described the diary. Bodenstein thanked her and ended the call, then tapped in another number.

'Bodenstein from K-Eleven,' he identified himself. 'I need to track down a vehicle involved in an accident.'

Pia gave him a quizzical look.

'The accident happened recently, on the K 772 between Oberursel and the B455. A black Porsche, registration F-AP 34 1. Yes, thanks, I'll hold.'

'What's up?' Pia silently mouthed the words, but Bodenstein motioned for her to hold on. He paced restlessly in the big office until the duty officer came back on the line.

'The vehicle was towed by H&K,' he said. 'Usually, they store the accident vehicle in their own garden until an insurance adjuster arrives.'

'Very good. So where is the vehicle now?'

The officer gave him the address of the towing service. Bodenstein turned to his two uniformed colleagues, who were sitting on a sofa in a corner of the office and slurping coffee. He gave them the task of looking for a diary in Karoline Albrecht's Porsche and bringing it to him in Höchst the fastest way possible. The two nodded and left, happy to have something to do. Then Bodenstein quietly informed Pia about what he had just learned.

Riegelhoff turned to them.

'I found what I was looking for,' he announced, taking a few pages out of a binder. 'This is the operating-theatre protocol from the organ explantation. The names of all the participants are on it.'

Pia went over and took the papers from him. She sat down at the table and began to read.

'Professor Rudolf, Dr Simon Burmeister, Dr Arthur Janning and – *Jens-Uwe Hartig*!' Pia gasped for air in disbelief. 'Boss, check this out! Hartig is listed here as one of the surgeons in the organ explantation of Kirsten Stadler. Why did he lie to us?'

She shoved the pages over to Bodenstein.

'Probably because we're still waiting for answers from the UCF, even today,' Bodenstein grumbled. 'I'll call Hartig and ask him.'

He tapped the speed dial for Hartig's number. Hartig didn't answer.

In the meantime, Pia wrote down all the names and demanded that Riegelhoff show her the other binders.

'Bring me all of them, please.' The lawyer shrugged, glanced at his watch, and then at his wife, still talking on the phone out on the terrace. 'I hope it will help you.'

'There are way too many.' Pia looked somewhat hopelessly at her list, which kept growing longer. 'And I bet we find another twenty names in that binder. Why were twelve surgeons necessary?'

'We're talking about a multi-organ transplant,' said the lawyer. 'To do that, it has to go fast. Sometimes five or six teams are working in parallel on a bod . . . uh . . . on a donor.'

'He can't possibly want to kill all of them.' Pia stared at the list of names.

'Maybe you can save yourself some work if the officers find the diary,' said Bodenstein as he looked at his watch.

'I'd rather not count on it,' Pia replied. She had an idea, and she looked at Riegelhoff. 'Stadler's objection was not to organ removal as such, but to the method and manner with which his wife was treated, isn't that right?'

Riegelhoff nodded.

'So we have to concentrate on the decision-makers,' said Pia. 'On anyone who gave false information to Joachim Winkler. Who at the hospital is responsible for such decisions?

Who speaks to the relatives of the patient? Do the doctors do this?'

'Sometimes,' replied Riegelhoff. 'But at a large hospital like the UCF, they have trained psychological personnel for such instances. People who arrange and coordinate the organ transplant.'

'So in the case of Kirsten Stadler, who was it?'

'I no longer remember.' Riegelhoff pulled over one of the binders at random and opened it.

'That'll take too long. It's almost ten thirty. We're running out of time.' Bodenstein shook his head. 'I'm going to call Professor Rudolf. Maybe he'll remember something.'

He went to the other end of the large office and tapped in Rudolf's number. This time he was more successful.

'Please leave me alone,' said the professor when Bodenstein gave his name. 'Kindly respect my grief.'

'That's what I'm doing,' said Bodenstein. 'The person who shot your wife has announced that tonight he will kill another person. In the meantime, we've learned that these murders have to do with events at the UCF that occurred ten years ago. At the moment, we're at the law firm that represented the UCF against Mr Stadler, and we've already come across some names. Whom did the Stadlers deal with at the hospital? For instance, what's the name of the person who was responsible for coordinating the organ removal?'

There was silence on the other end.

'Professor, please, help us,' Bodenstein said urgently. 'Prevent another person from dying.'

Rudolf hung up without a word.

'What a shithead!' Bodenstein cursed. 'That does it.'

'What are you going to do?'

Bodenstein punched in another number.

'I'm having him brought to the station,' he replied. 'I refuse to let him shirk his responsibility.'

He ordered a team to bring in Professor Dieter P. Rudolf. Then he put away his phone and gave Riegelhoff a chilly stare.

'In the meantime, have you remembered what Fritz Gehrke might have wanted from you?' he asked sharply.

'No,' said Riegelhoff, lowering his eyes.

'I hope you don't end up regretting this someday,' said Bodenstein.

'What am I supposed to regret?' asked the lawyer.

'The fact that you're refusing to give us crucial information.' Bodenstein turned round. 'Let's go. We're taking the documents with us.'

'And what about us?' Riegelhoff wanted to know.

'You can go on to your party,' said Bodenstein.

'But what if the sniper is targeting us? Will we have police protection, at least?'

'Sorry, can't do that,' said Bodenstein, shaking his head. 'If you'd been more cooperative from the start, then maybe the killer would be behind lock and key by now. That's the chance you'll have to take.'

They were done with dinner, Tafelspitz *with potatoes and green sauce. Now they were sitting round the table in the dining room and drinking California red wine, a 2010 cabernet sauvignon from the Napa Valley.*

He could read the label through the scope.

He could look at their plates, into their faces, at the backs of their friends' heads who were sitting with their backs to the window and still holding hands.

He could see every detail. The woman had drunk a bit too much, her cheeks were flushed and she was laughing a lot. She kept giving her husband loving glances, which he returned. Such harmony, such happiness. In the past, it might have moved him. In the past. When he had been like the man in the house. When he still had a family. Dreams. A future.

Snatches of words reached his ears, and laughter. The children were watching some sort of animated film and looked quite amused. An idyllic scene. A happy family in their new home, but after tonight, they would no longer be a family and they would never be happy again.

Now they were getting up. It was a little past eleven.

The women cleared the table; the men disappeared into the garage and came back with fireworks. The children jumped up and hopped round excitedly. He could hear their bright voices.

The men went outside on the patio, got the fireworks ready, sticking rockets into empty bottles, drinking beer, laughing. They had no idea that death awaited only fifty metres away.

The death that he would bring.

He was Death.

The first thing that Pia noticed was the handwriting. It was the same neat little girl's writing she had seen in the surveillance notes that she had found in Mark Thomsen's house. Pia had studied the piece of paper so long that certain graphological characteristics caught her eye at once: instead of dotting the *i*, the writer drew a little circle, and the writing slanted back sharply to the left, the way left-handers often wrote. She leafed feverishly

through the little black book. What should she look for? She
needed names, but where was the list that Karoline Albrecht had
mentioned?

Pia sat in the passenger seat of the unmarked car with
Bodenstein. The two uniformed officers had returned from
Höchst with blue light and siren on and turned over the diary
to him. They had also picked up the document binders from
Riegelhoff's office and stowed them in the boot of their cruiser.
Their boss had taken a quick look in the black book and then
handed it straight back to her.

'I can't make out the handwriting in this dim lighting, even
with my reading glasses on,' he said. 'Your eyes have got to be
younger.'

'Only slightly,' she replied, and borrowed his reading
glasses.

Mark Thomsen remained missing, Dirk Stadler had not
returned his call, and now Jens-Uwe Hartig also seemed to
have joined the ranks of those who had apparently been swallowed up by the earth. His house, his apartment and his shop
had been staked out, so far without result.

Just as Bodenstein slammed the boot shut, Pia found the
page. She jumped out of the car.

'I found it!' she exclaimed excitedly. 'Ms Albrecht was
right. She wrote out an actual death list. Listen to this.'

She quickly read off the names that Helen Stadler had
neatly numbered and listed.

1. Renate Rohleder (mother, dog)
2. Dieter Paul Rudolf (wife, daughter, grandchild)
3. Patrick Schwarzer (wife)
4. Fritz Gehrke (son)

5. Bettina Kaspar-Hesse (husband, children)
6. Simon Burmeister
7. Ulrich Hausmann (daughter)
8. Arthur Janning (wife, son)
9. Jens-Uwe Hartig (?)

'She even wrote down the addresses!' Pia shouted. She was shaking all over with excitement.

This was it! This was the breakthrough!

'Helen Stadler had spied on all the people she held responsible for her mother's death. And now someone is carrying out what she had planned. I just don't understand why Hartig's name is on her list, too.'

'We can mull that over later.' Bodenstein opened the car door on the driver's side and reached for the radio. 'If the sniper keeps to the same order, then the next victim is somehow related to Bettina Kaspar-Hesse. Give me her address.'

'Sterngasse 118 in Griesheim,' said Pia.

Bodenstein called station dispatch and told them the name and address, repeating the woman's name twice.

'Griesheim near Frankfurt or near Darmstadt?' he asked Pia.

'No idea, it doesn't say!' she shouted. 'Just ask them to find out where there's a street by that name.'

She decided to call Kai, and she managed to reach him.

'In Griesheim near Frankfurt, there isn't any Sterngasse,' one of the uniformed officers said. 'I know that after spending ten years on the beat in Frankfurt.'

'No, not Offenbach!' Bodenstein said at the same time, his voice vibrating with impatience in the microphone. '*Stern*gasse, not *Stein*gasse, good grief.'

'I have Kai on the phone!' Pia shouted to her boss. 'He's still at work and is running a search.'

'When you two finally locate the place, send someone out there, and you'd better call first and say you're coming. Tell the people there to turn off all the lights and get everyone into the basement until we arrive.' He ended the call. 'Get in, Pia. Maybe we can get there in time.'

Twenty to twelve. The man and his pal had set up all the rockets and fireworks; in the house, the wife was opening the champagne. Through the wide-open patio doors, he could hear the corks popping. The television was screeching with the broadcast of the New Year's Eve party from the Brandenburg Gate in Berlin.

The countdown started.

The children ran excitedly through the house; they'd put on their jackets. The friend went inside, perhaps to help the women with the champagne.

The husband stood on the patio, one hand in his jacket pocket, in the other holding a bottle of beer. He took a swig, tilted his head back, and gazed into the clear night sky, in which rockets were prematurely exploding here and there. What must he be thinking? Probably something beautiful. He was proud of his house, it was a wonderful evening, he was in a good mood during those final minutes of his life. Yes, he was doubtless going to die happy.

In the house, the phone rang.

'Who could be calling at this hour?' shouted the man's wife.

'Just pick it up. Maybe it's your parents,' answered her husband with a grin.

He turned round and was looking right at him.

Can he see me, here in the construction site, behind the cement sacks?

The phone stopped ringing.

He didn't look to the left or right anymore.

He put his finger on the trigger.

He had the man's face right in front of him, could see every pore.

'Ralf!' called the wife, her voice shrill. 'Ralf! Come inside!'

He breathed deeply in and out.

He crooked his finger and squeezed the trigger.

TUESDAY, JANUARY 1, 2013

The news reached Bodenstein just as he was turning off the A5 at Griesheim. He had to brake hard so he wouldn't drift out of the exit lane into the roadworks.

'You were right, boss.' Kai Ostermann sounded depressed. 'Ms Kaspar-Hesse was the next target. He shot her husband. Officers from Darmstadt arrived eleven minutes after they got the call, but unfortunately, it was the wrong address. The Hesses moved a month ago. Now they live at Tauberstrasse 18. They phoned over there, but it was too late.'

'Shit!' Bodenstein yelled louder than Pia had ever heard him, and banged on the steering wheel with the heel of his hand. 'Dammit, dammit, dammit!'

'Although the whole area was sealed off immediately, he seems to have made his escape,' Kai went on. 'Where are you now?'

'We'll be there in five minutes,' said Pia as she changed the target address in the satnav.

The tension of the past few hours turned into deep disappointment. All their efforts, all their hopes, had been in vain. Once again, the sniper had a head start on them.

'What about a helicopter?' Bodenstein shouted.

'It's New Year's Day, boss,' Kai reminded him. 'Because of the fireworks, there's a ban on low-flying aircraft.'

'Okay, we'll try again later,' he replied, having regained his composure. 'If you get hold of Kröger, please send him out to Griesheim, so we don't offend our colleagues.'

'Will do,' said Kai. 'Oh, yeah, in spite of everything: Happy New Year to both of you.'

'Thanks, Kai. And thanks for your help,' Pia said, suddenly tired.

As Bodenstein turned at the entrance to Griesheim off the North Ring, the first rockets rose into the night sky and exploded in wonderful cascades of coloured lights. As they drove round between the A 67 and the city, the fireworks really let loose. Beyond the sharp curve that the road made at this spot they reached the first roadblock. Bodenstein rolled down his window, showed the officers his ID, and was allowed through.

At the roundabout, he took the third exit to Elbestrasse, from which several cul-de-sacs branched off to the edge of the woods. Tauberstrasse was the fourth in a newly developed area, with scattered houses standing between empty plots. It was easy to see in which house the tragedy had occurred. They were confronted with the scene they knew so well after every crime or discovery of a dead body: the ME van, ambulances and police vehicles with mutely flashing blue lights. Bodenstein left the car by the last roadblock, and they walked the final stretch along the newly paved road. The cold air smelled of black powder. A hearse rolled past them, and up ahead, the first of the onlookers were gathering.

There was absolutely no doubt that this murder could be chalked up to the Taunus Sniper. Darmstadt's Chief Inspector Helmut Möller, who normally had nothing to do with murders and just happened to be on call, was elated to be able to turn the case over to Bodenstein. He brought them up to speed about the situation and agreed to let Bodenstein bring in his own evidence team.

'Appalling,' he kept saying. 'Simply appalling. I've never seen anything like it. Right in front of his kids and his wife, shot to death.'

Pia's phone rang. Christoph! She stepped aside and took the call.

'Happy New Year, my dear!' he shouted, in a great mood. 'Has your mobile network broken down again?'

'Christoph!' said Pia. 'Happy New Year to you, too. I'm still at work. There's just been another sniper murder. Can I call you back later?'

'Oh God, you poor thing,' Christoph said, full of sympathy. 'I'd hoped you'd be sitting with Kim at home, drinking champagne. Sure, call me later. I'm thinking of you.'

'Me, too. I miss you.'

Pia heaved a deep sigh, silently girding herself for everything that would happen in the next few hours, and followed her boss into the house. Once again, they encountered incomprehensible horror, pain, profound despair, screams and tears. She could hardly bear it. Bodenstein was as deeply affected as she was. Deep furrows had appeared on his face over the past few days. Nobody should be burdened past their breaking point. That was why psychological support was made available for first responders and police officers. The mental anguish of family members rubbed off on even the toughest and most experienced among them.

A blinding floodlight that was mounted up under the roof-beam and was motion-activated bathed the body of Ralf Hesse in glaring light. The man lay on the patio in front of a white wall, and the sight was truly horrifying. Blood, brains and bone fragments had sprayed onto the wall. The shot had struck him from the front, right in the face, and the bullet had ripped off half his head.

Pia looked round. She saw the rockets in the empty wine bottles that were stuck into the dirt of the garden that was not yet planted, a broken beer bottle on the terracotta tiles. Beyond the neighbouring empty plot stood the partial frame of a duplex.

'He must have fired from the house under construction over there,' she surmised. Bodenstein didn't react. He stood there in silence, his hands in his coat pockets, his shoulders hunched, his lips pressed together in a narrow line, as he stared at the dead man at his feet.

'What drives a person to execute five people in this way?' he asked. 'Murder and manslaughter in the heat of the moment, I can understand to a certain extent, but this . . . This sort of well-planned and executed killing is something done only by terrorists who are blinded by ideology.'

He raised his head. His gaze flickered.

'I've always managed to maintain a certain objective distance. But this time, I can't do it anymore. This time I'm taking what this bastard does personally. He's mocking us with these e-mails. God help him when we get our hands on him!'

Pia touched his arm. She knew what was going on inside him, and she shared his furious sense of helplessness.

'Let's go and talk to his wife,' she said, remembering with horror that day in July two years ago. She would never forget the all-encompassing fear when she found the dogs dead in the driveway and Christoph bleeding on the kitchen floor. And then she'd learned that Christoph's granddaughter Lilly had been kidnapped. For her, there had been a happy ending, at least as far as Christoph and Lilly were concerned, but Bettina Kaspar-Hesse would never be able to hold her husband in her arms or fall asleep and wake up next to him again.

'Yes.' Bodenstein nodded resolutely. 'Let's get this over with.'

They entered the house through the open patio door. The television was still on, showing people happily celebrating the new year in front of the Brandenburg Gate. Bodenstein took the remote from the table and switched it off. The dining room table had not yet been cleared; in the kitchen, dirty dishes were stacked up, and the dishwasher stood open. On a tray stood four champagne glasses and an open bottle.

A dark-haired man in his mid-forties spoke to one of the officers and then entered the house.

'I'm Darius Scheffler,' he said, introducing himself. 'My wife and I were celebrating with Ralf and Bettina. I've just been helping to take the children over to the neighbours' house.'

Although he, too, was clearly in shock, he answered all the questions that Bodenstein and Pia asked. Scheffler had set up the fireworks together with Ralf Hesse; then he went into the house to help the two women with the champagne.

'The phone rang,' he recalled. 'Bettina wondered who could be calling, and Ralf shouted that it was no doubt her parents. She picked it up, listened for a moment, then turned pale and yelled, 'Ralf! Ralf! Come inside!' and then . . then . . . I . . . I turned round and saw how Ralf's head . . . simply . . . disappeared. He fell against the wall and . . . the blood . . . the blood shot up like a fountain.'

He fell silent, took a few quavering breaths, then regained his composure.

'Did anyone else see what happened?' Pia asked.

'Yes, we all did,' said Darius Scheffler. 'When Bettina screamed, we turned round to look at Ralf.'

'The children, too?'

'No, not them. They'd already put on their jackets, and I managed to catch them both in time and keep them from running outside. They didn't see anything.'

'Where is your wife?' Pia asked.

'Upstairs, with Tina. I took the kids to the neighbours across the street so that they wouldn't have to see all this.'

'That was good.' Pia smiled briefly. 'Thanks for telling us your account. Please give your personal information to one of the officers. We'll be in touch with you later.'

They went upstairs. The doctor who had been summoned came over to them and explained in a low voice that the victim's wife was in a bad way, but she had refused any treatment.

'Her friend will stay with her,' said the doctor. 'And her parents are on their way over.'

'May we ask her a couple of questions?' Pia enquired.

'If you must.' The doctor was not enthusiastic about the

idea, and Pia felt worse than if she'd had to tell someone a loved one had died.

'Please wait here,' she told the doctor. 'We may need you in a moment.'

Bettina Kaspar-Hesse was sitting slumped on the bed in her bedroom upstairs, not crying, her whole body rigid, as if paralysed. Her friend sat beside her with her arm round Bettina.

'Mrs Kaspar-Hesse, I'm very sorry, but we do have to ask you a few questions,' Pia began after she introduced herself and Bodenstein. 'Is that all right?'

Stupid question. Of course it wasn't all right. But it was Pia's duty to ask questions, even when she didn't think it was wise.

'We have reason to believe that your husband was a victim of the sniper who has already shot four other individuals to death,' Pia went on, even though the woman showed no reaction. 'For this reason, we have to know whether you or your husband ever had anything to do with A&E at the Frankfurt University Hospital. Either in the past or recently.'

Bettina Kaspar-Hesse slowly raised her head. She stared at Pia uncomprehendingly; then she nodded weakly.

'I used to work there,' she said softly. 'Until my first pregnancy. Why do you ask?'

'In what capacity did you work there?' Pia ignored her question.

'I was the transplant coordinator,' said Bettina Kaspar-Hesse. 'For seven months, and then I got pregnant.'

'Do you remember a patient named Kirsten Stadler? She was brought in on September sixteenth, 2002 with a cerebral haemorrhage, then died and became an organ donor.'

Bettina Kaspar-Hesse nodded.

'Yes, I remember her well, because the day before I learned that I was pregnant.' The corner of her mouth twitched with a smile, but it vanished at once. 'What's the point of these questions? Why do you want to know? What does it have to do with what just happened?'

Her voice failed.

'Do you recall the names of any colleagues or doctors who were involved in the Kirsten Stadler case?' Bodenstein now asked.

'I . . . I don't know . . . It was so long ago.' Bettina Kaspar-Hesse kneaded her fingers. 'My boss was Professor Rudolf. Back then, Dr Janning was still there from the intensive care unit and Dr Burmeister. He was the head of transplant surgery back then, and he was really crazy, like a vulture. He used to chew me out if the patient's relatives didn't want to sign the consent agreement. So I would put a form down in front of them and say it was only the hospital admission form.'

Pia and Bodenstein exchanged a brief look.

'The doctors were pressuring me to persuade the patient's parents to release her for organ donation. To use any means necessary, because time was tight and they had a patient who urgently needed a new heart. So I did it. That was my job, after all. And on that particular day, I was feeling so upbeat and I wanted to do a good job. Later, the husband filed a lawsuit against the hospital, but I don't remember how it all turned out, because by that time I was already on maternity leave . . .'

She fell silent and looked from Bodenstein to Pia, wide-eyed. Suddenly she seemed to comprehend.

'No,' she whispered in horror. 'No! It can't be true. Please, tell me, that didn't have anything to do with my husband . . . my husband being . . .'

For a couple of seconds, she sat there stock-still, her gaze going glassy. Then she opened her mouth and uttered an inarticulate scream. She tore herself loose from her friend, fell to her knees, and pounded her fists on the floor, shrieking and shrieking until her voice hardly sounded human anymore. The doctor came running in and shot Pia a dirty look.

'Enough of this questioning,' he hissed reproachfully, as though Pia were doing it out of sheer enjoyment. She turned on her heel without a word and walked out. The suspicion that she might be to blame for her husband's death would haunt Bettina Kaspar-Hesse to her dying day.

On the way home, he thought about whether he should burn the shoes in the fireplace or stuff them in a rubbish bin somewhere. He had certainly left tracks in the mortar dust at the construction site. But it wasn't worth the effort. They were going to catch him anyway, and then he would confess to everything; they could save themselves the trouble of doing a lab analysis of his shoes. Every radio station was talking about the fifth victim of the Taunus Sniper.

It worried him a bit how fast the police had been on the scene, as if they had known where he would strike next. They must have worked out the connections, and that could jeopardize his plan.

He turned into the neighbourhood, the car bumping through frozen potholes that made the shock absorbers groan. All the houses were dark. On New Year's Eve, not a soul was round; they all preferred to celebrate at home, where there were neighbours they could wish Happy New Year.

That suited him fine.

He put the car in the garage and went inside. The house

*was nice and warm, and he noticed that he was hungry. After
he changed his clothes, he put a couple more logs on the fire
and made himself some scrambled eggs and bacon. He ate the
food right from the pan and turned on the TV. No official
statement from the police, only shots of the crime scene that
told him nothing. Blue lights, crime-scene tape, a hearse and
reporters looking solemn, saying the same things as they had
last Friday. They were again characterizing him as a psychopath, a monster. How unimaginative. Always the same
vocabulary. And incorrect. But soon they would know his
true motives. Whether they would understand them was
something else, but he had no doubt that someone somewhere
would secretly comprehend why he had been driven to act.
Why he could not let these people escape unpunished.*

*Four names were left on his list. Burmeister was next. He
was on holiday with his daughter, but was returning the day
after tomorrow, and then he would receive his punishment.*

It was two thirty in the morning when Pia's phone rang. Bodenstein was still talking to Kröger at the construction site; Pia stood
down below, smoking a cigarette.

'Hello, Henning,' she said in surprise. 'Did you and your
family have a Happy New Year?'

'You can make that singular,' he replied dryly. 'I spent the
night with Friedrich Gehrke.'

'Excuse me?'

'There was a little argument with Miriam when she told
me she preferred to visit friends. She didn't like it that I had to
go out in the early evening to deal with another dead body.
Since Ronnie, who was on duty, and I had nothing better to
do, we decided to clear out a couple of cold-storage drawers.'

'You are really incorrigible.' Pia shook her head and at the same time felt a little ashamed because deep inside, she felt a hint of malicious glee. Miriam used to be her best friend, but after she and Henning got married two years ago in something of a rush, their friendship had soured. It particularly rankled Pia that Miriam always acted as though she had succeeded in reining in Henning's excessive workaholic tendencies, which was the reason why Pia had divorced him. Obviously, this was not the case.

'So, listen up,' said Henning without going into detail about the spat with his wife. 'There are a couple of points that could be interesting. In the report from the crime scene, it states that Gehrke had burned papers in his open fireplace before he died. Is that correct?'

'Yes, that's right. Quite a lot, in fact. Why?'

'We found no soot particles in his bronchial passages or in the lungs or on the mucous membranes. Either he wore a protective mask or he wasn't present while the fire was burning.'

'What do you mean – "he wasn't present"?'

'Hold on. In the vicinity of the nose and mouth, as well as the upper and lower lip, we found skin desiccation and minor subcutaneous haemorrhages, as well as light irritation of the nasal and oral mucous membranes.'

'And?'

'We did a quick test in the laboratory and found that Gehrke had inhaled chloroform. In vivo, forty per cent of a one-time dose is broken down in eight hours by the lungs, and because of that, we have to examine the lung tissue, which will take only a moment.'

Pia was exhausted and couldn't help yawning. She couldn't understand what Henning was getting at.

'Would it be all right if you e-mailed us a report tomorrow?' she asked. 'I'm standing in front of a house in Griesheim. We've had another sniper murder.'

'I had a hunch you weren't celebrating New Year's with friends,' Henning replied, wide awake and unmoved. 'We just heard about it on the radio. So maybe you should listen to me after all.'

'Yeah, sure.' Pia sighed.

'I've come to the preliminary conclusion that Gehrke inhaled chloroform and then lost consciousness,' Henning continued. 'From Kröger's report, I couldn't tell whether a cotton-wool ball or a handkerchief soaked in chloroform was secured at the crime scene. In addition, subcutaneous bleeds on the back of the head and the nape of the neck indicate that he was being gripped hard.'

Finally the penny dropped for Pia.

'You mean that Gehrke was murdered?'

'Bingo, even though it took you a while. But I'll let the current corpse serve as your excuse.'

'And the insulin?'

'Someone could have given him the injection at any time. He was sedated and couldn't defend himself.' Henning didn't sound as though his marital troubles were giving him a headache. 'Chloroform isn't really in fashion these days, but it's marvellous for putting someone out for a while—'

'How certain are you?' Pia interrupted him. Bodenstein had come out of the construction site with Kröger, and both were now standing next to her.

'I'm fairly sure. But you'll still get all the lab results, of course.'

'Thank you, Henning. My boss just arrived. Talk to you again tomorrow.'

'What did the Lord of Death want at this hour?' Kröger enquired.

'He had nothing better to do tonight, so he performed a post-mortem on Gehrke,' Pia replied. 'He's pretty sure that his death was the result of foul play. Apparently, Gehrke was knocked out with chloroform. There were no soot particles in his lungs, which means he must have been dead before the documents were burned.'

'Another murder.' Bodenstein shook his head in resignation. 'That's just great. As if we have nothing else to do.'

'You guys should go home.' Kröger patted him on the shoulder. 'We'll finish up here. Whatever Dr Kirchhoff can do, I can do, too.'

'You're a screwball, Christian,' said Pia with another yawn. 'Come on, boss, let's go home. Tomorrow's another day.'

After he dropped Pia off at Birkenhof round four in the morning, Bodenstein drove home. His fury at the sniper and his own powerlessness had metamorphosed into a feverish unease. Since Inka preferred to sleep in her own bed after she came back from her emergency call, he had no reason to stay at home. He realized that he didn't have to take anyone into consideration. He didn't have to justify his actions or feel guilty for working on a holiday; there were no children to disappoint by failing to keep a promise, no reproachful looks. He could turn on all the lights in the house at five o'clock, start the coffeemaker, and take a leisurely shower and shave without worrying about waking someone up. Why, he thought as he stepped over to his wardrobe in the bedroom with a towel wrapped round his waist, would he want to change this situation? Living in a relationship seemed much more complicated than living alone; the drawbacks far outweighed the advantages. Even during the period after his divorce from Cosima, he'd enjoyed living alone; back then, the only thing that had bothered him was the lack of comforts in the coach house of the Bodenstein Estate. Now, on the other hand, he owned a lovely house, and being free felt like paradise.

Bodenstein enjoyed the freshly brewed coffee and the view out of the floor-to-ceiling windows of the entire Rhein-Main region. He wasn't the type of person who started the new year with a zillion resolutions, only to give them up in a matter of weeks. But at this moment, he intended to achieve three things in the year 2013. First, he would catch the sniper; second, end his relationship with Inka; and third, accept Gabriela's offer. No more self-doubt and constant giving in out of sheer laziness. This year, he was going to change a few things, and he was looking forward to it.

Feeling motivated, a little later he put on his coat, turned off the lights in the house, and went out to his car. They were close to reaching a breakthrough in the sniper case; his intuition told him that. Yet he was wary of having overlooked something, and that made him edgy. The investigation had been chaotic from the start, and the team was not working smoothly together. Every time he thought he'd understood something, new circumstances had popped up, a new murder happened, and all that talk about a perp profile had confused him utterly. Nicola's decision to bring in a profiler had simply been premature. Before they had even worked out what the murders were all about, they'd been distracted by psychological speculations that had to be revised the next day, and at some point, they'd lost their perspective. In the end, who was to blame for their failure to arrest the sniper yet? Why did more people have to die?

As Bodenstein drove along the streets of Kelkheim that were littered with fireworks debris, he thought about Chief Inspector Menzel, his former boss in Frankfurt. His motto was: *Remember everything that you heard or saw and follow the trail backwards.* The sniper simply hadn't allowed them enough time to think things through and to eliminate false starting points. He had hounded them forward, put them under pressure and they had let themselves be hurried, although in a murder investigation, nothing was more disastrous than haste, stress and exhaustion. Tired people make mistakes, drew the wrong conclusions and lost the thread. At least now they had names and knew what was driving the sniper. They could warn the individuals who were on Helen Stadler's list.

For days, Bodenstein had secretly been anticipating that the higher-ups would take him off the case that was attracting so much attention, or bring in some super-investigator from State Criminal Police headquarters to replace him, but that had not happened. Either they trusted him to get the upper hand in the case, or else there was no one else foolish enough to scorch his reputation with such an unpopular investigation. Failure was always bad for anyone's career; failure in the eyes of the public was professional suicide. But he had no intention of failing. On the contrary. Now that most of the pieces of the puzzle were on the table, they just had to put them together correctly. And they had to do it today.

Pia's eyes were watering from fatigue as she drove towards Hofheim shortly before 7 a.m. along the paved road that ran parallel to the autobahn. When she'd got home, Kim wasn't there, and her bed hadn't been slept in. After Pia Skyped with Christoph, she had nodded off on the sofa, but she wasn't able to enter a deep sleep. One nightmare had followed another, and round five, she received a cryptic text on her mobile, which Kim had no doubt sent round ten the night before in answer to her text. It had been delayed by the annual overload of the mobile network on New Year's Eve. *Okay. Call if you need me. Not drinking until 11. After that, we'll see! ;-) XO Kim.*

By six thirty, Pia gave up on sleeping. She had a shower, put on clean clothes, fed the animals, and took off again.

As she drove through the pitch-dark morning, she pondered what mistakes she might have made that could possibly cost Christoph his life. The offences of Renate Rohleder, Patrick Schwarzer and Bettina Kaspar-Hesse had not been capital crimes – they were human errors, long forgotten or repressed. But the decisions they made back then had injured other people so deeply that their actions became a boomerang that returned to punish them ten years later in the most horrible way.

A fox ran across the road, its eyes shining spooky green in the headlights; then it vanished into the dark.

No one went through life without occasionally hurting other people, now and then causing disappointment, problems and even outright harm. For almost any action that hurt someone else, there were rules for rectification, namely the penal code. Long ago, people took the law into their own hands, but that time was over. Even if many felt unjustly treated by the law, as a rule, they did not take up arms to exact vengeance. But that's exactly what the sniper was doing. He did not trust in the system of justice and the rule of law. Instead, he held to the biblical legal code: 'a life for a life, an eye for an eye, a tooth for a tooth, a hand for a hand, a foot for a foot, a brand for a brand, a welt for a welt.' He was meting out his own justice. What did his deeds mean? Your beloved for my beloved?

Pia's mobile beeped, and the thought that had flitted through her head evaporated. She called up Henning's text and read it as she drove. *Dr Hans Furtwängler, Cologne,* he wrote. *He had a lot to do with Rudolf, maybe he can help you guys out. Tel. no. follows.*

Dr Hans Furtwängler! Fritz Gehrke had phoned him before his death, and she had read the name in Helen Stadler's notebook. Kai had already checked out the old doctor and also asked him what he and Gehrke had talked about on Saturday evening for fourteen minutes. But she couldn't recall what Furtwängler had told Kai. She definitely needed to ask him again. She turned off the dual carriageway towards Hofheim and reached the station three minutes later. Kim's car was parked in the public car park, and it hadn't been there for long, because Pia could see tyre tracks on the frost-covered tarmac. Where had her sister spent the night?

Professor Dieter Rudolf was beside himself. Last night, the police had taken him into custody and locked him in a cell without giving him a chance to call anyone. On the way from the cell to the interrogation room, his shoes kept slipping off because he'd had to surrender his shoelaces, but the height of humiliation was that he'd had to hold up his trousers with one hand, since they were too loose without a belt.

'This is wrongful deprivation of personal liberty!' he yelled angrily at Bodenstein and Pia as he was ushered past them into the interrogation room. 'I'm going to lodge a complaint, you can count on that!'

'Shut up and sit down.' Bodenstein pointed to the chair across the table from Pia, who had already taken a seat.

'You'd better watch how you talk to me,' the professor retorted. 'I have rights!'

'In a society in which we have rights, we also have obligations,' Bodenstein countered with a cool look at the man sitting across from him. The professor's thin face was flushed and his Adam's apple hopped up and down. He was unshaven, and his white hair was sticking out wildly. The night in the cell had deeply shaken his ego, and he was reacting precisely the way Bodenstein had expected: with aggression and shouts. Men in executive positions liked to think of themselves as untouchable. Used to obedience without complaint from their subordinates, they had a hard time taking orders from anyone they would normally regard as beneath them.

'I know my rights!' Rudolf snapped in rage. 'I pay as much in tax every month as you make in a year!'

'Sit the fuck down!' Bodenstein thundered at the man, and he obeyed, in shock. 'We're not talking about tax here, but about moral obligations! You could have saved the life of an individual yesterday if you'd told us the name of your former colleague. Last night, the husband of the former transplant coordinator at the UCF, Mrs Bettina Kaspar-Hesse, was shot to death. Even more guilt to heap upon your conscience!'

The professor pressed his lips together, crossed his arms, and defiantly stuck out his chin.

'In the meantime, we've found out that you violated regulations in order to implant a new heart in the son of your friend Fritz Gehrke. The boy was very ill, and then Kirsten Stadler happened to fall into your hands. Ms Stadler was unfortunately blood type O. That means that her heart was a match for

Gehrke's son and coronary patient Maximilian. You cut short Ms Stadler's life by prematurely declaring her brain-dead,' Bodenstein said.

'The woman was dead anyway,' Rudolf argued. 'A day sooner or later, what difference did it make?'

'So you admit, with reference to Kirsten Stadler, that you—' Pia began in disbelief.

'I admit nothing!' the professor declared. 'There is nothing to admit.'

'Now, I want you to listen to me carefully,' Bodenstein took over, leaning forward. 'You are sitting up to your neck in shit. If you had been cooperative from the beginning, then perhaps we never would have discovered what we now know about you.'

'My wife was shot to death by this . . . this person.' The professor was stonewalling. 'I was in deep grief and utterly bewildered. You can understand that, can't you?'

'You weren't grief-stricken and bewildered enough not to try to do some damage control when you talked to Fritz Gehrke on the phone,' Bodenstein replied. 'I don't believe a word you're saying. You have violated your Hippocratic oath as well as the law. And proof of it has now come out. That's why Gehrke paid the relatives of Ms Stadler a large sum to drop the case. But there was a witness who did not keep his mouth shut, namely Jens-Uwe Hartig. He told the Stadlers the truth.'

'You have no idea what you're talking about.' The professor remained outwardly calm, but he was blinking his eyes rapidly.

'On the contrary, we're learning more by the hour.' Bodenstein glanced at the piece of paper with four names on it that

Pia had jotted down, and nodded brusquely. 'The lawyer Riegelhoff told us quite a few things and turned over all the documents from the lawsuit between Stadler and the UCF.' He leaned back and studied the professor's face intently. 'Our conversation with Mr Hartig was also extremely informative. Today, we will be talking to Furtwängler, Janning, Burmeister and Hausmann.'

A spark of apprehension appeared in the professor's eyes, and his mask of arrogant indifference began to crack.

No one said a word. Bodenstein and Pia simply stared at the professor. Abrupt silence was a tried-and-trusted technique. Most people couldn't deal with it, especially not after a tough verbal exchange. They would grow more nervous by the minute. Their thoughts would begin to race, and they would get tangled up in explanations, justifications, excuses and lies.

Professor Dieter Rudolf lost the power struggle after exactly seven minutes and twelve seconds.

'I want my lawyer,' he croaked, cowed.

'And you're going to need one.' Bodenstein shoved his chair back and stood up. 'I arrest you provisionally on suspicion of the negligent murder of Ms Kirsten Stadler.'

'You can't do that,' the professor protested. 'My patients need me.'

'They're going to have to get along without you for quite a while,' said Bodenstein, nodding to the officer standing by the door. Then he left the interrogation room with Pia.

Kim had stopped at a convenience store to buy sandwiches, and she now set the plate in the middle of the conference table. Present were Nicola Engel, Bodenstein, Kirchhoff, Ostermann, Altunay and Fachinger. Everybody reached for a sandwich. Pia grabbed a soft pretzel with cheese.

'Happy New Year,' Kim told her, taking a seat beside her sister.

'Thanks, same to you.' Pia smiled as she chewed, then lowered her voice. 'Where were you last night?'

'Later,' Kim whispered. 'By the way, you could have let me know and I would have come along.'

Before Kai could begin, Pia took the floor and told her colleagues about her conversation with Henning.

'We have to consider the possibility that Gehrke did not commit suicide, but was murdered,' she concluded. 'We'll be receiving detailed lab results ASAP.'

Kai had gone through Helen Stadler's notebook, which Pia had given him last night, and he'd made a list of people he wanted to phone. He had reached the ex-wife of Dr Simon Burmeister and learned that the doctor had been in the Seychelles with his seventeen-year-old daughter for two weeks and was expected back tomorrow morning.

Pia thought of something else.

'Remind me, Kai, what did Dr Furtwängler talk to Fritz Gehrke about the night before he died?'

'Apparently nothing in particular,' replied her colleague. 'They were old friends, and Gehrke had seemed in a melancholy mood. He attributed it to the death of Gehrke's son.'

'Do you believe that?'

'So far, anyway. Why?'

'Henning gave me a tip about Furtwängler. He apparently had worked a lot with Rudolf. And now I'm asking myself where their fields of expertise intersected: one was a cardiologist, the other an oncologist and haematologist.'

'I'll call him back.' Kai nodded and wrote himself a note.

Mark Thomsen's house was still deserted. There was a stakeout on it, just as there was on the Winklers' home and on Hartig's house and shop. A note on the goldsmith's door said that the shop would be closed until 6 January 2013. Hartig's house in Diedenbergen had also been checked out and searched. It was empty. Neighbours had told them that Hartig had begun the renovation, but work had suddenly ceased this past autumn.

The telephone on the conference table rang. Kai picked it up and then handed the receiver to Pia.

'Hello,' said a timid girl's voice. 'My name is Jonelle Hase-brink. I live in Griesheim, on Saalestrasse.'

'Hello, Jonelle.' Pia sat down and put the call on speaker so that everyone could hear. 'I'm Pia Kirchhoff with Kripo in Hofheim. How can I help you?'

'I think,' said the girl, 'that my boyfriend and I saw the killer.'

Everyone stopped chewing and stared at the telephone as if spellbound.

'My parents can't know about this, because ... they ... well ... They have no idea that I have a boyfriend.'

'How old are you, Jonelle?' Pia enquired, writing down the girl's last name and shoving it over to Kai. He typed it into his laptop.

'Fifteen.'

'You're still underage. That means your parents have the right to be present when you talk to the police,' said Pia.

'Can't we do it on the phone? Otherwise, I'll get in big trouble.'

'Hasebrink, Lutz and Peggy, Saalestrasse 17,' Kai said quietly.

'How good a look did you get of the man?' Pia asked.

'Not too good, I guess.' Jonelle was trying to back-pedal, now that she realized the possible consequences of making this call. 'But I saw him getting into his car. Maybe it's not that important.'

Pia looked over at Bodenstein. He gave her a thumbs-up and nodded.

'No, it's very important.' Pia tried to sound soothing. 'You'll help us a lot if you tell us exactly what you saw. We'd be happy to come over straight away, and it would be good if your boyfriend was there, too.'

'But how will I explain it to my parents? I mean, about Fabio?'

'Don't you think that they'd be proud of you two if you contributed to solving this series of murders? Plus, then you and your boyfriend wouldn't have to keep sneaking round.'

The girl hesitated.

'Hmm. Well, maybe you're right. When can you come?'

'We can be there in half an hour.'

Ten minutes later, Bodenstein, Pia and Kim were in the car heading towards Darmstadt. The construction site had clearly been the shooter's hiding place, as proved by the ballistic path of the bullet. And for the first time, the sniper had left traces behind. Kröger and his men found shoe prints in the dust of the construction site, along with a clear body print where he had lain. The sniper had lain in wait in the opening of a floor-to-ceiling window on the second floor. He had rested the rifle barrel on two sacks of cement stacked up. A perfect hiding place with a first-class view of the Hesse family's house.

Pia looked at her sister in the rear-view mirror. Kim was typing a text into her smartphone and smiling to herself. In Bodenstein's presence, she didn't want to ask Kim about where she had been last night. But she was curious.

'We'd like to keep you here one more night for observation,' said the consultant. 'A concussion and whiplash are nothing to trifle with.'

'I'm not planning on going skiing,' Karoline Albrecht said stubbornly. 'I can lie in bed just as well at home.'

'You were in a serious car crash,' the doctor argued, but he was already beaten. Of course he wanted to keep a private patient in the hospital a while longer, but Karoline was restless. At a little past noon, she had phoned Greta to wish her a Happy New Year, but refrained from mentioning the accident. She didn't want to upset her daughter unnecessarily. She hadn't been able to reach her father, because his mobile was turned off, and he didn't pick up the landline. Maybe he had put in earplugs and gone to bed, since he'd never been a fan of New Year's Eve and fireworks.

'I feel fine,' Karoline said to the doctor. 'I promise to take it easy. And if I feel worse, I'll come back.'

'As you wish.' He gave up. 'I'll have the discharge papers printed out. But you'll have to sign a statement saying that you're leaving the hospital at your own risk.'

As soon as he was out the door, Karoline got up. She felt a bit woozy, and she had a headache, but except for a couple of bad bruises and a cut on her forehead, she had survived the accident without injury. She went into the small bathroom and was shocked when she saw how pale she looked in the mirror. The left half of her face had turned purple, and under her eye, a fat blood blister had formed. Someone had put the clothes she'd been wearing yesterday into the wardrobe. It was rather disgusting to put on the stinking, blood-caked garments, but she could have a shower and change her clothes when she got home. Her phone rang. The number was unknown, but she took the call anyway. It might be the police or the towing company.

'Bodenstein. Good morning.' She recognized the sonorous baritone of the inspector. 'How are you feeling?'

'Good morning. I'm feeling pretty good, thanks. Because of the airbags, I have only mild concussion and whiplash,' she replied. 'I'm going home now. Were you able to get anything out of that notebook?'

'Yes, it's very informative. But I'm afraid that last night it was too late. Once again, the sniper was faster than we were.'

'Oh my God.' Karoline sat down on the edge of the bed. 'If I hadn't had that accident and could have delivered the notebook earlier—'

'It's not your fault,' the inspector interrupted her. 'And you're not to blame for Fritz Gehrke's death either. The postmortem showed that he had been sedated and then killed with an overdose of insulin. Later, a large number of documents were burned in his fireplace, which we thought he'd done to cover up something. But new information has now shed a whole new light on the destruction of the documents.'

One piece of disastrous news after another. In the meantime, she was so numb inside that she hardly felt anything with regard to dead bodies and murder. She had once read in a book that no one who had been touched by murder, no matter how casually, would ever be the same. That was certainly the truth.

'Your father was a friend of Gehrke's,' the inspector went on. 'Is that correct?'

'I have no idea whether they were actually friends,' replied Karoline. 'But they had known each other for a very long time, and Gehrke's firm financed my father's research.'

Her phone began to beep because of a low battery.

'In case this call is cut off, it's because my battery is running low. I left my charger at home.'

'Then I'll make it brief,' said Bodenstein. 'Last night we arrested your father. He's not talking and wants to have his lawyer present. Of course, that's his legal right. But it's important for us to find out what he talked about with Gehrke the night before his death and—'

His voice broke off; the battery was dead. Karoline stood up and tossed it in her handbag. Mama was dead. Papa in jail. The new year was starting out as badly as the old year had ended. She grabbed her coat and bag and went down to the nurses' station. There she signed a form that said she was leaving the hospital on her own recognizance. She longed to have a shower and get some sleep. But before she went home to bed, she would stop by her parents' house one more time.

By ten thirty, they were in Griesheim. Streets were still blocked off over a wide area, and the evidence team was busy reconstructing the sniper's escape route with the help of sniffer dogs. The Hasebrinks lived on the second cross street before Tauberstrasse, which had already been more densely developed, in a duplex that was painted red. Jonelle was a pretty girl with a snub nose, long straight hair and big wide eyes. Her boyfriend, Fabio, was a skinny guy with spiky hair; the kind of guy who wore jeans that were too loose, a baseball cap and trainers. But for the visit to his girlfriend's parents, he had dressed decently. He sat motion-less at the Hasebrinks' pine dining room table. Bodenstein and Pia had also sat down, and the two young people stared at them like convicts eyeing their executioners. The conversation was not flowing smoothly, which may have been due to the disapproving expressions of Jonelle's parents. They made no secret of the fact that they regarded Fabio as a disastrous boyfriend for their fifteen-year-old daughter. Finally, Pia asked the parents if they could speak to the teenagers in private. Kim remained with the parents. After that, things went better.

Jonelle and Fabio had been going out for four months. They had met quite often at the construction site on Tauber-strasse, where work had been stopped for almost a year because the contractor went broke. Last Friday, they had been there, too, on the second floor, because windows had already been put in, and it wasn't so cold up there.

'We just sat round talking,' said the girl, moving a strand of hair out of her eyes. 'There was a noise downstairs. We totally panicked because we thought, Oh shit, it's an estate agent or maybe the guy who owned the dump. We couldn't get out of there without being seen, so we hid behind a couple of cement sacks.'

'A man came up the stairs,' Fabio continued the account. 'We saw him through the steps. He looked all round and then went into the room that had a good view of the house across the way. He was in there a couple of minutes, then he went downstairs. We heard him walking round down there. After a while, he left. And we did, too.'

'What did the man look like?' Pia asked. 'What was he wearing?'

'Dunno.' Jonelle shrugged. 'I didn't look that closely at his face. But he was wearing all black, with a cap and hoodie.'

'Black jeans and a dark blue jacket,' Fabio said more precisely.

'I think he had a beard,' Jonelle said.

'He wasn't clean-shaven,' Fabio agreed. 'But it wasn't really a beard.'

'A moustache?' Pia suggested.

'Yeah. That's it.'

'How old was he? What's your guess?'

'Pretty old.' Jonelle looked at her boyfriend uncertainly. 'Around forty. Or maybe older . . . dunno.'

Pretty old? Thanks a lot, Pia thought.

'What happened then?' Bodenstein asked.

'He kept walking round, like forever,' said the boy. 'I thought, Hey, man, get the hell out of here. I had football training at four, and my coach is really strict if you show up late. When the guy finally left, we ran downstairs and got out of there. I left for training on my moped.'

'I wanted to go home,' Jonelle went on. 'But first I thought I'd stop and get something sweet at the HEM petrol station. So I'm walking up the Elbestrasse and at the roundabout at the North Ring, I see the guy in the car park next to the HEM garage getting into his car. An old Opel, dark blue or black. I noticed the number plate, don't know why. Maybe because it wasn't from round here. And the guy was acting so strange.'

She told them the number plate, MTK-WM 177.

'And you're sure it was the same man you saw in the house under construction?' Bodenstein made sure.

'Yes, a hundred per cent,' Jonelle said with a nod.

'You're a good observer, Jonelle.' Bodenstein smiled. Thanks so much to both of you for calling us.'

The two smiled a bit uncertainly, but with some pride. Someday, the story of their testimony and the criminal police would make them heroes among their friends. But Jonelle was still humming and hawing.

'Um, do you think you could talk to my parents?' she asked Bodenstein coyly. 'About Fabio, I mean.'

'I think Dr Freitag has already done that,' Pia assured the girl. 'You won't get into any trouble.'

He had to get rid of the car, and right away. The police had not only the number plate, but also the make and colour. How had they managed that? Where had he made a mistake? He'd been so careful to avoid being seen by anyone. He almost fell over when he happened to hear the news on the radio, and ever since, he'd been jittery. Dammit, they were right on his heels. Luckily, they had no idea where he was. He had to capitalize on his small head start, or he could forget about the rest of his plan, which he'd been following so scrupulously.

He drove up the hill towards Königstein. His palms were sweaty, and at any moment, he expected his car to be recognized and pulled over. He was scared. Not of being caught, and not of prison. He was afraid that he wouldn't be able to finish his list, that they would stop him before he did. There wasn't a lot of traffic on the roads. It was a bank holiday. New Year's Day. People were still in bed with hangovers, or they were afraid of being shot by the Taunus Sniper. Having a few cars on the road was good; that way there was less risk of being spotted. Anyway, a blue Opel Meriva would be easier to spot in light traffic.

But he had an exit scenario for everything in his plan, also for the car. And now he would carry it out exactly, instead of driving the car into the woods in panic and ditching it there.

It had started to rain. At first only a few drops, but now the slate-grey sky had relentlessly opened its floodgates. Raindrops were pounding on the roof and windscreen of the car, and Bodenstein had to set the wipers on intermittent to be able to see anything at all. For the past half hour, he and Pia had been sitting in the car, watching the house at Taunusblick 72 in the Liederbach development, where Wolfgang Mieger, the owner of the blue Opel Meriva with number plate MTK-WM 177, was registered. Nobody had seen him. The house seemed deserted. Junk mail was overflowing from his mailbox, and the path to his door was covered with fallen leaves. The blinds were rolled down.

The car's back door was wrenched open, and Cem now plopped down on the back seat.

'What shitty weather!' he cursed, brushing the wet hair back from his forehead. Like Bodenstein and Pia, he wore a bulletproof vest under his coat. It might be practical if anyone shot at him, but it was about as comfortable as a fur coat in summer.

'What did the neighbour say?' Pia enquired.

'Wolfgang Mieger has been in assisted living since Christmas of 2011,' said Cem. 'He has dementia and apparently no relatives to take care of him. His wife died a few years ago, and he has no kids. Since then, the house has been empty. Somebody comes to check on the house and mow the lawn in the summer, but the neighbour has never met him.'

'If we're unlucky, the stakeout will be a waste of time,' said Pia, huffing on her cold hands. While the police service vehicles did have automatic windows, luxurious extras such as heating when parked were not included. 'But if we're lucky, the sniper will be using the house as a hideout.'

Initially, excitement had gripped the whole team when the sniper was turned from a phantom into a person of flesh and blood by the testimony of the two young people. But now an intolerable tension had set in. So far, Bodenstein had received no e-mail message from the sniper with an obituary for Ralf Hesse. Tracking of yesterday's e-mail by the IT specialists at State Criminal Police HQ had indicated that it had been sent from an open WLAN, but so many of these unencoded URLs were no longer active. Most users protected their WLANs with passwords to prevent unauthorized use. Was the sniper starting to feel the pressure? Did he suspect that they had found Helen Stadler's notebook and were closer on his heels than he'd thought? And if so, how did he know that?

Ostermann had reached Dr Burmeister at his hotel in the Seychelles and informed him that he and his daughter would be met at the arrivals gate by the police. When Burmeister asked why, Kai had not replied, so Pia decided to go out there herself and talk to the doctor. Mark Thomsen was still on the loose, as was Jens-Uwe Hartig. Kai had informed one of the shop assistants of Hartig's decision to close the shop until January 6, and she was surprised. As far as she knew, Hartig hadn't had any plans to go anywhere over Christmas. The state attorney's office had approved a mobile phone localization warrant, but so far, Hartig's phone had been turned off and remained as untraceable as its owner.

'Could you please turn on the engine for a minute?' Pia asked her boss. 'I'm almost frozen.'

Bodenstein turned the key in the ignition. The engine

TO CATCH A KILLER

sprang to life, and the defroster cleared off the fogged-up windscreen. Then his phone rang. He put it on speaker.

'The Special Assignment Unit will arrive there in ten minutes,' said Ostermann. 'And Napoleon has turned up here. Should I get rid of him?'

'No.' Bodenstein's anger at Neff had abated in the meantime. 'Maybe he can be of some use to us. What does the notebook say?'

'It's more of a diary; she wrote down what she did each day in abbreviated form. Lots of everyday stuff. But I did find a couple of interesting items,' Ostermann said. 'Helen talked to Fritz Gehrke, Professor Ulrich Hausmann, Dr Simon Burmeister and Dr Arthur Janning, and she noted down precisely where and when. She also entered the exact same date for each: 19 December 2012. She didn't report much about what they discussed, and I can't really make sense of the entry 'Santex, blood type barrier, blood type O universal, Donor A to Recipient O – no, reverse yes, Insel Hospital Bern, Uni Clinic Zürich and even the address of the Federal Association of Physicians. No idea what all this is supposed to mean.'

'Let's ask her father when we finish up here,' Pia suggested. 'He should be back soon.'

'Have you located Janning and Hausmann?' Bodenstein wanted to know.

'No, sorry, not yet,' replied Ostermann. 'But I'll keep trying.'

'We definitely have to find out whom Karoline Albrecht got this notebook from,' said Bodenstein.

'Her phone is still turned off,' said Kai. 'I'll keep trying her.'

The radio began to make noise, and a raspy voice came through.

'Kai, it's starting,' said Pia. 'The SEK is there. Talk to you later.'

Pia and Bodenstein got out and walked down the street in the rain until they reached the SEK vehicles. They went over the exact procedure with the team leader. Three men would enter the property round Mieger's house through the back garden. Two officers were already posted there to make sure that nobody could approach or exit the house unseen. The other four officers would enter the house through the front door with Bodenstein, Cem and Pia, but first the garage door would be opened.

A few minutes later, the garage door had been opened without much noise, and what they saw was surprising. Or maybe not. In the garage stood the black SEK belonging to Mark Thomsen. Thomsen must have known Mieger from somewhere; maybe the old man was a member or sympathizer of HRMO. Somehow Thomsen must have heard that Mieger's house was vacant and his car stood neglected and ready to roll in the garage. For someone who worked at a security firm, the old-fashioned front door lock presented no problem.

'Thomsen was previously a sharpshooter with the GSG-9,' Bodenstein told the SEK leader. 'He should be considered armed and dangerous.'

The SEK leader informed his team, then ordered the attack. Within seconds, the front door was broken down, a stun grenade was tossed into the dark hallway, and ten seconds later, Mark Thomsen, who had been lying comfortably on the sofa watching a movie on his laptop, was taken into custody. When Bodenstein, Pia and Cem entered the house, he lay prone on the floor, dressed only in a T-shirt and jogging pants, his wrists bound behind him with plastic cuffs. Two of the masked

SEK men pulled Thomsen roughly to his feet. Jonelle and Fabio's description couldn't have been more precise: Thomsen was unshaven, slim, late forties, with a moustache. Over the back of a chair hung a pair of black jeans and a dark blue jacket.

'We meet again,' said Pia.

'Did you have to scare me half to death?' Thomsen said with a crooked grin. 'Why didn't you ring the bell?'

Bodenstein boiled over with anger when he saw the grin. The gruesome photos of the victims flew through his head, and he thought about the profound despair of the relatives. He had to stop himself from ramming his fist in the man's face.

'You're under arrest,' he said, trying to keep his voice under control. 'You will be charged with the murders of Ingeborg Rohleder, Margarethe Rudolf, Maximilian Gehrke—'

'Hey, what's the meaning of this?' Thomsen yelled, no longer grinning. 'You can't be serious!'

'I've never been more serious,' Bodenstein replied coldly. 'In your house we have taken possession of clear evidence that you are the sniper who shot five individuals.'

'What sort of evidence?' Thomsen said, shaking his head.

'The record of your surveillance of Maximilian Gehrke, for instance.'

'There are plenty more of these documents,' said Thomsen. 'Helen researched all of them.'

'Nonsense!' Bodenstein snapped. 'Where's the weapon?'

'What weapon?'

'The rifle that you used in all the murders.'

'I didn't kill anyone, and I'm sure you've already found my weapons and had them examined. I had nothing to do with this.'

'According to your documents, there is one rifle missing. Why did you take off and lock us in your furnace room?'

'Because . . . because I panicked.'

Bodenstein shook his head. Thomsen was certainly not the type to panic when the police arrived. He was lying.

'How did you get into this house?' asked Pia. 'How do you know Mr Mieger? And where is the car?'

'What car?' Thomsen was again playing dumb, and Bodenstein was sick of it.

'That's enough,' he snapped. 'Take him away!'

'I'm not the sniper,' Thomsen insisted, but Bodenstein merely turned on his heel and left the house.

Dirk Stadler was still on his way back from Southern Bavaria and wouldn't be home until round 8 p.m. Bodenstein wanted to wait with the questioning until someone from the state attorney's office was present. He didn't want to make any mistakes that a clever lawyer could later turn to Thomsen's advantage in court. The true merit of this decision emerged only an hour later, when an anonymous tip came in about a garage on Toni-Sender-Strasse in Sossenheim in response to a call for information on the radio. The blue Opel they were looking for was inside garage number 601. Bodenstein sent a patrol over, and Ostermann tracked down who had rented the garage. After a few phone calls, he got hold of someone from the property management company who told him that garage number 601 had been rented in October 2012 by a Markus Thomsen, who had paid the rent in cash for a year in advance.

With over a thousand houses and nearly as many garages, of course, they didn't know every renter personally, said the man, almost apologetically. The garage was empty, but Bodenstein had it sealed and asked Kröger to do a forensic examination of the space as soon as possible.

'So now we'll have a connection between him and the car,' he said in grim triumph as he took his seat at the conference table. 'I'm eager to see how Thomsen's going to try to weasel out of that.'

'He doesn't want a lawyer,' Pia told her colleagues. She had just spoken to the suspect.

'His choice.' Bodenstein shrugged, then clapped his hands. 'People, with a little luck, we've caught the sniper today, and you'll be able to leave work on time.'

'That would be something,' said Kai. 'We all need it.'

He tapped Karoline Albrecht's phone number for the umpteenth time and finally got through.

'I've already seen that you've tried to get hold of me several times,' she said, instead of saying her name. 'Sorry, my battery was totally dead.'

'I don't want to take too much of your time. But it's important for us to find out who gave you Helen Stadler's notebook.'

Ms Albrecht hesitated for a moment.

'I discovered that Helen's Facebook page is still active,' she answered. 'And that's how I found her friend Vivien Stern, and we met in Frankfurt.'

'Facebook!' Kai moaned. 'Why didn't I think of that?'

'What did you talk about with her?' asked Bodenstein.

'She said that Helen was on the track of a huge case. She was convinced that they let her mother die so they could get at her organs. Helen wanted to clear up everything that happened back then.'

'How close were Helen Stadler and Ms Stern?'

'Apparently, they've known each other since their school

days, and later they went to college together in Frankfurt. Helen always left her notebook with Vivien so her father or her boyfriend wouldn't find it. Her boyfriend seemed to be putting a lot of pressure on her. He wanted to get married straight away, but she didn't. Helen and Vivien were planning in secret to go to the States to study. When Helen's boyfriend got wind of that, he threatened Vivien and even beat her up. She has a real fear of that man, that's why she didn't dare give the notebook to the police. She asked me not to mention her name, but I told her I couldn't promise her that.'

'Do you have a phone number for her?' Bodenstein asked.

'No, I'm afraid not. She's flying back to the States the day after tomorrow. She just came over to see her parents for Christmas. And then she realized for the first time that there was a connection between Helen's investigations and the murders.'

'How so?'

'She read the names in the paper. Ingeborg R., Maximilian G., Margarethe R. That's what Helen christened them.' Karoline Albrecht paused briefly, as if trying to imagine the conversation. 'Helen didn't trust anyone after she found out that her father had received a million euros from someone for retracting his lawsuit against the hospital. That came out because the tax authorities showed up at her father's house. Afterwards, she began her own investigation. She was supported by a friend whose name I've forgotten.'

'Mark Thomsen?' Bodenstein offered, impressed by the memory of the woman who'd had a traffic accident just yesterday.

'Yes, that's it,' Karoline Albrecht confirmed.

'Why does Vivien Stern suspect that Helen was murdered?'

'She's convinced that Helen had no reason to commit suicide. She claims Helen was absolutely euphoric because of the upcoming trip to America and the results of her investigation. Vivien suspects that her boyfriend killed her because she wanted to leave him.'

'There is some suspicion that your father let Helen's mother die so her heart could be transplanted. Did you know that?' Bodenstein asked after a moment. He could hear Ms Albrecht sigh.

'Yes, I knew that.' Her voice sounded bitter. 'That's why my mother was shot before my daughter's eyes. If it's true, I'll never forgive him.'

'Henning, it's me, Pia. Sorry I'm calling so late.'

'No problem. How late is it, anyway?' he said.

'Eight thirty.'

'Oh, I haven't paid any attention to the time.'

Pia had to smile. A typical Henning reply. Had he and Miriam buried the hatchet? Maybe their quarrel yesterday hadn't been the first, because lately Henning seemed to have been at the Institute from morning till well into the night. Something she remembered only too well from when she was married to him.

'Tell me, could you please have another look at the postmortem report on Helen Stadler?' she asked her ex. 'We suspect that she was pushed from the bridge in front of the train and didn't jump. Maybe there were some marks on the body that could be reinterpreted.'

'I'll have another look and call you back,' Henning promised. 'Are you making any progress on the case?'

'Today we arrested a suspect,' said Pia.

'Congrats.'

461

'Tell me, your informant who wants to remain anonymous, could it be Dr Arthur Janning?' she asked.

'How did you come across that name?' Henning countered, and that was answer enough for Pia.

'Helen Stadler seems to have done some investigating on her own. She spoke to almost everyone and wrote it all down in her notebook,' Pia explained. 'Including Janning.'

'You're right, he's the one,' Henning confirmed. 'He's now the chief of staff at the UCF. In my opinion, he had nothing to do with the Stadler case back then, but the patient had been in the ICU, of course, so he did hear about what happened.'

'Helen Stadler compiled a sort of hit list of nine names, and Janning was one of them. Five of these people, or their relatives, are already dead,' Pia revealed. 'That's why we're afraid that Janning might be the sniper's next victim.'

'Oh,' was all Henning said.

'We're convinced that other inappropriate actions were taken at the UCF, and Helen had found out about them. The fact that everyone is afraid and that documents were destroyed at Fritz Gehrke's house, whether by him or by someone else, confirms our suspicion.'

'Then watch out that Rudolf doesn't leave Germany,' Henning advised her.

'He already missed his chance,' replied Pia dryly. 'He's been locked up at government expense since last night.'

Dirk Stadler seemed to have just arrived home. His small suitcase still stood in the hall.

'Please come in,' he said politely to Pia and Bodenstein.

'Thank you.' Pia smiled. 'How was Bavaria?'

'Peaceful.' Stadler returned her smile. 'Judging by the

TO CATCH A KILLER

debris on the streets, it must have been considerably louder here.'

He shut the front door.

'Last night we had another fatal shooting,' said Pia.

'I heard it on the radio,' said Stadler. 'But you don't still believe that my son had anything to do with it, do you?'

'No, we don't,' said Bodenstein. 'We arrested someone today.'

'Oh, that's . . . That's great. Congratulations.' Stadler seemed both surprised and pleased. 'So how can I help you now?'

'The man is denying that he's the perpetrator, of course. So we still need to uncover more evidence and a motive. We're obviously dealing with murders for revenge and retaliation. And we also know the basic motive. But there's probably a lot more behind this than what we know at present.'

'I see.' Stadler switched on the lights in the living room. 'Do you mind if I sit down? My leg . . . after that long drive from Bavaria . . .'

'Please do,' said Bodenstein with a nod. He and Pia followed Stadler, who massaged his knee as he listened attentively to Bodenstein sum up the story of Professor Rudolf and Fritz Gehrke's son.

'You knew that Gehrke was an old friend of Rudolf's, didn't you?' Bodenstein asked.

'I thought it was something Jens-Uwe made up.' Stadler looked exhausted. His cheeks were sunken and his eyes had a feverish gleam. 'Jens-Uwe was disappointed and angry, and he wanted to ruin Rudolf. He viewed me as an ideal person to cause trouble for Rudolf and make the whole matter public.'

'So you didn't really want to file a lawsuit? Why did you change your mind?' Pia wanted to know.

'I've already told you,' replied Stadler. 'My father-in-law was pressuring me. He kept harping on about it. But the more he went back and forth with the lawyers, the more obvious it became to me that we didn't have a chance. Even if we won the case, it wouldn't have brought my wife back to life. I just wanted to be left in peace.'

'You told us that you received fifty thousand euros in compensation from the UCF,' Pia prodded him, remembering her conversation with Henning about his anonymous informant. 'Was that the total amount?'

Stadler sighed in resignation.

'No,' he admitted. 'From Fritz Gehrke I got an additional one million euros.'

'*A million euros?*' Pia repeated, feigning disbelief. 'Why so much?'

'Because I agreed to retract my lawsuit. A trial lasting a year would have ruined me. The money gave me the opportunity to secure a good life for my children.'

'So Gehrke bribed you,' Bodenstein stated. 'Why?'

'I think it's more likely that he wanted to soothe his guilty conscience by making the payment. His son could go on living, but my wife had to die,' replied Stadler calmly. 'He didn't need the money, but I did. I put it into a Swiss bank account, which was a mistake. Because one day, the tax inspector showed up. My account and my name were on a certificate of deposit. I had to pay back taxes and a fine. Of course, my children, who hadn't known about the money previously, then found out all about it.'

'How did they react?' Bodenstein enquired.

'Erik didn't care. He just said it was stupid of me to take money under the table,' Stadler replied. 'Helen, on the other hand, was furious and accused me of taking hush money. She said I had implicated myself. We discussed it over and over until she understood why I acted as I did.'

'When was that?'

'Two years ago.'

Bodenstein and Pia exchanged a glance. Two years ago was when Helen had started keeping her notebook and doing her research.

'Did you know that your daughter started keeping a sort of diary at that time?' Pia asked.

'Yes. She had kept a diary when she was a child, but stopped when she was sixteen or seventeen. After that, she limited herself to making daily notes.'

'Your daughter was convinced that the doctors did not use all possible means to treat your wife,' Pia said cautiously. 'She thought they had let her die in order to harvest her organs for transplants.'

'But that's nonsense,' replied Stadler wearily. 'We've already discussed that.'

'Nonsense or not, it's what she believed, and that's why she began investigating on her own,' Pia continued. 'She was putting pressure on people. And rather intense pressure, at that.'

'No, I just can't believe that,' Stadler emphatically protested. 'That can't be true. My daughter was emotionally very unstable; she never would have dared do something like that.'

'She spoke to the director of the UCF, to Fritz Gehrke, Professor Rudolf and another doctor at the hospital whom she felt was responsible. She seems to have given each of them an ultimatum.'

'An ultimatum? What do you mean?'

'Presumably, she wanted them to make public the truth about the circumstances of your wife's death. The ultimatum had a deadline of shortly before Christmas,' said Pia. 'But three days after the last conversation, she took her own life.'

Pia's mobile buzzed. A text from Kai. *I found Vivien Stern*, it said. She debated whether to ask Stadler about her daughter's friend, but decided to wait until she spoke to the young woman.

'She also had no plans to get married,' Bodenstein added. 'Apparently, she was afraid of Mr Hartig, who was trying to control her life and restricting her actions.'

'That's crazy! Jens-Uwe loved Helen!' Stadler shook his head, flabbergasted. 'It's true that she would have preferred to postpone the wedding a bit, because she wanted to go to the USA and study for a year. I approved because I thought it could have a positive effect on Helen if she did something completely new and got away for a while. Jens-Uwe agreed with me on that.'

'Then why did he stuff her full of drugs?' Pia asked.

'Who told you that?' Dirk Stadler gave the impression that he could no longer cope with any more news of this sort.

'We learned that from a reliable source,' Pia said evasively.

'On top of that, your daughter had quite different plans,' said Bodenstein. 'She drew up a list of people whom she held responsible for her mother's death. And she started observing these people, spying on them and recording their routines for months at a time. She was obviously assisted by Mr Thomsen. In his house, we found a record of the surveillance of Maximilian Gehrke. We assume that Helen wanted to call these individuals to account. After her death, someone else took over the project.'

Stadler looked at Bodenstein, and for a fraction of a second, his eyes revealed the pain for which there were no words, the grief he had carried round with him for more than ten years, and from which he could not free himself.

'And who might that be?' he asked in a toneless voice. 'Who was supposed to . . . "take over"?'

'Someone who is a very good marksman,' replied Bodenstein.

'Thomsen?'

'Possibly. By the way, does the name Wolfgang Mieger ring a bell?'

'Of course.' Stadler nodded wearily. 'Wolfgang was one of my work colleagues, until he fell ill with Parkinson's and then dementia. Three years ago his wife died, and he had no children. But how did you come across him?'

'We arrested the suspect inside his house.'

This piece of news left Stadler speechless for a few seconds. He straightened up.

'I have a key to Wolfgang's house,' he said quietly. 'Since he went to the old folks' home in Königstein, I've been stopping by the house from time to time and taking care of the garden. Helen often went with me. Occasionally, she'd go there alone to empty the mailbox and check on things when I didn't have time.'

'When were you there last?'

'Sometime before Christmas. Yes, about two weeks ago, when it was so cold. I wanted to check on the furnace.'

'Do you ever use Mr Mieger's car?'

'No. It stays in the garage, and the registration hasn't been renewed.'

'Unfortunately, that's not true. Someone has been driving it.'

'But that's impossible. The car is neither registered nor insured.' Stadler grimaced, got up, and limped past them to the sideboard in the hall. He opened a drawer and handed them a car key. 'Here. That's the key to Wolfgang's car. If anyone is driving it, it's without my knowledge.'

'Could your daughter have had a second key to the house? A key that she may have given to Thomsen or Hartig?' Bodenstein asked.

Stadler had to lean on the sideboard for support.

'My God. Yes, that's possible,' he admitted. 'I've been missing one of the front door keys for months.'

'Do you know where Mr Hartig might be staying?' Pia asked.

Stadler shut the drawer. For a moment, there was an awkward silence.

'No.' Stadler shook his head. 'Since Helen's death, I no longer have any contact with him.'

'But last Friday you talked to him on the phone for over an hour.'

'Yes, that's true. He wanted to wish me a Happy New Year. And then we spoke for a while.'

'About what?'

'About this whole case.' Stadler made a vague gesture with his hand. 'About the fact that you suspected him and had searched his house and studio. And about . . . Helen. It would have been her twenty-fourth birthday.'

*

468

When they left Stadler's house, the rain was still coming down in buckets.

'I remember the days when I could count on you bringing along an umbrella,' Pia grumbled as she pulled up her hood, though it was too late to do any good.

'I've got one in the car. Want me to get it?' Bodenstein offered gallantly.

'Nah, never mind.'

They ran to the car with their shoulders hunched, avoiding the biggest puddles. On the way, Pia's phone began to ring, and she took the call despite the rainwater running down inside her sleeve.

'You guys might be right,' said Henning in her ear. 'Helen Stadler's body was in a rather bad state, but the upper extremities were almost unscathed. At the time, the case was considered a suicide, which is why the bleeds on the upper arms were probably dismissed as contusions. But it could be that she had been held tightly by someone. She was a petite woman. For a strong man, it would have been no problem to push or throw her over a bridge railing.'

Pia could feel her heart beating faster.

'What about her clothes?'

'They must still be in the police evidence lock-up. But there's one more thing.'

'Yes?'

Bodenstein opened the passenger door for Pia and she slipped inside.

'Even when the death is the result of a suicide, we do a thorough post-mortem, as you know. Under the fingernails of the left hand, skin particles were detected, also dismissed at the time. If there is now some suspicion that her death was not a suicide, and that a third party was involved, then you should see to it that the clothes and everything else are sent to the lab.'

'I'll take care of it straight away. Thanks, Henning.'

Bodenstein turned on the engine, then turned up the heat and fan full blast. Pia told him what Henning had said.

They drove through the darkness for a while in silence.

'I've got such a funny feeling,' Pia said.

'About what?'

'I'm not sure,' she said with a shrug. 'Viewed superficially, Stadler was completely believable. He seemed stunned, but also fairly candid with us. There's nothing I can point to at the moment. He admitted the thing with the hush money from Gehrke, as well as the call from Hartig. And the story about Mieger's house sounds credible. He doesn't seem the least bit flustered or nervous. And yet . . . I'd like to have him watched.'

'Stadler?' Bodenstein shot her an astonished look. 'Why? How are you going to justify that to the state attorney?'

'By saying that he still has the strongest motive of anyone.' She raised her hand when her boss wanted to argue. 'I know, I know, he's not physically capable of the shootings, and he has alibis. And unlike Thomsen and Hartig, he knows nothing about firearms, but all the rest fits so well.'

'Come on, Pia.' Bodenstein shook his head. 'Wolfgang Mieger was a colleague of Stadler's; Helen knew the house and had access to the key. She told Thomsen about the house and gave him the key. He had nothing to lose. That's what fits. Thomsen is our man, no doubt about it.'

Pia was staring out the window, deep in thought.

'Does Stadler know that Hartig was a doctor at the UCF on Professor Rudolf's team?' she asked.

'Why didn't you ask him?' Bodenstein countered.

'Why me?' Pia took her boss's question as a reproach. 'You could have asked him yourself.'

'I assumed you had some reason for not asking him about it.'

'The only reason was that I didn't think of it.' Suddenly Pia felt overwhelmed by all the questions she'd asked in the last few days without getting any real answers. So many suspicions, speculations and unexplained circumstances on the one hand, and so many excuses and lies on the other. She could no longer see the forest for the trees.

'You know what I still wonder about?' she said as they passed the Rhein-Main thermal baths. 'How did the conviction for tax evasion affect Stadler's job? Isn't he an official who works for the building commission of the City of Frankfurt?'

'Could be. In any case, he's a civil servant.' Bodenstein nodded. 'A while ago, the head of a local tax office was removed from the civil service because he had reported false income tax figures over several years. Although it had nothing to do with his job, it was a serious breach of duty.'

'How do you know about things like this?' Pia was baffled.

'I read the papers,' Bodenstein grinned.

'At nine thirty p.m. on New Year's Day, we won't be able to get hold of anyone in the Frankfurt city offices.' Pia yawned loudly. 'And I'm as hungry as a bear and dead tired.'

In the middle of her yawn, she stopped, as she suddenly remembered the text message from Kai.

'Shit!' she exclaimed, pulling out her mobile. 'Kai sent me a text earlier when we were at Stadler's. He found Vivien Stern. Maybe he's already talked to her on the phone.'

'Would you please stop yawning? It's contagious,' said

Bodenstein as he turned into the car park of the police station. 'We still have to question Thomsen.'

'Oh, that can wait till tomorrow.' Pia yawned so hard that her jaw made a cracking noise. She opened the passenger door. 'He's not going anywhere.'

'You're right. Let's call it a day,' said Bodenstein. 'Good night.'

'Good night, boss.' Pia slammed the door and went over to her own car. Bodenstein backed out and turned round. As he pulled out of the car park to the street, he was probably more tired than he'd ever been before in his life.

WEDNESDAY, JANUARY 2, 2013

Condor Flight DE 303 from Mahé had landed on schedule at 6:30 a.m. He looked once more at the arrivals board. Terminal 1, Gate C, unchanged.

There was plenty of activity at Frankfurt Airport as usual, so anyone standing round with a suitcase did not stand out. He took a seat in the coffee shop across from where passengers from Gate C would enter the arrivals hall, ordered a cup of coffee, and leafed through a newspaper that had been put out for guests. He looked like a man on a business trip. There were thousands of them in the airport. He scanned the headlines about the Taunus Sniper, but the rest of the paper didn't interest him much. Over by the gate, four uniformed policemen were posted, and next to them stood the blonde policewoman, Ms Kirchhoff. She looked as tired and burned out as he felt. She must have had a long night, and he was to blame for that.

It would be over soon. He would complete his plans and justice would be served.

He stirred his cup of coffee although there was nothing to stir, since he didn't take milk or sugar. But from a distance, it looked convincing when someone absent-mindedly stirred their coffee while reading the paper. Kirchhoff kept looking round, and her gaze passed over him a few times, but she didn't seem to recognize him. He was a master of disguise, and his average-looking face was an advantage. He was neither tall nor particularly good-looking, and in public that was the best protection.

A dark-haired woman and an elderly grey-haired man appeared, and the inspector went over to speak with them. The brunette was nervous, wringing her hands, twirling a strand of hair in her fingers and rummaging in her handbag. They were standing apart from the other people waiting, looking at the gate from which the passengers were gradually emerging. Men, women, children, teenagers. Families, somewhat exhausted from the long flight, but suntanned and visibly relaxed after a holiday in the Seychelles. Many were being met by friends and relatives. Waving, laughing and hugging, glad to see one another. Burmeister and his daughter were almost the last to appear and were immediately greeted by the police. The girl, who he knew was sixteen years old and named Leah, said goodbye to her father. The two embraced and exchanged a few more words. He stroked her cheek and gave her a kiss. Then Leah went over to the dark-haired woman, her mother, and took her by the arm. Burmeister paid no attention to her. Kirchhoff spoke to Burmeister, but he kept staring after his daughter.

He drank the rest of his coffee, which had turned cold. He was having a hard time staying calm. So much depended on the next few minutes. Soon he would know whether he should let plan A play out or switch to plan B.

Burmeister and his daughter were among the last passengers from Condor Flight DE 303 from Mahé to come out of the gate. They pulled suitcases behind them.

'There she is!' called Burmeister's ex-wife excitedly. She had been waiting together with Pia, and now she waved with both hands. 'Leah, Leah, over here!'

The girl was supposed to take the train from Frankfurt to Düsseldorf, but in view of the situation, it would have been irresponsible to allow her to travel alone. Yesterday, her mother had instantly assured the police on the phone that she and her husband would pick up Leah at the gate in person. The three now exited under the curious gaze of several onlookers. They were accompanied by two police officers, who took them to their car and then escorted them to the Wiesbaden Kreuz. Pia didn't want to take any chances.

Dr Simon Burmeister was an extremely good-looking man in his early fifties. His thick dark hair was combed back, he was suntanned and sporty, with a striking face and the self-confident air of a man who was thoroughly aware of his social position and physical attributes.

'Dr Burmeister? I'm Pia Kirchhoff from Kripo in Hofheim,' she introduced herself. 'My colleague spoke with you.'

'Right now I need a good cup of coffee. The swill on the plane was disgusting,' he said in lieu of a greeting, and waved to his daughter, who blew him a kiss. Then he briefly scrutinized the two uniformed policemen and finally looked at Pia. 'What's all this about?'

Burmeister grabbed his suitcase and headed straight for the coffee shop, which was located a few metres from the entrance to the arrivals hall. Like it or not, Pia had to chase after him.

'One proper German coffee, please,' he said to the woman, placing a ten-euro note on the counter. Then he seemed to remember his good manners. 'Would you like one, too?'

'No, thank you,' replied Pia indignantly. 'Are you ready to listen to me now?'

Burmeister grabbed his cup of coffee and took a sip.

'Ah, that's better,' he said with a smile, and the laughter lines made his face look friendlier. 'So, you now have my un-divided attention.'

The news of the sniper's series of killings had made it all the way to the Seychelles, but Burmeister's smile vanished, and he even forgot to drink his coffee, when Pia rapidly explained the connections.

'Your name is on the sniper's hit list, and he has already killed five people,' she concluded. 'We need to talk to you, and we want to protect you.'

'You want to *protect* me?' Burmeister regarded her with eyebrows raised. 'How do you plan to do that?'

'We'll assign you two bodyguards who will stay with you until we catch the sniper,' said Pia. 'In addition, you would—'

'Out of the question!' Burmeister interrupted her, grabbing his coffee and case and heading for the exit. 'That's all I need! Strangers constantly following me, even to the toilet? Absolutely not. I can take care of myself.'

'Did you hear what I just told you?' Pia stepped in front of him to block his way. 'Do you think I came out to the airport at six a.m. just for fun?'

'I appreciate your concern,' Burmeister countered. 'If I

understood you correctly, this sniper has previously always targeted relatives of the people who are on this list. So you'd do better to protect my daughter.'

'That's precisely why your ex-wife picked up your daughter here today. Who else is close to you? Who could be in danger?'

'There's no one else who is close to me,' Burmeister said.

'Do you have a girlfriend?' Pia persisted.

'No, no one steady.' The doctor finished his coffee and tossed the empty cup into a bin. 'I work long hours and I value my freedom. Now I have to go. I have an appointment at ten at the clinic.'

Pia was getting more and more pissed off because this arrogant jerk wasn't listening to her.

'Dr Burmeister, you need to take this matter very seriously,' Pia said. 'We think the perpetrator is a relative of a former patient of yours, and he is bent on retaliation. Only twelve hours after she was admitted to your hospital, Kirsten Stadler's heart and other organs were removed, but the documentation that would have justified this action officially was falsified. Perhaps no one would have noticed, but a doctor from your team was unable to reconcile these actions with his conscience. So he filed a complaint against you and Dr Rudolf with the hospital administration and the Federal Association of Physicians. Despite all this, the matter was successfully swept under the rug.'

Finally Burmeister looked at her. His expression remained unchanged, but he had turned pale beneath his suntan.

'Kirsten Stadler's husband was paid a large sum of money by Fritz Gehrke to keep quiet, and the young doctor at the hospital was bullied into silence,' Pia went on. 'The whole matter seemed settled until Kirsten Stadler's daughter began to make inquiries. She spoke to Professor Hausmann, Professor Rudolf, Dr Janning, Dr Furtwängler and to you. And she noted the date and time of each conversation.'

Burmeister turned up the collar of his jacket because of the blasts of cold air coming through the automatic doors.

'She gave you an ultimatum with a deadline of Christmas. That was when she was going to turn over the whole story to the press, if all of you refused to admit to what had gone wrong back then. Are you aware that Helen Stadler took her own life in September?'

'I had not heard about that,' said Burmeister.

Pia considered this statement a lie, but decided not to comment.

'What did Helen Stadler want from you?' she asked.

Burmeister took a step to the side and scratched his head.

'She levelled several vague accusations at me,' he said. 'The whole matter had been cleared up long ago, but she didn't want to accept that. She was quite confused. After she had called me at least thirty times, I asked her to leave me alone, or I would report her for harassment.'

'Did she threaten you?' Pia asked.

'Yes, but I didn't take it seriously.' He made a dismissive gesture, but his nonchalance was clearly feigned. 'As I said, this matter had been resolved, a settlement had been reached and the family received a generous payment.'

Pia doubted that he in fact took such a casual view of the matter. Burmeister was an ambitious man and the respected chief physician of Transplant Surgery at the UCF. He also had a remarkable reputation as a surgeon. For him, everything was at risk should he be revealed to have acted unethically or with intent to deceive: he could lose his job, his future, his own good reputation, and ruin the reputation of the hospital itself. Helen's curiosity had no doubt been a threat to his very existence. A man like him, with such a great need for admiration, could not live without an excellent reputation and the recognition of his peers.

'Now you know the story and why we're concerned,' Pia said in conclusion. 'We can offer you our protection, but we can't force you to accept it.'

'Thank you for the heads-up and your candour.' Burmeister managed to force a smile. 'I'll think about all this, then get back to you.'

'Oh, and one more thing.' She had purposely left this part till last. 'Your former superior, Professor Rudolf, is at present in police custody under suspicion of negligence in the death of Kirsten Stadler. We have also spoken to Drs Hausmann and Janning, and Mr Gehrke.'

'Indeed? And why is that?' Burmeister's expression turned steely. But underneath was a flicker of fear.

'I think you know why,' replied Pia. 'Cancel your appointment and come with me to the station. Perhaps you can help us.'

That last sentence was a mistake. Pia saw the steel and worry in Burmeister's eyes change to relief. Whatever it was the doctor was afraid of, she had clearly revealed that she had no idea what it might be. Damn!

'Thanks for your offer, but I think I can take care of myself just fine.' He glanced at his watch. 'I have to go. It was a long flight, and I have to be at the clinic by ten.'

Pia shrugged and handed him her card, which he ignored with a disparaging smile.

'As you wish,' she said. 'It's your life.'

*

Kirchhoff had spoken to Burmeister for almost twenty minutes. He had no idea what they discussed, but she seemed annoyed. She shrugged, offered him her card, which he did not take, and then walked off with the two uniformed officers. He was relieved. Plan B would have been much more complicated; now he didn't have to alter anything or improvise. Burmeister was an arrogant idiot and believed he was untouchable. And that's exactly what he'd been hoping for.

Now he had to act fast. He grabbed his mobile at the same moment Burmeister did and left the building. Burmeister followed him only a moment later, talking quietly on his phone with a strained expression.

He stopped outside, went a little further, looked round. He was looking for a taxi, and here came one. It stopped next to Burmeister. The driver popped the boot open from inside and then got out to load the suitcase. Burmeister got into the right rear seat.

He couldn't repress a satisfied smile. Despite the warning that Kirchhoff had most definitely given the doctor, the mouse had arrogantly stepped right into the trap. He walked round the taxi, opened the left rear door and climbed in next to Burmeister.

'I have no alibi,' Thomsen repeated, still refusing to have a lawyer present. 'I've already told you that.'

'And I've told you that it's looking bad for you,' replied Bodenstein. The most contradictory feelings were raging inside him. Less than half an hour ago, Thomsen seemed only seconds away from confessing, but now he'd changed his tune. They needed to get a confession from him, because even though the chain of evidence against Thomsen had almost no holes, Bodenstein still lacked the positive proof that would dispel any remaining doubts.

'You have no evidence that'll stand up in court,' replied Thomsen with a nonchalance that irritated Bodenstein because it was true. His colleagues on the night shift told him that Thomsen had stretched out on the bed in the cell in the evening and fallen into a deep, calm sleep only minutes later. Nobody who was guilty ever managed to do that. But as a former member of an elite police unit, Thomsen had received top-flight training. He knew exactly how to behave to fool his opponent. Could he possibly be a psychopath, someone who had no conscience and felt no guilt?

'Oh, yes, we do, we have plenty!' Bodenstein said, sweeping aside his own doubts. 'You are an excellent marksman. And we have proof that you spied on Ingeborg Rohleder, Maximilian Gehrke, Hürmet Schwarzer, Margarethe Rudolf, Ralf Hesse, Simon Burmeister and Jens-Uwe Hartig over a period of several months. We found all the documents in the paper recycling bin at the firm where you work. You disposed of them there when you brought back the dog. The car belonging to Mr Mieger, whose house you were using as a hideout, was seen in the vicinity of one of the crime scenes. And it was also seen in a garage in Sossenheim that you had rented.'

'That's not true.' Thomsen shook his head. 'I didn't rent a garage or use the car.'

'In the garage, we found an empty water bottle with a perfect set of your fingerprints,' Bodenstein went on. 'How do you explain that?'

'I can't,' replied Thomsen honestly. 'But I had no reason to rent a garage. And I've never been to Sossenheim in my life.'

'You planned this whole action way in advance.' Bodenstein chose not to comment on Thomsen's objections. 'You used Wolfgang Mieger's car for transportation to the crime scenes. But you made a mistake with the garage. That is going to be your downfall.'

'I told you once already that Helen was tailing all those people,' Thomsen said. He sat calmly on his chair, his hands resting in his lap, and returned every look with no excessive blinking or sweating. 'It went on for months.'

'Yes, we know that. But she didn't do it alone. She had help from you. And after her death, you turned her plan for revenge into reality. You have no alibi for any of the times of the shootings. On the evening when Mrs Rudolf was shot, your shift ended at six p.m. When Maximilian Gehrke and Ingeborg Rohleder were shot, you worked the night shift. We've already checked out everything. And you locked us in your furnace room so you could destroy all the documents in peace and quiet.'

Bodenstein felt his frustration growing. They were going round in circles, repeating almost word for word what they had already said several times.

'How do you know Mr Mieger?'

Bodenstein already knew what Thomsen would answer, but he let him repeat it. Maybe he'd eventually get tired, forget a detail, and give himself away.

'I don't know him personally. He was a colleague of Helen's father. They used to work for a structural engineering firm, doing large-scale projects abroad. Stadler and Helen took care of him when his wife died and he developed dementia. I remembered his house when I locked you in the cellar. At first I wanted to go to the Winklers' house, but I thought you'd probably look there first.'

'Which brings us back to the question of why you disappeared. If you're innocent, you have nothing to fear.'

'It was a knee-jerk reaction,' said Thomsen, the same answer he'd given three times before.

'Where did you get the key?'

'Helen told me that she had hidden a house key under the birdbath next to the garden shed.'

'I'm afraid you don't understand the gravity of your situation, Mr Thomsen,' Bodenstein now interrupted the cycle of repetitions. 'We suspect you of having murdered five individuals! The evidence against you is overwhelming.'

Thomsen merely shrugged.

'Why would I do that? Why would I shoot anyone?'

'To carry out Helen's plan.'

'Bullshit.' Mark Thomsen shook his head. 'My life is screwed up enough. I'm not going to risk spending the rest of my days in the slammer by translating the fantasies of a mentally unstable young woman into reality.'

'Where is Mr Mieger's car?'

'No idea. I didn't even know he owned one.'

'You were seen with that car,' Bodenstein reminded him, well aware that it was only a supposition.

'Impossible. The witnesses must have seen somebody else. Jens-Uwe, for instance. God knows he had more reason to carry out Helen's plan than I did.'

'Helen wanted to break up with him,' said Bodenstein. 'She was afraid of him, and you knew that, because you helped her kick the pills that Hartig had been giving her.'

No reply.

'Why did Hartig give Helen those pills? Why was he controlling her every step?'

'You're going to have to ask him that.'

'Come on, Mr Thomsen!' Bodenstein exhorted him. 'Why don't you give up and tell us the truth? Why did you flee and hide out in Mieger's house?'

Thomsen sighed.

'I couldn't risk landing in investigative custody before I had done something that required urgent attention,' he said, changing the choreography of the interrogation. 'At first I thought you were just going to ask me a few questions and then leave, but then I realized you were going to arrest me. So it was really a knee-jerk reaction on my part.'

'What did you have to get done?' Bodenstein asked insistently. 'And where?'

Mark Thomsen rubbed his unshaven cheek.

'It had absolutely nothing to do with this whole affair. When you and your colleague were at my place, I got a phone call. You may remember that.'

Bodenstein nodded. He had a vivid memory of the growling dog and the change that had come over Thomsen after that call.

'The call was from Holland. I had to go to Eindhoven immediately.'

'What for?'

'To prevent a messy business.' Thomsen returned Bodenstein's look without flinching. 'I also wanted to talk to Burmeister as soon as he returned from his holiday. But now the police can do that.'

'What did you want to talk to him about?'

Thomsen stared at him for a long time, and Bodenstein's hope of wringing a confession out of the man melted away.

Only now did he comprehend how firmly convinced of success he had been.

'I recently found out that Burmeister was in Kelsterbach on September sixteenth,' Thomsen said once Bodenstein no longer seemed to be expecting a reply. 'His car was caught by a speed camera that day on Kirschenallee. Only a hundred metres further on was where Helen supposedly fell from the pedestrian bridge onto the commuter train tracks.'

Bodenstein was speechless for a few seconds.

'How did you find that out?'

'I may have been out on my arse for a while, but I do still have some connections on the force.' Thomsen shrugged. 'The last thing I want is to help the police. I certainly haven't forgotten getting the boot. After twenty years of risking my life a hundred times, the bastards at internal investigations twisted my words and made me the scapegoat. But I still don't want to see criminals get off scot free, and that's why I did a little snooping. I'm fairly sure that the sleazy Dr Burmeister killed Helen because she found out something that would have destroyed his reputation.'

It was nine o'clock when Bodenstein left the interrogation room and stepped next door. That was where Pia, Kai, Neff and Kim had been following his conversation with Thomsen through the one-way mirror.

'He's not the sniper,' Bodenstein said gloomily as he sat down on a vacant chair and stared through the window at Thomsen. 'He's just a frustrated ex-cop who has a big grudge against us. Damn it, we got the wrong guy.'

Nobody contradicted him.

'We'll have to check whether he's telling the truth about Burmeister's car.'

'I'll do it,' said Kai.

'How'd it go at the airport?'

'Burmeister refused any protection,' said Pia. 'I kept trying to convince him, but he doesn't want our help. He had an appointment at ten o'clock at the clinic that was more important to him.'

'All right, then. All we can do is warn him,' said Bodenstein. 'What about Dirk Stadler? Where's he?'

'He hasn't left his house since last night,' said Neff. 'We've had him staked out round the clock since you and Ms Kirchhoff were there.'

Oppressive silence. Instead of nearing their goal, they were at another dead end.

'I can't think any more until I get something to eat.' Pia stood up. 'I'll run over to the bakery. Want anything?'

They all gave her their orders, except for Kim, who was busy on her smartphone and smiling dreamily.

'Want to come along, Kim?'

Hearing her name gave her a start, and Pia was amused to see her expression. No matter what happened in the world, life went on, and love found a way even amid murder and manslaughter.

'So, tell me where you were on New Year's Eve,' said Pia when they were sitting in the car a few minutes later. 'I don't have the energy for another interrogation, so don't keep me guessing.'

'I was at Nicola's,' said Kim.

'That's what I was afraid of. And?'

'And nothing. We just had a good time talking.'

'About what?'

'About everything.'

'Come on, now. This is like pulling teeth. Is she into you?'

'I think she likes me,' said Kim, who actually blushed a little. 'But she has no experience with women.'

'Or with men lately?' Pia teased her.

'Successful women like her have a hard time finding a man who doesn't view her as a competitor. I know that from personal experience,' said Kim, defending the object of her desire.

'Well, I must be lucky that I'm not so successful,' said Pia.

'You and Christoph are equals,' said Kim. 'But most men can't tolerate their partner working more and maybe even making more money than they do. That's why my last relationship ended. And not just because he couldn't stand it that I had to deal with the worst criminals day in and day out. That was only an excuse. For two long years, it hadn't bothered him at all. By the way, did you know that Nicola was once engaged to Bodenstein? They were going to get married, but then Cosima came between them.'

'Yes, I know.' Pia turned down Elisabethenstrasse when the light turned green. 'But honestly, I'm interested in my boss's love life only as it pertains to you. Because I'm afraid she's going to show up with you at our family celebrations.'

'At what family celebrations?' Kim had to laugh. 'But we'll go out to dinner together once this case is solved.'

'Well, that's going to be a while,' replied Pia. 'Mark Thomsen isn't the sniper.'

'I agree with you on that,' said Kim. 'All the evidence against him can be viewed differently.'

'I just wonder why he locked us in the cellar and then disappeared.' Pia put on the indicator and turned into the parking garage at Untertor in central Hofheim.

'But he told you why. He knew you suspected him, and he wanted to keep from landing in a cell before he took care of something and had spoken with Burmeister,' said Kim. 'If he really had something to hide, he wouldn't have called the police to tell them where you were.'

Pia nodded. Bodenstein had been so carried away with the idea that Thomsen was the sniper that he'd paid no attention to this mitigating detail.

'As Oliver correctly said, Thomsen is a frustrated ex-cop who got a bad break in life,' Kim went on. 'I believe him when he says he has no wish to spend the rest of his life behind bars. He's definitely not stupid.'

'But why did he clear out his house and throw Helen Stadler's notebook in the bin? If he has nothing to hide, why would he do that? Is he covering for somebody? Maybe the real sniper?' Pia stared at her sister as though Kim's expression might give her the answers to her questions.

'Just think about it, my dear sister,' Kim said. 'What does Thomsen care about more than anything?'

Pia drummed her fingers on the steering wheel and stared at the ugly facade of the Buch department store.

'This HRMO thing,' she said after a moment.

'Precisely. The HRMO people's biggest complaint is with the inhuman way the relatives of organ donors are treated in some hospitals. They want to denounce these practices, which means they need publicity,' replied Kim. 'The situation seems to have been particularly bad at the UCF.'

'Right,' said Pia with a nod. 'Bettina Kaspar-Hesse described Burmeister as a vulture. They more or less forced her to deceive the Winklers so they could get at Kirsten Stadler's organs. And it was definitely not an isolated case.'

'I think that was Thomsen's primary concern. Not Kirsten or Helen Stadler. I'm pretty sure that he and Helen were on the track of something else, something that Furtwängler, Gehrke and the lawyer were mixed up in. You need to talk to Furt- wängler again. Ask him straight out what he was up to with Rudolf and why he had to leave the UCF back then. I believe that's the key to the mystery.'

Pia's stomach rumbled loudly in the silence.

'But first I need a whole bunch of calories,' she said. 'Come on, let's get some fodder for the pack.'

Her father had been arrested because the police suspected him of killing a woman who was married and had two children. He hadn't stabbed, shot or strangled her; no, he just let her die, although he could have saved her life. Why had he done that? He was a doctor, a good doctor, a man who lived for his profes- sion. How had he been able to reconcile something like that with his conscience? *Out of greed and vanity.* That's what the Judge had written after shooting her mother, as retaliation for what her father had done to the woman. Was it the first time he'd done something like that? Did he want to be celebrated as a healer by those whose lives he had saved with a transplanted organ? Or was it just the first time he'd been caught snuffing out one human life prematurely in order to save another? How could a person presume to make such a decision? The dead had no lobbyists. The relatives seldom doubted what doctors in the hospital said, especially when confronted with an eminent surgeon such as Professor Dieter Paul Rudolf, who assured them in his calm, understanding manner that there was no more hope.

Karoline Albrecht sat as if frozen at the dining room table in her parents' house. She didn't know what to do. Her father, whom she had admired all her life and whom she had loved almost desperately, was a murderer. Selfish and without a conscience, he had abused her trust and lied to her. Instead of admitting what he had done, he tried to cover it up. That's how he'd spent the past several days, instead of grieving for his wife and arranging for her funeral. How despicable. He had lied and schemed, using any means available and acting without scruples. Why had he done all that? For money? For fame and praise?

Karoline closed the binder in which she had discovered the correspondence between the development board of Santex and her father. She got up, aching all over. But even worse was the pain in her soul. There was nobody she could talk to about all this. She longed for someone to pour out her heart to, someone who would understand how terribly lonely she was. Her mother, the only anchor she'd had in life, was gone. She had no close female friends, and no boyfriend or lover she could call. She had a house in which she did not feel at home, a job that meant only money and professional success, and the responsibility for a traumatized daughter.

The best thing would be to call a taxi to take her home, and simply go back to bed. Or she could take Mama's car. Karoline stiffly pulled on her coat; she had neglected to put on the awkward cervical collar this morning after her shower. In the top drawer of the sideboard, she found the key to the BMW. She left the house and activated the remote on the key ring. The garage door opened with its familiar clatter. An acrid burnt smell struck her nostrils but quickly dispersed. Where did the stench come from? Had a marten caused an electrical fire under the bonnet of one of the cars? For a moment, she hesitated, then walked over towards her mother's BMW, stumbling over something soft.

'Shit!' she exclaimed. She almost fell on her face, which wouldn't have helped with her concussion. She bent down and saw a blue rubbish bag leaning against the rear tyre of her father's black Maserati. Karoline picked up the bag to move it aside, and grimaced. This was where the smell was coming from. She curiously opened the sack and found to her surprise some of her father's clothes. A dark-grey cashmere pullover, a shirt, a pair of grey slacks, a pair of shoes. She stared at the clothes in bewilderment. Why had her father stuffed them into a rubbish bag?

Like lightning, the words of the inspector flashed through her head: *In Gehrke's house, a large number of documents were burned in the fireplace.* Karoline leaned against the book of the car because her knees were about to buckle. *It's important for us to find out what he talked about with Gehrke the night before he died.*

There was a click, and the light in the garage went out. Karoline stood quite still, thinking. The pieces of the puzzle, which had previously been whirling round in her head, suddenly came together.

It was not easy to find an open Wi-Fi anywhere. Even in döner *shops, Turkish cafes and cheap hotels, they had started protecting their Internet connections with passwords. Today he didn't have time to drive to one of the two places in central Frankfurt where he could simply log on from the pavement, but now it no longer mattered. He went into a cafe and was surprised to see that he was almost the only patron. That wasn't* good, *but it was too late to turn and walk out. The waitress was already heading his way. He hung his jacket over the back of a chair, ordered coffee and a piece of Frankfurt crown cake, and asked for the password.*

'*Simple,' she said and winked 'It's 123456.'*

'*I might be able to remember that,' he said with a smile. 'Thanks.'*

At the table across from him sat an elderly couple. Were they staring at him, or was he just imagining things? He shouldn't underestimate how suspicious people had become. With a little bad luck, the police could catch him, just as the goal was nearly within reach. Good thing he'd left red herrings all over the place. If the police had found the garage, they would also find the bottle with Thomsen's prints on it. He sent off the e-mail even before the coffee and cake arrived. His heart was pounding. The old couple glanced over at him again and whispered to each other. Jeez, he was seeing ghosts everywhere. He had to get out of here. He didn't care what they thought of him. He put a banknote next to the plate, not even touching the cake or the coffee, grabbed his jacket, and left.

'But if it isn't Thomsen, then who is it?' asked Kathrin Fachinger after Pia had explained to her colleagues point by point why she doubted that Mark Thomsen was the sniper. They were sitting at some laminate tables covered with coffee stains. They'd shoved the tables together in the special commission centre. The team members were morose, bleary-eyed and hopelessly exhausted after being hit by one defeat after another for over two weeks. The energy of the first few days had long since vanished, along with their fighting spirit and firm conviction that they would soon catch the perp. Bodenstein took a soft pretzel from the tray containing Pia's purchases from the bakery as he looked at the weary faces of his team. After his conversation with Mark Thomsen, he'd been filled with a mixture of despondency and angry defiance. He felt oddly disoriented, and his sense of time was off due to lack of sleep and no fixed daily routine. Both were terrible conditions for doing systematic work. The situation was taking a toll on everyone; they had all become thin-skinned. Even Kai Ostermann, normally steady as a rock in the surf, was reacting with swift irritation.

'So we're left with Hartig,' said Kai as he ate. 'He's my favourite anyway.'

'What about Winkler?' Cem suggested dubiously.

'Neither one,' said Pia, shaking her head and glancing at Bodenstein. 'It's somebody else. He fell through the cracks for us before, but he still has the strongest motive.'

Where did this woman get her energy? She couldn't have got much more sleep than he had, but she looked alert and sharp, remembering small details that he had forgotten.

'There's so little evidence pointing to him,' Kai said, because he knew whom Pia was talking about.

'Whom do you mean?' Nicola Engel asked Pia. She was the only one eating her cheese sandwich in a civilized manner from a plate.

'Dirk Stadler.' Pia wiped her hands on a paper napkin and crumpled it up. 'Even though Thomsen appeared to be the perfect perp, my gut tells me that he's not the sniper. He's too . . . perfect. It'd be too easy, and easy solutions always make me suspicious.'

Bodenstein had to admit that Pia's argument was valid.

'My impression is that somebody has been deliberately planting clues that pointed to Thomsen. The rented garage, for instance. All it takes is an e-mail and a stranger putting a couple of euros in someone's hand, who couldn't care less about any of it, and bingo – you've got a rental contract.'

'But how do you explain Thomsen's prints on the water bottle that was found in the garage?' Kröger asked sceptically.

'For Stadler and Hartig, it wouldn't be much of a problem to get hold of some object with his prints on it,' Pia countered. 'They all know one another and have met before because of Helen. Who knows how old that bottle is?'

'Dirk Stadler is severely disabled and can hardly walk,' Neff remarked. 'Besides, he has alibis for the times the crimes were committed. He was working.'

'Have you checked that out?' asked Pia, raising her eyebrows.

'Yes. Well, not directly.' Embarrassed, Neff avoided her gaze.

Everyone turned to look at him.

'What's that supposed to mean – "not directly"?' Bodenstein's voice was cold, but his eyes were blazing. He had ruled out Dirk Stadler as the possible perp because he was firmly convinced that the man had airtight alibis for the times of the shootings. 'You did the research on the guy, and when I asked you if you'd double-checked all the info, you told me "of course"!'

'I Googled his name.' Neff blushed to the roots of his hair. 'And it said online that he works for the City of Frankfurt in the building commission. It even gave the phone number.'

'So did you call them?' Bodenstein's anger, which had been slowly flowing through his veins, converged in his stomach like a fiery ball.

'N-no.' Neff was squirming in his chair.

'The Internet retains every piece of information, no matter how old.' Kai couldn't resist the gibe. 'It could be a very old page from the cache.'

Without waiting any longer, Pia picked up the phone on the table and asked the operator to connect her with the building commission of the City of Frankfurt.

It was deathly quiet in the room while they waited for someone to answer.

'Eckel, Frankfurt Building Commission,' a woman's voice said on the speakerphone.

'Pia Kirchhoff, Hofheim Criminal Police,' she replied without taking her eyes off Neff. 'I'd like to speak to Dirk Stadler.'

It seemed to Bodenstein as if a black hole opened beneath his feet when the woman replied that no employee by that name had worked in the office.

'Are you quite sure?' Pia asked. 'Who is your superior?'

'Dr Hemmer. The department head.'

'Please connect me with him.'

It took a while before the man picked up and confirmed that Dirk Stadler hadn't worked for the City of Frankfurt for the past two years. There had been irregularities.

'Are you referring to the judgement concerning tax evasion?'

'Yes, that was the reason,' the office manager admitted.

Pia thanked him and hung up.

'How was I to know that it was old information?' Neff tried to defend his mistake. 'I'm here only as an adviser, not an investigator. This is really not my job, and I thought someone would double-check the information. Ostermann does that sort of thing all the time and—'

Kai gasped angrily, but before he could say a word, Bodenstein completely lost it. He slammed his palm on the table, and Neff stopped in mid-sentence.

'You accepted this assignment; you even volunteered for it! You bragged about your excellent connections, and I *depended* on you. Teamwork means relying without question on everyone involved. Don't you get that? If I could do everything by myself, I wouldn't need colleagues or a team. Through your gross negligence, you caused us to stop focusing on Stadler. That is an investigative disaster that can never be put right. I promise you, Neff, if it turns out that Stadler is the perp, then I will personally make sure you lose your job.'

He shoved his chair back and stood up.

'Pia, call Dr Burmeister at once. We're taking him into protective custody,' he commanded. 'Kai, Cem and Kathrin, you go and research everything you can find about Dirk Stadler.'

Those who had been given assignments got up and left.

'But I really—' Neff began. He would probably have pleaded 'not guilty' in court even if he were caught redhanded, with a bloody knife in his hand, standing next to a corpse. Bodenstein took advantage of his height as he looked down at Neff.

'Shut – your – mouth,' he said menacingly. With his inflated view of his own abilities and his arrogant narcissism, this man had brought nothing but unrest to his team. And it turned out that he had even obstructed the investigation. 'Get out of my sight. Right now. Before I do something I'll regret.'

Then he turned on his heel and left the room.

Standing in the corridor, Pia tapped in the number of Dr Simon Burmeister's mobile. The blood was rushing so loudly in her ears that she could hardly formulate a clear thought. Would her theory be proved right? When she called Stadler on Friday, shortly before Hürmet Schwarzer was shot, he had claimed to be at the Frankfurt Main Cemetery, checking the durability of gravestones. Why had she simply believed him? But why would she have had cause to doubt him? On Friday evening, she had again spoken to Stadler, and she tried feverishly to remember how the man had behaved. Burmeister did not answer his phone. It was twenty past ten, so he was probably at his meeting. Pia went to her office and sat down at her desk. Kai appeared only seconds later.

'That sleazy bastard tried to shove the blame onto me,' he complained furiously, plopping down on the chair behind his desk. 'He puts on a good show, I'll give him that. Talking big, refusing to be pinned down, uttering stupid, superficial psychobabble.'

He was really pissed off, but Pia had no words of solace for her colleague, because she felt exactly the same way. She was annoyed because she had relied on Neff and had been taken in by Stadler, even though from the start, her intuition had been warning her to beware.

In her mobile phone, she searched for the message from Henning with Dr Furtwängler's phone number. She rang the doctor in Cologne, but she got his wife, who claimed that her husband was out and did not own a mobile.

Pia ended the call. She no longer felt like listening to lies and excuses. Once again, she tapped in Burmeister's number. Still no answer. So she called the UCF and demanded to speak to Dr Burmeister. She was put on hold for a long time, but finally someone from the hospital administration answered.

The woman sounded irritated as she reported that 'Dr Burmeister has not yet arrived. But we expect him any moment. He's scheduled to perform an important operation at ten.'

Pia was suddenly filled with foreboding.

'Are you sure he's not there?'

'That's what I just told you,' the annoyed woman snapped. 'Do you think I'm incompetent?'

'Dr Burmeister's life is in danger,' Pia said insistently. 'As soon as he arrives at the clinic, have him call me straight away. And now I need phone numbers for Dr Janning and Professor Hausmann.'

'Those gentlemen are still on holiday,' the administrative woman informed her in a cool voice. 'I am not authorized to release any information—'

Pia hit the roof. 'Listen, this is an emergency!' She no longer bothered to sound polite or friendly. 'In case you misunderstood: I am Chief Criminal Inspector Pia Kirchhoff from the Homicide Unit of Kripo Hofheim. We have already had five murders; we are trying to prevent two more! Now, give me the goddamned phone numbers *at once* or I'll have you arrested for obstructing a police investigation!'

The woman finally seemed to understand. Clearly intimidated, she rattled off the phone numbers. Then Pia hurried over to Bodenstein's office. Before she could knock, he opened the door, and she almost fell into his arms.

'I can't get hold of Burmeister,' she told him. 'He hasn't shown up at the hospital yet, although he—'

'Ms Albrecht just called me,' Bodenstein interrupted her. 'She found documents in her father's house, and clothes that reek of smoke.'

Pia, who was worrying about Burmeister, didn't understand.

'We're going to Oberursel.' Bodenstein pulled on his coat as he walked. 'Hurry up.'

'But we can't just—' she began, but Bodenstein didn't let her finish.

'Gehrke supposedly burned documents,' he said impatiently. 'But no smoke particles were found in his bronchial passages and lungs. Either he was wearing a face mask or he was already dead when the documents were burned in the fireplace. Rudolf's clothes reeked of smoke, and Ms Albrecht found a document binder that obviously came from Gehrke's house.'

'I see.' Pia postponed the calls she was planning to make until later. 'Give me a minute to get my things.'

'Fritz Gehrke was the victim of a cover-up.' Karoline Albrecht got straight to the point. 'When he worked out what my father had done, he had to die.'

On the big dining room table lay the document binder that she'd found in her father's car, and next to it a mobile phone and other papers. Her exhaustion was evident on her face, yet she presented the facts that her investigation had uncovered with a precision that won Bodenstein's respect. She had dismissed his polite enquiry as to how she was feeling by saying simply, 'I'm all right.' The left side of her face was swollen, and a bruise stretched from temple to chin, but even this disfigurement couldn't ruin the remarkable symmetry of her face. He wondered how she would look when she laughed.

'The search for my mother's murderer isn't the focal point of my interest,' she said. 'That's your job. I want to find out what my father did, and why my mother became a victim. The truth is, my father gave the order to stop Kirsten Stadler's respirator. Part of a diagnosis of brain death is the so-called apnoea test, in which the patient's ability to breathe unaided is tested. He is disconnected from the respirator, and if he does not start breathing within five minutes, that is one of the indications of brain death. Kirsten Stadler was still breathing unaided in the first test as well as the second. Normally, the tests must be carried out no more frequently than twelve hours apart, and by doctors who have nothing to do with an eventual explantation. Are you following me?'

Bodenstein and Pia nodded.

'The first offence against existing laws in the case of Kirsten Stadler was that these tests were performed a few hours apart. The reason for this was her blood type. It was determined that she was blood type O, which meant that her heart would be a match for any recipient.'

'The blood type!' exclaimed Pia. That was what had been hovering for days on the edge of her consciousness, but she hadn't been able to put it into words. She now remembered her conversation with Henning. In answer to her question of whether Professor Rudolf might have transplanted organs for money, he had explained that especially for a heart transplant, this would be as good as impossible because of the incompatibility of the blood types. 'You can't simply transplant a heart into any recipient; the blood types have to match. A to A, B to B, and so forth. The one exception is blood type O. A donor heart having this blood type will match with any donor.'

'Correct.' Karoline Albrecht nodded. 'Blood type O was the death sentence for Kirsten Stadler. With the tacit consent of the head of intensive medicine, at the behest of my father all life-support measures were shut off. An hour later, her brain was irreversibly damaged due to lack of oxygen.'

'How do you know this?' Bodenstein asked.

'As chance would have it, the head of intensive medicine phoned,' replied Karoline Albrecht. 'Dr Arthur Janning wanted to speak to my father. He and my father used to be good friends, but Kirsten Stadler's case had turned them against each other. There had already been incidents which he unfortunately chose to ignore, but this case was the last straw.'

'But why did your father take these measures?' Pia asked. 'That was murder!'

'What's one murder compared with the Nobel Prize in Medicine?' Karoline Albrecht snorted. 'That's my father's cynical world view. I always admired my father for his skill, but he was acting out of completely different motives than I'd assumed. Maybe this wasn't the first time he'd let a person die to gain access to a donor organ.'

'Kirsten Stadler had to die so that he could implant her heart into the son of his friend Fritz Gehrke,' said Pia.

'Precisely.' Karoline Albrecht nodded and heaved a great sigh. She seemed to have reached a point far beyond any emotion. There was no other choice but to proceed, no matter how horrible the truth might be. 'But there must be an even bigger story behind all this. My father did not help Maximilian Gehrke out of pure friendship, but because he feared that Gehrke's company, Santex, might opt out of funding his research projects.'

She slapped her hand on one of the files.

'These binders come from Gehrke's house,' she said. 'I don't know what the documents prove, or whether they prove anything at all. There are protocols, documentation of transplantations, patient documents and the complete correspondence between my father, Dr Furtwängler and Fritz Gehrke.'

'What did Furtwängler have to do with your father?' Pia asked.

'He was the haematologist.' Karoline Albrecht shrugged. 'His speciality was human blood. He and my father had done research together in Cologne. Exactly what sort of research, I don't know.'

Bodenstein cleared his throat.

'And why do you think that your father killed Gehrke? Why now, after so many years?'

'After I told Gehrke about the sniper's motives by showing him the obituary, he must have got straight on the phone. Dr Janning told me that he spoke with him in great detail on Saturday afternoon and confessed to him everything that had been weighing on his soul for years. After that, Gehrke must have been beside himself, so he called my father.' Karoline Albrecht pointed to her smartphone. 'That's my father's secret mobile phone, which I found in his safe. Gehrke called my father at round eight p.m. on Saturday evening.'

'He drove over to his house, knocked him out with chloroform and injected him with an overdose of insulin,' Pia spun the thread further. 'Then he searched through all the documents, burned most of them, and took these binders home with him. It was supposed to look as if Gehrke, in desperation, had wiped the slate clean and then committed suicide.'

'And he almost succeeded,' said Karoline Albrecht, her voice breaking as she stood up. She went to the window and looked out into the garden. 'Sheer ambition drove my father to walk over dead bodies. Even the body of my mother.'

She folded her arms, choking back sobs, but otherwise keeping her emotions under iron control.

'For what he did to my mother, my daughter and me, he deserves to go to Hell,' she blurted out. 'All the suffering he caused is not balanced out by the good he undoubtedly did. And the more I learn about his intentions, the clearer it is to me that he never viewed the patients as individuals. He saw only the opportunities their deaths presented for himself. His empathy was never genuine. All he ever cared about was recognition, fame and honour. I hope he'll spend the rest of his life in prison.'

Her face and her bearing hinted at the powerful emotions she had managed to suppress with an admirable amount of self-control. Rage, pain, disappointment, grief.

'If we can pin Gehrke's murder on your father, then he will sit in prison for a very long time,' said Bodenstein. 'But so far, we have only circumstantial evidence, which a clever lawyer could easily tear to pieces.'

Karoline Albrecht went back to the table, opened her leather-bound Day-Timer and took a note out of it.

'I know that I should have left this to you, but I . . . I've had someone investigate a couple of things,' she said quietly. 'This is the address of a witness who saw my father coming out of Gehrke's house at 12:35 a.m. on Sunday morning. One of Gehrke's neighbours who had let his dog out late in his back garden. He gave a good description of my father. Along with the documents and the clothes that smell of smoke, you should have enough evidence.'

'What did Rudolf do?' Pia puzzled when they were back in the car and Bodenstein had started the engine. 'In his research, was he trying to overcome the restrictions of blood type?'

'Sounds a lot like Dr Frankenstein.' Bodenstein was sceptical.

'But it's plausible. Why else would he have worked with a haematology expert like Furtwängler? Helen Stadler could have stumbled across what he was doing. The keywords she jotted down all fit the topic.'

'And Burmeister and Hausmann are doctors who had an interest in keeping the UCF current with the latest in medical research,' Bodenstein said. 'It would elevate the reputation of their clinic incredibly and also bring in cash. But then Rudolf became unsustainable and he had to leave the UCF. The trigger may have been the Kirsten Stadler case.'

'And this Dr Janning, who was friends with Rudolf earlier, had got everything off his chest when he visited Gehrke's house and told him the truth,' said Pia. 'But Janning is still on Helen's hit list, and most probably on the sniper's as well. Why?'

'Because in her eyes, he was partly to blame for her mother's death,' said Bodenstein.

'I'm going to phone Hausmann and Janning right now.' From her rucksack, Pia dug out the piece of paper on which she'd written their numbers.

'Be careful,' Bodenstein warned her. 'We still don't know enough to confront them with Rudolf's story. If they are co-conspirators, they're also accessories and might destroy evidence.'

'They did that long ago,' Pia countered.

She chose Professor Hausmann's number first. He answered and frankly admitted he'd been alerted that Pia might call. That wasn't good, but she had expected as much. Pia explained why she was calling.

'Why did Professor Rudolf leave the UCF? What really happened?' she demanded to know.

'Just a moment, please.'

She heard footsteps; then a door closed in the background.

'We were always having trouble with him,' said the professor in a pleasantly deep voice. 'Rudolf had a dictatorial management style that no longer fit in a modern clinic. There were ever-increasing protests from the doctors and nurses. Finally, I had no choice but to ask for his resignation and cancellation of his employment contract. It was the only way to obtain peace and quiet in the administration of the hospital.'

'So that was the reason?' Pia insisted. 'Not the Kirsten Stadler case in the autumn of 2002?'

Hausmann hesitated for a fraction of a second.

'That case certainly escalated the strained mood,' he said, elegantly extricating himself. 'A young doctor from Rudolf's team had complained to the hospital administration and the Federal Association of Physicians after he had criticized Rudolf's decisions and was subsequently warned off.'

'What did the complaint involve?'

'I don't recall the details. It was probably mainly a matter of personality conflicts. Rudolf was a difficult character, and self-confident young doctors did not have an easy time with him.'

Pia was sure the first two sentences were lies.

'What did Helen Stadler want from you when she visited you last August?' she asked.

'Who visited me?'

'Kirsten Stadler's daughter. According to our information, she spoke to you a few months ago.'

Again a tiny pause.

'Ah yes. The young lady. Right now I don't recall.'

Pia didn't believe him for a second. 'I assume she tried to blackmail you, because she had obtained internal details from Dr Hartig that you would have preferred to keep confidential. But that is of no interest to us. I'm sure you've seen in the media that in the past fourteen days, five individuals have been shot to death. We have now determined the motive of the perpetrator. All the victims had some connection to the Kirsten Stadler case via relatives. That puts you in a key position, because three of the five victims had some connection to the UCF. You need to cut short your leave ASAP and talk to your secretary. If she had notified you a few days ago, when we first tried to reach you, we might have been able to prevent two of the murders.'

'What should I do?' asked the professor, and he suddenly sounded extremely anxious.

'Make public the facts surrounding the death of Mrs Stadler before the press does. The news will reach the sniper, and perhaps no more people will have to die.'

'But that . . . that isn't something I can simply do,' replied Hausmann.

'Why not? Whom are you afraid of?'

'I'm not afraid,' the professor argued. 'But I'm only an employee of a hospital belonging to a foreign corporation that does not particularly like negative headlines.'

'There will be negative headlines anyway,' said Pia. 'I can only advise you to come back and do some damage control.'

'Yes, I . . . suppose . . . I can . . . ' stammered the administrative director of the UCF.

'Oh, and Professor,' Pia said, pretending that she had just remembered something else. 'The sniper has not yet been caught. If you have loved ones who mean something to you, you really ought to warn them.'

With that, she hung up. Then she tapped in the mobile number of Dr Arthur Janning. He answered on the fifth ring. She also asked him what Helen Stadler had wanted to discuss, and like Hausmann, he beat round the bush.

'Your name has come up in connection with the death of Kirsten Stadler ten years ago,' said Pia, and enumerated once more the victims of the sniper. 'Someone in your family or you yourself could be next. Are you completely indifferent to the danger?'

'No, of course not,' Janning replied uncertainly.

'Professor Hausmann told me what Rudolf did at the UCF back then, and why he had to go. The case has broken wide open, and the media are going to jump on it. Why won't you help us?'

'Hausmann did what?' Janning began in a surprised voice. 'What do you expect? What am I supposed to do?'

'Wrong question. You should be asking: Why is my name in Helen Stadler's notebook? Why don't you tell me what she wanted from you? What did you do or neglect to do in 2002?'

No reply.

'We're going to find out, whether you cooperate or not,' said Pia. 'We can only protect you from the murderer who has your name on his list if you work with us.'

'What kind of list?'

This time Pia didn't reply.

'Where are you right now?' she asked instead.

'In Cortina d'Ampezzo,' replied Janning. 'With my family. But we're coming home tomorrow.'

'Check in with us when you arrive. You'll be given police protection.'

She hung up and at the same moment her phone rang.

'We found Wolfgang Mieger's car,' Kai Ostermann told her. 'It was in the car park at the Main-Taunus Centre, the key still in the ignition. I informed the evidence team and they'll bring it to the crime lab.'

'Very good.' Bodenstein nodded. 'Anything else?'

'Yep.' Kai's voice sounded tense. 'Unfortunately, nothing good. I got hold of Vivien Stern and learned something about Dirk Stadler that you're not going to be happy about.'

Twenty minutes later, they were sitting in Bodenstein's office.

'Vivien Stern was actually a close friend of Helen Stadler's. They'd known each other ever since they were ten years old.' Kai consulted his notes. 'In the summer, they often went to a weekend cabin somewhere in the Taunus hills that belonged to a friend of her father's. A man who was ill.'

'Wolfgang Mieger?' asked Pia.

'I have to assume so.' Kai nodded. 'Like Stadler, Mieger came from East Germany. He got out just before the Wall was built. They didn't know each other, but since they worked at the same company, they eventually got to be friends. Ms Stern told me that Stadler had been in a frogman brigade in the East German People's Army and had fled across the border by swimming forty kilometres across the Baltic Sea to the island of Fehmarn in West Germany. I checked it out and learned that Stadler had won several medals. For three years in a row, he was the best sharpshooter in the People's Army.'

For a moment, you could hear a pin drop.

'I don't believe it,' Bodenstein muttered.

'After that,' Kai went on, 'I thought I'd look into why Stadler has a disabled badge. We assumed he had difficulty walking, but that's not true. He has a badge because of mental problems. Neither his family doctor nor the Frankfurt city doctor had heard about him having difficulty walking.'

'He played us for fools!' said Pia in surprise.

'He wasn't lying when he said he hadn't been in the German Federal Army.' Bodenstein shook his head. 'He was in the East German Army. Damn it! Why didn't I think of that when Neff said he came from Rostock?'

'By the way, he doesn't have a sister in Southern Bavaria,' Kai added. 'In all of Kempten, there's nobody with that surname. And the people who have the same telephone prefix have never heard of a Helga Stadler.'

Bodenstein was just as surprised as Pia.

'Neff has it coming,' he grumbled, grabbed the phone and dialled the number of Erik Stadler's company. But when he answered, Bodenstein hung up.

'What was that about?' asked Pia.

'I had an inspiration,' replied Bodenstein, placing a call instead to the officer who was watching Dirk Stadler's house in Liederbach.

'Nothing happening,' said one of the officers. 'A little after eight the blinds rolled up, that was all.'

'Okay,' said Bodenstein, who had a bad feeling. 'I'd like the two of you to go up to the house and ring the doorbell. Then phone me back.'

As they waited for the callback, Pia tried once more to reach Dr Burmeister, but his phone was now turned off. Bodenstein's mobile rang. The two officers had rung Stadler's bell several times, but no one came to the door. These geniuses had just now discovered that someone could easily slip from the back garden into the neighbour's garden without being seen from the front.

'Check the garage and talk to the neighbours,' Bodenstein ordered in a voice he was controlling with effort. 'And I want a callback at once, got it?'

He hung up, puffed up his cheeks and exhaled slowly.

'The bird has flown the coop,' he said soberly. 'Kai, please send out an APW for Dirk Stadler and his vehicle.'

'Will do.' Kai got up and left Bodenstein's office.

'He brazenly lied to us about his fictitious sister in Southern Bavaria.'

Pia still couldn't believe that she'd been taken in so easily. 'He was so . . . so believable.'

'You can say that again. He was absolutely certain that we didn't suspect him. And he needed only two more days, namely until this morning. He needed to wait for Burmeister to come back from holiday. Remember how he jotted down that phone number?'

'Yes, why?'

'He wore gloves to do it.'

Pia thought back.

'You're right,' she recalled. 'He was just about to load his luggage into the car, and it was cold. But he could have taken off his gloves in the house.'

'And he didn't. Because he didn't want to leave fingerprints or DNA on the piece of paper.'

'But we could have found that anywhere in his house.' Pia frowned in thought.

'As I said, he was stalling for time,' said Bodenstein. 'He

knew that he had left traces at one of the murder sites, and that sooner or later, we would find Mieger's car, which he no doubt had used. But as long as we had no match for the prints, we would first have to decide he was a suspect and then get a search warrant for his house. And maybe he thought his prints might be in a database somewhere.'

'We did a routine computer search on him, and nothing turned up. Except for a couple of incidents in Flensburg, Dirk Stadler is a totally blank page, never in trouble with the law.' Pia shook her head. 'So he made up this sister just to give himself an alibi.'

'Quite possibly.' Bodenstein nodded. 'And his son would surely lie to us, too, or warn him. That's why I broke the connection before he could pick up.'

The phone rang again. The officers had asked a few neighbours, but no one had seen Stadler drive off. Most of them didn't even know him and had to think hard. His garage at the end of the row of houses was empty.

'You think that Stadler is our man?' Pia asked.

'Yes,' replied Bodenstein with a dark look. 'You and your intuition were right from the beginning. He planned the whole thing meticulously, betting that he would be the focus of the investigation. That's why he was prepared for all the questions.'

'We should have found out much earlier that he no longer works for the City of Frankfurt,' Pia remarked.

'But we didn't.' Bodenstein stood up and went to the door. 'He anticipated this risk by believably acting like he was disabled; he even told me on the phone that he was at the cemetery at the moment. Besides, he made sure we had no time to think things over. Maybe Hartig and Thomsen are in cahoots with him and deliberately steered suspicion onto themselves to gain Stadler some time.'

'So what do we do now?' asked Pia, following him into the hall.

'We inform the commissioner and the team,' said Bodenstein. 'Then we have to find this weekend cabin that Helen Stadler's girlfriend mentioned. And we have to find Burmeister.'

Kai came round the corner, his laptop under his arm. He had heard Bodenstein's last sentence.

'That's no longer an issue,' he said excitedly. 'This time the sniper sent two simultaneous e-mails to the newspaper. Faber copied them both to me. The first is about Ralf Hesse. The second, you have to see for yourselves.'

Everyone stared mutely at the gruesome photo that Kai had projected onto the big screen in the conference room of the special commission. It showed a dark-haired man in a white T-shirt with a panicky, pain-stricken expression on his face. He was strapped to a table in the operating theatre. His arms and legs were restrained, but his right hand lay on his chest, cleanly severed at the wrist, and the stump of his arm had been expertly bandaged.

'That's Dr Burmeister.' Pia had to fight off the rising nausea. A wave of helpless rage rolled over her, and she didn't know who made her more furious: the sniper or Burmeister, who had so carelessly dismissed her warning.

'They must have caught him at the airport or at the front door of his house,' she surmised.

'"They"?' Dr Nicola Engel asked.

'Hartig and Stadler,' Pia replied. 'I'll bet you anything

they're working together. And there's something else that indicates Hartig has something to do with this.' She pointed to the
photo. 'He was a surgeon, and a rather good one, before he
picked a fight with Rudolf and Burmeister.'

'So he, too, has a reason to take revenge on Burmeister,'
Bodenstein put in. 'A very personal reason.'

'Okay.' Nicola Engel nodded. 'How shall we proceed?'

'The APW for both suspects has already been issued,' said
Kai. 'Their houses are staked out, and we're looking for both
cars. The IT specialists at State HQ are tracing where the last
two e-mails from the Judge came from. And we went through
the property records looking for Mieger's weekend cabin. It
must be somewhere near Kelkheim. Vivien Stern remembered
that on the way there, they stopped at an ice cream parlour
located right behind the S-Bahn tracks.'

Pia again read the text of the obituary for Ralf Hesse. RALF
HESSE HAD TO DIE BECAUSE HIS WIFE IMPLICATED HERSELF IN
THE COERCION AND ACCEPTANCE OF THE DEATH OF A HUMAN
BEING BY EXERTING PSYCHOLOGICAL PRESSURE.

What would Bettina Kaspar-Hesse feel when she read that?
Wouldn't it be better to withhold from her this cynical accusa-
tion of guilt? Yet she might hear about it anyway, just as
Gehrke had.

'When were the e-mails sent?' Bodenstein enquired.

'Both within a minute of each other,' said Kai. 'Between
eleven fifty-two and eleven fifty-three a.m.'

'Burmeister left Frankfurt Airport at round seven this
morning.' Pia stood up and stepped over to the map on the
wall. Coloured pins marked the crime scenes. 'Assuming that
they kidnapped him from there, they would have about four

hours to transport him somewhere and amputate his hand. So they must be somewhere in the vicinity of Frankfurt.'

'I'll check the security cameras at the airport in front of Terminal One,' Kai said, nodding.

'Take a look at this,' said Christian Kröger, who had been studying the photo. 'I turned up the brightness on the image, and look what's in the background.'

Everyone looked at the big screen.

'Those tiles. It looks like an old butcher's or bakery,' Bodenstein suggested.

'Or a large kitchen,' Nicola Engel added. 'Can you sharpen it up at all?'

'I'm afraid not. The quality and the resolution of the photo aren't very good,' said Kröger.

'So we should look for abandoned buildings with large kitchens and butcher's shops within a radius of about one hundred kilometres,' Cem suggested.

Finally something was happening in the investigation. While the team brainstormed, Pia was thinking. It was terrible that Burmeister had fallen into the clutches of the sniper, but she had no reason to reproach herself. He had chosen to ignore all her warnings. Hartig had been missing for days. And Stadler had never been in Southern Bavaria, but he wasn't in his house in Liederbach either. Where did the two men hide out?

Wolfgang Mieder's Opel had been in the garage unit in Sossenheim when it wasn't in use. Maybe the sniper had switched back and forth between the two cars – a very clever idea. Thomsen hadn't rented the garage, but maybe Hartig or Stadler had; neither one of them liked Thomsen. It was easy to assume that the two had laid down a false trail that led to

Mark Thomsen. For every dead end the police were lured into, the sniper gained more time.

'Is Thomsen still in custody?' Pia asked the team .

'Yes. He was transferred round noon to the provisional prison,' said Kai.

'Everybody, listen up, please!' said Pia, standing up. 'I'm sure that Thomsen knows the location of the weekend cabin. And we need to protect Professor Hausmann and Dr Janning, and their relatives, from Dirk Stadler.'

'What do you propose?' Bodenstein straightened up.

'We can cancel the stakeouts at Stadler's and Hartig's houses,' Pia said excitedly. 'Instead we should tap their phones, as well as the landline and mobile of Erik Stadler, in case he's involved in this with his father. Somebody has to call Hausmann and Janning and ask them about any relatives who might be in danger. In addition, we have to ramp up the pressure on Rudolf. Bring him to the station and show him the photo of Burmeister. Do the same with Thomsen and ask him about this weekend cabin.'

'Understood!' Bodenstein stood up. 'Start with Thomsen. And I want to talk to Helen Stadler's friend.'

'She's due to fly back to the States this evening,' said Kai.

'She'll have to postpone her trip,' Bodenstein decided. 'She has to come here, ASAP. And please print out some copies of Burmeister's photo.'

Dr Nicola Engel followed Bodenstein and Pia out to the corridor.

'Is there anything I can do to help?' she asked.

'Yes,' Bodenstein answered dryly. 'Keep the big picture in

mind. Because right now, I think I've lost all sense of perspective.'

Mark Thomsen knew about the Ranch, as Wolfgang Mieger's cabin was called, because Helen had recounted with enthusiasm the happy days she had spent there. It was located in the popular weekend getaway area between Fischbach and Schneidhain. He couldn't remember the exact address, but Kai found it in a matter of minutes by doing a land registry search for the city of Kelkheim. Several patrol cars were dispatched at once and an SEK action was ordered for Eibenweg, because it was presumed that Stadler or Hartig was holed up inside and armed. Cem and Kathrin phoned Hausmann and Janning and then checked to make sure that Vivien Stern hadn't simply taken off to America before Bodenstein had spoken with her. In the meantime, Bodenstein, Pia, Kröger and Kim drove through the leaden-grey day to Fischbach. Along the hard shoulder, rubbish bags had been piled up next to overflowing bins. The waste attracted rats and foxes, which even in broad daylight boldly dashed across the eerily deserted streets. Many people had either left town for a while or barricaded themselves in their houses and apartments. Most of the cars they passed going the other way were police patrol cars. Commuter train and bus schedules had been cancelled for days, newspaper and post delivery as well as rubbish removal was still suspended, and delivery drivers and construction workers refused to work. Numerous shops and restaurants were closed, and in the supermarkets, only skeleton crews were working because many employees preferred to call in sick rather than risk being shot on their way to work.

The thermometer had again dropped below freezing. The hoarfrost on the bare branches and twigs had created a true winter wonderland, but none of them even noticed. Pia drove straight through Fischbach, turned onto the B 455 towards Königstein, and then into the weekend cabin region two kilometres further on. They passed the Fischbach Tennis Club, their car bouncing over the unpaved road. With a loud cracking sound, the tyres broke through the ice on the puddles filling the potholes.

'Turn in here!' Kröger pointed at a street sign. 'Number 19.'

Several uniformed police officers were waiting along the street as requested, and Pia pulled in behind a patrol car. A little later, the SEK from Frankfurt showed up and secured the property and house.

'The house is empty,' the team leader informed Bodenstein ten minutes later. 'You can go inside.'

'Thank you,' said Bodenstein with a nod.

Number 19 was a small, unobtrusive cabin situated among huge fir trees. The garden, surrounded by a tall yew hedge and a rusty chain-link fence, ended abruptly at the edge of the forest. They entered the property through a squeaky gate that hung between two stone pillars overgrown with lichen. On the weather-beaten mailbox they saw a barely legible handwritten sign with the names of the owners: *Wolfgang and Gerda Mieger.*

'In the winter, there's not much happening here,' Bodenstein said. He had grown up only a couple of kilometres away. 'It started with a few huts, and gradually houses were built with electricity but no sewer network. Most of the houses were built illegally.'

'Mieger's dacha – a perfect hideout,' Pia remarked. 'Especially this time of year.'

'Don't touch anything,' Kröger reminded her unnecessarily.

The little cabin had wooden shutters and a porch with two steps leading up to it. Three wooden wagon wheels formed the railing, which did give the cabin the look of a ranch house. In front of the porch was a chopping block with fresh wood chips strewn round it.

Bodenstein and Pia pulled on booties and gloves and went inside the cabin, which consisted of one big room with a kitchen niche. Two doors led off to the left and right. It smelled musty and of stale smoke. Bodenstein felt like he was in a wooden coffin: pine floor, closed shutters, the walls and ceiling panelled with tongue-and-groove boards. He inspected the kitchen area. In the sink were a saucepan, a plate and dirty utensils, and on a plastic drainer two clean glasses and another plate. The small refrigerator was full of groceries. The ashes in the fireplace were still lukewarm. He opened the door to the small room on the right side. The bed in there was unmade, with clothes and dirty underwear scattered about. Bodenstein turned round. On the kitchen table were newspapers, and on a pine cabinet stood an old-fashioned tube TV.

He stopped in the middle of the room, closed his eyes for a moment and balled his hands into fists. He could physically feel the presence of Stadler. The man's words *I am a pacifist* still rang like mocking laughter in his ears. Pia, Kim and Christian Kröger were walking about in the cabin; the dull pine floor covered with a faded runner rug creaked under their feet.

'Boss!' Pia's voice tore him out of his musing. 'Have a look at this!'

He opened his eyes, followed her to the room to the left of

the living room, and stopped in the doorway as if rooted to the spot.

Neatly lined up in rows on the wall were photos of the victims, pieces of street maps and satellite photos. In the filing tray on the desk were dossiers on every single victim and their circle of friends and relatives. In a cardboard box were five empty file folders, each labelled with a name.

Outside the cabin, Kröger circled round and found the spot where Stadler dumped the ashes from the fireplace. He seemed to have taken the rubbish with him, because the eighty-litre dustbin was empty and overgrown with moss.

'He burned a pair of shoes,' Kröger announced. 'But the soles survived. We'll compare them with the shoe prints we found at the construction site in Griesheim.'

'What should we do now?' Pia asked.

Bodenstein thought hard. He couldn't afford to allow even the tiniest mistake, or he'd be taken off the case. And the press would tear him and his team to bits.

'We'll wait here for him. He's got to come back eventually,' he decided. 'Can the front door be closed?'

'The lock suffered a little damage,' replied the SEK leader. 'But we can close the door so that nothing is noticeable at first glance.'

'Good. Christian, take pictures of everything, but don't mess anything up.'

Those last four words under different circumstances would have made Kröger blow up, but he merely nodded and got to work. The SEK team took up positions in the neighbouring gardens and in the woods behind the house. Two plainclothes officers had already found an unobtrusive spot to station themselves in the car park of the Fischbach Tennis Club at the entrance to the weekend area. They would alert the leader of the SEK team when Stadler drove past.

Ostermann called. The e-mails from the Judge had been sent from a Wi-Fi connection in a cafe in Unterliederbach. He had already sent a patrol over there to quiz the staff.

'We need to interrogate Erik Stadler and his girlfriend,' Bodenstein mused out loud as he headed back to the car with Pia and Kim. 'Their computers, laptops and smartphones must be confiscated. And I also want the two Winklers brought to the station.'

'But if they turn out to be involved and they're suddenly incommunicado, Stadler might be warned off,' Pia remarked. 'He'd probably assume that we'd talk to his son and the Winklers first. If they've agreed to phone each other at regular intervals, he'll think he still has plenty of time, as long as he's able to reach them. If he can't, he'll kill Burmeister and Hartig and go underground.'

Bodenstein scowled.

'Besides, none of them will say a word if they're in on it,' Pia added. 'It's better if we gather all the facts and think them over so we don't miss anything.'

Bodenstein's phone rang. Ostermann again. He put it on speaker.

'We've looked at the video from the surveillance cameras at the airport,' said Kai. 'Between six thirty and seven thirty a.m. The plane from the Seychelles arrived at Gate C in Terminal 1. Burmeister got into a taxi that pulled up next to him when he came out of the arrivals hall at six fifty-eight. Then a second man got in the back seat. The number of the taxi is legible. We're checking it now.'

'So they nabbed him right at the airport,' said Pia in disbelief. 'While I was talking to Burmeister, the sniper must have been very close.'

She tried to recall the situation in the arrivals hall. There wasn't much going on compared to the departures hall. Even as Pia was speaking with Burmeister's ex-wife and preparing herself mentally for the conversation with the doctor, she was also carefully observing all the other people in the waiting area. Except for a few airport employees and four or five business travellers in the coffee shop, she saw only people meeting friends and relatives. So the sniper must have been in disguise.

'Is there also a surveillance camera in the hall? One that would show the gate and the coffee shop?' Pia enquired.

'It's possible,' replied Kai. 'Since the bombing in 1985, there's hardly a corner that isn't on closed-circuit TV.'

'The sniper must have been one of the men in the coffee shop,' Pia decided. 'Could you please check that out?'

'Sure, will do. See you later.'

Pia shifted into gear and drove off.

'I know that soon we'll be getting a message telling us where Burmeister's body is,' she said bitterly.

'Wrong,' Kim put in from the back seat. 'They won't kill him. They'll just mutilate him so he can never work as a surgeon again. In principle, the amputation of his right hand has already done that.'

'We couldn't protect him or any of the other victims,' Bodenstein said sombrely. 'We've always been one step behind.'

'The whole time we've had two stories running simultaneously,' said Pia, ignoring her boss's reproaches. 'First, of course, we have the circumstances surrounding the death of Kirsten Stadler. That case had been swept under the rug, but is on record, and as such, not a secret that absolutely had to remain one. But the reason behind the UCF's stubborn stonewalling is really what Helen Stadler was trying to track down. To this day, only a very small circle knows about it: Rudolf himself, Janning, Hausmann and Burmeister. The official reason for Rudolf's departure was purportedly his authoritarian management style and the problems that allegedly resulted. But this morning, Burmeister had sheer fear in his eyes until he realized that I was bluffing. The same for Janning. When I told him that Hausmann had told me everything, he stopped short and switched to one-syllable answers.'

'That's why Helen Stadler had to die,' Kim suspected.

'Then Hartig as her murderer makes no sense,' Bodenstein interjected.

'That depends. He could have been in on the Kirsten case,' said Pia. 'Or maybe she found out that he was on Rudolf's team, and threatened to tell her father.'

'I think Vivien Stern has pegged Hartig as Helen's murderer because she's personally afraid of him,' said Kim.

'That's my view, too,' Bodenstein grumbled.

Pia turned left onto the B455. Ostermann called again as they were driving through Kelkheim.

'The taxi was reported stolen this morning,' he said. 'But – and this is the good news – it has a satnav chip, so the taxi company found it only two hours later.'

'Where?'

'Now the bad news: in front of your house, boss.'

'Pardon me? Bodenstein was baffled. 'This shithead is playing games with *me*?'

'A clear display of power,' said Kim.

'The taxi went straight from the airport to Ruppertshain,'

Kai recounted. 'The taxi company thought it was a regular trip at first, until the driver radioed in and said he'd been put out of action with a blow to the head and left in the woods near Unterschweinstiege. The company has a hundred and thirty taxis on the street, and at the taxi garage this morning, only a young female dispatcher, who didn't immediately understand what was going on.'

'He took an enormous risk by hijacking a taxi,' said Pia. 'The drive from the airport to Ruppertshain is about thirty-five minutes. That means they arrived round seven thirty. Before that, they must have stopped somewhere to transfer Burmeister from the taxi into one of their cars. At about noon, the e-mail with the photo was sent. Doing an amputation and treating the wound takes time. So they must be somewhere in the vicinity.'

That was really no help, because 'in the vicinity' included one of the most densely populated areas in Germany. Several hundred uniformed officers were searching abandoned buildings all over the Frankfurt region, and an APW was running on radio, TV and the Internet for Hartig and Stadler, but it was like searching for the proverbial needle in the haystack. At a recent seminar, Bodenstein had listened to arrogant colleagues from Berlin saying that the Lower Taunus was merely the 'unsophisticated provinces'. This condescending attitude angered him every time, because there was probably no region in Germany that was less provincial than the Rhein-Main area, which included Frankfurt Airport and so many banks and multinational corporations. But today he wished he actually were working in the provinces. Then he'd have to search only a couple of villages with ten farms, a school and maybe two gyms. The instant that thought popped up, his brain made a connection that he'd overlooked until now.

'Of course!' he shouted excitedly, making Pia jump.

'You want me to have an accident?' she said gruffly.

'Stadler worked for years at the building commission. That means he knows all the public buildings in the city. Museums, schools, gyms, swimming pools and so forth. We can narrow our search to the city limits of Frankfurt.' He tapped in Ostermann's number, wanting to alert the team to his idea. But before he could say a thing, Kai told them another piece of news.

'Are you guys on your way here?' he asked. 'We just got a new e-mail. This time no photo, but there's a video file attached.'

'I'll tell you straight off, it's not for the faint of heart,' Kai warned them, loading the eight-minute video to project on the big screen.

Burmeister's face, distorted with fear, appeared in close-up, his eyes almost popping out of his head. Nothing remained of the vital, self-confident man with the laughter lines round his eyes who had warmly embraced his daughter at the airport.

'No!' he begged desperately. 'No, please, please, no! You can't do this! Please! I . . . I have money, I . . . I'll do anything you want, but please not my hand, please!'

The camera panned from his face across his torso to his left arm, which was strapped to a base and professionally tied off above the elbow.

Pia felt sick. She turned away, shuddering. She wished her ears were plugged, because Burmeister's screams of pain were unbearable. She couldn't stand it any more, so she pushed through the crowd of officers, ran down the corridor, and left the building through the back door. Outside, she sat down on the top step, breathing deeply and fighting the nausea and the rising tears of rage. With trembling fingers, she got her cigarettes and lighter out of her jacket pocket, but she couldn't manage to light the cigarette. She could have saved Simon Burmeister! Why hadn't she simply taken him into custody? The bitter sense of failure grew with each breath she took. She leaned back against the cold wall and closed her eyes. She didn't even look up when the door opened and someone sat down beside her.

'It's not your fault.'

Bodenstein had apparently regained his composure.

'Yes, it is,' said Pia. 'I should have made him come with me.'

'You can't help someone who doesn't want help.'

'Oh, if only I'd flown to Ecuador with Christoph.' Pia wiped away the tears with the back of her hand, opened her eyes and tried once more to light a cigarette.

'I'm glad you didn't go.' Bodenstein gently took the lighter from her hand and the cigarette from her mouth, lit it and handed it back. Then he took one for himself.

'Why did we make so many mistakes?' Pia asked despondently. 'Why didn't we look on Facebook for any of Helen Stadler's friends?'

'Because we didn't have time to think things through,' replied Bodenstein. 'He left us no time. He kept putting out false leads. I'm quite sure he deliberately picked the Christmas season for his series of murders, because he knew we wouldn't discover a lot of the information in time.'

'He made such a . . . normal impression.' Pia blew smoke into the cold air. 'I almost felt sorry for him, idiot that I am. My intuition failed me completely.'

'Wrong,' said Bodenstein, shaking his head. 'From the start, you knew something wasn't right about him.'

They sat next to each other for a while, smoking and not talking.

'This is no time to get discouraged,' Bodenstein said at last. 'You and I, we've fought so many battles together; we're going to win this one, too. We're right on his heels. Burmeister was his last victim. All the rest are safe.'

'Still, I have a nagging feeling that we've missed something.' Pia flicked the butt into the bushes. Bodenstein stubbed his out and crumbled it absent-mindedly between his fingers.

'I have the same feeling,' he admitted. 'But I know that I've done everything in my power. We're just people, Pia, not robots or superheroes. And people do make mistakes.'

They looked at each other.

'Where do we go from here?' Pia asked.

'Rudolf has just arrived. He's going to have to watch the video, a hundred times if necessary, until he breaks down,' replied Bodenstein. 'But first we'll put the screws on Thomsen. Kai has e-mailed the photo of Burmeister to Janning and Hausmann, so they'll understand how serious the situation is. Hausmann has a daughter who works at a bank in Frankfurt. We're giving her police protection.'

He stood up and gallantly held out his hand to Pia. She gave him a crooked grin.

'Time for the last battle.' Bodenstein smiled. 'Today we'll get him.'

Mark Thomsen looked at the photo and the video.

'Finally.' A faint smile flitted across his face. 'The pig got what he deserved.'

'What's that supposed to mean?' Bodenstein wanted to know. 'Are you still not telling us something?'

'No. I really don't know who the shooter is,' replied Thomsen. 'Until the shot was fired from the high-rise, I was guessing it was Erik. But not after that. No mere sportsman could have made that shot.'

'Why is he doing that to Burmeister? Why did he change his strategy?' Pia pressed him.

'No idea,' Thomsen said with a shrug. 'Burmeister and Rudolf are megalomaniac bulldozers.'

Pia exchanged a quick glance with Bodenstein.

'Rudolf and his old pal Furtwängler spent years searching for a drug that could change the blood type of a live patient. Innumerable laboratory animals died in hundreds of experiments. In the end, at least three human beings died, too. Rudolf and Burmeister transplanted hearts into these patients, deliberately choosing donors who had a different blood type, after they had initially been treated for weeks with specific drugs. The experiments were financed primarily by the pharmaceutical giant Santex. Fritz Gehrke, who was chairman of the board of Santex, was not entirely unbiased in terms of his involvement. He hoped that Rudolf would succeed and thus save his son's life.'

Thomsen paused for a moment.

'The testing of the drug was still in the animal testing phase, but Rudolf and Burmeister started using it on their own patients. These individuals were utterly desperate and knew they would die unless a miracle occurred. Rudolf convinced them that he could bring about this miracle, but it failed in every case. The organ recipients survived the transplants for only a few hours or days, then died in torment when their bodies violently rejected the organs. The number of unreported cases might have been even higher, but Hartig, who was on Rudolf's team, knew about three for sure. After that, Gehrke wanted to resign as chairman of the board of Santex. The experiment seemed to be foundering, and Rudolf and Burmeister panicked. If their process succeeded someday, then there would be no more problems with incompatible blood types, and they would be able to save many more human lives. In addition – and this was probably a more important reason – Rudolf would certainly have won the Nobel Prize.'

'And then Kirsten Stadler happened to be delivered to the hospital. And she was blood type O,' Pia said.

'Precisely.' Thomsen nodded. 'Rudolf and Burmeister manipulated the brain-death examination, removed her heart and implanted it in Gehrke's mortally ill son. Everything went well, Maximilian recovered rapidly and Gehrke, told by Rudolf that the drugs had worked, extended his engagement in the research. But then there were problems with Kirsten Stadler's family. Rudolf wanted to hush up everything and told Gehrke that Kirsten Stadler could have survived. Gehrke probably felt guilty and offered the Stadlers money, a lot of money. At this time, Hausmann, the medical director of the UCF and formerly a good friend of Rudolf's, also learned about the background of the three deaths and intervened. Perhaps Rudolf would have succeeded in sweeping it all under the rug if Hartig hadn't spilled the beans about procedures at the clinic. Then the old friends fell into a disagreement and Rudolf had to leave the UCF. The hospital reached a settlement out of court with the Stadlers, and Gehrke paid an additional million euros in hush money to Dirk Stadler.'

'How do you know all this?' asked Pia.

'I am in contact with the relatives of two victims of Rudolf's megalomania,' Thomsen replied. 'They had no courage, no money and no opportunity to complain about him or the hospital. But based on their information and Hartig's stories, Helen and I have begun to research it.'

'So you do know of specific cases.'

'Yes. With names and dates,' Thomsen stated. 'About a year ago, Helen went without telling me to talk to Gehrke, Rudolf, Hausmann, Janning and Burmeister. She had learned about the million euros shortly before and was beside herself because her father had sacrificed the truth for money. For her, the money was unimportant, nor did she feel bound by the agreement not to talk about it to which Dirk Stadler had consented. She threatened to go to the media with it, specifically with this blood type story that she knew about thanks to Hartig and me.'

'That would have caused a gigantic scandal,' Bodenstein put in.

'No doubt. But not only that,' Thomsen said. 'It would also have been a disaster for the reputation of the entire field of medical transplants, which has already suffered considerably from the scandals of recent years.'

He rubbed his chin between thumb and forefinger.

'The UCF mafia was afraid of Helen because they knew that she was in contact with Hartig, and he would definitely be a credible witness before a court. They knew nothing about me. They had no choice but to eliminate the threat. So they did.'

Thomsen laughed. A bitter snort with no mirth in it.

'They were the ones who killed her, obviously.'

'Why didn't they threaten Mr Hartig, then?' Bodenstein

wanted to know. 'He's a lot more dangerous than Helen Stadler.'

'Hartig had no interest in making the case public. And there is still his father, who plays in the same league as Rudolf and Company. That was his protection.'

'How can you be so sure that Helen was murdered?' Bodenstein was still not completely convinced.

'Would you kill yourself if you were just a hair's breadth away from solving the greatest problem of your entire life?' Thomsen asked. 'She was euphoric, overjoyed and feeling more alive than ever before. She was just about to emerge from the shadow that had hung over her and her family for half her life. She'd even summoned the courage to tell Jens-Uwe that she didn't want to marry him before spending a year in the States. She had applied for a student visa and been accepted as a visiting student!'

'How do you know all this?' Pia asked.

'Helen kept almost no secrets from me,' Thomsen replied.

'But the plans that she devised!' Pia shook her head. 'She spied on people and kept real surveillance logs. Why didn't you stop her?'

'At first, I even helped her,' Thomsen admitted. 'I even did research on the people involved. We never wanted to cause anyone harm – on the contrary. But then Hartig found out something about it, and it got out of control. He was utterly obsessed with putting pressure on his former colleagues.'

'Why?'

'I don't think he ever got over the way they'd treated him,' said Thomsen. 'From a moral standpoint, he'd acted altogether correctly, and for that he was punished.'

'But I don't understand why Hartig first told Helen everything, then stuffed her so full of pills and controlled her to such a degree that she grew fearful of him,' Pia countered. 'That doesn't make any sense at all.'

Thomsen was silent for a long time; then he sighed and looked up.

'He never told Helen anything about it,' he said despondently. 'It was me. And that's how this whole ill-fated story first got started.'

Pia glanced quickly over at her boss.

'Up until that point, Helen was firmly convinced that she was the only one who could have prevented her mother's death,' Thomsen went on. 'For her, it was like a deliverance when she realized that it wasn't her fault, but the doctors'. Maybe she would have let it go at that if Hartig and I hadn't been there. Jens-Uwe fell in love with her, and she skilfully extracted every detail out of him, goaded on by her father, her grandfather and me. For all of us, there was only one idea and one intention – revenge! Each of us had his own personal motive, but in the end, we all wanted the same thing: to bring the truth to light. We're to blame that the dust won't settle on the case.'

'And Hartig? What did he do?'

'He only gradually realized what would happen if Helen found out what part he had actually played in her mother's story. To his credit, he regretted it bitterly. But he did do it.'

'He did do what?' Bodenstein asked.

'Kirsten Stadler's heart was the first one he was allowed to remove and transplant,' said Thomsen. 'It was his first organ transplant in a promising career as a transplant surgeon. He did everything right, but at the time, he knew nothing about the circumstances.'

'How do you know that?'

'Because he told me about it once. Many years ago, when he gave his first talk at HRMO. Before he'd met Helen in person. It was a perfect storm that eventually led to more people dying.'

'Who came up with the idea of killing the relatives of the people involved?' Pia wanted to know. 'What did you have to do with that?'

Again, Thomsen thought for a moment before he replied.

'I wanted to bring to light the truth about Rudolf's human experiments,' he said. 'So Hartig seemed the right choice as informant. He and I might have been able to manage it on our own. In two cases, we had names and evidence, after all, and there were witnesses who would have testified. But then Helen got involved, and her family, and the whole thing turned highly emotional. In the case of her mother, there hadn't been any evidence or a credible witness, but now she had one.'

'Hartig.'

'Exactly. And he couldn't slow her down. I couldn't either. I tried, but she did whatever she liked. Hartig's tool of choice was psychopharmaceuticals, while mine was limited support of her plans. I thought I had everything under control, but I was wrong.'

'Helen's father was in the National People's Army of East Germany,' Bodenstein remarked.

'What?' Thomsen gave him an astonished look.

'We suspect that Dirk Stadler is the sniper,' Bodenstein said. 'Do you think he would be capable of something like that?'

Thomsen frowned, pondering.

'I never would have thought of Dirk in that connection, but now that you mention it . . . He suffered a lot after his wife died. His whole life ended. Maybe that's why he held on so tight to Helen. He didn't want to let her go, because he was afraid to be alone.'

Thomsen's comment contradicted what Stadler had told them.

'Wasn't it the other way round? That Helen clung to her father?' Pia asked.

'She was too weak to tell him that she wanted to live her own life.' He sighed. 'For half her life, she'd hoped that his personality would change, or that he'd find another woman. That he'd be able to return to a normal life once the past was cleared up and the guilty were punished. But Dirk seemed satisfied with the way things were. He pictured the two of them together forever. He had shut himself off from the outside world and lived only in the past. That's also why he hated me so much. He was afraid I might take her away from him.'

'I should think Hartig would have been an even bigger threat,' Bodenstein said.

'No. Dirk had the upper hand because of Hartig's guilt complex. Hartig and Helen kept allowing him to manipulate them and subject them to emotional blackmail.'

'So did Stadler know that Hartig was once part of Rudolf's team?'

'Yes, of course. Hartig must have told him when he convinced him, together with Winkler, to join the suit against the UCF. Everyone knew except Helen.'

All at once, they saw everything they knew about Dirk Stadler in a completely different light. They had paid so little attention to him that they hadn't noticed the dark, damaged side of his character.

'Why did the Winklers break off contact with their son-in-law?' Pia asked.

'Joachim and Lydia disapproved of the way Dirk lived with his daughter. They thought it unhealthy. Helen slept in the same bed with him, they watched television holding hands, and they did everything together. She was undoubtedly utterly fixated on her father, and he prevented her from leaving the nest. Viewed from outside, Dirk always acted like he wanted to protect her, but in reality, just the opposite was true. Helen's death finally pulled the rug out from under Dirk's feet. He thought she had killed herself because she could no longer live with the guilt surrounding her mother's death.'

Everything Thomsen said sounded plausible and also happened to confirm Karoline Albrecht's suspicions. The picture was finally complete. Still, Bodenstein was furious.

'Why are you only telling us this now, Thomsen?' he brusquely admonished the man, whom he had almost come to like. 'Why didn't you lay all your cards on the table right away? You would have saved yourself and us a lot of trouble – and maybe even prevented the killing of Ralf Hesse and the maiming of Dr Burmeister!'

A mocking glint appeared in Thomsen's eyes.

'Save Burmeister? That's the last thing I'd want to do,' he replied coldly. 'And considering the way I was treated by the police force, the way they kicked me in the arse, I had no reason to help you in any way.'

'So why then this sudden change of heart?'

'I don't want any of these bastards to get out of this

unscathed,' Thomsen admitted. 'They should get the punishment they deserve.'

Professor Dieter Paul Rudolf was sitting at the table in the interrogation room like a bored guest at a coffee klatsch, his hands in his trouser pockets and his legs crossed. He had watched the video without batting an eye, totally unimpressed by the gruesome fate of his former colleague.

'When can I get out of here?' he asked after responding to all their questions with stubborn silence.

'The way it looks, never,' replied Pia. 'The state attorney's office is preparing an indictment for at least three counts of murder against you. Your days of playing golf and doing heart surgery are over, as well as your dream of the Nobel Prize.'

Rudolf looked at her for the first time.

'What is all this nonsense?' He took his hands out of his pockets and sat up straight. 'Do you have any idea whom you're talking to?'

'Certainly.' Pia glared back at him. 'We've learned a great deal about you recently. You lied when you claimed you could make no sense of the sniper's e-mail, and that you'd never had a problem with a patient's relatives. We also know that you and your former chief physician, Burmeister, precipitated Kirsten Stadler's death so you could transplant her heart into Fritz Gehrke's son. We know your motives. We know that Gehrke threatened to withdraw his funding because your ambitious research had failed to produce results. We know that you used the medication, which was still in the animal-testing stage, on human beings, and that those patients died.'

Rudolf's pale cheeks flushed with anger.

'Your vanity would not tolerate the failure,' Pia continued

to provoke him. 'You were carried away by the idea of being the first surgeon in the world to succeed in transplanting hearts across the blood-type barrier. You had your eye on the Nobel Prize: fame and honour and a huge sum of money. You were utterly ruthless. You regarded Kirsten Stadler, with her O blood type, as a gift from heaven. The woman was of no more importance to you back then than your old friend Burmeister is now, or the death of your wife—'

'Shut up!' Rudolf growled in fury. His hands were beginning to tremble.

'For you, the organ donors were merely raw material, your patients only means to an end, and you treated your subordinates like shit.' Pia didn't take her eyes off him, alert to the slightest reaction from her opponent. 'But then all your grandiose plans were brought down by an unimportant young doctor who could no longer stand your contempt for humanity and your arrogant megalomania. Jens-Uwe Hartig reported you to hospital management and the Federal Association of Physicians. And because of that, you had to resign from the Frankfurt University Clinic.'

'I helped thousands of people!' Rudolf protested. 'I made pioneering discoveries in the field of organ transplants, and you . . . you bigoted little cop, you're dragging it all into the dirt! All of you are completely clueless! I have the vision and the courage to implement new ideas. Men like me have always made advancements for mankind. Without us, people would still be huddling in caves. Sacrifices are inevitable.'

'Men like you damage the entire medical profession!' Pia countered sharply. 'You have killed innocent victims. You will go down in the history of transplant medicine as a ruthless, greedy criminal. People will be horrified and will throw your books in the recycling bin.'

Her words struck his conceited soul like a blow of the sword. Pia could see the effect on Rudolf's face. He was intelligent enough to realize that she was right.

'A doctor who feels so little empathy for his patients would do better as a carpenter,' she continued relentlessly. 'The results wouldn't be so bad when an experiment fails.'

'I'm not a failure!' Rudolf snarled. A vein throbbed in his temple and beads of sweat had formed on his brow.

'Yes, you are,' said Pia. The pity in her voice brought the professor to white heat. 'In every respect, both professionally and personally. You'll be an embittered old man by the time you get out of prison.'

Dieter Rudolf's face was twitching uncontrollably, and he rubbed his palms on his thighs.

'Who pushed Helen Stadler in front of the train?' Pia asked unexpectedly. 'Was that how you were trying to cover up your failure?'

The professor stared at her, full of hate.

'I wish I had done it!' he croaked. 'I wish I'd killed that little slut who wanted to destroy my life's work, but regrettably, it wasn't me.'

Spit sprayed from his lips, and his knuckles turned white.

'Who was it?' Pia asked, unmoved. 'Tell us. If you cooperate, it could go a lot easier for you.'

'You can kiss my arse!' the professor exploded. 'I want to call my lawyer right now.'

Pia and Bodenstein stood up.

'You'd better look for an expert in criminal law,' Bodenstein advised him. 'You're going to have to answer in court for several counts of murder.'

'You haven't got a thing on me!' Rudolf yelled, now beside himself with rage. 'Not a damn thing!'

'Oh, yes, we do,' Bodenstein said with a cool smile. 'You were seen on Saturday night leaving Fritz Gehrke's house after you knocked him out with chloroform and killed him with an overdose of insulin.'

'How can you accuse me of something like that?' The professor wasn't easily cowed. 'Fritz was my friend.'

'Friendships can be broken if one friend lies to the other,' replied Bodenstein. 'In your house, we found clothes that reeked of smoke. In your car, there were document binders that belonged to Mr Gehrke, and a bottle of chloroform. And in your safe, we found a mobile phone that you used to make a lot of calls in recent days. Your daughter was very cooperative.'

Rudolf turned as pale as a corpse.

'She planted that evidence because she hates my guts,' he claimed. 'I want a lawyer. Right now.'

'What a disgusting character,' Pia said with a shudder after they'd left the interrogation room. 'He doesn't give a damn about Burmeister.'

'A megalomaniac who has lost all touch with reality,' replied Bodenstein. 'Narcissistic and blinded by ambition.'

'If he hadn't lied to us, we would have got wise to Stadler much sooner. That made me so mad, I just had to provoke him.'

They walked down the hall to the conference room.

'Whom are Riegelhoff and Furtwängler afraid of? All this

happened ten years ago.' Pia stopped next to the fire door by the stairwell.

'I can understand the anxiety Furtwängler must feel, or the director of the UCF,' Bodenstein said. 'A scandal like this could ruin the reputation of a clinic or hospital, especially when people find out it was covered up.'

'Then the lawyer must feel the same,' Pia said with a nod. 'He was actively involved in the cover-up and must be afraid that he'll be disbarred or even end up being indicted. Bribes and hush money may have changed hands. Who knows?'

Bodenstein opened the glass doors, and a moment later, they entered the conference room. Several colleagues were startled out of their lethargy, while others kept dozing. Dirty dishes, empty glasses and bottles covered the side tables along with pizza boxes. The room was stuffy and it was as quiet as a church. Seeing his exhausted team, Bodenstein fervently hoped that the investigation would soon be over and they would have a chance to rest.

At one table, the state attorney in charge, Nicola Engel, Kim and Kai Ostermann were talking quietly.

Bodenstein and Pia sat down and reported on their conversations with Thomsen and Rudolf.

'Stadler will kill Hartig as soon as they're done with Burmeister,' Bodenstein concluded. 'And then this whole scandal may remain unresolved, because the others will keep their mouths shut in order not to incriminate themselves.'

'But why would Stadler do that?' enquired Engel sceptically. 'The way it looks right now, Hartig is an accomplice.'

'Stadler doesn't view himself as a murderer. He sees himself as a champion of a just cause,' Bodenstein replied. 'He used

Helen's research to take revenge on those who caused him and his daughter harm. He followed his plan rigorously, without leaving any evidence behind. But then something changed.'

'What?' asked State Attorney Rosenthal, a large bald man in his mid-forties who was known for his shrewd intelligence.

'He attacked Burmeister,' replied Bodenstein. 'Not the man's daughter or girlfriend or ex-wife. Why? Why did he change his strategy, which had worked perfectly so far?'

'Maybe he found out something,' the state attorney suggested.

'That's what I think.' Bodenstein nodded. 'But what? And from whom?'

'From Hartig?' Pia mused.

'No, I suspect it was Vivien Stern, Helen's friend,' Bodenstein said. 'An outsider who may have given him a new perspective, which made him decide to include Hartig in his plans.'

'Cem and Kathrin are still at Stern's place,' Kai said. 'She refuses to come to the station.'

'When did we talk to Stadler about his daughter's notebook?' asked Bodenstein.

'Yesterday evening,' Pia said.

'If Vivien Stern told Stadler that Hartig wanted to prevent Helen at all costs from going to America, then Stadler had to accept that Hartig's relationship with Helen was based on sheer calculation,' said Bodenstein, laying out his theory. 'Hartig had used the Stadlers by encouraging the hopeless suit against the UCF. But when Helen began to poke round in the old case, backed by Thomsen, Hartig had to restrain her, because otherwise she would discover what role he'd played in the death of Kirsten Stadler. That's why he started giving her drugs. I'm certain he would have stuck her in a psychiatric institution, and she would never have been able to get out. Someone – if he didn't do it – then solved the problem by pushing Helen in front of a train. But Hartig had never dreamed that Helen's family and Thomsen knew she was afraid of him.'

'The girl ended up in the hands of two psychopaths who had failed at everything in their lives,' Pia added. 'The only person who could have saved her was Mark Thomsen.'

'So why didn't he?' asked Kai.

'Because he may have underestimated what had gone on between Stadler, Hartig and Helen,' Bodenstein said.

'All this is nothing but speculation,' State Attorney Rosenthal interjected, shaking his head.

'For the time being yes,' Bodenstein said. 'But these speculations are based on solid police work, the way it was done a hundred years ago – without genetic fingerprints and such frippery. Kai, please call Cem. He has to ask Ms Stern whether Stadler phoned her yesterday.'

'But you're of the opinion that Stadler and Hartig worked together when it came to Burmeister, aren't you?' asked the state attorney.

'Yes, definitely,' Bodenstein confirmed. 'Hartig is an excellent surgeon. And Stadler filmed the whole thing.'

Kim hadn't taken part in the conversation. She was watching the video of Burmeister's hand amputation a few more times on Kai's laptop.

'This linoleum floor you can see in the video bothers me,' she now said. 'They don't have that type of floor in kitchens and butcher's. Way too slippery when dealing with water and fat. But I did notice something else. Look at this.'

She turned the laptop round to show them the frame on which she had paused the video. Everyone looked closely.

'Here!' Kim tapped on a point in the background. 'That's a wooden bench, and there are clothes hooks along the top. Now the type of floor makes sense. They're in the locker room of a gym.'

'A school gym. That's possible,' Kai agreed. 'All the schools are still closed for the Christmas holidays. And schools don't have night watchmen like office buildings do, since no cash is kept on-site.'

'Excellent,' Bodenstein praised Kai. 'Inform the patrols in the field to give priority to checking out schools with gyms on the west side of Frankfurt. Find out how many schools there are, and keep in mind that Stadler is far from finished with his campaign of retaliation.'

'Bull's-eye, boss,' said Kai Ostermann as he hung up the phone. 'Stadler did call Vivien Stern last night, probably shortly after you left. He wanted to know what Helen had told her about Hartig, and what happened afterwards. He also asked about what happened on September sixteenth, the day Helen was killed by the train. Naturally, I asked Ms Stern about that, too, and she admitted through her tears that Helen was supposed to meet someone who was going to tell her the truth about her mother's death. Ms Stern had a bad feeling and wanted to accompany Helen, but she refused. She said she had it all under control.'

'And then what?' Engel prodded. 'Whom was she supposed to meet?'

'A doctor from the UCF,' replied Ostermann. 'But unfortunately, Helen didn't tell her friend who it was.'

Somebody had opened a window to let in some fresh air. No one was dozing any more.

'That confirms what Thomsen told us,' said Pia. 'An ice-cold murder in order to save the hospital's reputation.'

'Which could have remained undiscovered,' Engel added.

'We have a genetic fingerprint from the swabs of Helen Stadler's body,' said Kröger. 'If we get saliva samples from Hausmann, Janning, Rudolf and Burmeister, we can run a DNA comparison.'

'So, it's not merely solid investigative work like the police did a hundred years ago,' said State Attorney Rosenthal with a wry smile. 'Still, good job.'

'We also received the security video from the airport,' Kröger went on. 'I'll play it on the big screen.'

Everyone watched the video as if spellbound. The frame included the exit door and the short loading zone by Gate C in the arrivals hall. The coffee shop was clearly visible.

'Stop!' Pia shouted.

Kröger paused the playback and zoomed in.

Two Asians were sitting at a table; next to them was a man reading a paper, and way in the background were two men occupied with their smartphones.

'It must be the guy with the newspaper,' Pia said. 'He's sitting at an angle so he can see the whole hall.'

Kröger let the video roll in slow motion. To the casual observer, the man was simply a businessman with a moustache and horn-rimmed glasses, reading a newspaper and drinking coffee. But on closer observation, you could see that although he was turning the pages of the paper, he was neither reading nor drinking the coffee. What was happening in the hall was claiming his full attention.

'In any case, it's the same man who gets into the left rear seat of the taxi a few minutes later,' said Kai. 'There's no doubt about it. Tie, glasses, moustache – everything matches.'

'Well, congratulations,' said the state attorney. 'Now all we have to do is catch him.'

He had hardly uttered these words when the officer on duty opened the door of the watch room and yelled across the hall: 'They got him!'

Everyone jumped up as if electrified. A wave of excitement flowed through the room, affecting even lazy Ehrenberg.

'The Frankfurt police have found his car behind the gym of the Ludwig Erhard School in Unterliederbach.'

Finally things were moving. Bodenstein doled out assignments, and everybody knew what he had to do. Within half an hour, one of the most extensive police actions of all time was underway in the Rhein-Main region. In and round Unterlieder-bach, all the streets, main roads and rural roads were blocked off. Every vehicle was stopped and searched. Even the slip road to the A 66 autobahn was blocked off, as well as Königsteiner Strasse, which led out of the city to Highway B8 and the auto-bahn. Not a mouse could have escaped unseen from the west side of Frankfurt. Nicola Engel and Ostermann coordinated the action because Bodenstein wanted to be on the scene.

'Christian, you come with us, but send two of your men over to the UCF.' He already had one foot out the door when this occurred to him. 'They have to confiscate something from the offices of Hausmann, Janning and Burmeister that will serve as a DNA fingerprint. The state attorney has promised to get warrants for you ASAP.'

'We're on it,' Kröger confirmed, and grabbed his mobile. 'Let's go! Good luck!'

Four patrol cars were already waiting out front, with blue lights flashing and two-tone sirens going, to escort Bodenstein, Pia and the evidence team to Unterliederbach. During the journey, the police radio chattered quietly, and Pia made one phone call after another from the passenger seat. Bodenstein glanced over at her. He could see the tension in Pia's face. She was taking this case personally, just as he was. On the steps of the station, he'd seen her crying, which moved him deeply because he couldn't recall ever seeing her weep before. Not even during the case two years ago, when Christoph's granddaughter had fallen into the hands of the child abuser and Christoph himself had been injured by the man. Since then, she'd grown more sensitive. Bodenstein felt a need to console her, take her in his arms and reassure her that in the past two weeks, she had performed at a superhuman level. But that wasn't something he should do, not even in an exceptional emotional situation like this one. He was her boss and had to behave correctly at all times.

After Pia spoke to Karoline Albrecht and had sent a unit to the professor's house in Oberursel where she was staying, she called Hausmann and checked to hear if he and his family were safe. Janning, too, was spooked after seeing the photo of Burmeister.

'We're here at home and won't leave until you give us the all-clear,' he assured her.

All hell had broken loose on the police band.

'What sort of idiot is this Rudolf, anyway?' Pia had her phone clenched between her knees and held on tight to the armrest of the door because Bodenstein was taking the bends so fast. 'Just to keep from losing the sponsor for his crazy experiments, he lets a woman die. And without giving a thought to the consequences. Then this man who's over sixty doesn't have the guts to admit to his crimes. Not even the death of his wife made him stop and think.'

'Quite the opposite. Out of fear of being discovered, he even killed his old companion and supporter,' Bodenstein added. 'It's unbelievable.'

He followed the two patrol cars, which were thundering along the right shoulder of the road past the cars in the traffic jam, with blue lights flashing and sirens wailing. At the exit to Unterliederbach, they were stopped for a moment and heard over the radio that the school was already locked down.

'They broke in through one of the doors,' a voice croaked from the radio. 'What should we do now?'

'Don't wait for us. Go in,' Bodenstein decided. 'We're stuck here at the autobahn exit. If the injured man is really in there, he's going to need medical attention fast.'

'Copy that. Understood.'

Bodenstein's fingers were drumming impatiently on the steering wheel. His emotions kept shifting between hot and cold. He had a bad feeling that once again they were going to arrive too late.

When they arrived at the school building, it was all over, and Bodenstein's foreboding proved true. The disappointment that the perps had escaped was written all over the faces of the officers. They had found Burmeister in one of the locker rooms of the gym, and the doctor was already with him.

'I can't go in there.' Pia stopped short.

'I'll do it,' said Bodenstein. 'You take care of the car.'

She gave a grateful nod and vanished into the darkness,

while he went into the gym with Kröger. The familiar smell of locker room sweat underlay the sweet, metallic smell of blood. The doctor and the paramedics were taking care of the injured man.

'How's he doing?' Bodenstein enquired from the doorway. He was trying to convince himself that he didn't want to disturb any evidence, but in reality, he was afraid of having to look at what he'd already seen on video a couple of hours earlier.

'We've stabilized his circulation. Now we'll take him to the hospital in Höchst,' the doctor told him. 'Both his hands were amputated, and rather professionally at that. But it's too late to reattach them.'

'Why?'

'Well, just have a look,' the doctor replied. 'I've been doing this job for fifteen years and thought I'd seen everything. But things just keep getting worse.'

Bodenstein gathered all his courage and stepped into the locker room. The linoleum floor was covered with pools of blood that had already dried. Burmeister lay on a bench, bound with nylon straps like the ones used to secure suitcases. He was unconscious.

Bodenstein swallowed hard. A shiver ran down his back when he saw the stumps of arms and the bloody bandages. In the long years he'd been with the homicide division he'd seen plenty of gruesome things, and he wasn't easily upset. But the sight of the severed hands lying on the floor like a carelessly discarded pair of dirty socks cut him to the marrow. This image of the most brutal, profound contempt for humanity became seared into his mind, and when he imagined what must have happened here a few hours before, his stomach turned over. One of the paramedics sliced through the nylon restraints. Burmeister moaned and started to move.

'All right, he's coming round,' said the doctor, and Bodenstein made his escape.

No sign of Stadler or Hartig. Stadler's silver Toyota was parked at the edge of the schoolyard, not far from the gym, which had been broken into with a crowbar. A helicopter circled over the area, and behind the police cordon, the usual crowd of curious onlookers had gathered along with early arrivals from the media.

Bodenstein sat down on the edge of a concrete planter and wiped the cold sweat from his brow. Stadler was gone. The blood on the floor of the locker room had congealed; the first amputation had taken place several hours ago. Time enough for Stadler and Hartig to be far away by now. They had left the car on purpose as a renewed taunt, a clear message aimed directly at him: *You're too slow, Bodenstein!*

The towing service arrived and loaded the silver Toyota onto a flatbed truck. Pia came walking slowly across the schoolyard.

'Who knows what sort of car he's driving now?' she said as she stopped in front of Bodenstein.

'Maybe Hartig's car.' All the energy had seeped out of his body, and he felt like his feet were encased in concrete blocks.

Burmeister was wheeled out of the gym on a stretcher to the waiting ambulance. Cameras flashed, and a floodlight cut through the darkness. Bodenstein was still trying to banish the sight of the severed hands from his mind.

Suddenly he thought about Karoline Albrecht. He hoped

she was safe from Stadler. Good thing that Pia had sent a pair of officers to guard her. He didn't know why, but he felt somehow attracted to this brave, strong woman with the unusual green eyes.

'They have to be heading somewhere,' Pia said more to herself than to him. 'It's cold, and they can't spend the night in the car. And we're watching all their hideouts.'

'Maybe they know of some that we don't.'

'Come on, let's get out of here.' She stuck her hands in her jacket pockets. 'All we can do is wait for Stadler to surface somewhere or fall into our net at a roadblock.'

'You're right about that.' Bodenstein swallowed his disappointment and stood up. 'Let's go.'

The roadblocks had been lifted, and traffic was flowing normally again. Pia, who was driving, was just about to turn from Königsteiner Strasse onto the autobahn heading for Wiesbaden when Bodenstein's mobile rang. It was connected to the hands-free unit in the car.

'Target has just turned into the development,' said the SEK leader with whom Bodenstein had arranged to use their mobiles instead of the police radio. 'Sitting alone in the car, a dark-coloured Volvo, registration MTK-JH 112.'

Pia reacted like lightning: she flipped off the indicator, stepped on the accelerator, and continued straight ahead past the Main-Taunus Shopping Centre. She was familiar enough with the area to know the fastest route.

'He's alone, driving Hartig's car,' Bodenstein said. 'That may mean that he's already killed Hartig.'

She sat behind the wheel, her face pale, and didn't argue with him.

Bodenstein informed Ostermann and then fell silent, equally exhausted and tense. The emotional roller coaster, alternating between hope and disappointment, had taken its toll, and he could feel his heart hammering against his ribs. This job is not healthy, he thought. Good thing he had another option. He was so sick of chasing criminals. He was fed up with blood and death and despair – fed up with being lied to and treated like he was stupid. But what bothered him most was the fact that he had relied on Neff, a stranger who wasn't even part of his team.

'Target is still sitting in the car,' said the SEK leader from the speakers. 'The engine is turned off. Maybe he suspects something, but he won't get away from us now. We've blocked off every street, and the sharpshooters are in position.'

'Is he really sitting alone in the car?' Bodenstein asked as Pia drove their police car at 170 kilometres an hour up the dual carriageway despite the thickening fog.

'Positive. Do we move in?'

'No, not yet,' Bodenstein replied. 'Let him get out and step onto the property. As soon as he makes a move towards the house, grab him. And remember, we need him alive.'

Pia slowed down, took the bend to the left, and turned right at the intersection in Hornau onto the Gagernring. Visibility was no more than fifteen metres.

'Turn off here,' said Bodenstein, pointing to the left. 'We'll take this shortcut. It'll save us ten minutes.'

'Target is still in the car,' reported the SEK leader. 'You can hardly see your hand in front of your face, it's so foggy.'

'Then move in as soon as it's possible,' Bodenstein ordered, hoping that they wouldn't encounter a bus on the narrow road and have to reverse.

He got out, locked the car, and went over to the rusty garden gate. The hinges squeaked when he opened it. He was tired. Bone tired. Countless nights without sleep had him longing for a hot shower and a bed. No phone, no people, no words. No need to keep thinking. He walked up the flagstone path to the veranda and bent down to pick up the key from under the doormat. Suddenly it was bright as day. His heart skipped a couple of beats from the shock. He turned round. For a few seconds, he was totally blinded and closed his eyes.

'Hands above your head!' someone yelled, and he obeyed. 'Get down on the ground! On the ground now!'

Suddenly everything round him came to life. Men emerged from the fog, dressed in black and masked. Voices, footsteps. They grabbed him by the arms, pulled him to his feet and frisked him. Then he was shoved back to the ground, his arms brutally yanked behind his back and his wrists cuffed. His heart was racing and he broke out in a cold sweat. Although he had expected a situation like this, it was still terrifying to experience it for real. But he would make it through. He had to. At least until the early morning.

The news that the action was successful reached Bodenstein and Pia as they were driving through Fischbach.

'No resistance,' the SEK leader told them. 'Target was unarmed.'

'Very good. We'll be there in five minutes.' Bodenstein leaned back in relief and briefly closed his eyes. He waited until his heart rate calmed down a bit, then tapped in Ostermann's number.'

'They've got him,' he said. 'He didn't put up any resistance.'

'Finally we can sleep again.' Pia gave a wan smile. 'Thank God.'

They turned into the community of weekend cabins and left the car on Eibenweg. They walked through the thick fog to the end of the cul-de-sac, which was brightly lit with flood-lights. The black SEK vehicles and several patrol cars blocked the street. Black-clad figures were running round, as well as several uniformed officers. Hartig's Volvo was parked close to the hedge surrounding the property. Bodenstein and Pia stepped through the gate and went up the path. Stadler lay on the ground in front of the steps to the porch, his hands bound behind his back.

Bodenstein, who in the past several days had often imagined how he would feel when he stood facing the sniper, was surprised that he simply felt nothing. Relief at most, but neither anger nor hate. That would probably come later, during the endless interrogations that awaited them. Now he was just glad the nightmare was over.

'Let him get up,' he said.

Two SEK men pulled the man to his feet. He was blinking in the harsh light. Bodenstein heard Pia next to him inhale sharply. He stared at the man standing in front of him and recognized him, but his mind refused for a fraction of a second to accept what he saw. Before him stood not Dirk Stadler, but Jens-Uwe Hartig.

THURSDAY, JANUARY 3, 2013

Four in the morning.

Since his arrest, Jens-Uwe Hartig hadn't said one word.

Pale and mute, he had sat on the plastic chair in the interrogation room, persistently avoiding any eye contact and staring with bloodshot eyes at the tabletop before him. He hadn't reacted to requests or threats, and finally Bodenstein had cut off the interrogation shortly after midnight. In the boot of the Volvo, the rifle had been secured, a Steyr SSG 69 with a telescopic sight, silencer, and infrared proximity sensor, along with the appropriate ammunition. No all-clear had been sent to Janning, Hausmann and their daughters, because Stadler was still on the loose. Even without his sniper rifle, he was still dangerous.

Almost no one had gone home. Bodenstein was asleep in his desk chair, Kim lay wrapped in a blanket on the carpet in Pia's office. Pia had phoned Christoph and now sat at her desk; the small TV on a shelf of document binders was turned on but with the sound off. Kai sat across from her, his feet up on his desk and his chin on his chest, snoring quietly. It was dark in the office except for the bluish flicker from the TV and the light coming in under the door from the corridor.

Pia couldn't sleep. Although she was dead tired and her eyes were burning, her mind was wide awake and wouldn't let her rest. She aimlessly scrolled through the channels. On N-TV, they were showing repeated views of the police cordons and the gym in Unterliederbach, along with archive photos of Simon Burmeister. Reporters in the foggy darkness were talking into microphones; without sound, their exaggerated mimicry looked ridiculous.

They had assumed that Stadler would kill Hartig – was it now the other way round? In the end, was Dirk Stadler not the sniper after all?

She would probably never understand what motivated

people to deceive, abuse and kill other people and still believe they could get away with it.

With a yawn, she kept flipping through the channels. She wanted a cigarette but was too lazy to get up and go downstairs so she could go outside to smoke. A commercial channel was running an old horror potboiler with zombies in a cemetery. She was just about to zap onward when a thought flashed through her mind. Abruptly she sat up. She jumped up and went to Bodenstein's office and shook him by the shoulder. He woke with a start.

'What's going on?' he whispered groggily.

'I think Dirk Stadler is at the cemetery,' Pia said softly.

Bodenstein yawned and rubbed his eyes.

'Which cemetery?' he asked in confusion.

'At his daughter's grave,' Pia said excitedly. 'He fulfilled his mission – otherwise, he wouldn't have left the rifle in the boot. Come on, let's go and see!'

It took Bodenstein a moment to gather his wits. Then he nodded.

'Maybe you're right,' he said at last. 'It's worth a try.'

They drove in silence through the darkness and the thick fog, which reflected the headlights and swallowed up everything else. The windscreen wipers swept the rainwater back and forth. Fifteen minutes later, they reached the Kelkheim main cemetery, and Pia pulled into the first parking space. Bodenstein took a torch out of the boot. They entered the cemetery, walking slowly along the rows of graves. The thin beam of the torch felt its quivering way along the ground. Pia noticed a draught, and something brushed her hair. She ducked, her heart pounding hard.

'What was that?'

'Only an owl,' said Bodenstein, who was walking in front. 'Careful, the branches are hanging pretty low here.'

Unexpectedly, the bare branches of a weeping willow came out of the fog and slapped Pia in the face. When she looked up, Bodenstein had vanished in the fog. All round, she saw only darkness and sinister-looking bushes. Her heart beat faster.

'Where are you?' she called out, annoyed because her voice sounded so anxious. Footsteps crunched on the frozen sand.

'Here.' Bodenstein gave her a concerned look. 'Everything okay?'

She wanted to say, *Yes, of course,* but that would have been a lie. She was freezing and touched her service weapon in the holster on her belt. Bodenstein held out his arm to her, and she gratefully took it.

'We're almost there,' he said, turning onto a narrower path. 'It's right up ahead.'

He held the torch higher. Pia's mouth turned as dry as dust; she gripped his arm tighter, then let him go and drew her pistol. On the slab, reclining against the gravestone, lay a motionless figure.

'Mr Stadler?' Bodenstein shone the torch beam on the man's face. Dirk Stadler lay on his back, barefoot and dressed only in a T-shirt and jeans. His eyes were closed, and a layer of ice had formed on his eyelashes and eyebrows.

Pia put away her pistol.

Bodenstein squatted down and put two fingers on the man's carotid.

'Too late,' he said, looking up at her. 'Once again, too late.'

Dirk Stadler was dead.

*

Dawn was breaking. The blackness of night was turning a lightening grey. Bodenstein and Pia were standing on the path, silently watching as the men from the mortuary placed Stadler's body in a coffin and took him away. They had naturally called the ME, but he merely confirmed what Bodenstein had already determined. Stadler was dead; he froze to death between one and two in the morning. He had folded his jacket and pullover into a neat pillow and had drunk a whole bottle of schnapps. Drunken people freeze faster, which he had obviously known. Dirk Stadler had planned his death perfectly. Hartig had let himself be arrested, buying Stadler the time he needed.

The undertaker came over to Bodenstein and handed him a folded envelope.

'This was in the inside pocket of his jacket,' he said. 'Your name is on it.'

'Thank you,' Bodenstein said with a nod and scrutinized the envelope addressed to him before he tore it open and took out the letter.

My dear Mr Bodenstein, it read in neat handwriting,

When you read these lines, I hope I'll already be dead. What I have done is inexcusable, but not inexplicable. The decision to kill innocent people in order to cause their loved ones the same pain that my daughter, Helen, and I have suffered was not an easy one, but it was carefully considered. The person responsible for this tragedy is Professor Dieter P. Rudolf, whose contempt for humanity in his striving for fame and honour led him to walk over dead bodies. Including the body of my devoted and beloved wife, who fell into the hands of this monster with no conscience. No less guilty is Dr Simon

Burmeister, who regarded the patients entrusted to him not as human beings, but as means to an end. My daughter, who had tracked down the unethical actions of these two men, paid with her life because of her wish to know the truth and resolve this matter.

But in the end, I have failed from a moral perspective just like those I punished. They played God, and I did, too. I incriminated myself and must now appeal to the highest authority in the faint hope of finding forgiveness. I alone planned and carried out all the killings. No one but me committed any crimes or violated any laws.

It was never my intention to be in the public eye. I regret having imposed such high costs on this country, which took me in with open arms and was always good to me. My original intention was to surrender to justice, but I have decided instead to quit this life voluntarily. In my will, I have stipulated that my estate shall devolve to the state, in order to cover at least some of the costs precipitated by my actions. I die in the hope that justice will call all those to account who have incriminated themselves.

Yours sincerely,
Dirk Stadler
2 January 2013

Bodenstein shook his head and handed the letter to Pia. Then he stuck his hands in his coat pockets and, head bowed, walked back through the fog to the car.

Epilogue

Saturday, June 8, 2013

White tents on the green lawn, happy people at tables and on benches, with a marvellous, cloudless sky of early summer overhead. The aroma of barbecued meat hung in the air, mixed with the indescribably sweet scent of freshly mown grass.

'This is exactly how I'd imagined our wedding,' said Pia, smiling at Christoph. 'A really lovely party!'

'The loveliest party for the most wonderful woman in the world.' Christoph wrapped his arms round her and held her close.

In February, they had officially announced their marriage, although they had decided long before to celebrate their wedding with a casual summer party at Birkenhof. Pia had no desire for a white wedding dress; she thought it was foolish at her age and for her second marriage. So she was now celebrating with family and friends. Starting at noon, they had been barbecuing, drinking and laughing. Christoph's daughters were there, and Lilly and her parents had flown in from Australia for the party. Henning and Miriam, who had patched things up after the crisis on New Year's Eve, were there, too, along with many of Pia and Christoph's friends and colleagues. Even Pia's parents had come, since she had re-established contact with them after the fiasco at Christmas. Christoph had used his charm to work his magic on her mother.

'I need to replenish the barbecue,' he now said, giving Pia a kiss. 'Can you manage without me for a moment?'

'Only with a heavy heart.' She grinned and went over to the table where her colleagues were sitting. Bodenstein had brought his daughter Sophia, who was romping about with Lilly somewhere on the farm. He had broken up with Inka Hansen earlier in the year.

In September, the trial of Professor Ulrich Hausmann for the murder of Helen Stadler was due to begin. Once again, it was forensic technology that had provided the evidence. In the lab, it was determined that the skin particles found under Helen Stadler's fingernails belonged to Hausmann. It was Simon Burmeister's Porsche that was captured by the traffic camera in Kelsterbach, but in the photo, it was clearly his boss who was behind the wheel. When arrested, he admitted that on 16 September 2012, he had pushed Helen Stadler off a bridge in front of a high-speed train.

Professor Dieter P. Rudolf was indicted for the murders of Kirsten Stadler and Fritz Gehrke and charged with negligent manslaughter in at least three additional instances. He was facing possible life in prison. Even Dr Simon Burmeister, despite his disability, could not count on escaping prison time. He would have to answer for at least three counts of negligent manslaughter. Dr Arthur Janning, who had given his tacit agreement to shut off life support for Kirsten Stadler, was indicted by the state attorney as an accessory to murder.

On the same day that Stadler's body was found, Mark Thomsen was set free. He went on to write a book about the death of his son, the Kirsten Stadler case and the exposure of the machinations of Rudolf and Burmeister. The book became a bestseller.

Erik Stadler had his father quietly buried in his sister's grave.

Jens-Uwe Hartig was tried on suspicion of grievous bodily harm to Dr Simon Burmeister, but since his participation could not be proved, he was acquitted for lack of evidence. He sold his goldsmith's studio and moved out of the area.

Karoline Albrecht had broken off contact with her father for good. Pia had learned this in passing from Bodenstein when he told her about the offer that his mother-in-law had made him. Supposedly, he had received advice on the matter from Ms Albrecht, but Pia suspected there was more to it than that.

'So are you going to quit your job?' Pia had asked Bodenstein, stunned by the news.

'Only if you want it,' he replied.

'Oh no, not me,' Pia had said. 'I'm quite happy the way things are.'

'Then I'll stay,' he'd said with a grin. 'Our boss might not agree to me moonlighting anyway.'

A car came through the open gate.

'Who could that be?' Kai asked.

'The later the evening, the lovelier the guests.' Pia got up from the bench. 'That's Kim's car.'

'I thought she wasn't coming,' said Christoph.

'And look who she brought with her,' said Pia with a smile when she saw Dr Nicola Engel getting out of Kim's car, looking unusually casual in a white shirt, jeans and moccasins.

'Did you invite our boss?' asked Bodenstein in surprise as he stood up.

'The invitation said "and guest", if you recall,' Pia replied. Kim and Nicola came over to them.

'Please excuse us for arriving late, Ms Kirchh . . . uh . . . Ms Sander.' Nicola Engel winked at Pia. 'I'm going to have to get used to the new name. And you must be the happy groom?'

'The ecstatic groom,' Christoph corrected her, shaking hands. 'Great that you could join us.'

He waved to one of the caterers they had hired for the party.

'Every new guest is a new reason to drink a toast!' Christoph said with a laugh, putting his arm round Pia. The champagne flowed freely, and they all clinked glasses.

'By the way,' said Nicola Engel. 'There's a good reason for our late arrival. I got a call from France, and then had to inform the state attorney's office. Last night in Paris, someone was arrested who we'd thought was dead. He was recognized by a young woman and positively identified. Then the French police arrested him even though he had a diplomatic passport and a new name.'

'Don't keep us in suspense,' said Bodenstein.

'Dr Marcus Maria Frey,' said the commissioner with a smile that was more relaxed than Pia had ever seen from her. 'The wheels of justice turn slowly – but they do keep turning.'

'That definitely calls for a toast – and before the champagne gets warm,' Bodenstein said. 'Cheers!'

'Hey, when are you going to kiss the bride?' Kai called out, and the other guests happily took up the chant.

'Kiss the bride! Kiss the bride!' they shouted.

'Just a moment.' Christoph took Pia's glass and handed it to Bodenstein along with his own. Then he took Pia in his arms.

'I love you, Ms Sander,' he whispered, looking tenderly into Pia's eyes.

'And I love you, Mr Sander,' she replied with a smile.

Beyond the Taunus hills, the fiery red sun was sinking as the guests clapped and whistled their approval. Could there ever be a more perfect moment for a kiss?

Acknowledgements

My biggest thanks go to my editor, Marion Vazquez, who during the development of the plot was always available with helpful suggestions. She also put the final polish on the manuscript.

I thank Susanne Hecker for her critical feedback in the initial stages, which often put me on the right path.

Also a gigantic thank-you to my first readers, who gave me support, advice, and constructive criticism in the early phases of doubt: my mother, Carola Löwenberg; and my sisters Claudia Cohen and Camilla Altvater; my agent, Andrea Wildgruber; and my friends Simone Schreiber, Catrin Runge and Vanessa Müller-Raidt.

I thank Mr Reinhard Sturm for the opportunity to participate in a 'crime-scene inspection', and Chief Detective Inspector Andrea Rupp for helpful comments regarding police work.

I thank all my professional advisers for tips and comments and ask their forbearance with my occasional exercise of literary freedom in modifying facts to fit the story.

Thank you to everyone at the publishing house of Ullstein Verlag for their wonderful cooperation once again.

I would also like to thank my readers all over the world who enjoy my books, for their tremendous enthusiasm and for giving me the motivation to keep coming up with new stories.

A big thank-you to my US editor, Daniela Rapp, and my publisher, St Martin's Press, for the great trust and the fruitful collaboration. A thousand thanks to my American translator, Steven T. Murray, and his wife, Tiina Nunnally, who have once again succeeded beautifully in translating my words.

And finally I would like to thank the most important person in my life: my partner, Matthias Knöss, who offers me such attentive and unselfish support, always encouraging and advising. He makes it possible for me to concentrate completely on my work. Thank you, my darling.

Nele Neuhaus, July 2014

ICE QUEEN

by Nele Neuhaus

A serial-killer thriller about family, revenge, power and buried secrets from a time in history that still haunts the present.

When holocaust survivor Jossi Goldberg is found dead near his house in Frankfurt, a five-digit number is discovered scrawled in blood at the scene of his murder. The post-mortem reveals that the victim has an old tattoo on his arm which connects him to Hitler's SS, making detectives Pia Kirchhoff and Oliver Bodenstein question Goldberg's true identity.

The victims of two subsequent murders are then found to be linked to Goldberg – but what is the secret they all shared that the killer is desperate should go no further? And what else happened at the end of the Second World War in Europe which is yet to be uncovered?

Pia and Oliver follow a trail which leads them back to the dark days of wartime, in the hope that they can find an eyewitness who may be able to come forward with the truth.

BIG BAD WOLF

by Nele Neuhaus

On a hot day in July, the body of a sixteen-year-old girl is pulled from the River Main near Frankfurt. She has been brutally attacked and murdered, but no one seems to miss her and no one seems to know who she is.

Investigations lead to an isolated children's-home in the mountains, and to a TV presenter whose research took her too close to the wrong people.

As investigators Pia Kirchhoff and Oliver von Bodenstein dig deeper, they uncover a web of lies and deceit in the midst of a middle-class idyll. And then the case gets personal . . .

extracts reading groups
competitions books new
books discounts extracts extracts
competitions discounts
books new extracts events
reading groups events books discounts
events extracts books reading groups
new extracts reading groups
books new titles reading groups
interviews events
reading groups events extracts extracts books
books extracts discounts events new
new books events interviews books
discounts events new events new books extracts

www.panmacmillan.com

extracts events reading groups
competitions books extracts new books